I0823568

PRAISE FOR

# THE SAUNDRA GRAY AFFAIR

"What a terrific, page-turning, enlightening book! It's well-plotted and well-written, suspenseful until the very end, and revealing about politics and the human heart. Highly recommended."

—**James Fallows,** former White House director of speechwriting and *New York Times*–bestselling author of *Our Towns*

"Captivating! Dan Yager has worked in DC politics for more than fifty years, and *The Saundra Gray Affair* brings the pitfalls, pressures, and drama of that world vividly to life. Much more than a murder mystery, this book is a rare and brilliantly plotted window into the messy realities of life in Washington."

—**Steve Gunderson,** former congressman (R-WI, 1981–1997)

"An intriguing reflection on the moral dilemmas that can beset politicians and those in their orbit, including close aides and the fourth estate . . . *The Saundra Gray Affair* draws you into politics in the nation's capital and small-town America, hot issues of the late twentieth century, party polarization, and the policy wrangling of centrists. It is also a really good read, with fun plot twists and surprises, and a nostalgic romp through sixties culture of sex and rock 'n' roll."

—**Wilma B. Liebman,** former Democratic member and chairman, National Labor Relations Board (1997–2011)

"Dan Yager is a fifty-year veteran of the Washington policy world, and it all shows in this riveting debut novel. Those who remember Gary Condit and Chandra Levy will be taken back in time to that period, and those who didn't experience it will understand what it was like."

—**Tevi Troy,** former senior White House aide and author of *The Power and the Money: The Epic Clashes Between Commanders in Chief and Titans of Industry*

"Dan Yager's debut novel is a page-turner! Combining elements of a political thriller with a whodunit story, *The Saundra Gray Affair* will keep you on the edge of your seat. His story contains illuminating insights into how decisions get made and how congressional offices deal with constituents and the often prying media."

—**John Faso,** former congressman (R-NY, 2017–2019)

"In *The Saundra Gray Affair*, Dan Yager brilliantly captures the mysterious world of Capitol Hill: the secrets, the unwritten rules, and the often impossible battle between public expectations, personal ambitions, and political realities that is the US Congress. Dan wraps it all in a murder mystery spanning forty years, with multiple surprise endings—all while leaving the reader with a moral dilemma to contemplate."

—**Steve Bartlett,** former congressman (R-TX, 1983–1991)

"*The Saundra Gray Affair* is an engaging political saga that reveals how the combination of a media circus, innuendos, and gamesmanship can destroy the career of a conscientious and effective congressman. Yager's work is as much a warning as it is an insightful look into how politics works—or doesn't work—today."

—**Mike Madrid,** cofounder of the Lincoln Project and author of *The Latino Century*

*For my lifelong partner, Linda,*
*who has taught me every aspect*
*of the meaning of love.*

www.amplifypublishing.com

*The Saundra Gray Affair: A Novel of Politics*



Author photo by Jeffrey McGuiness



For more information, please contact:
RealClear Publishing, an imprint of Amplify Publishing Group
620 Herndon Parkway, Suite 220
Herndon, VA 20170
info@amplifypublishing.com

Library of Congress Control Number: 2024927662
CPSIA Code: PRV0225A
ISBN-13: 979-8-89138-538-2

Printed in the United States

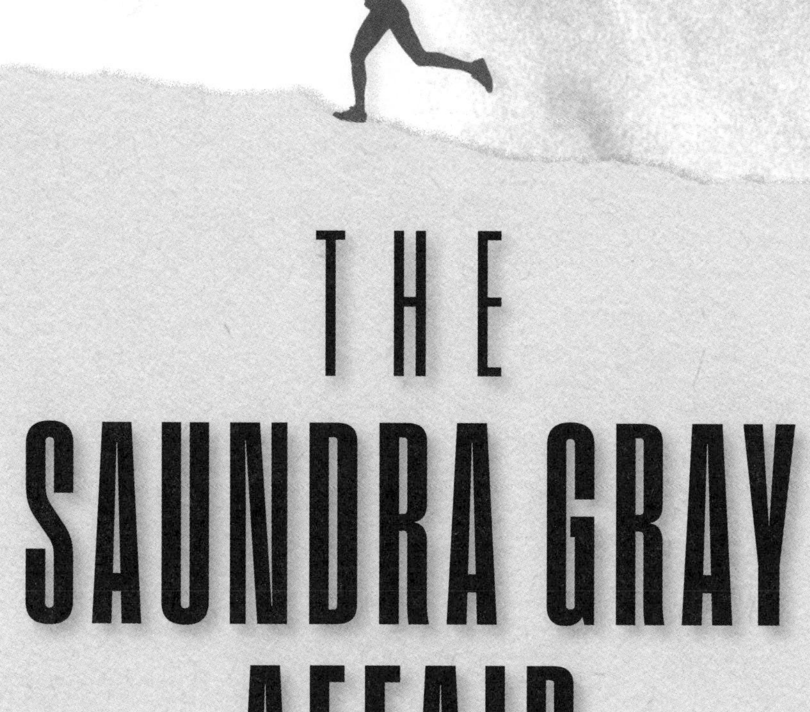

# THE SAUNDRA GRAY AFFAIR

Daniel Yager

"There are few things wholly evil or wholly good. Almost everything, especially of government policy, is an inseparable compound of the two, so that our best judgment of the preponderance between them is continually demanded."

**–Abraham Lincoln**

"The great enemy of truth is very often not the lie—deliberate, contrived, and dishonest—but the myth: persistent, persuasive, and unrealistic. Too often we hold fast to the clichés of our forebears. We subject all facts to a prefabricated set of interpretations. We enjoy the comfort of opinion without the discomfort of thought."

**–John F. Kennedy**

# CAST OF CHARACTERS

**J.D. Clay**, Democratic congressman from Iowa

**Faith Clay**, his spouse

**Wally North**, Congressman Clay's administrative assistant (chief of staff)

**Isaiah Stone**, Pulitzer Prize–winning journalist for the *Des Moines Register*

**Starr Fox**, entrepreneurial Soviet émigré

**Rose Budd/Naomi Bridgewater/Naomi Bridges**, student working her way through law school as a prostitute

**Saundra Gray**, law student working as an intern in Congressman Clay's office

**Dr. Aaron Gray and Mrs. Lynne Gray**, Saundra's parents

**Emily Norton**, Saundra's roommate

**Judy Carricutt**, former staffer to Congressman Clay

**Ray Collins**, US Department of Justice official

# AUTHOR'S NOTE

Readers who remember the sensationalism around Representative Gary Condit's alleged affair with Chandra Levy, an intern who disappeared in similar circumstances to those of the character Saundra Gray, will likely wonder about the connection with this book.

The Levy case was certainly an inspiration for this novel, but the book in no way seeks to shed any light on what happened in that case. There are some similarities with the public record, but there are far more glaring differences.

It's important to note that Condit has denied having an affair with Ms. Levy as well as any involvement in her death. Even more importantly, no compelling evidence has ever been brought forward of a connection between him and her disappearance.

For a personalized account of the Condit affair and its portrayal by the media, readers can look to the 2016 book *Actual Malice* by Breton Peace and Condit and *Finding Chandra* (2010) by *Washington Post* investigative reporters Scott Higham and Sari Horwitz.

PROLOGUE

# A FINAL NOTE FROM WALLY NORTH

*March 2014*

My dearest Gloria,

I know you feel like killing me, but obviously I've already taken care of that. And now that you've found this, I feel like I owe you an explanation.

First, the cancer wasn't getting any better. The pain and the treatments were becoming intolerable. It was going to end sooner or later, so why not cut it short while I could still handle the pain? Pain is nature's signal to take care of something, isn't it?

Second, I didn't want to see my medical expenses cut into that nice nest egg we've built. A memorial service (if that's what you want) and crematory fees will be a whole lot less expensive.

Okay, you already know all that, but there's more that you don't know, and I figure you'd better hear it from me first.

You remember all that agony I went through with J.D. and the "missing Saundra" scandal back in the nineties? As I said at the time, what happened to him could just as easily have happened to Kennedy (especially him), Eisenhower, FDR, Jefferson, and the many other American heroes whose human frailties were exposed later on. I know I convinced you he got screwed over, and, eventually, everything turned out fine for us with the lobbying job in downtown DC. Not every top advisor to a disgraced member of Congress has fared so well, even when they're seemingly vindicated like J.D. was. Here we are more than two decades years later, and I was certain it was all behind us.

But as it turned out, after J.D. died, a reporter—Isaiah Stone—started digging around. I never told you, but there was a lot more to Saundra's disappearance than anyone knew, including you. The truth is, neither J.D.'s role nor mine was as simple as it seemed. I'm hoping that by taking myself out, Stone will decide to let it go. After all, he was actually an admirer of J.D.'s, and with both of us now gone—along with most people having forgotten about Saundra's disappearance—why would he bother pursuing it?

I considered telling you the truth before leaving this world, but I knew it would only make you question my reasons, and you'd try to stop me. Suffice it to say that, by taking myself out, I am hoping to spare you and the family being dragged through the mud. If you knew the full story, you would understand why, as the Bard's Danish prince would say, I am choosing not to be.

Already missing you,

Wally

# PART ONE

A few years ago, with little more public notice than a few obligatory obituaries, former Iowa Democratic Congressman J.D. Clay's life came to a violent end that remains shrouded in mystery. He had served in Congress from 1981 to 1991 and had many great legislative accomplishments, but that's not what the obituaries immediately gravitated toward.

Rather, it was his central role in the media-fed public frenzy surrounding the disappearance of a young intern in the nation's capital—a situation in which he was initially suspected of playing some role. Her body was eventually found, and the perpetrator was identified by circumstantial evidence following his suicide. But this was revealed too late for Clay, well after defeat in his primary. Though Clay was exonerated, those headlines were much smaller and nowhere near the front page. So, most people probably remember him as being guilty of the crime or having some direct

country—one who rises above partisan rhetoric in order to accomplish something, even if it means compromising. He did this on numerous occasions, whether the issue involved employment protections, environmental restrictions, regulation of large corporations, or any number of other areas where partisanship can paralyze needed action.

But now I have to ask myself: Did my genuine admiration for Clay prevent me from performing my role as a journalist with the right degree of probity and skepticism? Perhaps.

Recent events caused me to do a little quiet digging into what Clay's real role was and what I have learned is both disturbing and embarrassing.

First, let me make it clear that I have learned nothing that leads me to suspect Clay of either committing or conspiring in the murder of Saundra Gray. There is nothing connecting Clay with her murderer and my

ONE

# A NECESSARY DISCIPLINE

**J.D. Clay**

*November 1960*

"I'm very sorry, Mrs. Clay, but J.D. . . ."

"Jean," Mom interrupts. "It's Jean. Come on, Ruth, we've known each other our whole lives." This didn't need to be said. In most small towns in Iowa, everyone knows everyone their whole lives.

"Okay." Ruth Warrick, principal of Mitoka High School, holds her gaze on me when she says it, then lowers her eyes to the paper bearing my indictment.

"I'm sorry . . . Jean . . . but we are going to have to suspend J.D. for a week. We cannot have that sort of language and behavior from one of our students toward a teacher. You do see that, don't you?"

I might as well not even be sitting here. My mind and eyes both wander. Warrick's office is a disciplined, well-ordered room with Lincoln and Washington sternly officiating by portraiture. *Can a principal survive if her office shows any disarray?* There is a prominent display of Harvard Classics on her bookshelf, and I doubt she has read any of them. My grandmother, who was a teacher, also had a set and told me anyone who read every volume would be the smartest person in the world. The fact that no one ever does probably doesn't matter. They are there to acknowledge the significant contributions of Aristotle et al. to the gene pool of Western education.

Until now, I have never really looked closely at Warrick's owlish face surrounding her tortoise glasses. Did her pinched mien appear after all the rejection and shaming that come with her job, or was it there before?

Outside, students are walking to their cars in the parking lot. Her window is right next to the walkway, and I'm obviously the afternoon's main attraction. Was the window's placement architecturally deliberate? In some ways, the "principal's office" is the twentieth-century scholastic equivalent of the pillory, especially with a parent's accompaniment.

My name is scattered above the din at times. By now, they all know what happened in Mrs. Housely's classroom. Most students quickly avert their gaze after making eye contact with me through the window. Except Faith, walking slowly and holding her books to her breast. She winks in support, and, in honor of this solemn occasion, I make sure my lips don't betray my inner smile.

Mom purses her lips, taking her time before responding to Warrick's questioning. She is still wearing her blue dress, her uniform for our family's drugstore. This nod to orthodoxy contrasts with her lengthy dark hair, worn like the folk singers from Greenwich Village she listens to at home. Dad likes both the music and the hair.

"Ruth, I certainly do not condone J.D. calling his teacher a 'damn fool.' It was insubordinate, and he knows not to swear around adults. Let me ask, though: What if he just would have called her a racist?"

Warrick's eyes flash, and she has to notice my appreciative glance at Mom. She pats her own primly balanced hair hat—perhaps to emphasize her difference from Mom. And their differences are not just visual. Mitoka's elections are secret ballots, like every other Iowa jurisdiction, but anyone in our small town can tell you how most Mitokans vote just by looking at them. Warrick most definitely voted for Eisenhower, while our family car proudly sported a Stevenson bumper sticker.

I once asked Dad why we were Democrats when almost everyone else in the town was Republican. He laid out a few key issues but then said it was also because we don't let our friends decide our political views. Then he added: "But they are still our friends, because that's far more important."

While Mom and Mrs. Warrick go back and forth, I review the events of the day in my mind.

---

Even though we are far removed from it in lily-white Iowa, there is a lot of racial tension in the country right now. Most of my classmates are oblivious to anything in the outside world that doesn't have anything to do with baseball. Most of them are Cardinals fans, so they would probably say "the Negro problem" is getting Ernie Banks out when they play the Cubs. As they grow older, they will probably fit right into the parochial environs of Mitoka. But there are a few of us who pay close attention to the news, even if it's just watching Huntley and Brinkley.

Teaching about the Civil War in a high school social studies class in the midst of this would be a challenge for any teacher. Out of all the teachers at Mitoka High, Mrs. Housely should be the last person doing this. I am only a month into my junior year, and I barely know her, but she is clearly tainted by her past.

Not that she is unpleasant. She has a broad, welcoming face that, combined with her voluble Southern accent, seems to always be saying, "Come on over for some pie." From a distance, her blue eyes seem warm, but up close they can pierce like Stonewall's sabre.

Her Dixie roots are underscored by the bright-colored, billowy dresses she wears. I know about her from Mom and Dad, since they know pretty much every teacher and where they came from. She is the daughter of a small-town mayor in Mississippi. Her maiden name was Saverna Stuart.

"J.D., I want you to take the position of the South," she says after announcing the class will hold a "mock" debate on the pros and cons of

Southern secession. Her steely smile fixes on me as she holds a ruler firmly in her right hand.

I am taken aback. She has to know my family's Democratic leanings. Is she taunting me or using this as a teaching moment? Seems like the former.

"I'm sorry, Mrs. Housely, I don't think I'm ignorant enough to do a good job with that." I try to keep a straight face while looking directly at her. She taps the ruler into her left palm. It is forceful enough to cause her wattled arms and pendulous bosoms to ripple—but certainly not in an erotic way.

We hold each other's stares, and I can feel the stillness in the room. The other students are frozen in place.

"Actually, J.D., many of our country's smartest and most honorable leaders were very eloquent in defending the South's position. In fact, many schools, buildings, and bridges are named in their honor." She nods pointedly at me, her eyebrows forming a crescent over the black rims of her glasses.

"So, they actually defended slavery? Is that what you want me to do?"

Housely clears her throat.

"Well, of course, it wasn't just about slavery. The states felt they should make their own decisions on a number of things. But even slavery, in its day, could be defended by some very reasonable arguments, even if they wouldn't work today. In fact, you could say many nigras would have been better off as slaves than they are today."

The offensive word, with her strong pronunciation of the first syllable, strikes me. She clearly has unlearned the other, more objectionable, variation starting with N somewhere between Natchez, Mississippi, and Mitoka. Probably corrected by some liberal Yankee college professor in Ames. I used that word once with my mother and was immediately sent to my room. I have never used it again, even among my friends, where it is common usage.

"Mrs. Housely, is that the word you use for Negroes? I don't think that's a real word, is it? I mean, you're the teacher."

She stiffens while I try to remain expressionless, hoping it masks my insolence. I know I am right up to the border at this point.

She takes a deep breath, obviously trying to measure her words.

"Okay, *Negroes* or *coloreds*, whichever you prefer. J.D., I think one could look at a lot of things happening in our country and find it reasonable to argue that both white people and coloreds were a lot better off under slavery. I'm not saying I agree. Just that the argument could be made."

I think twice about it, and then go ahead with it anyway: "Only a damn fool would argue that."

Now I am well aware that, while she can get away with saying "nigra," I cannot get away with saying "damn." I still wish I could have used a stronger term.

The closest thing to capital punishment in an American school is suspension, preceded by the capital crimes trial of the principal's office. So, less than ten minutes later, here I am sitting in Mrs. Warrick's office.

---

Mom makes sure we are outside hearing distance from the school before she turns on me.

"Did you really have to call her a 'damn fool'?"

"Technically I didn't. It was a general reference."

We are walking briskly toward home. Midday in downtown Mitoka between meals means we have the sidewalks to ourselves.

She stops again and turns to me. Something about this feels forced, and I'm not as intimidated as I should be. Okay, I got capital punishment. But I have received far worse from her for far milder transgressions, like missing an assignment or even forgetting my table manners at Grandma's Sunday dinner.

"But you had already made your point, J.D. I'm proud of you for that, but calling her a name turned it from a debate to impertinence. Since she was the teacher and you were the student, guess what—you handed her a victory."

"No, I still won the debate because I was right, and she was wrong. And she's a Southern bigot who deserves more than I gave her."

Mom isn't jumping to her defense, and we are not saying another word on the walk, hoping a dinner conversation with Dad will resolve the issue.

---

"What in the world are you doing here, J.D.?"

Mrs. Housely looks genuinely shocked to see me sitting in the front row of her empty classroom the following day, thirty minutes before the opening bell.

"I came to apologize."

A slight triumphant smile. "Okay, thank you, but you should not be here, young man. You are suspended."

She reverts to a frown—maybe forced—and is standing above me with arms folded. I'm not moving.

"Was there more?" she asks.

"Actually, yes. I was going to see if we could work out some kind of deal."

Her big face opens wide into a hearty laugh, which almost seems genuine.

"A deal? And exactly what leverage do you have, boy, to try to talk me into a deal? You shouldn't even be sitting here right now."

Through her stern demeanor, I see a sign of intrigue from my impudence.

"Mrs. Housely, I have no leverage. Instead, I want to appeal to your reason. You are my teacher, and I respect your wisdom and compassion."

I recite the last words very carefully, trying not to sound too scripted. I reflect on the stories my parents told me about Housely's extensive work with the town's charities, including one to help find American homes for Korean orphans.

She's not moving, and her frown reflects contemplation more than an attempt at intimidation.

"Okay, try me."

I clear my throat. "Here's my idea, Mrs. Housely. I'll be taking my suspension. And when I return to your class, the first thing I will do is apologize to you in front of everyone."

Her furrowed brow smooths. "Okay, so far, so good. These are things you should do anyway, though. What am I supposed to do in return?"

"You assign the class a book to read. It's called *Native Son* by Richard Wright. I read it last summer, and it opened my eyes to the Negro experience in America. Since then, I have learned a lot more. Do you know about Emmett Till?"

Her face becomes a puzzle.

"Of course. But isn't that book written by a Communist?"

"I don't know. The book's not about Communism, though there are Communists in it. I don't think that's really important, because the author isn't trying to convince the reader to become a Communist. The important thing is I don't think anyone could read it without it changing their view of Negroes."

"Negroes," she repeats, avoiding the disguised epithet she had used in class the day before. "But you're asking me to assign a book to the class that I haven't even read. Honestly, J.D., would you really expect me to do that?"

Reasonable point, as expected.

"Sure. I assume you would read the book, too. If you don't agree with me, you don't have to assign it, and I'll go ahead with the apology anyway. My parents told me you are one of the smartest people in town who does a lot of good things, so I'll respect your decision."

"Apparently not such a damn fool after all." The frown is now arched eyebrows.

I let her statement hang, not sure how to respond. Until she smiles and holds out her hand.

"We have a deal, J.D."

---

My suspension is over, and I appear in Housely's classroom a half hour before the opening bell. She is already sitting at her desk and invites me to take a front-row seat. I notice she is not wearing the usual flowery Dixie attire but is far primmer.

"I read the book, J.D."

"Okay, what did you think?"

The soft tone of her voice belies the frown on her face as well as the words she speaks. "J.D., do you really expect me to assign a book to my class about a murderer who is sympathetic to Communists? Do you have any idea how their parents would respond?"

"But it's a classic. I think it won several awards, and the author got a lot of critical praise."

"And he got a lot of flak, too!" Clearly, she did more than just read the book. "J.D., this is a high school in the middle of Iowa with a lot of very conservative people sending their kids to my class. You want me to put my job on the line?"

I could have anticipated this reaction and am surprised my parents didn't make the same point. I feel like a fool.

"Okay, so I guess we don't have a deal."

"That's not what I said," she corrects me. "I'm going to suggest a different deal."

"Okay."

"I still want to have the debate, and I want you to defend the secession like I said, whether you are 'ignorant enough' or not."

"I don't think I can do it, though."

"Yes, you can, J.D. You are one of my smartest students, and you have a very bright future ahead of you. Your classmates like you and admire how you stand your ground on things. But part of education is to understand where others who are not like you are coming from. As a future leader, that's a good lesson for you."

Her praise catches me off guard. Class is starting in ten minutes, and I am hearing students gathering in the hall.

"Well, I guess I don't have much choice. Unless I want another suspension."

"You don't have a choice, but I'm not through." She stands and walks directly in front of me. "J.D., you aren't the only one who can learn from this. I think your classmates could learn something, too. So, I am going to assign to you a report on Emmett Till, which I then expect you to deliver orally to the class. You can make it whatever you want to. It can just be about the facts of the case, or it can be about what it means, or both. It's up to you. Just no swear words," she adds with a slight smile and moves in front of her desk.

I'm wishing for more time before the other students begin streaming in so I can process what I've just been tasked with. Throughout the exchange, her demeanor only slightly changed, unlike my impression of her. She looks back and takes two steps toward me.

"I don't think I owe you an apology, but I do want to thank you," she says with a lowered voice. "You have to know that I grew up in a very different situation than you did. I was taught a lot of things by my parents and relatives that I should probably unlearn. Maybe that book was the first step. I look forward to learning from your report."

I get up to go to my usual assigned seat, but she stops me.

"One more thing, J.D. You taught me something, and I want to make sure I do the same for you. Starting at about your age, we go through the rest of our lives trying to believe we've got it all figured out. It gives us comfort in a chaotic and unpredictable world. Then the older you get, the more you discover how much you don't know—and it's usually stuff you need to know to evolve as a person. But you may not realize that until it's too late. Even at my age, I made that mistake, but you caught me. Take that from me if you take nothing else. If you do, you will grow faster than most of the rest of us."

## TWO

# THE SILVERMOON DRIVE-IN

**J.D. Clay**

*October 1961*

"What the heck, J.D.?"

I know I have gone too far the moment Faith removes my left hand from her right breast. "Hell" would only be used by Faith in a religious context, so I know she means it, even though her hand was not nearly as forceful as her voice.

We immediately return to the awkward silence that has blanketed the entire evening. In fact, ever since I asked my long-standing best girl friend (not *girlfriend*) on a first date, our relations have been awkward. If I had just kissed her, that would also have been awkward, but we could still easily revert to our recent platonic ignorance. Me trying to take things to "second base" will now make that impossible.

The next part is going to be difficult. Of course, we can go back to watching Warren Beatty and Natalie Wood, who seem to be no surer of their own relationship. The way it was advertised, *Splendor in the Grass* seemed like it could be the perfect love story to help me redefine my relationship with Faith. Little did I know, the movie was more about the challenges of romance than romance itself.

*So, who will start the conversation? Are we going to just watch the rest of the movie and drive home in silence?*

Finally, Faith speaks up. But first, even though the car is running and keeping us warm, she buttons the rest of her dull gray overcoat to just below her chin. Does she really think she can hide her beauty with the dreary clothes and hairstyles she maintains? The picture is completed by the brown wool sweater underneath the coat and sturdy green skirt that obscures her figure. But she could never hide the splendid sweep of her raven hair across the purity of her forehead and the tenderness of her mouth and chin over a porcelain neck.

And those eyes. She always seems on the verge of tears, even while laughing. There's a profound loneliness in her eyes that my mere friendship cannot relieve.

"J.D., am I just supposed to be your latest conquest? Now that you've gone through all the other pretty girls in Mitoka?"

The Silvermoon Drive-In Theater is bustling as usual on a brisk fall evening, despite the occasional drizzle. A rowdy group three cars over grows louder as they work their way through a smuggled case of beer, a teenage talisman at drive-ins everywhere. The sick smell of oversaturated popcorn grows stronger, and I'm starting to wish we had parked even farther from the concession stand.

Meanwhile, Beatty doesn't seem any surer of himself than I do. Ever since I asked Faith on a drive-in date, the ease of our relationship has faded. Since the first grade, we have been soulmates in every way, though our physical relationship has been limited to basketball in my driveway and an occasional Ping-Pong battle in her basement. Our closeness has been built upon interests, authors, and, most importantly, values. Okay, I won't be overly modest here. We are probably the two most intelligent people in our age group. I suppose we were destined to either be close friends or bitter rivals. How close, though?

We also share similar social views, coming from two of the few Democrat families in town. But our liberality has different roots. Because of my parents, I have grown up in a rich intellectual landscape, while hers grew out of her parents' overseas missionary deeds before they started a family. Theirs is an odd, somewhat puritanical, progressivism, but it is every bit as genuine as my own family's.

As we grew older and saw our friends increasingly separated by gender into various social clusters, we have somehow maintained this closeness. Naturally, this generates predictable assumptions among others. Whenever I ask another girl out, she invariably questions whether it is okay with Faith. So when I finally did ask Faith out on a date a couple of weeks ago, she was the only one who was surprised.

"Why? Is everyone else busy that night? If you just need someone to hang out with, that's fine," she had said, her demeanor very nonchalant.

When I said, "No, it's an actual date," her look was anything but nonchalant. And it was to a drive-in movie, no less. The favorite make-out date of all young men! But she did say, "Okay."

In the weeks following that request, there has been little that is direct about our dealings. In fact, we have found it so hard to talk when we see each other at school that we've been carefully avoiding each other.

I turn on the wipers as the light rain quickens, adding a metronomic beat to the soundtrack. She is still looking at me, awaiting a response, and it appears to be fixed.

"Not sure what you mean by 'gone through' them," I rebut.

"Name one good-looking girl our age you haven't taken out in the past year."

"What does that have to do with us?"

"You tell me. I know what some of them are like and their reputations. And I know yours as well. But I thought you and I were just friends, so I ignored it. Everybody knows I'm saving myself, which, of course, means few guys want to take me out. Am I just your final challenge before heading off to college?"

Before I can answer, she throws open the car door, pushes open the umbrella she had pulled from the floor, slams the door shut, and heads off to the concession stand. Doesn't seem like it's just nature calling.

Minutes later, she's back, closing the door only slightly more gently than she had opened it, and sits silently for a bit, keeping her coat buttoned to the top.

"How much longer is the movie?" she asks, knowing that Warren Beatty isn't even close to resolving his dilemma over being infatuated with a girl well below his "station."

"Faith, I do not view you as a potential 'conquest.'" I'm looking directly at her, but she is still fixed on the big screen. I grant Beatty is better looking than me, but that's not it.

*How can I pull this back to the honest relationship of our youth?* Right now, I need that more than anything physical.

"How do you feel about me?" I ask.

"Meaning?"

"Are you happy with us just being friends?"

A slight frown that eases immediately. She's cooled off.

"Well, I'm not happy right now about anything. But I've always been happy with being your friend. Since when—first grade? That's a long time. Okay, now I'm a woman and can offer something more than just friendship. I think I'm pretty. I get it. But if we're just friends, where does a date just months before our lives are about to move on fit in?"

"Because I think I really do love you," I blurt. This was no sudden realization. It started, subconsciously at first, when she began to mature. But I'd always been able to separate that from our friendship because there were permissible outlets with other girls. I've never gone "all the way" with any of them, even though I probably could have with a couple of them if I pressed hard enough. My father had once told me it takes a long time for guys to figure out when the Golden Rule—in a physical sense, of course—does and does not apply to sex. I'm still learning. Plus, it has only taken a few teen pregnancies in Mitoka for our parents to make an easy case to us on the virtues of celibacy. But there are still two more bases between first and home.

My profession of love seems to stun her. Her eyes raise momentarily, and she seems to soften, but then some internal defense mechanism sets in.

"What's different?" she asks. "Is it because I now have to wear a bra and I didn't in grade school?"

By now, I'm used to her occasional clinical reference to sex. She has never had any problem discussing it with me, as long as it remains clinical. In fact, it's been great having a girl I can do this with while navigating adolescence. When she shared the news of her first period, I didn't think twice about it until I realized that not only was I the only boy she had told this to but maybe the only other boy my age told that by any girl.

But I couldn't ignore the fact that the bra, and what it held, actually had made things different for a long time. I just had refused to acknowledge it to myself until recently. But she had asked the right question after all. Do I, in fact, love her, or do I just want her body? Also, are the two separate, anyway? What about the fact that there are girls whose bodies I want even more, but I have no other feelings for them? Does that make it different with her? Is it that there is something different about her that goes beyond physical or even intellectual attraction? Though I don't believe in fate, is there some destiny that connects her and myself?

"Well, do you think you love me, Faith?" The reflection from the drive-in screen gives her blue eyes a sheen. Her anger is completely gone.

"Take me home, J.D.," she says quietly but with an air of finality. I don't push back.

I drive her home, and, though we are going away to different colleges, I'm still wondering if this is her final answer. Or was that even actually an answer? I resolve that on our first time home for the holidays, I will ask her out again.

THREE

# SPOOLEY'S

J.D. Clay

*October 1963*

Open Mic Night always packs the crowd in at Spooley's like swarming golden shiners, and tonight is no different. The backup band, as usual, is the Cyclones, with my fraternity brother Paul Sahm on bass. Open Mic originated during the late fifties' folk obsession but in recent years has catered to the Burgoyne State students' preferences for rock 'n' roll and smooth pop.

Everyone in northern Iowa knows Spooley's' claim to fame. In February 1959, the Buddy Holly Winter Dance Party tour bus stopped in Burgoyne the night before heading on to Clear Lake for Buddy's last concert and his doomed chartered flight to Moorhead, Minnesota. A prominent member of the tour, Ritchie Valens, was bored after the band ate dinner at Paul's Diner and wandered over to check out the local scenery. According to the legend, a couple of folk singers were covering The Kingston Trio's "Tom Dooley." With his brown skin and accent, Valens would have stood out in a roomful of WASP students. One of them finally asked him who he was and why he was there. The upshot was Valens borrowed a guitar and played acoustic renditions of "La Bamba" and "Come On, Let's Go." Now they sure as hell knew who he was.

Spooley's has milked the legend for all it is worth, eventually doubling its size and dubbing the stage "The La Bamba" with a large picture of Valens as a backdrop. Reportedly, there is a move among some of the local denizens to change the city limits signs to include "Home of Ritchie Valens's Penultimate Concert." It's been held up by the dispute over how many people driving into Burgoyne would know what the word "penultimate" means.

The Cyclones can play almost any genre, giving them the upper hand against other local bands for the primo Saturday night spot. Sahm is the resident "beatnik" in my fraternity, constantly quoting Kerouac and Ginsberg but cultivating a three-inch-high well-lubed pompadour to embellish the Cyclones' image. He told me that the gig doesn't pay much, but the exposure has made the Cyclones the most in-demand band in northern Iowa.

The band has just finished its initial set and is taking a break before opening up the mic. They closed with a rousing version of Chuck Berry's "School Days" with the crowd chanting "Hail! Hail! Rock 'n' roll!" in open defiance of their parents and other detractors.

After propping his bass on the stand, Sahm works his way over to the table regularly commandeered by my fraternity brothers.

"You still going to do it?" Sahm asks me. "Microphone has your name on it, pal."

"Only if you insist," I respond. I feel like modesty requires me to play hard to get, but it has always been my secret desire to try my luck as a rock 'n' roll singer. I discovered I could sing in the high school choir and a couple of school musicals. But the only musical groups in Mitoka were a barbershop quartet and a polka band of some competence. The musical inclinations of the town kids are thus disenfranchised, and we haven't had enough solidarity to challenge the local order with the hedonistic sounds of Berry and Gene Vincent.

In contrast, Sahm and the other Cyclones are from urban areas, mostly outside Iowa, where they lived under no such strictures, enabling their revolutionary musical pursuits. In fact, a couple of band members were so mutinous that their parents deliberately sent them to Burgoyne State, thinking northwest Iowa would be a sanctuary from the jarring iniquities of an ungrateful generation.

Sahm had no such disability to work with, coming from a family of musicians, including his father who did well as a jazz drummer when he wasn't being an accountant for a large Chicago firm. His dad felt rock 'n' roll was just a cartoon version of its roots in what used to be called "race music." But he remembered his own parents' scorn of his music's departure from the saccharine sounds of Rudy Vallée and Victor Herbert. Al Jolson, in insulting blackface, was the closest they came to racial tolerance.

Sahm had heard me sing during a drunken singalong with the radio one night at the fraternity and had been impressed with the quality of my baritone. He asked me to perform at an upcoming open mic, and I agreed but needed a few weeks to put together two songs, the number performers were allowed to sing. I had seen too many people get up and wing it in performances for which they were too drunk to be embarrassed. Granted, the crowd is typically forgiving of anyone who has the courage to perform. But those with a modicum of talent get a more vociferous reception, and I clearly wanted to fall within that camp.

As Sahm and his bandmates returned to The La Bamba, the din grew into a buzz embellished with a few shouts. I had asked to go second because I've noticed it usually takes the first act a while to draw the crowd away from its isolated conversations. I went through the lyrics of the songs two more times in my head. I have had to memorize lyrics before for school musicals, but it has been a while, and I'm afraid of blanking out on stage.

First up is a nervous coed struggling through "Surfer Girl" with a voice better suited for other songs. Her self-effacing smile seems to ask the audience not to look directly at her, a request easily granted based on her performance. I notice that Valens's eyes in the picture seem slightly diverted, as if even he is impatient for the next act. The band members saunter through the backup, mostly just strumming chords.

I'm wondering why it is always okay for women to sing songs in the role of a man but not vice versa. It would be fun to try "Judy's Turn to Cry" without starting rumors. The coed is doing much better with "If I Had a Hammer"—as is the band. It occurs to me that anyone who can carry a tune probably has a shot at a hit record as long as they can just find a song fit best for their voice.

The coed finishes strong, and the applause is starting to ebb as Sahm announces, "Okay, folks, I want to introduce my fraternity brother, the righteous Mr. Clay. You all know him from his frequent pontificating on the issues of the day. Who knew he could sing, too? If it works, maybe he'll just stick with that and leave his other opinions to himself."

This comment draws both guffaws and cheers from the crowd. My activism on civil rights issues has generated a healthy mixture of followers and detractors, and both seem to be well represented this evening. I had decisively lost the election for student government president that fall. My frat brothers attributed it to my "commie pinko leanings," while those genuinely in the "commie pinko" camp abandoned me because I failed to criticize President Kennedy as a "red baiter" in the debate before the election. As everyone knows, these involved critical issues the student government would have to address.

I stumble on one of the steps up to the stage, and a heckler shouts: "Apparently, we won't be hearing 'Walk Right In.'" I ignore the comment and am now standing at the microphone staring at an abnormally silent crowd. I know most of them and figure they think they know me as well. I've seen many performers try to be someone else. That never works when I give a speech, so why try anything different here?

I've told the band my two songs, and the first starts acapella, so I ask the tall bespectacled keyboard player, whose pompadour is only half that of Sahm's, for a note and hum it quietly to myself.

The dead silence is both frightening and inviting. *Okay, here we go.*

"Here's my story, sad but true . . ." I know the band will jump in at the right time since every band can cover "Runaround Sue."

I can read the shock on their faces, so I'm hoping it sounds as good to them as it did to me. My voice soars through the song's intro, and before I know it, the entire room is adding the "hape, hape" backup to the verse, along with the crescendoing "ahhs" just before the bridge. When I go into the final verse, I motion the band to stop playing as the crowd carries the song with me to its conclusion acapella, including an improvised finale as a substitute for the fade in Dion's version.

The room goes silent. Then erupts. They are ready to blow the roof off the place, so I probably shouldn't follow with Gene Pitney's "Only Love Can Break a Heart." When I shake my head at the band they seem to know what I mean, so to keep it going I go right into the next one, which I know they've played many times.

"Welllll be-bop-a-lula, she's my baby . . ."

This one goes even better, and as I'm singing the song I notice a coed at the front of the stage with dangerous eyes I can't pull mine away from. It is as if the rest of her body hangs from those eyes like curtains. I read somewhere that one of the reasons Chuck Berry is such a magnetic performer is because he keeps constant eye contact with individual crowd members so that they feel he is singing only to them. I force my gaze on others in the crowd, but it keeps getting pulled back to her.

When I close with "she-he-he's my baby now," the room explodes, and even the jaded bartenders and waitresses join in the bliss. As I try to step down from the platform, three audience members join together to push me back up despite my protests.

I should have ignored them and stopped right there. My attempt at "Only Love Can Break a Heart" is tolerated at best. Ballads are not my forte, and this time the audience lets me descend. But my embarrassment at the letdown is short-lived, as numerous attendees, even a fair number who seem sober, shower me with praise.

I rejoin my fraternity brothers at the table and accept their applause, trying not to display the adrenaline rush. I notice that Dangerous Eyes has moved back to the bar and is talking quietly with another coed, but she's occasionally looking over at me.

She has an interesting allure, wearing her hair in a slightly elongated pixie framing her face. She is wearing a black shift that ends just above her knees. It is not terribly revealing but tight enough to draw attention. Those eyes, bearing only the slightest trace of makeup, make her captivating in an intellectual manner that most men would pass over. I can't do that. Even when she returns my gaze, I do not look immediately away as one might with a more casual attraction.

"J.D., do you know her?" asks Jim Gettys. As the captain of the football team, Gettys fashions himself as the resident expert on all things female. Of course, to him "all things" has a very narrow definition.

"Who?"

"Come on, man, it's pretty obvious."

"Okay, so what?"

"Do you know who that is?"

"I think I had a class with her, but I'm blanking on her name."

"That's Astrid Gilbert."

"Okay, yes that sounds familiar."

Gettys leers but thankfully refrains from licking his lips. "You really don't know anything about her?"

"She's attractive. Looks pretty intelligent, too."

"She's a total slut, man. Easy as they come. I see her staring at you. Go for it."

I glare at him.

"Jim, would you go to bed with just any girl?" I hold up my hand. "Wait. I'll answer it for you. Yes. Does that make you a slut? Meanwhile, do you know anything else about her?"

I don't have to look to know my other frat brothers are rolling their eyes. My progressive views in the smug bastion of a Midwest fraternity have led to a few clashes, but they have long since learned that I don't easily back down when challenged. I also pick my battles and often bite my tongue, but their boorish views of the other sex annoy me.

Before Jim can object, we are interrupted by Sahm, who has just joined the table after the band takes its second break.

"Holy shit, J.D. You tore the place up."

"Well, I probably could have avoided the lame Gene Pitney attempt."

"Man, nobody is going to remember that. You had the place in the palm of your hands."

"Thanks, I felt pretty good about the other songs."

"Pretty good? To say the least. Say, the other guys in the band were asking about you. We could use someone for the hard rockers we do. No one's really got the edgy voice for those. Want to sit in again with us for a few of our gigs?"

"Hey, twist my arm. I need to learn a few more songs, though."

"We can give you the list. Berry, Jerry Lee, Eddie Cochran. You know all that stuff. And probably more if you want to add some."

"Of course, sure, let me know what you need and when."

"Man, you had charisma up there," says "Horse" Harper, one of my other brothers who has just joined us at the table. His long face and large sensitive eyes mean he was born for that nickname. "You drew the attention of every single person in the room."

"Okay, well, I've got an okay voice."

"It wasn't your voice, man. It was you. It's like your entire soul was naked up there and we knew just enough about you to want to know more."

"Not sure what more there is to know."

"Everyone else who gets up there tries to be someone else. They try to be Elvis. They try to be Brenda Lee. Anyone but themself. You were just you. Nothing to hide."

"I guess that's not hard because I'm really not anyone else."

In my nervousness, I realize I've consumed quite a bit of water and beer, and it is catching up with me. I excuse myself and head toward the men's room. It has a long line, so I head out into the cold damp air to the one-holer at the back of the building. Thankfully no line at this one.

When I open the door to leave, Astrid Gilbert is standing in my way.

## FOUR

# TABLE TALK AT THE BIRD'S EYE

**J.D. Clay**

*February 1964*

"It's definitely yours."

Astrid Gilbert sits across from me, her elbows resting on the worn tabletop in our booth. Despite the many times we have slept with each other, we have rarely literally slept together, so we've almost never gone together for breakfast. Certainly not on a Tuesday morning. Her call to my room in the fraternity house had awakened both me and my roommate, who had glared at me from his pillow. She had cut off my whispered complaint, simply saying: "Meet me at the Bird's Eye in ninety minutes."

I had arrived at the restaurant about a half hour before she did. The Bird's Eye is located on a corner in a residential area, and I had wondered why she picked a place rarely frequented by our fellow students. By Burgoyne standards, it was high-end. Blue hair prime rib fare for dinner.

Amid the clinking of plates and clatter of the kitchen, I had gazed around the room at the establishment's various trophies. Despite the distancing between townies and students, Burgoyne State is clearly a source of local pride for the townspeople, given our stellar record in athletics. There are various autographed pictures around the room, including a signed Pittsburgh Steelers jersey of Stosh Hammer, one of a handful of alumni who made it to the NFL.

My reverie had been broken the moment Astrid joined me in the booth.

She didn't mince words with her claim.

"How do you know?" I ask, then instantly realize this sounded like an unintended accusation.

"I'll try not to be insulted by that question, J.D. You are the only guy I have been with for the past four months. Does that surprise you?"

Since the night at Spooley's, I've heard from several people about her multiple relationships. Most of my fellow students look down their noses at "libertines." Few use that classical word, though. "Easy" or "slut" are far more likely. That did not deter me. Astrid is one of the smartest people I have ever met—a straight-A dean's list student likely to accomplish great things long after the epithets have been forgotten. Nor does she seem to be overly concerned about her reputation. It is probably that self-assurance that attracts me to her as much as any of her physical attributes. If not for Faith, I could probably love Astrid, even if it is an obvious dead end. It would be far more adventurous and challenging.

Until that night at Spooley's, I had had few relationships with other students, none of which had been deeply intimate. When we left for college, I was still waiting for Faith's answer to my question, holding out hope. We do get together when we're home, and I haven't encountered anyone who could take her place.

But what followed that night at Spooley's has been one of the most exhilarating relationships I have ever had. I am drawn to Astrid's intellectual power as much as anything, as we talk about a wide range of things, including civil rights (on which we mostly agree) and Cold War politics (on which we mostly don't). With Faith, I share a set of values and goals. But with Astrid, I share interests and viewpoints—perhaps even more so than with Faith. I have realized all along that things with Astrid will inevitably come to an end, but that has never dampened my enjoyment of the relationship.

Until this morning. I had assumed that, with her liberated attitude, monogamy was anathema. She has continued her comfortable flirtation with other guys, and she has never seemed jealous of my flirtations. With Astrid, jealousy would be an anachronism. I also assumed that she was protecting herself, like more and more women were doing. I usually took precautions, but not every single time.

"So, you just assume that I was sleeping around?" She says it loud enough for the table next to us to notice. It is an elderly couple that very quickly downs their coffee and departs.

I'm staring at a broken yolk and wondering why of all things I decided to order eggs this morning. Astrid seems to be stabbing forcefully at her sausages. It is not a day for subtle metaphors.

I now realize I have been a constant for her. I could say the same, even though Faith continues to dominate my thoughts. Thus, in a spiritual sense, Astrid, not me, had been the faithful one.

Her stare is fixed on me.

My next question is both obvious and insulting, but I have to ask: "Didn't you take precautions?"

She shrugs. "Sure, most of the time, but you weren't exactly Hector yourself."

"Huh?"

"Hector. Troy. Trojan. Get it?"

I forgot she had a classics minor. Her accusatory demeanor is gone, and she is now more of a doomed coconspirator.

"Yes, I get it." My next obvious question: "What are we going to do about it?"

Of course, there is one daunting option. My parents have always insisted that if I ever "get a girl into trouble," I will marry her. They assume that's their decision, but, without ever contemplating it as a serious possibility, I have always assumed I would do the noble thing anyway.

She frowns and shakes her head.

"We? What are *we* going to do about it? It seems like I'm the one left holding the placenta. And no, that's not funny."

She says the word "placenta" loud enough to gain the attention of another one of the Blue Hairs. I'm feeling like the most important drama of my whole life is being played out in a theater with an unwilling audience. I quickly finish my eggs and ask the waitress for the check. We walk out trying not to pick any words out of the din.

Some freshly fallen snow from the night before results in less foot traffic on the way back to campus. We pretty much have the sidewalks to ourselves, but the resulting winter hush is a blanket that makes silence easier than conversation. But we need to finish this, so I force things.

"I guess I'm feeling like I have some responsibility here, both physical and moral," I say. "That's obvious, isn't it?"

For the first time in the conversation, she softens.

"Not to a lot of men."

"I'm not a lot of men."

"That's only partially true," she says matter-of-factly. "For the most part, all guys—including you—are just walking photocopy machines looking for ways to duplicate themselves."

"What's a photocopy machine?"

"Never mind. You get my point." Fortunately, her point comes across as more an observation than an accusation.

"Okay, I get I'm just a little more than a bit player here, but you had some urgency in getting us together. Clearly you're not writing me off altogether. What are you—as opposed to *we*—going to do about it?"

"I'm not going to have it."

I come to a halt as she keeps walking. There was neither defiance nor remorse in her voice.

"That's illegal," I say, with neither defiance nor remorse, and hasten to catch up with her.

"Yeah, well, the law is out of touch with reality. It's also illegal in many places for whites to marry Blacks. Believe me, I'm not the first person I know who has had to deal with this, so I can easily find out where to go."

She lets that sink in before adding, "It would be very chivalrous if you paid for it."

It occurs to me that I would not get very far with her by pointing out it would make me an accomplice in her crime. She would just say I already am, which would be at least partially true. Blurred legal distinctions don't seem to make much difference anyway at this point.

"Okay, but it's not just illegal. It's also wrong."

Now she stops walking and turns, looking me directly in the eyes.

"Ah, the Great Liberal has spoken. I love all your flowery words about how civil rights go beyond race and include women. Did you leave your soap box back in your room?"

The campus has been sharply divided over the Civil Rights Movement. At least among those who follow public affairs. Everyone knows I persuaded my fraternity to pass a resolution banning discrimination. It had met only token resistance because it is largely symbolic anyway, with no Black students enrolled at the school. But symbols can make a difference.

"Okay, sorry, abortion is just not an issue I've given a lot of thought to," I acknowledge. "Guess I pretty much assumed I would never have to deal with it."

"Suspect most men haven't. Women think about it all the time. Does that surprise you?"

She starts walking again, at a brisker pace, as if she doesn't care what my answer will be.

"No, I guess it shouldn't. Far less of a theoretical concern for them. And you're more likely than me to know women who have quietly dealt with it. They're not going to go around broadcasting it."

"No, just a bunch of incorrigible criminals, I guess."

We continue walking in silence until the campus comes into view. That will end the conversation, so I try to hurry things to a resolution.

"Well, look, regardless of what the law should say, it's still taking a life. That just seems wrong." I take the plunge. "Why don't we just get married?"

Her look of surprise turns quickly into a giggle, which turns into torrents of laughter that other pedestrians, now mostly students, notice. She finally regains her composure as I escort her to a bench far enough off the sidewalk.

"So, unless you and I have a radically different view of marriage, I guess that's a pretty clear no," I acknowledge.

"'Why don't we just get married?' You might as well ask, 'Why don't we just go to the movies tonight?' 'Why don't we just go get a grilled cheese down at the student union?' Are you shitting me?"

"But it is the right thing to do instead of taking a life."

"'The right thing to do'?!" she repeats forcefully and grabs my arm and points her finger at me. "J.D., right now I am torn between contempt and admiration for you, and I don't know how to put it into words. But let me try. First, the contempt. We don't even know when this other life *begins*. Certainly not in any sentient form for a while anyway. It hasn't even reached the larvae stage as far as I know. Meanwhile, what about *our* lives? Think of everything we each hope to accomplish and how that would cut things short while you went off to some job in a drugstore while I stayed home with the diapers."

Since it was clear my offer was a nonstarter, my sense of guilt expands proportionate to my sense of relief.

"You said something about admiration," I remind her.

"Look, J.D., I really like you," she continues. "Well, I guess I've pretty much proven that. You are a really smart, caring guy, and I actually know you well enough to know you don't just say things to get through the moment. If I said yes, you really would go through with this."

I had convinced myself of that as well.

"You are probably going to build a very nice life for some lucky woman. But I have to have someone I really love, not just someone I like a lot, so that woman is not me. The marriage would be doomed to divorce, and do we want to put a child through that?"

"Okay, well, have you thought about adoption?" Of course, she has, but I just want to know why she rejected it.

"Sure, I thought about it. I also thought about what it would do to my education, my reputation back home, my relationship with my parents. Ever since my older sister was killed in a car accident, I've been their prize, even if I usually don't deserve to be. This would crush them. Should I go on?"

"I guess not."

For a person so typically self-assured, she is now showing a brief glimpse of fear. I am waiting in vain for her to say something.

I finally speak, "Well, I can't really stop you from doing this."

"No, you can't. But you also don't have to wash your hands completely of it. You can pay for it. I'm also going to need to travel somewhere away from Iowa. Would be nice to have someone who cares go with me."

I readily agree to both.

FIVE

# A NEW STAR IN CONGRESS

**Isaiah Stone**

*March 1982*

When I walked to the offices of the *Padua Patriot* this morning, I assumed it would just be another day covering the courthouse, a school board session, or any number of other dull venues assigned to a struggling reporter of a small-town newspaper. Anything but this.

"You want me to do a story about that new congressman who wrote a song about . . . uh . . . boners?" I ask my editor, the legendary Charlie Kane.

I know any assignment on politics can help my career, but I don't see how covering yet another flaky politician will give me the boost I need. We don't do sarcasm or cynicism, however well deserved.

"The song is not about erections," Kane insists, peering over his bifocals. I love working for Kane. He is right out of central casting with thinning hair parted in the middle, a bow tie, and suspenders. To cap things off, he has a pipe that only seems to leave his mouth for a sneeze or yawn, but it rarely emits any smoke. Oddly, the bow tie, which in so many other men marks pretention, makes him even more endearing.

And indeed, he is the real deal. His modest office belies his national prominence. An autographed picture of him and Ernie Banks. A black-and-white picture of Scottish coal miners that I assume were ancestors. An imposing photo of Teddy Roosevelt—Kane's only political hero—standing in front of a moose. A bust of William Allen White, an iconic

Midwesterner cut from the same cloth. But there is no sign of his Pulitzer Prize or congratulatory photos with well-known nonsports celebrities. Any visitor to his office would have no idea of his accomplishments. He likes to be underestimated.

"This Congressman Clay's song was called 'Hard On,' wasn't it?" I ask, stifling a smirk.

"No, the song was called 'Heart On,'" Kane clarifies giving a hard pronunciation of the T, despite the pipe that grows from his lips. "I'm guessing you never really listened to it."

"When that song came out, 'Rubber Duckie' was probably my favorite song. Nope, never paid much attention to it."

Kane clears his throat while resting his pipe on his desk.

"Okay, then just listen to these lyrics about a paraplegic soldier returning to his sweetheart after being given a Purple Heart:"

*While I carried that gun beneath those faraway skies*
*My memories carried your bluest of eyes*
*Now these silver wings carry me back over the sea*
*So in your loving arms I know that I will soon be*
*Well, the damage from that bullet can't keep us apart*
*And I know you'll still love me with my new metal heart*

He stops singing and gives me an inquiring look. "Not bad singing, huh, for someone whose melodic career ended with eighth-grade music class? That's just the verse. Now here's the chorus that almost everyone in the country could sing at the time:"

*Ribbon of purple and a gold border, too*
*With a picture of George hung on more than a few*
*I hope it makes up for what did not make it through*
*The best I can do is have my heart on for you.*

Kane's voice quavers on the final line.

"Sorry, Isaiah, I didn't mean to lose it there. My brother got a Purple Heart for losing a leg in Nam, so the song really hit home for me at the time. Meanwhile, it didn't hurt that Clay himself earned a Silver Star for his own service there. That's probably why the censors looked the other way on the double entendre."

I am not at all surprised that Kane can sing so soulfully. Honestly, there's very little about the man who hired me as a favor to my father that surprises me anymore. He won the Pulitzer after blowing the lid off a zoning bribery scheme involving the Padua mayor and half the city council. It received a lot of attention outside Iowa—disproving the "Andy of Mayberry" image of bucolic small-town innocence. It didn't sit well with the local gentry—even those uninvolved—but it gained him a level of respect (and fear) that few small-town editors carry.

Meanwhile, he has gained national prominence through his coverage of Iowa politics, a focal point since Jimmy Carter leapfrogged the other presidential contenders by carrying the caucuses in 1976. Politically, Iowa is a fascinating blend of extremes, moderates, and powerful interests on all sides of most issues. The *Patriot* is second only to the *Des Moines Register* as the ultimate word on Iowa politics.

But Kane has always done all the political reporting himself, leaving the local news to me and a more senior (and far less ambitious) reporter. The fact that he is assigning me a political story is a welcome sign of confidence. Is he also thinking of me as a potential successor? I'm encouraged by both, but the latter is out of the cards for a Chicago boy who is all too eager to leave the suffocating strictures of a small Midwestern town. I know why someone would choose to stay here. It's the security of small-town predictability. I may look for that when I'm Kane's age. But much as I admire Kane and love working for him, a good political story could help me break out of here.

Our reverie from the lyrics is broken by a noisy scuffle in front of the abortion clinic across the street. We go to the window and see yet another young woman trying to enter, standing nose to nose with the demonstrators.

These encounters have become increasingly common since Reagan's election has emboldened opponents of the Supreme Court's *Roe* decision. The clinic was set up soon after that decision, and it primarily serves the out-of-town coeds at Padua State. Permanent Padua residents would presumably go to another town to protect their reputation. The pro-lifers have established a "watch team" during business hours that, among other things, photographs the women who come and go.

I can see the distress on Kane's face. The paper has never taken an editorial position for or against *Roe*, which has caused demonstrations by both sides at the paper's office. We have been alternatively called "latent baby killers" or "the Pope's patriots," a reference to Kane's devout Catholicism. Kane tells me he has tried writing an editorial with a nuanced view of the decision but has tossed each draft for being *too* nuanced. He vows to keep trying, but the editorial has never materialized.

"With the opening of the new memorial in DC, this reminds me of some of the clashes we saw during Vietnam," Kane observes. "Not as many people in the demonstrations but even more intense. Funny how *Roe* was decided around the time the war was winding down. I guess there always has to be something that divides us."

"Do we as journalists have a role somewhere in there?" I ask.

"Not at all sure. On issues like abortion, what more does anyone need to know before making what is really a moral choice? But, yes, in other areas, we can play a strong role in at least establishing the facts. After Nam, who else is anyone going to listen to? Certainly not the government."

"Hope so. And it seems like the advances in communications technology they are projecting could really help wipe out widespread ignorance and miscommunications. I mean, twenty years ago, who would have ever anticipated faxes and Xerox machines? What's next? Maybe there's room for optimism."

Kane looks at me with raised eyebrows and a half smile but doesn't speak. I know it's time to get back to work.

"Okay, so J.D. Clay is a one-hit wonder from a few years ago," I note. "I'm betting outside his district even those who remember him from the song would hardly take him seriously."

Kane starts filling his pipe—something I have never witnessed—but will he actually light it?

"They probably don't, but maybe they should," he responds. "From what I am hearing from my sources in Washington, he is starting to make waves. Doesn't fit the expected mold of a Democrat. Pisses off the unions and others on the left for not toeing the line. Even rattles the leadership by trying to move policies toward the middle against their wishes. That's pretty uncommon for a first-term congressman. But a lot of people think the Democratic party has gone too far left since its big wins following Watergate. Carter's tried to fix that, but his failure to do so helped Reagan and now things have gone too far right. People may be looking for someone like Clay."

"So, other than making a record, what did he do after the war before getting elected?"

"He returned to his family drugstore business. You also know his name from the Clay Drugs drugstore chain in this part of Iowa. That's probably where you get your condoms."

I ignore the dig. Kane often kids me about my bachelorhood in a town where nearly everyone marries not long after completing their education.

"I hadn't made the obvious connection. So, he's a successful businessman?"

"Well, his father is the one who grew the business, but the name recognition didn't hurt J.D.'s political aspirations."

Kane finally lights his pipe—another subtle sign of trust?

"Isaiah, I want you to check this guy out. He might be the real deal."

"I'm not going to do a puff piece, Mr. Kane."

"That's not what I'm asking. I always try to tell it like it is, so I expect nothing less from you. You're going to need to do some traveling for this, Isaiah. Not to DC. We'll let the *Register* worry about the DC angle for now. I think there's an opportunity for us here."

He takes a puff and lets this soak with me.

"We need to explore his district," he continues. "I want to know how this guy is playing among the voters themselves. I can guarantee you, come primary season, he's going to have a lot of the far lefties nipping at his heels for being an apostate. Of course, that would play right into the Republicans' hands on recapturing the district, but the extremes never seem to factor that in."

"What if I don't like what I see? He probably has a lot of fans, but I would want to call things as I see them if he's just another opportunist trying to look different. That may not be well received by a lot of our readers."

"Isaiah, rest assured I am not looking for a puff piece. I want an honest portrayal, and if there are warts, so be it. That's why you are perfect for this since you don't have a lot of bridges around here to burn."

"Okay, boss, if this guy is the real deal, as you say, it's going to have to be proven to me."

## Rep. J.D. Clay:
## Can the One-Hit Wonder from Mitoka Produce More Hits?

by Isaiah Stone, *Padua Patriot,* April 12, 1982

I was riding next to Congressman J.D. Clay in his 1972 Ford pickup. We were paying visits to some of the most remote parts of his northwestern Iowa district—one of the largest districts in the Midwest. It stretches from the outskirts of the Omaha–Council Bluffs metropolitan area and almost two-thirds of the way across the state. That's a lot of farms and small towns—like Clay's hometown of Mitoka—and a lot of diverse points of view and needs.

“Smell that? Any idea what it is?” Clay asks, as we pass a leafy field.

I take a guess at oats, which draws a chuckle.

“So you’re not from Iowa, I guess. That beany smell is from soybeans.”

He then explained how he can tell what crops are growing next to the road just by the odor. It reminds me of a wine and whisky connoisseur who claims he can identify fruits in the bouquet and flavors of his beverages. It all smelled like farmland to me.

Clay is just over halfway through his first term and is gearing up for reelection in a district that has seldom elected Democrats, even moderate ones like him. In a Republican-dominated year led by Ronald Reagan, Clay was a rare Democrat who’d unseated a Republican—Don Shyla. He did, however, get some help from Shyla—after twelve terms, he had been smug enough to assume that he could survive a bribery indictment. Still, few expect the freshman congressman to be as lucky in his first reelection attempt. Key Republicans in the district, who had bided their time for years waiting for Shyla to step down, see this as the opportunity they’ve been waiting for.

Clay’s congressional stint is not his first flirtation with fame. Even those who didn’t know his name before probably remembered his band, The Cyclones, for which he was the lead singer. If not the name of the group, most would remember their hit, “Heart On.” The song about a disabled Vietnam vet returning home to his sweetheart with a Purple Heart touched a nerve with the public. Even those in the older generation who blanched at the double entendre were moved by its poignancy and respect for its subjects. The fact that Clay himself was a decorated Vietnam vet made it even more compelling.

And a compelling story his is. He was awarded the Silver Star after he risked his life by flying his helicopter into heavy enemy fire to evacuate the wounded aircrew of a downed helicopter. As he was rescuing other soldiers, they told him their wreck had destroyed a number of homes of people who had played no part in the war. Clay returned and saved four Vietnamese children whose home was in flames that had killed their parents. This display of heroism won him the admiration of many war opponents. Clay has reportedly kept in touch with the families who adopted the children, sending them birthday and Christmas gifts every year, though he avoids discussing it publicly.

In addition to the hit song, the Clay name was already well known throughout the area because of a chain of drugstores owned by his family. His grandfather had opened the first Clay Drugs in Mitoka in the 1920s, and his father expanded the operation to another fifteen stores sprinkled throughout the region. Those stores are now managed by J.D.'s wife of seventeen years, Faith, who worked there as a teenager.

J.D. and Faith were married right before he left for Viet Nam, but their relationship went all the way back to their childhood growing up together as close friends.

"We never really dated until after we both went away to college and got together back home during breaks," Faith says with a smile. "He figured it out a lot sooner than me; it took me a long time to realize that we were more than just friends. I came from a very strong religious background—my father is a minister—and I initially resisted any long-term relationship. He persisted and finally won me over. He went away to Nam right after the wedding, and I wondered if I'd done the right thing. Supporting his political role while running the family business has been a challenge, but it has its rewards, too."

Clay shares his first name—James—with his father but has always been called J.D.—for James Daniel—to distinguish himself from his dad. The acronym stuck—a good fit in Washington, the City of Acronyms.

Clay's looks don't hold him back, either. On his best days, he looks like Gregory Peck, or sometimes Gary Cooper, Montgomery Clift, or even Cary Grant. If he hadn't gone into politics, he would have been a movie mogul's dream. He speaks with a firm, authoritative voice that quells any dissent. If he was an extremist, his forceful manner could draw comparisons with the deplorables of recent history. But the only thing he seems to be extreme in is moderation.

The Democratic leadership in the House is watching Clay's election closely, knowing that "leaning Democratic" could easily turn into "toss-up," depending on whom the Republicans nominate. His moderate leanings can be a thorn in the leadership's side. However, if his election helps secure the Democrats' hold on the House, they can look the other way. One reason why many give Clay a good chance of holding an otherwise solid Republican district is because he often votes like, well, a Republican. That's often an annoyance to Speaker "Hap" O'Connor but tolerated because he knows anyone who voted 100 percent with the party could never hold that seat for the Democrats.

Meanwhile, after only one year in Congress, Clay is increasingly viewed as a leader among the moderate Democrats who are always at risk on partisan issues. Instead of consistently voting with Republicans, he very often uses his unpredictability as leverage to modify legislation, moving it toward the center, thus capturing not only the moderate Ds but a few Rs as well.

A good example was the reauthorization of the food stamp program as part of last year's Farm Bill. Despite being a critical piece of legislation for Clay's constituency, he and his followers threatened to vote against it over a provision that would have allowed strikers to receive food stamps. The Speaker could have allowed him to offer an amendment on the House floor to delete that provision, risking an embarrassing leadership loss while exposing its members to a divisive debate over whether the party is beholden to organized labor. Instead, the provision was pulled from the bill before going to the floor.

The move received little national attention, but Clay got a lot of credit in his district for not only standing up to the liberals who wanted to "subsidize the labor bosses' strikes" but also for ensuring passage of the bill many of them depended on for its subsidies to their own livelihoods.

"One of the reasons I ran was to try to get some rationality in the political process," Clay claims. "So much of Washington is all about whose side you are on. A lot of those in my party think just because something is a 'Republican idea' they need to vote against it. Republicans have the same mindset. But my constituents sent me to Washington to fix their problems, not to score points. That's what football games are for, with one winner and one loser. In my view, we all need to be winners, regardless of the score."

When I suggested that a lot of people in both parties wondered why he didn't simply switch parties, he dismissed the notion offhand.

"First, if you look at my voting record, I vote with the Democratic leadership a solid majority of the time. Maybe around 80 percent, but I'm not keeping score." (According to this reporter's research, it is actually 81 percent, so he probably does keep score.)

"But the question really goes a lot deeper," he continues. "A lot of centrists, like myself, both within and outside Congress, decide on their party affiliation by their reaction to the extremes on both sides—the mythical party 'base.' Instead of worrying about which one they agree with most, they gravitate toward the one whose fringe scares them the least.

"I can use myself as an example. I really don't like how unreasonable the far left can be, even though I generally agree with their broad objective of a just and generous society. They are unreasonable, they push for any kind of change regardless of how disruptive, and they castigate anyone who doesn't agree with them 100 percent. But they don't scare me that much because at least they still believe in the American system. They just think they can improve on capitalism without destroying it.

"But the far right does scare me. They are often driven by hatred and suspicion of anything or anyone different from the status quo. Even though they aren't necessarily racist—and most of them certainly aren't—the reality is that racists align themselves with them. I could never be in a party with a base that includes people like that."

But Clay still thinks the extremes play an important role.

"We need the far left to keep pushing for change and getting us out of our cultural comfort zone to address inequities. But we need the far right to ensure a measure of caution, so we don't go too far. What happens if you give too much control to one of these extremes, though? You either get something like the Jim Crow South—or worse—or you have the guillotine of the far left Jacobins who executed anyone who questioned any aspect of the French Revolution."

In his view, it's the job of those in the middle to find the right balance.

"If the moderates prevail, society continues to move forward at a measured pace. At least in my state, I think centrist Democrats are the most effective in playing that role, but certainly there are centrist Republicans who do as well."

As we traveled around his district, this moderate viewpoint was reflected in conversations with many voters. One voter told me she usually votes Republican, and she disagrees with a lot of J.D.'s "liberal views." But she admires how he is "his own man."

With her, it doesn't hurt that he is pro-life, which is consistent with her strong religious views. In Washington, this is a thorn in the side of many of the liberal organizations that generally support Democrats. It has also made him a pariah with feminist organizations, even though Clay downplays the issue when it is raised.

"Look, I have all the sympathy in the world for a woman who winds up in a situation where she is considering whether to end a pregnancy—especially if the man involved is unwilling to own up to his own role and responsibility. That is a very tragic situation. But it still is the taking of a life, and I just can't go along with that, absent very extraordinary circumstances like a rape or a threat to the life of the mother. I'm not rabid on this. I fully respect the other point of view, but I just can't be at peace with myself if I endorse a policy that takes a life at any stage."

When I asked him if he would agree with calling women who have abortions "baby killers," he visibly blanched at the epithet. Clearly, he struggles with the issue and is uncomfortable discussing it.

Meanwhile, not all of his constituents appreciate his careful approach to issues. Carrie Jones, a lifelong Democrat who heads up the child nutrition programs in Council Bluffs—the only truly urban section of his district—is adamant and not reluctant to be quoted: "He is a Democrat in name only. His vote last year for Reagan's cuts to the school lunch program was heartless. I know he doesn't see a lot of poverty in most parts of his district, but it's here and we need Democrats who are committed to the war on poverty that Lyndon Johnson started."

It should be noted that the cuts were part of a much larger package that was aimed at reducing overall spending in several areas. In fact, in his House floor speech before voting, Clay said he didn't necessarily agree with all the bill's provisions, and he even singled out child nutrition as one of those areas.

If anything sets Clay apart from most of his Democratic colleagues, it is his commitment to containing the budget across the board. While that endears him to many of his fiscally conservative constituents, not all of them are willing to be as unselective.

One voter said, while he admires Clay's service in Viet Nam, "he seems to have abandoned the fight against Communism. He talks about cuts in military spending and does not support the president's efforts to contain Communism in Central America. What he doesn't seem to realize is we are now engaged in a global war that will eventually decide whether we can continue to live in freedom. We don't have to have Moscow launching a missile attack on Washington to make that real. It's already there."

In fact, Clay has taken no position on how the United States should deal with the encroachment of Communism in Central America. Like many of his Democratic colleagues, he has remained silent.

I finally asked him the question that always lingers with a rising star in DC—how far did he expect to go? The ultimate prize?

"Hey, right now, I'm just really enjoying this gig and hoping it is not another 'one-hit wonder.' I'm pretty low on the charts, but maybe with a bullet. Even if the voters don't want to buy my stuff, I want to make some pretty good music while I have this job. No matter how far my political career goes, even if it's just until the next election, I want to leave office knowing the country is better off for me having served."

# PART TWO

A few years ago, with little more public notice than a few obligatory obituaries, former Iowa Democratic Congressman J.D. Clay's life came to a violent end that remains shrouded in mystery. He had served in Congress from 1981 to 1991 and had many great legislative accomplishments, but that's not what the obituaries immediately gravitated toward.

Rather, it was his central role in the media-fed public frenzy surrounding the disappearance of a young intern in the nation's capital—a situation in which he was initially suspected of playing some role. Her body was eventually found, and the perpetrator was identified by circumstantial evidence following his suicide. But this was revealed too late for Clay, well after defeat in his primary. Though Clay was exonerated, those headlines were much smaller and nowhere near the front page. So, most people probably remember him as being guilty of the crime or having some direct

country—one who rises above partisan rhetoric in order to accomplish something, even if it means compromising. He did this on numerous occasions, whether the issue involved employment protections, environmental restrictions, regulation of large corporations, or any number of other areas where partisanship can paralyze needed action.

But now I have to ask myself: Did my genuine admiration for Clay prevent me from performing my role as a journalist with the right degree of probity and skepticism? Perhaps.

Recent events caused me to do a little quiet digging into what Clay's real role was and what I have learned is both disturbing and embarrassing.

First, let me make it clear that I have learned nothing that leads me to suspect Clay of either committing or conspiring in the murder of Saundra Gray. There is nothing connecting Clay with her murderer and my

If all of this
in her eventu
protect her. B
as he could
Not a murder
his repeated a
with Gray.
disingenuous
better term.
forward with
obstructing
identification
prolonging
those who kn
And one
"irrelevant"
happened ab
Gray and the
and had result
But how do
if there was a
he had spok
politically, bu

SIX

# A RELATIONSHIP FORGED

**Wally North**

*January 1984*

The cornfields of Iowa are scrolling by as I am ferrying Congressman Clay to the next campaign stop. He's been quiet all morning and, while outwardly friendly, has kept his distance from me while I carry out my campaign driving duties.

Even though I haven't let on in my calls back home to Gloria, I still haven't decided whether I did the right thing by leaving my stable job with the trade association to volunteer with the long-shot presidential campaign of Iowa Congressman J.D. Clay. Stable, yes, but a low-level job with the National Association of Pizza Shop Owners (yes, NAPSO) just did not seem like a ticket to the kind of glamorous, influential position I was hoping for in DC. The only thing rising in the job has been our credit card debt.

After graduating with a political science degree from Iowa State, I set off with my new wife Gloria to what I thought must be the most fascinating place to work in the United States. I quickly learned that the best starting place for a generalist like me was something on "the Hill" (i.e., Congress). Gloria took a job with the phone company while I pounded the halls of Congress with my rather lean résumé. When we needed more to pay the bills, I took a quick position with NAPSO as a legislative assistant. It paid almost as well as a Hill job, but the work—basically monitoring legislation and regulations for my boss, the NAPSO lobbyist—gave me no exposure to the real influence wielders.

That's when Dad volunteered to help. He knew a guy who knew a guy who knew the top dog in Congressman Clay's office—his administrative assistant, in congressional parlance. Turned out they didn't have any open positions, but Clay now had his sights on the White House. He had made a bit of a name for himself in his first term with a successful amendment to the Defense Bill in the House aimed at cutting "waste, fraud, and abuse" in the Department of Defense in the midst of a huge increase in funding. He generally supported the increase but parroted Reagan's rhetoric about a bloated federal government back at the hawks, who had a hard time opposing it.

Very ambitious indeed for a second-term congressman to run for president, but an obscure governor from Georgia had proven in 1976 that the primary system could make just about anyone with modest credentials a contender. And it all started with the Iowa caucuses, which provided instant name recognition for any Iowa politician.

Not surprisingly, no one but Clay himself gave him a squirrel's chance in a kennel, so he was starting out on a shoestring. He needed a driver who knew Iowa, someone willing to leave a well-paying job for a long shot at power in a new administration, and an understanding spouse who'd tolerate them sinking even deeper into debt while her telephone operator job became their only income—for a while. (No kids—yet at least.)

So that's why I'm driving the congressman from a rotary meeting in Marshalltown to a fish fry in Waterloo a week before the caucuses. Despite our distance, he's at least been as polite as one would expect from any politician. At the outset, he asked me about my own background and aspirations—without any promises about helping me fulfill them—and it turns out we do have a few shared interests beyond politics—mostly music, movies, and history. When we meet with voters, he always makes it a point to introduce me, emphasizing my Iowa roots. But that is clearly a ploy for political gain. Most of the time while I'm driving, he is buried in local papers, issue briefings, and other staff memos.

He will occasionally mark up the latter with a red pen, dashing off notes in the margin, presumably to the sender. Every once in a while, he mutters "fucking liberals," or, in a slightly louder voice, "fucking conservatives." I guess that is for the more respectable Republicans, because sometimes he says, "fucking fascists," or, even more emphatically, "fucking fascist assholes."

One thing I have been able to add to my Iowa geographical repertoire is the location of pretty much every pay phone in the state. This is the only way J.D. is able to get constant updates from his campaign staff, mostly his press secretary Darby Randolph, who will be waiting for us at the fish fry.

While stopped at Howdy's Gas and Grub in Grundy Center, it doesn't take long for a couple of young women to approach J.D. on his way in. In any small town, the appearance of a celebrity—and that would be pretty much anyone who has been on TV—can quickly turn into "an event." We are not in J.D.'s district, and his cinematic looks alone would be a draw, but even the most apathetic Iowa voter can't ignore all the publicity around the caucuses, so the young women know who he is. I can overhear their questions, which have nothing to do with policy. He finally gets rid of them—politely—by saying he needs to call his wife—his usual ruse in these situations.

A couple of stray dogs, sensing the excitement, have wandered into the lot, but they quickly realize there is no food involved, so they move on with their quest. There is one other car at the pump, driven by an elderly man with a cane. He starts to wave and then recognizes J.D. and crawls back into his car. His "Love It or Leave It" bumper sticker explains everything.

I fill the tank and go in to buy a Fry's Five Centres bar to tide me over until the fish fry. The look on the woman's face behind the counter makes me wonder if she had boiled muskrat for breakfast. I return to the car, and, Five Centre's being one of my favorites, I savor each separate flavor as I work my way through the bar. I reach the black currant part when J.D. returns to the car half ashen, half pissed.

"Godammit," he says as he slams the door shut.

He takes a long pause as his face grows redder. I'm not asking. I start the car, but he slaps the dash.

"Don't. Just pull over to one of those parking spots. I need to think."

I do as he says. We sit in silence while his face starts going through the seven stages of something. When he gets to about the fifth, he turns to me.

"Okay, kid, give me your take on this." It is the first time he has ever said anything to me without smiling. Is he really asking for advice or just testing me? Either way, it seems like a good sign for long-term employment possibilities.

"Here's the deal, Wally." He uses my name, and his Gary Cooper eyes are piercing mine—another good sign. "There's a story circulating that my father was in the Ku Klux Klan, based on a picture of him and another kid holding a rifle with a well-known Klansman in the twenties. It's being circulated by the *Des Moines Jewish News,* and I'm being called upon to renounce my father and change the names of our drugstores, which he founded, as you know. According to Darby, there is a flock of reporters in Waterloo waiting to press me on it. What do I do?"

I don't want to overload him with questions, but I need a little more.

"Is the picture real?"

His sigh has a hint of resignation. "Well, the picture definitely could be. There was a guy my grandfather's age named Clay Sumner who was eventually convicted of burning a synagogue. Darby says the older man is identified in the picture as the local Grand Dragon, even though he isn't pictured in robes. The other guy apart from my dad is probably Clay's son, Judd. Dad was the same age and probably hung out with him on occasion. I do remember Judd. Definitely a recalcitrant conservative. He owned Mitoka's leading building company. Probably built a quarter of the houses in town."

"Your dad has passed on? Was there ever any hint he belonged to the Klan?"

"Absolutely not. Both my parents believed strongly in equality and taught me accordingly. Race, religion, you name it. They were actually pretty outspoken and pissed a lot of the townsfolk off with their Stevenson, Kennedy, and Johnson signs. Even lost a few customers because of that. There is no way my dad would have been in the Klan. But how do you prove something didn't happen sixty years ago?"

It isn't a rhetorical question. He starts pinching the top of his nose. Right below a pensive squint.

The whole thing seems pretty flimsy to me. "Isn't the burden of proof on them? So, don't they need more than just a picture?"

"Of course they would, Wally, if I was just an ordinary congressman. And, meanwhile, to be crass, I have very few racial or religious minorities in my district, so it would take a whole lot more than that to present any threat to my congressional career. Shit, I may actually pick up a few votes with some of the right-wing dipshits in my district."

"But you're running for president."

"Precisely."

"And those minorities form a big part of the Democratic base."

"Correct, and most of them will go with Mondale anyway, but they aren't as predictably liberal as a lot of people think. And if I mishandle this, I could lose all of them and a lot of others who may be looking me over to see if I have what it takes."

"Still, this seems pretty easy to refute."

"Agree, so why should I be worried?"

A shift in tone tells me he has moved from the final stage of whatever into cold analytical mode. Does he really need any more help from me, or is this just a test?

I start to ask something, but he tells me we just need to think about it for a while. He starts the music cassette, which is playing "[I'm a Fool to Do Your] Dirty Work" by Steely Dan, and turns it up loud enough for us to feel it. When the song finishes, he shuts it off and turns to me without saying a word.

I clear my throat. "I guess it isn't so much whether you refute it but how you do it. Could this be a trap to get you to say something insensitive that can be taken out of context?"

He smiles and raises his eyebrows in mock innocence.

"A trap? In a presidential race? Surely not."

"Right. I guess Nixon didn't have a monopoly on dirty tricks after all."

This time the smile is warmer and even seems to be bordering on respect.

"Okay, political genius. So, what do I say to this phalanx of vultures in Waterloo?"

We spend the next thirty minutes honing his message. When we are done, I feel like he could have done it himself, but his probing questions made me feel like I was also part of the process. It seemed like he was not only testing his message but also me.

When he turns the music back on—appropriately, "Born to Run"—I know he is ready to hit the road.

Halfway to Waterloo, he tells me to stop in Dike, and we find another pay phone at Cougar Dave's Food & Spirits. He doesn't say who he is calling, but when he returns to the car, he has a grim look on his face. He was again stopped by well-wishers—in this case, a middle-aged woman and her attractive daughter, who couldn't take her eyes off J.D. He gave them the obligatory five minutes and then returned to the car. It is clear he didn't want me to ask so we drive in silence the rest of the way to Waterloo.

As we pull up to the Ramada in Waterloo, we see Darby holding off a larger group of reporters than had been expected. Obviously, the allegation is the news of the day. J.D. waves to Darby to let them approach. He walks to a spot on the lawn and makes sure all have gathered. The questions start coming at him quickly, and he holds his hands up to quiet them.

"Is everyone here? You got the cameras rolling? Okay, thanks, I'm going to address the news from this morning one time and one time only. So, I want to make sure you all get it.

"I am aware that there is a picture that appears to be that of my father in the company of a very notorious leader of the Iowa Ku Klux Klan back in the twenties. I believe the other person in the picture is that person's son, who grew up with my father and who, like my father, passed away a while ago. This picture is as newsworthy to me as it is to you. It was taken long before I was born.

"I am aware that in the twenties, the Klan was a major force in Iowa. I never knew that man in the picture—Mr. Clay Sumner—but I know he was the Grand Dragon in Iowa and at one time was accused of burning a synagogue. In fact, he was acquitted, but I'll leave it to historians to determine whether it was an impartial trial. He was a bad man. I did know his son was a friend of the family, as is typically the case in any small town where people grew up going to school together. My father loved to hunt, and I suspect this was taken on a hunting trip that had nothing whatsoever to do with Mr. Sumner's abhorrent activities."

I whisper to myself: "Keep making it about your dad."

He continues in a different, stronger voice. "But let's forget about Sumner, whose life clearly calls for condemnation. How about my dad, who isn't here to defend himself? I can only talk about the James Clay I knew who, along with my mother and my wife Faith, have made me what I am today. Even if I thought there was one ounce of racism or religious prejudice in his body, I would still ask that he be judged as an entire person, in view of all he did for his community, his employees, his country, and, not the least, his family.

"But I don't have to go there, because I know that my father was a tolerant, open-minded person who taught his children to respect all people and judge them the same no matter what their color or religion. And I think my life and my record in public office bears that out.

"So, no. I am not going to renounce my father or do anything to change the proud name of the family business. This picture has nothing to do with my campaign, which is as committed to racial equality as any other campaign. Thank you for listening."

One of the reporters shouts: "Do your drugstores employ any colored people?" An obvious answer would have been that they would, but there are very few Negroes in that part of Iowa. But J.D. deflects it by saying he is through with questions on the incident. A few similar questions are shouted, but he ignores them and turns instead to a question from Isaiah Stone of the *Des Moines Register* about his views on farm policy. As a regular subscriber to the *Register*, I've been impressed with Stone's work, and J.D. has told me he is someone to watch. J.D. is not unbiased. Stone wrote a very favorable profile of J.D. for the *Padua Patriot* during his first term in Congress.

I don't get to talk to J.D. at all the rest of the day, with his more senior advisers dominating his time at the all-day event.

---

We pulled out of Waterloo early this morning and are on the long drive to the southwestern corner of the state.

Yesterday went very well for J.D., and I feel like I helped him, but I am feeling no sense of camaraderie this morning. It's like I am back to square one, with the silence soaked up by Jackson Browne, Little Feat, and John Prine.

When it looks like he will not be saying a word until we get there, I punch off the music and break the silence: "I thought that went well yesterday. You seem to have put that issue to rest."

"Yeah," he responds sullenly, then punches the music back on.

I keep driving for a while but decide to test my new bond with him.

"Rest of the day go okay, you think?" I shout over the music.

"Yeah, sure, the rest of the day was fine."

I hit the off button. "Then what the hell's the matter, J.D.?" I say it like a family member. His testy look chastens me. I miscalculated.

"Sorry, none of my business."

He keeps staring at me. Finally, he breaks the silence. "Actually, I will tell you if you promise to keep it to yourself."

"Of course."

"You know that gas stop we made yesterday where I left you for a while?"

"Sure."

"I put in a call to my mom to get her take on the Klan thing. I also wanted to give her a heads up in case she got any calls, which she hadn't yet at that point."

"Was she aware of the picture?"

"No, but she sure as hell remembered Judd Sumner and his dad, neither of whom she had much regard for."

"I get it with the dad, but I thought his son was a good friend."

"It's like anything else in a small town. When you grow up with someone, go to all the same classes, play together on the same teams, go to each other's weddings, and so forth, you know the drill. It isn't really about being friends. You're stuck with each other. You have a bond, which is as much about shared experiences and community as it is any personal feelings toward each other. So, of course they were close, regardless of whether it was friendship."

"I'm guessing the son was no different from his father?"

"Well, he never headed up the Klan, but in all other respects, he wasn't any different. And he had a particular thing about Jews. I forgot he had lost a brother in the war, and Mom said he blamed the Jews for his loss."

"He thought that was all we were fighting about? Not that that wouldn't have been a good reason anyway, but I thought most people back then thought the war was about defending against tyranny and stopping the spread of fascism—not specifically about what was happening to the Jews."

"Well, people like him don't exactly think like Arnold Toynbee. Why he would blame all of Jewry for the loss of his brother instead of Hitler is anyone's guess, but that was how he looked at it."

"Okay, so he was wrong to blame the Jews. That's still him, not your dad."

"And that's where it gets complicated. Judd Sumner was a very powerful person in Mitoka. His construction company built almost everything in the town from 1940 onward. Couple years after the war, a Holocaust survivor was relocated to Mitoka. Single guy. No family. As it turns out, he was also a pharmacist in Poland before the pogroms."

"Nice fit for Clay Drugs."

"Indeed. Mom said we didn't really need any new pharmacists, but my dad agreed to help him anyway and bring him on."

"Okay, your dad still sounds like a hero to me."

"He was, right up to the point where Judd Sumner walked into the store one day to fill a prescription and found a Jewish pharmacist who could barely speak English. Judd got impatient and started berating him, calling him a 'kike' and who knows what other insults. Well, this guy was pretty tough after surviving the camps, and he started shouting at Judd, probably in Polish, causing a major commotion. The next day, my dad fired him. Apparently, there was some allegation of a prescription not being handled right, jeopardizing customer safety, but Mom's pretty sure it was at Judd's behest. The Jewish guy wound up moving somewhere else, and we have no idea whatever happened to him."

I think about my own parents, who have been great role models for me. Respect and fairness to others regardless of who they are have always been what they've shown me, but what compromises have they made to get them where they are?

"Okay, so that's still your dad but not you."

"That's not the point, Wally. If you're just talking about yesterday and me doing damage control to the campaign, you're right. We got through it. But I'm still upset about what I learned about my dad. For everything he taught me about bigotry, at a critical point, he didn't have the guts to stand up to it when it counted."

He shakes his head in disgust and punches the music back on—"Easy to Slip" by Little Feat fills the space between us.

I assume it's over, but he seems to want to make it a teaching moment.

"The problem is, Wally, shit like the Holocaust, Jim Crow laws, and lynchings happen not just because of the actual perpetrators, but because so many others let them happen. Good people stand by and refuse to say or do anything in order to protect their own situation. And then they feel good about themselves by sending money to some liberal group or voting for the right candidate. As long as people are so chickenshit about this, no amount of lawmaking will correct the problem.

"And that's where I don't know what my own role is. I ran for Congress so I could solve the world's problems. This is a huge one. What can I do? Should I have gotten into this yesterday? And what would my solution have been?"

He reverts to silence again for a moment but then can't let it go.

"What is frustrating is everyone looks to leaders to fix these things. But they don't realize that to fix things like this, they have to fix it themselves. To some extent the laws can go after the bad guys. But sometimes it's the good guys that are as big a part of the problem. They can't just sit back and wait for the law to fix things."

That's it, I guess. He turns the music back up. Jackson Browne's solemn poignancy is just right for the moment. Just before hitting the halfway point in Des Moines, we stop in Dewey Falls at Hogs and Dogs Diner for a sandwich and a call in to Darby. The smiles and handshakes that greet J.D. from the other diners lift his spirits. When we return to the car, J.D. tells me to drive on but doesn't turn the music on.

"Wally, thanks for yesterday. That was very helpful. But there's a lesson in this if you want to stick with politics."

"Sure, J.D., always eager to learn."

"After all was said and done, there actually was a very small grain of truth to the story, even though it wasn't revealed in the pictures. If you stick with politics, you will have to deal with a lot of anecdotes, which is what most of the news is. And just because they aren't false doesn't make them true, either. Mastering that distinction is one of the great challenges in politics."

SEVEN

# J.D. TAKES A STAND

**Wally North**

*August 1986*

I'm making good progress on responding to the fifteen constituent letters in my inbox when our administrative assistant, Park Thatcher, buzzes me. Since my promotion to J.D.'s legislative director, I've been able to pass most of this routine work to the legislative correspondents who report to me. But I still handle the tricky issues that don't fit a standard response.

Before Thatcher buzzed me, I was looking for one from someone who has sold several designs to Fruit of the Loom and Hanes. They're proposing a National Underwear Day. In the two years I've been on J.D.'s staff, I've become as adept as any legislative correspondent at "sharing" our various constituents' concerns—regardless of how ill- or well-fitting.

"You need to get in J.D.'s office," Thatcher orders. "He's about to meet with a bunch of faggots. He asked for me to join him, but I told him I have an important call with a major donor. I'll let you figure out whether you want to shake hands with them and expose yourself. Pretty sure they're here to talk about more money for AIDS research or some such bullshit. Keep in mind there is no political upside to helping them, so by all means do not let him make any promises."

"Well, it's pretty clear now that just shaking hands is okay, so I'm fine with that. I'll be right there."

"Sure, if you believe the research they paid for. Just no promises, okay?"

"Got it." I'm happy for the relief from the pile of letters, even though I know the afternoon mail will likely add at least another five letters.

Five minutes later, I'm sitting in J.D.'s office with an unusual mix of folks. Vic Basile of the Human Rights Campaign Fund (HRCF) is the spokesperson. He is dressed very conservatively in a dark suit with a multicolored tie. I assume he is probably gay, but he does not have any of the obvious stereotypical mannerisms.

That is not as true of some of his cohorts. John White of Manly, Iowa, (of all places) is the token constituent (required in every successful lobbying visit), and he is wearing a pink suit with very loud socks over multicolored Oxford shoes. He is more than a little bit effeminate, and I wonder if he still lives in Manly. Probably not. He gives me a wink that is more jocular than seductive, and I'm glad Thatcher decided not to take the meeting.

Other than someone dressed as a woman with the unmistakable hint of a two-day stubble, the others could raise suspicions about their tendencies from someone like Thatcher, but none are as obvious as White.

Ignoring Thatcher's warning, I shook hands with each of them when introduced. It was a large group seated around J.D.'s coffee table, so I took a seat behind him.

After the obligatory pleasantries, Basile goes into a long intro with a lot of data about the spread of AIDS and its impact, including a significant number of cases in Iowa.

J.D. holds his hand up, interrupting the speech.

"Look, Vic, you don't have to convince me. I completely agree this is a public-health disaster that is only going to get worse, and I feel for the folks in the gay community who are endangered."

Basile stops, eyebrows raised.

"Okay, uh, sorry I didn't realize you felt so strongly about it. You haven't really said anything publicly regarding your position."

He's right. Since I've been in the office, the issue has heated up, but I have never heard J.D. address it. On that, he's pretty typical among the other moderate Democrats in tough districts.

"Yes, I've kept quiet. As you can imagine, as a Democrat in a Republican district, I have to be careful. Unfortunately, there is a lot of homophobia in rural Iowa."

Basile shrinks and is about to launch into the gracious "thanks, anyway" mode that all good lobbyists are adept at. Some of his colleagues glance at him with "we told you so" raised eyebrows. But J.D. raises his hand again.

"But that doesn't mean I'm not willing to help. In this case, my constituents are just wrong, and maybe if I take a position, I can get them to look at this differently. Tell me what I can do."

Basile lights up. He immediately reaches into his briefcase to produce a paper laying out the HRCF's agenda and hands it to J.D., who looks at it quickly and passes it to me.

"I'll let Wally read this, but let's get right to the chase. What are the two or three things you want most?"

Basile stammers a bit and then ticks off the priorities: more federal funding of AIDS research, creation of an AIDS Commission by the president, and expansion of federal and private health insurance coverage of AIDS prevention and treatment.

"Where do you need the most help?"

Basile is still scrambling like someone whose car ran out of gas in the middle of Wyoming and all of a sudden has five cars stopping to help.

"Well, there is a bill introduced by Congressman Henry Waxman of California that would provide funding to the states to help with treatment of HIV-positive people. As you know, he chairs the Health Subcommittee, and he's looking for cosponsors. So far, he has only Democrats on the bill except for one Republican, a liberal from New York. If you joined as a cosponsor, maybe other moderates in both parties would be more amenable, given the level of respect you hold."

He is right about that. Since I became J.D.'s legislative director, I've gotten a number of calls from other staffers of moderate Democrats wondering how he was going to vote on controversial issues. Clearly, they didn't want their bosses to be out there by themselves. Joining J.D., whose thoughtful independence is renowned, would give them some cover.

"Sure, I'll have Wally take a look at the bill and add my name—assuming it looks fine," J.D. promises. "I don't like to cosponsor bills without looking at the fine print, but I'm sure if Henry is good with it, so am I. Anything else? Cosponsoring is easy. What is Reagan doing about this? When his friend Rock Hudson died, he called it a 'top priority,' but I don't think he's done much to make it one."

"Yeah, we are looking for some Republicans to put the heat on him but haven't had much luck."

"Well, what if a moderate Democrat from a conservative district sent him a letter urging him to do more, with a few suggestions? Maybe I could even talk a few of my colleagues into cosigning it."

Basile's face visibly broadens. He's stunned, and then he gets excited. There is now a buzz in the room with his colleagues audibly whispering to each other.

"Well, sure, if you would do that. We can draft something for you."

"No, I never let outside groups do my writing, but if you can give me some suggestions and some specifics, we'll draft something, and you can look at it before we send it around."

"Honestly, Congressman, that would be terrific. If I can just make one other suggestion, it would be most helpful if it wasn't just a letter quietly sent over to the White House. I'm not sure Reagan will even respond, but if there was some visibility, that could add considerable influence to our position."

J.D. frowns. Just as Basile is about to go into his "thanks, anyway" mode, J.D. responds.

"Sure, we'll do a press release and coordinate with you on publicity."

Basile starts to rise, but then he sits back down.

"Maybe there is one other important thing you can do for us. Our annual conference is being held in New York next week. We're looking for speakers who wouldn't be among those expected. Would that be possible?"

J.D. pauses, frowns, and then shakes his head.

"Let's hold off on that for now. Honestly, that just may be too much visibility. Come back next year on that."

Basile smiles and nods.

As the group leaves the office, I notice Thatcher standing in his doorway observing all the excitement that accompanies a highly successful lobbying visit. I assume they saved the high-fives for the hallway outside the office. Once they are gone, he looks at me sharply and jerks his head toward J.D.'s office.

We enter and J.D. is back to reading a staff memo to prepare for his next meeting.

"What the hell happened in here?" Thatcher asks.

J.D. doesn't flinch.

"We're going to help them."

"How?"

"Cosponsor a Waxman bill and send a letter to the president asking him to do more."

"The hell you say? You and what other moderates?"

"Far as I know, I'll be the first. Hope it brings more along."

Thatcher clinches his teeth and doesn't speak for several beats. It's clear he wants to launch into something but is holding himself back.

"So what district are you planning to run in next year after you lose in November, J.D.? Do you know how many of our folks this is going to piss off? Do you have to do this right before going into the campaign?"

"Park, I think the people most likely to be offended by this are those I was going to lose anyway. Maybe I have a little more faith in the people that sent me here than you do."

"Oh yeah, this will sure help you get the faggot vote, and as we know there are a hell of a lot of those in rural Iowa."

I realize I have not been working for J.D. long enough to have seen the level of anger I am now seeing. In his case, his facial expression with a lowered voice does the shouting.

"Park, do not ever use that word again in this office, not with me or anyone else. I honestly don't care how many gay constituents there are in my district, but I suspect there are more than you would think. I'm here to do more than just play the game. If an issue is important enough, like this one, I have to rise above political pandering and do the right thing. Now go back to your desk and worry about all the other matters I rely on you for. Wally and I will take care of this one."

I let Thatcher proceed first out of the door but once he is out, J.D. grabs me and whispers, "Once he's through with you come back in."

Thatcher doesn't want to play it out in front of everyone, so he leads me to the men's room down the hall, makes sure no one else is in it, and screams at me for ten minutes. He already has other epithets he can use without violating J.D.'s admonition. I tell him I ultimately work for J.D., not him, and that's where I get my orders.

When we leave the men's room, Thatcher pulls out a cigarette and leaves the building with it, making it easier for me to go right into J.D.'s office.

"You okay?" J.D. asks me.

"I guess so. I'm not sure how long I can work for him. He had given me specific orders not to let you promise anything. Guess he thinks he's the congressman."

J.D. puts his hand on my shoulder, a rare move for him.

"You don't need to worry. He'll be out of here soon. This is really just the tipping point. Brilliant guy with great political instincts, but we just aren't always in sync. Suspect he can find a nice home with a Republican member."

"That's good to hear, I guess. He's hard to work for, but at least he's the devil I know. Thanks, J.D." I turn to leave, but he stops me.

"Wally, he is right. This is not the best political move by me, and it will add another issue my opponent can use against me. But aren't you wondering why I'm willing to take that risk anyway?"

"To do the right thing, right?"

"Well, of course, and it is the right thing, but there's more."

"Okay."

He starts to speak but holds up.

"My wife's brother is dying of AIDS," he says with a slight break in his voice.

"Seriously? I didn't know."

"No one does, other than her and me. As you may know, she comes from a very religious family, with her dad being a fundamentalist preacher. Her dad doesn't like my politics, so we rarely speak. Her brother's name is Matthew Mark, from the first two books of the New Testament, but we call him M&M. I always thought he was different. Not so much effeminate as very troubled. Not long after we were married, he announced to her parents that he was gay and moved to Minneapolis, which is more receptive than rural Iowa."

"How is Faith doing?" I have never really spent any time with his wife, but it seemed okay to call her by her first name. "Your wife" just didn't feel right under the circumstances.

"It's a struggle. She's pretty religious, too. Loves her brother but has had a hard time accepting it. I'm not real religious, but I try to tell her God probably accepts people for who they are. She struggles but, unlike her parents, she's stayed in touch and has come to agree with me. He works in a mission, helping homeless people. He's been with a few other men, so it was probably just a matter of time. You have to wonder if gay people got married and had kids like the rest of us, it wouldn't be as risky. What is there to bind them to a single relationship?"

"Well, that's probably never going to happen. I guess you have to keep quiet about this."

"For now, yes, so please don't tell anyone. But it's just a matter of time before he goes, so when he does, it'll get out. I'll let others make the connection with what I'm going to do on the issue. It's one of those things where my personal experience is driving my policy position, rather than any independent assessment. Having said that, it is taking me to a place where I need to be.

"I'm also wondering if this is more than just a health care issue. The public reaction and negativity to people who are the way they are is bringing back memories of the civil rights struggles years ago, which haven't been resolved. Maybe this is the next wave. But we're not there yet, I suppose."

He puts his hand on my shoulder again and looks like he is about to break up, so I nod and turn to leave quietly.

But he stops me at the door.

"One more thing, Wally. Do you want to be Park's replacement?"

EIGHT

# A DANGEROUS FUNDRAISER

**J.D. Clay**

*August 1986*

I hate fundraisers. Absolutely fucking despise them. Along with all the fundraising phone calls, they just take time away from what I really came here to do, not to mention having any semblance of a personal life.

Actually, it's not just the fundraising itself; it's the whole dependence on money and the temptations it creates. I like to think I always vote for what is right—from both a policy and a political perspective—and the money comes after the fact: "We appreciate your work and want to sustain it by helping your campaign." Unfortunately, the public sees it more like, "If we support your campaign, we expect you to vote with us." Well, that's not me, but, with the amounts of money involved, managing appearances is challenging, especially since I have so many colleagues who are not nearly as conscientious.

It's even more challenging in my case because I get a hell of a lot of money. That's not because I'm a whore. It's because I'm in a swing district with more Republican voters than Democrats, so I have to run an aggressive, expensive campaign to survive. Of course, it also means that whomever my Republican opponent is gets a lot as well, and it turns out to be a bidding war between the two parties. Regardless of which side they are on, they don't really care who me and my opponents are; they just want the seat to keep or acquire a majority in the House.

It's not surprising that most of my money comes from the usual Democratic sources. In addition to the party itself, it comes from: unions, progressive interest groups (other than the women's groups that despise my pro-life position), liberal wealthy donors, and so forth. They know I won't always vote with them, but I usually do, and they know a lot of those errant votes help me hold the district.

And I do get money from other sources. A lot of the work I do is for parochial concerns of Iowa and my district that have nothing to do with ideology. So, I get a lot of money from Iowa businesses, especially agriculture, but some from major corporations as well who appreciate that I don't always vote in lockstep with my Democratic colleagues.

So, here I am at the National Democratic Club three blocks from the office hobnobbing with a bunch of lobbyists. I actually like a lot of them. Moreover, lobbying in its purest form is healthy for democracy. What the hell do I know about energy policy and a lot of other complicated areas I have to vote on? Even more concerning is the utter lack of real-world experience among the squadrons of Hill staffers we rely on. Brilliant, well-educated people but, given the low level of pay, for most of them this is their first job before moving downtown or to a government agency.

The key is to have reliable sources on both sides of an issue so we can predict how our votes will impact real people and their livelihoods. Sadly, balanced input is not always available, but it's still better than voting in the dark.

My fundraiser is being hosted by the National Farmers, who typically give me high marks for my voting record. Why wouldn't I? I represent a hell of a lot of farmers, and they often know better than I do what is good for them.

The Farmers' top lobbyist, Claire Comingore, is running the show tonight. She is brilliant, stunningly beautiful. And dangerous. My staff and I have worked closely with a lot of the people on her team, but I have had minimal personal interaction with her. And that's a good thing, apparently. I have been warned by some of my colleagues that she has a way of, shall we say, using her beauty to help achieve some of her professional goals. Her affairs with various powers that be in DC have gone largely unnoticed by the public (if not their spouses), and, being single herself, she has avoided any personal repercussions.

Claire introduces me to the crowd, and I give the usual spiel, which goes over well. Having a fundraiser in August is unusual, but, since I have to be in town for an important meeting, the timing is actually pretty good. There are no other competing fundraisers, so anyone else who is stuck in DC for August recess had little choice but to attend.

After my talk, a lot of people bail, but Claire and I have to stick around for the whole thing. She pulls me aside in an area where no one can eavesdrop. She's wearing a blue business suit that has the façade of prim but the aura of aphrodisia. Her proper white blouse is unbuttoned low enough to expose a baby's-bottom of cleavage. I need to force continuous eye contact, which I've gotten pretty good at in DC.

"Great job, Congressman, and we really do appreciate your continuing support," she says.

"Oh, happy to help you folks. You are an easy one, given the district, and you have one of the best teams to work with."

She smiles and touches my right hand, which is hanging very close to my thigh, giving her an opportunity for a slight brush over it.

"Don't I know it. On ag issues, I really do think we have the best. As you know, I used to work up here for the Ag Committee and we try to get the best of the staffers who work for it."

"Well, you do."

"I agree, but I really think, given your importance on the committee, you and I really do need to work more closely together."

She gives my hand a squeeze and a slight lift that makes me briefly wonder where it is headed. I pull it back.

At this point, she's definitely got my attention. If I were single, I probably would not hesitate to take the bait and may not even have any biological choice in the matter.

So, I invoke my usual defense when this happens (and it happens a lot in a city of beautiful, liberated women). I think of Faith. I'm not going to say in what manner I think of her in these instances. That's between her and me. But it usually works.

"Sure," I say. "My office door is always open for you, and there are a lot of issues we need to work together on. Call Edna in my office anytime. I'll be back in DC when we reconvene, so any time after that would work."

She gives a slight frown that is more of a tease than an admonition.

"Of course, but I was actually thinking you and I should have dinner sometime so we can really get to know each other. Hey, I wasn't able to eat any of the hors d'oeuvres passed around, so I'm pretty hungry now if you're up for someplace nearby."

I'm watching Faith in the bathroom after she gets out of the shower. God, she is beautiful.

"Actually, I've really got to run. I have an early flight back to Des Moines tomorrow, so I'll probably grab a chicken pot pie from the freezer."

"No worries, but my offer stands," she says with a wink and steps close enough to nudge my thigh with her knee.

I back off. Need to make things clear here.

"You know, Claire, I would love to do dinner. Maybe the next time my wife, Faith, is in town, we could all get together for dinner along with whoever you are seeing. That could be fun. I think she would really like you."

My turn to wink.

She smiles.

"Sure, I would love to meet her. Thanks again for doing a great job tonight."

"Thank you, Claire." I'm pretty sure the dinner will never happen.

I look around and see the room is probably empty enough that I can finally bail. I notice a redheaded woman standing at the bar whom I've seen before. Maybe a lobbyist for one of the unions. I wouldn't give it any mind, but it seems like every time I've looked at her this evening, she's been looking at me and then pulls her eyes away. Stunningly beautiful, of course. What else?

As I start to head for the door, I see she is making a line for me. She gently touches my back.

"Congressman, I wonder if I could have a brief word on one of our issues. I'm Mary Moorehead from the United Food & Commercial Workers, and there's a food safety issue I wanted to bring to your attention."

"Mary, very sorry but I've really got to run. Call Edna in my office and see if we can set something up. Or talk to my assistant, Wally North, who is standing over by the bar. He can probably help you."

As I leave, I don't bother to look back to see if she's going to talk to Wally. It was probably very innocent, but my guard is still up after Claire.

Damn, that was close.

NINE

# FAITH'S BRUSH WITH DEATH

**Wally North**

*September 1986*

I am three weeks into my new position as J.D.'s administrative assistant, which is the chief of staff. (My parents thought I had been demoted into a clerical job until I explained the odd Capitol Hill nomenclature for this role.) My brief turn as his legislative director only barely prepared me for a role that seems to combine the floor of the New York Stock Exchange, the NFL playoffs, and a meatpacking plant. Like anywhere else, the higher up the ladder you go, the tenser things get.

I can see clearly now why Park, my predecessor, wasn't going to last too long in J.D.'s office. Although things in Washington do get cutthroat, maintaining integrity and a moral compass are paramount to J.D.'s office.

It was probably just a matter of time before I moved into the top role after bonding with J.D. on his ambitious presidential campaign trail.

I do seem to thrive with the pressure. J.D. seems to be coasting to reelection to his third term, so I should be set for at least two more years. The session is wrapping up, so there are a number of bills moving quickly to the House floor that have to be finished prior to adjournment.

Being one of the more proactive members, J.D. has a number of things going on. A couple of amendments to the farm and defense bills that are up this week. A pesticide hearing by his Agriculture Subcommittee that he is chairing—including a witness from our district. In addition to his own fundraiser, he has three others by his colleagues he will attend this week.

Last night, we had had a very successful fundraiser at Bullfeathers, a Capitol Hill favorite for such events, and J.D. was in top form. I was offered a few toasts on my new position. Unlike many staffers, I try not to let stuff like that go to my head. It's the position they are sucking up to not the person.

J.D. asks me to come into his office as the staff is settling in for the day. I heard his voice break when he called, and I see his head buried on his desk as I walk in. He looks up with an ashen face. His lower lip bobs up and down, and I'm unsure if he's stifling a sob or trying to pull out words.

"Faith." He manages to get out. "She's been shot . . . They're not even sure she's going to make it."

This stuns me. Coming from a small town in Iowa, violent crime has never had a presence in my life, though I have been concerned about the high crime rate in DC and whether my family is safe here.

If I have this reaction, how must J.D. be feeling? Not getting rattled is a big part of my job. I need to get the bare facts, then get him the hell back to Iowa.

"How did it happen?"

"A robbery attempt in the Mitoka store. Apparently, some deranged addict was desperate for a fix, and she happened to be the one at the counter. She started asking questions, and he pulled the trigger. Bullet went right through her."

"J.D., we've got to get you back there right away. We'll get you on the eleven o'clock direct to Omaha, and we'll have someone at the airport to get you to Mitoka as fast as we can."

He appears to digest this and nods at first, then shakes his head.

"I have amendments on the floor. I'm chairing that hearing, and I have another fundraiser. What the hell?"

"Forget about the votes, J.D." I can tell he needed me to say that. "People will understand. We'll get on the phone with Congressman

Shorter's office to see if he can sit in as chair for you."

J.D. is glued to his chair. Uncharacteristically inert.

"You don't need anything, right? Straight to the airport?" I almost literally lift him out of his chair.

"Can you take me?"

"Of course, but we need to get going."

As we are leaving the Rayburn House Office Building parking garage, J.D. launches into an extended soliloquy about Faith. I can tell it is more for himself than me.

"Wally, I just couldn't be where I am without her. When I decided to run for Congress, we had to figure out who was going to run the business. I had been calling the shots, and she helped a lot, but she went through a very high learning curve before taking over. As it turned out, she had a keener business sense than either of us realized, and she has actually grown the business, adding five more stores."

I need to keep him talking.

"And I'm guessing with you away, raising the kids has also been a challenge."

"Well, at least they've grown enough to be at home alone after school. And Mom has been really helpful, too. At least until she started declining." He looks out intensely at the sea of taillights in front of us. "There's a lot of traffic. We going to make it for my flight?"

I'm also a little concerned, but that's a worry he doesn't need to keep him talking.

"She's a big part of your support, too, right?"

"Are you kidding, Wally? Everyone in Mitoka knows her, and she regularly travels around to the other stores as well. In some ways, her political skills are better than mine. And we both get good marks for customer service. There are a lot of people in the district who can't stomach some of my votes, but they vote for me anyway because they see it as a vote for both of us. That just can't be replaced."

J.D. has often said to me his twenty-four-hour days as a congressman are only exceeded by her twenty-six as a business owner, parent, and wife.

He starts to break up but regains composure as we pull up to departures. His initial shock has turned into fear as he stares into a potential abyss that may not include Faith.

TEN

# A LATE-NIGHT RESCUE

**Wally North**

*November 1987*

The ringing phone cuts through my nightmare like a siren oblivious to any other earthly dangers. I think it rings a couple more times before Gloria finally nudges me. The clock says 1:00 a.m.

"Mr. North, this is Sergeant Walter Milton with the DC police. I'm very sorry to disturb you," a husky voice says through the receiver in our bedroom.

Gloria needs her sleep, so I cradle the phone and have just enough time to get to the kitchen phone before the call will be cut off.

"Sergeant who?" I ask again, a bit confused and breathless from the quick transition.

"Walter Milton, sir. The name may be familiar because my daughter works in your office."

Willow is one of our few staffers not from Iowa. This is often the case in the Capitol Hill offices where a lot of members of Congress hire local DC people—primarily women—for clerical jobs that involve little contact with constituents. Willow was an early hire. Very loyal and a hard worker. God, I hope she's okay.

"Oh yeah, Willow. She's great. She all right?"

"Oh, she's fine, sir. That's not who I'm calling about. It's your boss, Congressman Clay."

It's been a little over a year since the shock with Faith. She fought to survive after the shooting, and J.D. fought alongside her—sort of. He spent weeks juggling his campaign with hospital visits, barely scraping by with sympathy votes and sheer luck against an opponent so outdated he was still railing against the New Deal. Faith came through, but not without scars. Paralyzed from the waist down, she's now confined to a wheelchair. The woman is tough as nails. Only a few months later, she returned to managing the drugstores—although on a part-time basis at first. J.D. might still be the face of the district, but Faith has become the soul. But between the rehab and the adjustments at home, their life hasn't just changed—it's shrunk.

And now this.

"Is he okay?"

"Well, physically yes, he's fine, but he's in a difficult situation. I'm with him here outside an apartment building in Northeast Washington."

J.D. lives in Northwest. Northeast has a lot of rough areas. What the hell? I hear a lot of ill-defined noise in the background.

"Why in the world would he be in that part of town?"

"Let's just say where I am is a very popular place for, shall we say, some needy men." That could mean a lot of things.

"Oh, Christ. Are drugs part of this?"

"No, not that. He's actually quite sober but very much afraid. He's sitting quietly in the back of my patrol car."

"Is he under arrest for something?"

I hear Milton's police radio in the background. A lot of numbers and locations but nothing distinct.

"Well, he could be . . . technically. There was a dispute between a customer and one of the other girls, which escalated to gunshots. At least one person is dead and several others are injured. He was in one of the other rooms but wasn't able to get out before we arrived."

"Are you going to arrest him for solicitation?" I'm hoping he isn't, or else he wouldn't be calling me.

The background noise is growing stronger, and he muffles his phone to shout something to another officer.

"We could, but we've got to give this murder case the top priority. And right now, the congressman and other, uh, customers, are kind of a distraction."

"Well, what do you want me to do? Or under the circumstances, what can I do?"

His voice lowers into a forced whisper.

"If you could come down here as soon as possible and get him, that would be great. If I take him into the station, we'll have to book him. But we need to get him out of here right away. If word gets out that we protected some white guy, it wouldn't look good, especially a member of Congress. I'm thinking mostly of Willow here. I had to tell her what's up to get your number, but she will be discreet about this, I can assure you."

He gives me the address, and by three, I am navigating the streets of Northeast Washington with a senior member of Congress quietly sitting in the passenger's seat.

As we drive through the streets of "the other DC," we hear gunshots in the distance. A glow comes from an alley where a group of men with thick blankets covering their shoulders surround a blazing trash can. Various genres of music ebb and flow as we pass cars with powerful speakers serenading the neighborhoods. I feel very privileged.

J.D.'s eyes are fixed straight ahead, not locked on anything specific. I keep waiting for him to break the silence, but he is leaving me no choice.

"J.D."

"What?"

"You have to explain this to me."

One of the least desirable aspects of being a member of Congress's administrative assistant is you often have to force discussions that neither of you want to have. You have to probe, scold, press, and push the envelope as far as you can without going so far as to lose your job. It's like those bad heist movies with the triggering lasers pointed all different directions between the robbers and the famous diamond. Up to this point, J.D.'s personal life has been relatively smooth, other than Faith's accident, but I have heard enough stories from other AAs to know I have been charmed until now.

"What's to explain? You don't know why a guy would go to a place like that?"

"No, I really don't. Why you would is not at all clear. Even if you weren't playing with political fire, you wouldn't need this. Please tell me this is some onetime-only wild hair deal."

His long, vacant stare through the windshield is not reassuring.

"So, I guess it wasn't," I conclude.

But he still retorted, "I wish it was that easy."

"What, this didn't teach you a lesson?"

I hear a slight quaver in his sigh. The tension has lifted slightly as we have entered a safer part of town.

"Look, Wally, you have a beautiful wife, and I assume from everything you've told me, all is well with your relationship. But you don't have a wife who is bound to a wheelchair. And meanwhile, with no reflection whatsoever on your looks, you probably don't have women throwing themselves at you constantly like I do."

I have been to enough events and in enough meetings with J.D. to know exactly what he is referring to. As much as we all like to think Washington runs exclusively on brain power and social skills, it is overrun with beautiful women. That beauty can come in handy professionally (not in the "oldest" sense, of course), but some women simply like to bask in the glow of powerful men. In other words, it's very easy for a congressman to get laid. They just have to be careful with whom.

"Look, Faith and I love each other very deeply. Despite all the temptations, throughout our marriage before the accident, I was absolutely true to her. It was not easy here in DC, but I never strayed. That all changed with the accident, and she knew it. This may surprise you, but she has told me 'pay to play' is fine. She would prefer that to having to compete with all the talent running around on Capitol Hill and K Street. She has had enough conversations with other congressional wives to know the carnal landscape here and how a lot of wives—like Jackie Kennedy did—just look the other way. She doesn't want to know the details, but as long as she knows it is purely physical and that love is not involved, she's fine with it. So, we've come to an agreement."

"Well, I'm pretty sure she wasn't thinking about one where you are hanging out in cathouses in the most dangerous parts of town."

"You mean the parts where no one knows or gives a fuck who I am? And no, we don't get that far in those conversations. Like I said, she doesn't want to know."

I struggle with the notion that any wife, especially one as strong in their religious beliefs as Faith, would be okay with this.

J.D.'s remote stare suggests the conversation is over as far as he is concerned, but I can't let it go.

"So, you're not going to stop doing this?"

"Look, goddamn it—Wally, I know myself too well. Sure, I could tell you right now I will stop, and that's easy because at this moment that's the last thing I want to think about. But as soon as those breezy lobbyists start fanning the flames again, I'm going to be looking for some outlet, and it sure as hell isn't going to be with them. I owe that to both myself and Faith."

"Even if it means flirting with a front-page *Washington Post* headline?"

"Shit, Wally, I don't know. Look, you do a very good job of looking after me. Why don't you figure something out?"

I guess I need to do some homework.

# ELEVEN

# STARR FOX

**Wally North**

*November 1987*

"Mr. North, shall we start by being completely honest with each other?"

Starr Fox startles me by using my real name, instead of the one I had used to set up the meeting. I really didn't want her to know who I was. When she called me "meester" and said "ve" instead of "we," it made me even more wary.

The name I gave her assistant on the phone was Hugh Duffy. She had said to meet her in suburban Dumfries at the restaurant Cervantes, a gourmet Spanish eatery. I was ushered to the best table in the place on a terrace overlooking the clientele.

Dumfries is thirty-five miles deep into Virginia at the southernmost limits of the metropolitan area. I had wondered why she wanted me to travel all the way out here, but it occurred to me that, this far from downtown DC, I probably wouldn't bump into any familiar faces. Very few Hill staffers want to add the additional two hours of commuting to what is already a very long day, so it seems unlikely we'll see anyone of consequence.

I was skeptical there was anything genuinely gourmet in blue-collar Dumfries, but I assumed there were plenty of modest eateries out there that bandied the label about. I assumed the closest thing to genuine Spanish food in this neck of the woods would be the Taco BellGrande at the Taco Bell I passed on the interstate. So I'm surprised to see a well-dressed crowd and a menu that includes *guiso del día* and *pulpo a la gallega*. The prices are lower than downtown DC, but so are the rent and taxes.

"Why are you calling me that? That's not the name I gave your assistant."

"It is your name, no? If we do business with each other, we must be honest, yes?"

"Look I assume 'Starr Fox' is not your real name, unless there is a pocket of Dodge City descendants in Russia."

She raises her index finger and looks at me as if I am a puppy that just soiled her rug. "No Rus. Ukraine. Big difference. Someday we will show Commie bastards where crayfish is wintering."

"Huh? Are there crawdads in the Ukraine?"

"Sure, but is expression we use for revenge. And, by the way, is not 'the Ukraine.' Is Ukraine. Rus sees us as region, but we are country. Someday separate, we hope."

"Got it. Wow, that's where Chernobyl is, right? Is your family okay?"

"Maybe okay, maybe not. No communication with them since I left. Very tragic. Rus will pay someday."

She still doesn't give me her real name, but I decide not to press.

"How do you know my name?"

She smiles conspiratorially.

"Mr. North, if we do business, you learn quickly there is little I do *not* know about my clients. And, believe me, you will be happy for that. Information about clients helps avoid making porridge."

As I'm trying to figure out what "making porridge" means (perhaps someday we'll have portable translators like on *Star Trek*!), we are interrupted by the waiter, who is dressed, albeit tastefully, like a flamenco dancer and whose name on his "Bienvenido" badge is "Arturo." I am kind of disappointed we don't get the matador at the next table named "Santiago," because he has a much nicer smile.

Arturo asks me if I have had a chance to look at the menu. I can deduce from his accent he is also Ukrainian (not Russian).

I had been connected with Starr through a lobbyist for one of the meat-packing companies, who is a good enough friend of J.D. to avoid any additional questions. The inquiry could also have been for me as far as he was concerned, but he really wasn't concerned. He is too good of a lobbyist to want to burn any bridges with loose lips.

But I had thought I could keep myself out of it with the fake name.

I order the *paella maresco*, which turns out to be delicious. Starr has something that looks like a bean stew that, based on my high school Spanish, doesn't seem to resemble anything I'd seen on the menu.

"So, Wally. Okay to call you Wally?"

"Sure." I give up.

"Business would be for you or another?"

"Not me, someone else, but I'd prefer not to name him. We can do all this just between you and me."

I realize after our earlier exchange that probably isn't going to work.

"Wally, we know where you work. Name seems obvious. Must protect myself as well as others in operation. Just need to confirm."

I continue to wonder if the whole thing is a mistake and if it isn't too late to back out. But what other options do I have if I don't want to be driving through Northeast DC again some night? I also genuinely want to help save J.D. from himself. So, I give her J.D.'s name and describe the whole situation.

While we are talking, I notice a few people passing her, exchanging glances, but no words. Applebee's this is not.

After listening very carefully, she asks a number of logistical questions. How often? His place or somewhere remote? Point of contact? Preference of hair color and other physical attributes? All the usual details in a typical business arrangement.

She seems relatively satisfied with my answers, which is not surprising given the variety of client situations she must have to deal with. She isn't writing anything down, but I can tell it is all going into her mental database. Very intelligent woman!

We sit silently eating our food. I start to say something, but she holds her hand up like a crossing guard, and I realize she is quietly calculating.

Then she looks straight at me. "So, before we go further, have one more dot to put over letter. Will quote you amount of monthly retainer. Probably will make your face pale, but recognize under lying stone, water does not flow. Or, how you say, 'no gain if no pain.' Understand what you get. Not buying a cat in a sack. Classiest, cleanest, most beautiful women in town. Most do this on side. Otherwise have very respectable professional jobs, you know. We arrange situations where no one finds out what is up and have very strict confidentiality rules for workers. 'Mute as a fish,' as we say."

She holds her hand up, and her face grows stern. "Believe me, rules enforced so no one would want to break. Twenty years without a breach. Be clear on this: not a one-woman operation. Workers know the rules and respect them. Works as well for them as for me. They do whatever to protect arrangement. Let me stress, they do whatever it takes."

Her demeanor is scary enough to convince me. "Okay, that's obviously exactly what I'm looking for. How much?"

When she tells me the amount, I feel like she has just punched me in the chest. I have no idea why I ever thought it would be anything less than an enormous sum. Apparently, the look on my face makes up for any reply.

"Think about your need," she said. "Something steady, risk-free, no tar in honey. Attractive girls who not make him feel dirty. Smart girls in safe places who know his. Or can keep going to cathouses in Anacostia. Short time before front page of *Washington Post*, eh?"

"I can't disagree with you. The problem is that is simply money we don't have. Obviously, we can't pay this legally out of the office budget, but even if we could, that kind of money just isn't there. And I doubt J.D. has that kind of money on his own."

She smiles when I use the word "legally."

"You think this is first time I have this conversation? I know more than you don't know. If he can't afford, have to find some rich donor who is close enough friend to not judge. Can just pay me directly. Can even set up a code so his name never comes up. Maybe they just buy very nice jewelry from me for wife or lover or whoever. All just between me and them, and congressman just has winning way with beautiful, smart young women. Which I'm sure he does."

She smiles and lets me mull it over. I think about all his various connections. There are some wealthy donors in the district and even a few lobbyists whom we could probably squeeze this out of, but it certainly wouldn't be legal. As if any aspect of this whole thing is. I know he has a very wealthy cousin he grew up with and is still close to. Are they close enough for this?

While I am pondering, she continues.

"Be sure I have several clients with same arrangement. Lot of powerful people in this town who work on K Street make big money. Plenty of folks out there who would love to have congressman in their debt."

Which is exactly what I want to avoid.

"Look, I get it, but this is sounding a lot more complicated than I thought it would be. I'm going to have to get back to you."

"You know where to find me. But, please, not wait for too much water from sea. Best to move on. Now I am squeezed lemon. Must go home, get sleep." She asks "Arturo" for the check.

As I get in my car in the parking lot, I see Starr return to hers. It is too dark to tell, but it looks like a Mercedes-Benz AMG Hammer, one of the most expensive cars out there. When the driver comes around to let her in the back seat, he makes no attempt to hide his shoulder pistol holster.

I have a lot to think about on the long drive home, wondering whether I might not be a whole lot happier in a job slinging hash at a diner somewhere in downtown DC.

---

"My boss says your boss has worked something out to help with his, uh, marital challenges," says the AA for a very conservative Republican who billed himself as a strong champion of "family values."

It has been a few months since we began our arrangement with Starr Fox, and I am a bit thrown off by the abrupt statement. *Maybe this arrangement isn't as discreet as we think*, I think as I hold the telephone receiver loosely.

The AA provides a bit more context than I wanted to know. Apparently, this conservative's values aren't so strong in this case, because his marriage is on the rocks, and his wife is only staying with him to save his political career. Not out of any sense of loyalty but because she, too, enjoys the trappings of being a local celebrity. Meanwhile, "Mr. Family Values" recently disentangled himself from a dangerous liaison with a lobbyist.

The staffer's own loyalty does not go so far as taking the trip to Dumfries himself, so I agree to help arrange something. (Probably safer for me, anyway.) As one of the wealthiest members of Congress, his boss would not have the same financial challenges that we faced.

A month after I help set this up, an envelope with a key and a post office box number arrives in the mail. The box contains a package from Volpe Enterprises with a very large amount of cash and a note that says, "There's more where this came from." As soon as I recall from Latin class that *vulpes* is the word for fox, I make the connection. I also quickly figure out that trying to return the money to this organization is not an option. And, after all, it *is* cash.

This ends up being the first of several calls from other offices, and since then, the envelopes have become a regular source of income. With mounting debts from a modest Hill income and looming college tuitions, how could I turn it down?

Do I feel any remorse about my part in this arrangement? The enterprise will go on with or without me, right? I am the barnacle, not the whale, right? I am helping to save marriages, right? Maybe even my own.

My family's plummeting into debt could certainly lead me to desperate measures of a more reprehensible sort. There are so many worse courses of action I could be taking.

Meanwhile, I handle the money for the family, so Gloria has no idea.

TWELVE

# ROSE

## J.D. Clay

*June 1989*

The moment she walked through the door of the cabin, I could tell she was different from the others. It's been over a year since this arrangement started, and the setup has worked well. The three-room cabin in the woods near Sugarloaf Mountain is a bit of a drive, but it is so far off the beaten path that my trips here have drawn no notice.

The assurances of confidentiality have proven true so far. Moreover, the girls are uncommonly beautiful, refined, and, as arranged, always different. Personal questions are out of bounds, but I have little doubt they are pursuing other careers and making good money doing this. I assume most are doing it out of financial despair, but maybe for many of them it's just good money. How would I ever know what would motivate any woman to do this? I try to keep my distance, and they do too, which seems to be the best way for this to work.

But this one feels different.

Not an arresting beauty like the others. Nice body, but nothing extraordinary. In a montage of photographs, hers would not stand out. But, in person, it doesn't take long for a certain magnetism to hold the view. Her slightly wavy dark hair frames the smoothest of skin with a slight brown tint, suggesting some Hispanic blood. Almond-shaped brown eyes fix on the viewer. Her brief smile betrays some slightly irregular teeth, and its brevity implies an unnecessary self-consciousness. The imperfections do not detract from her beauty but add interest.

There is an allure when her person is taken as a whole. There is a self-assuredness that stands in contrast to her reason for being there. Yes, she shows submission but without any sense of inferiority. Ironically, she is the conqueror. With other women, I may have withdrawn from that. But I seem to want to be part of her world. *Is this the kind of charisma that draws people to me?*

I have looked forward to these encounters. The peaceful cabin miles away from the frenetic quorum calls, fundraisers, and demanding constituents is no small part of that. It provides an air of taste (if not dignity) to the occasions. The cabin lies at the end of a long, graveled drive whose turnoff is barely noticeable from the main road. In fact, on the first occasion, I whizzed past it twice, having to rely on my odometer to determine the precise mileage point at which the turn occurs.

The cabin's interior belies its rustic exterior. It has a full kitchen with a well-stocked refrigerator and wine cabinet, in case any customers wanted to accompany the proceedings with a meal, even one with a crimped conversation. The furnishings are similarly accommodating, especially those in the bedroom. It would be nice to spend a relaxing weekend here with Faith on one of her occasional trips to DC. But that won't happen.

I refuse to call these trysts "making love," since there is no love whatsoever involved. All the other terms—*intercourse, sexual relations, cohabiting*—just sound too clinical, and "sleeping together" is plain inaccurate.

After we finish whatever I want to call it and catch our breath, I ask her again what her name is, even though I know it is fake.

"Rose."

"Pretty name. It fits you. Last name?"

"Budd."

"Like the movie?"

"Yes."

"So, you've actually seen *Citizen Kane*?"

She smiles at the apparent rebuke after making a show of being offended.

"Yes, I have *actually* seen it. A lot of people have seen it. Including all those critics who call it the 'greatest movie ever made.'"

"Well, I guess I just assume most people your age would be more into the latest Tom Cruise or *Saturday Night Live* spinoff."

"So, you didn't think a 'working girl' like me would be sophisticated enough to know that movie?"

I'm now feeling very boorish, but why should I care about offending her if I'm never going to see her again?

"Sorry. So, you like movies?"

She stands up to get dressed, and I take one last look at her nakedness. Take away her personality, and her body would seem very ordinary. Of course, breasts on almost any woman in almost any form attract a man. Of course, I'm drawn to them, but their simple purity is the allure. It's more the maternal comfort and nourishment that they represent, not the eroticism. Her Venus triangle is earthy with an imperfect outline. She has an appealing face adorned by the long locks of her raven hair, but, again, nothing that would accompany a cosmetic commercial. Like Faith, her beauty has an enduring quality that I predict will survive aging's etchings.

"Yes, I love movies," she replies. "That one in particular."

"Why?"

"Well, I think it says a lot about how we view famous people. It's a collection of bits and pieces of information that all supposedly fit into a puzzle. I mean, that's the motif of the movie, the jigsaw puzzle, right?"

"Yes, the way the story unfolds is what made it famous as much as all of its other innovations."

She is now fully covered in the plain business casual attire she had arrived in.

"Right," her voice quickens as if she is excited about the evening going beyond her carnal obligations. "But even then, we are limited to the most interesting bits and pieces about Kane. Yet, like most of us, most famous people's lives are overwhelmingly boring. Eating, sleeping, reading the mail, watering the plants. It's only those few things that are noteworthy that define the person in the public's eye."

While buttoning my shirt, I think about my own "bits and pieces," which are still playing out. She continues her musings as I pull on my trousers.

"I suspect most people are a mix of good, bad, and boring. And, if you are famous, you are going to be defined by those instances that are the most interesting. If they are bad, you'll be remembered as a bad person, and vice versa. Even Kane must have done some good things, even though the movie doesn't really dwell on them. If those had been the only things the public knew, he'd be remembered as a good person. Hitler was supposedly good with children. Lincoln was probably an asshole to his wife, given her condition. But neither of those defined the person."

As she talks, I wonder how she could do what she does with such aplomb and no apparent sense of shame or regret. But is that just a cover? I assume most of the women in the service need the money so badly they had to suppress any fears about their reputation. Yet, she gives no appearance of such qualms.

I'm intrigued by her intellect and want to keep this going. "Well, those are examples of people with huge legacies that are going to define them no matter what else they did."

"Certainly, but the vast majority of people, even celebrities, don't have that kind of legacy. What if what I did tonight was the only thing people knew about me? Guess I know how I'd be remembered. You too, and you really are a famous person . . . sort of."

I'm taken aback. All of this is supposed to be surreptitious. No real names exchanged.

"How would you ever know that?"

She smiles as if she has just checked a chess piece. “Oh, believe me, I know you are a congressman. You even ran for president once. The average person may not recognize you, but anyone who follows politics closely would.”

“Well, that’s a little scary.”

“Oh, don’t worry. Remember, you have something on me as well,” she says with a wink.

“Only if you plan to be famous someday.”

A barrier seems to rise as she seems to no longer be speaking to me but herself.

“I want to succeed in whatever I do. Fame would be nice, but not from doing this, unless I want to be the next Sally Salisbury.”

“Who?”

She starts, as if suddenly remembering I’m here.

“She was a prostitute in London in the early 1700s who actually became a celebrity by serving a lot of famous people. I did a little research before I took this on. Didn’t end well for her. Died in prison after stabbing a client.”

She starts gathering her things, but I’m not ready for this to end.

“This obviously is not your day job—sorry about the pun. What do you do?”

She pauses, her hand lingering on the edge of her bag as if weighing her options. Her shoulders stiffen slightly, but then she exhales and sets her things back down. Instead of sitting beside me on the couch, she lowers herself into the chair with deliberate precision, her posture upright and poised, as though creating an invisible barrier.

“Let’s just say I’m studying to be something more than just a body.”

“That’s good to hear, because you do seem like someone who has a lot to offer.”

Her lips curve into a small, hesitant smile, her fingers brushing over the arm of the chair as if grounding herself. “I think I just proved that.”

“That’s not what I meant. I know there are a lot of things you can’t tell me, but maybe there are some things we can talk about. What other movies do you like?"

"Mostly the old classics. *The Grapes of Wrath* is a favorite. That 'I'll be there' speech Henry Fonda gives at the end is so moving. It makes me cry every time."

She holds a blank stare into the distance when she says this and makes me wonder if it was more than just a movie to her.

"Yes, I agree. I grew up lucky, in a fairly affluent family, but I can only imagine what those folks went through."

"I may know a little about that." She gives a half smile with enough vacancy that I can now see the connection with the movie. I am pretty good with accents, and hers, though somewhat masked by cultivation, suggests somewhere in Appalachia.

"What draws you to the movies?" I ask, deciding to steer away from a more personal question.

With this, she stands up and pretends to examine the various contents of the cabin. She seems to be talking more to herself than me as she looks at a picture of a medieval castle above the fireplace.

"As a kid, I dreamed of being a performer," she shares as her eyes are still lost in the picture. "I put on shows for my family, and they were so poor that was about the best they could do for entertainment other than TV, and we didn't even have cable."

She remembers I'm there and does a brief mock of a tap dance ending in open arms and a bow, followed by a stage smile. I dutifully clap.

"Is that what you want to do with your life?"

She sighs and fumbles with her keys. "That's not really what I'm studying for, but I always look for opportunities on the side. Performing for people is really what I am best at."

"How about music?" I ask.

"I'm actually a pretty good singer, but I don't have broad tastes. Pretty much just country. Merle, George, and Hank Jr., a few beers, and a good dance partner."

"What about jazz?"

"Nah, just can't get into it. Might as well play kroncong."

"Huh?"

"It's Indonesian urban music. Picked that name up from an article I read about Indonesia. Funny how some words stick with you."

"Have you ever really tried to like jazz?"

"Well, I've sure heard stuff by Miles Davis, John Coltrane, and others. I know who they are, but I just can't get into it."

"Let me tell you my theory."

I am aware that most people could probably care less about the musical theories of a politician, but she seems genuinely interested. *Is it genuine or paid for? Is it intellectual curiosity only, or does she really care what I think?* Either way, I am enjoying the conversation, even though a conversation wasn't what I'd paid for.

"Think about different kinds of liquor," I begin. "Wine, scotch, bourbon, or even a really good ale. If you're a kid or even an adult who has never had a drink, you drink it like you drink a soda pop and immediately spit it out. But eventually you realize if so many people think it is good, you must be missing something. So, you keep trying, and you eventually learn that it's all about the part of your mouth where you feel the drink. Maybe the top of the tongue, under the tongue, the back of the mouth, or even the aftertaste."

The irony of talking about tongues in this situation is not lost on me, but she is now deadly serious, with her steady gaze fixed back at me.

"When you find where in your mouth the drink is appreciated, you start to cultivate an experience and enjoy it," I continue. "As you know, we call it an 'acquired taste.' Music is the same way. Different kinds of music touch different parts of the brain. Children's music touches the most receptive parts, so that's why kids immediately like 'On Top of Old Smoky' and others. Or even Beatles songs, which are so accessible at the outset and then eventually reach different levels as you listen more. That's what makes them timeless."

"That's true. I don't remember ever not liking the Beatles."

"You like country because you automatically direct it to that part of your brain without thinking about it. You probably grew up around it, given where you are from . . ."

She holds up her hand and forces a stern look. "You don't know where I'm from. Nor can I tell you."

"Okay, lucky guess. But now consider jazz, heavy metal, kongcong—whatever is alien to your brain."

"*Kron*cong, with an r," she corrects me with a smile.

"Okay, kroncong, whatever. With jazz and a lot of classical music—because they are so complex and nuanced—it probably takes longer to find that place. That's why they are for most people an acquired taste, but once you get there, it just feels so good—even better than the easy stuff like country and kids' music."

We are staring into each other's eyes, delaying her departure. She inadvertently drops her car keys, and the jingle of their fall breaks the spell. She picks them up and stands to leave, but not with any sense of certainty.

I can't let it go.

"Tell you what, let's do this again, and next time I will bring you a few jazz albums that are accessible. You have to promise to listen to each of them five times—not in a row. Let them sink in. If I pick the right ones, I'm pretty sure at least one of those will connect, and that could be your bridge to that part of your brain. Deal?"

She frowns and shakes her head. But there is no sense of certainty in that, either.

"Next time?"

"I think I get to make a request. I really want to see you again. Is that okay?"

"I guess. This is going to sound kind of weird, but I have a rather busy schedule. Tonight worked out for me, but it could be hit or miss any other time."

"I'll make the request and tell them to give me options."

"I guess I should be flattered that I was that good."

She is probably thinking of the sex, but I'm not. I don't want her to feel her skills are being insulted, so I decide not to correct her.

"It's been really terrific. Better than I ever could have imagined."

We again stare at each other for a long time before she breaks the silence.

"Sorry, I really have to get going or I have to charge you double. That's the rules. I have to leave first, so they know I'm okay."

It just occurs to me that the service has a surveillance system. No surprise.

"If I want you again, I can just ask for Rose?"

"That should work. Will depend on scheduling, as I said."

"I get that. I can wait, if need be."

Her smile is genuine, clearly not part of the service.

"I like your smile. Reminds me of my mother," I tell her.

"Oh, I guess we do Oedipus complexes, like every other service."

"No, it's not really that. There's a quality there that you share with her. Comforting. Understanding."

"Good to know. I'll see if I can market that."

THIRTEEN

# A CALL HOME

**Naomi Bridgewater**

*June 1989*

I release a brief sigh of relief as I put down my pen, rise, and walk over to the desk to turn in the test. Corporation Law is not one of my best courses, but I figure I'm confident I will pass, and, at this point in my law school career, that is all I need. As most law students can attest, you really only need to survive that first year—during which I had thrived. Making your grades after that isn't that big of a lift.

As I'm leaving the testing room, I feel a tap on my shoulder. It's Joe Cotton, who sat next to me in Conflicts of Laws. We've spoken briefly a few times, but I've never paid much attention to him. Clearly, he's more interested in engaging now than I am. *How do I politely brush him off?*

"Can I walk with you?"

"Sure." I wonder if my attempt at showing no enthusiasm is a little too obvious.

"Not sure how I did," he says. "That was really tough, especially that director liability issue."

"Agree. That probably was the toughest one. I connected my answer with the corporate charter, but I'm not sure I got it either."

Most small talk in law school begins with the task at hand. Women are outnumbered seven to one. Modesty does not prevent me from realizing I am one of the most attractive, despite my attempts to underplay my beauty. Hard as I try, I can't go beyond sparse makeup and ill-fitting clothes to actually try to make myself ugly. Homely is my best bet, but this is not the first attempt by a male classmate—or female for that matter.

Other students are gradually emerging with varying signs of relief and consternation as we continue down the corridor. The hallways of a law school after a test are not unlike those of a small hospital, with a mixture of joy (childbirth), anguish (death), and, most often, anxiety (awaiting the lab report).

Joe strikes me as a typical George Washington University law student. His accent sounds like New England, and his attire suggests family money. I seriously doubt he has ever spent the night in an Appalachian double-wide. When we get to the bottom of the steps of Stockton Hall leading into University Square, I give it a shot.

"Well, good luck, Joe. Guess I'll see you at the next one."

I make a deliberate turn down a sidewalk that puts him squarely behind me, but he persists.

"Which way you headed?"

"I really have to get back to my apartment and start booking for the next one."

"Okay, I was thinking maybe we can get together for a drink and possibly dinner later. Sounds like you will need something to relax with." I flinch when he touches my shoulder, which I hope he notices.

"Joe, I really appreciate the invite, but I am totally booked with my studies from now until the end of the semester, and then I'll be heading home."

"Sure. By the way, where is home for you?"

"Oh, it's really not far, just a couple hundred miles away." Which could be any number of major cities within easy driving distance from DC. I have managed to mask my distinct accent, but I can't get rid of all traces of the South, so I figure most assume somewhere downstate Virginia or the Carolinas.

Joe fixes his gaze on me with a squint, waiting for more. When he doesn't get it, he says, "Okay, well, travel safely then. Hope we have some classes together next semester. Good luck on the test results."

I am sorry to disappoint him, but he won't have any trouble finding someone else. He is good looking and obviously comes from money that would be good to marry into. If I let him get close, he would eventually learn my secret. And he probably came from one of those families that run background checks on their children's relationships if there is any suspicion.

When I get back to the apartment, I dutifully call Mom.

"Hi, Mom, it's Naomi."

"Oh, honey, it is so good to hear your voice. How is my young lawyer doing?" Hearing her deep-woods drawl reminds me both of what I miss and what I am trying to escape.

"I'm not a lawyer yet, Mom, but I guess one step closer. I took one of my hardest tests today, and I think I did well enough to pass. Just twelve more months, and I'll be ready to join the world's second-oldest profession." The irony doesn't escape me.

"I am so proud of you, Naomi. Your father and I would never have thought we would have a lawyer in our family, not to mention a college graduate."

"Take some credit yourself, Mom. You pushed me hard, and hopefully it will pay off someday."

I know the usual question is next.

"Honey, I am so proud of you, and your father would be too if he was still alive. But I feel so bad that I'm not being much help to you. School is so expensive, and Washington is not a cheap place. Are you really making enough money at that restaurant to get by?"

"Oh, yes, Mom." I again pray that she will never come visit and ask to go to "that restaurant."

I haven't told her that I've been cast in a play at the Arena Stage, because I know she would want to come see it. I haven't yet figured out how I am going to juggle that with classes and the other job, but I'm not letting go of my wish for a performing career. The stage and screen are far more alluring to me than drafting wills and filing motions. But it isn't a sure thing like a law degree.

"Well, gee, honey, it must be a really nice restaurant to be able to help you pay for law school. I just can't imagine. Maybe someday I will drive up to DC and treat you to dinner there. I'm sure they just love you."

"That would be great, Mom, but, believe me, there is no way we could afford to eat there. It's a hundred bucks a person, if you can believe that a restaurant could ever be that expensive. The tips are sure nice! Anyway, I'll be done soon and coming home for the break. The food here is okay, but I can't wait for some shoofly pie."

"We'll have that your first night back. Just let me know when you leave so I'll know when to expect you. How's that old beat-up Impala doing?"

"I think it can hold up until I get that first fat paycheck at a prestigious law firm. Thanks, Mom, and give Sis and Puffy a big hug for me. See you soon."

After we hang up, the other phone rings.

"This is Rose."

"Rose, you have a reservation at the Liberty Inn this evening at eight. Mr. Johnson will join you."

"Thanks. I'll be there."

FOURTEEN

# ROSE, AGAIN

**J.D. Clay**

*July 1989*

Rose should be here in about an hour. I arrived early to begin cooking a spaghetti dinner and line up some music. The cabin has an excellent stereo system, so I brought *Saxophone Colossus* by Sonny Rollins; *Djangology* by Django Reinhardt; *Straight, No Chaser* by Thelonious Monk; and, of course, *Kind of Blue* by Miles. All good intros to jazz. I'll give them to her at the end of the evening, as promised, with the suggestion that she give them four more listens.

I am wondering if the first two encounters were just in the moment. Will I continue to feel this attraction beyond the physical? How will she respond to what I'm going to tell her? It will be a surprise, but hopefully not an unpleasant one. The crunch of the gravel outside mainlines right to my stomach. *Why am I so uptight about this?* I can't let that show.

She is again dressed in a nice business suit, as I have requested, with just enough red to bring out her raven locks.

Having breezed into the cabin, she stops abruptly when the aroma of the tomato sauce hits her. With a slight frown, she surveys the spread on the table with a bemused look.

"Dinner?"

"I thought it would be nice. I hope you haven't eaten."

"No, I never do until afterward, but I guess it's late enough."

She stands for a moment as if waiting for something, brushing her hand through her hair. An embrace and a kiss? When they don't happen, she edges awkwardly toward the dinner table. Awkward but not nervous.

She sees the bottle and two glasses.

"I can't join with that." Her tone is business-like.

"I figured but thought I'd try," I acknowledge. "There's some sparkling grape juice for you."

"That's fine. Water, too. Can I help?" My dismissal prompts her to find her place at the table, where she rearranges her setting. Twice. She clears her throat but doesn't say anything. I guess I need to get the conversation going while I finish preparing dinner.

"When is your birthday, Rose?"

"You know I'm not supposed to provide you any details like that."

"Maybe I'll want to remember it someday."

"I guess you see this becoming a regular thing with us?"

"It could. I checked into it, and that can be part of the deal. I'd like to, if possible."

"I guess I should be flattered." Her smile is slightly uneasy but not forced. From the moment she walked in, her body language has suggested a friendly openness, which I take as a sign of mutual affection. But I have to assume the suggestion of something permanent raises a warning flag for her. Arrangements like this by definition are temporary.

"You should be flattered. I really like you."

"I like you, too. But then that's not an essential element of this commercial transaction."

"'Commercial transaction'?" I scoff. "Do I get a receipt? If I don't like the service, do I report it to the Better Business Bureau?"

"Good luck with that."

If I can't know her birthday, I can at least search for clues.

"What's the first movie you remember?"

"*Robin Hood.* The Disney cartoon, not Errol Flynn and Olivia de

Havilland."

"I wonder if anyone even watches that one anymore."

"It's better, I think. The Disney movie works for kids, though. I think my sister and I were sitting in the back seat at the drive-in for it. Pretty sure it was a double feature. They stayed for the second one, but we both fell asleep. I do remember staying awake long enough to fall immediately in love with Robert Redford."

"First popular music you remember?"

"I know what you're doing, but I guess I can safely answer. Aretha Franklin or something else Motown."

"'Something else Motown'? Sorry, Aretha isn't Motown. Motown was a production company with a distinct set of artists that sounded nothing like Aretha. Actually—" Her raised eyebrows and deep sigh shut me off. I don't want the evening to turn into the old guy lecturing the young lady on "how things used to be."

"Well, everybody considers her Motown," she retorts. "Isn't that all that really matters? Why does it need to be so precise?"

I can't let that one go. It has nothing to do with our age difference.

"Well, I think that's what's wrong with a lot of people when it comes to music and a lot of other things as well. What's wrong with being precise?"

She grins, warming to the intellectual challenge, as I put the dinner plates in place.

"Because I think music and any other art can sour if it is overthought. If I'm at a disco and I want to hear Aretha—or Otis Redding or Marvin Gaye—it's much easier for me to just say to the DJ, 'play some Motown.' According to you, I should say, 'please play music by predominantly African American performers who recorded between 1963 and 1972.'"

"You mean sixties R&B?" I say while pouring our drinks. She takes a few bites of her meal and quickly swabs her lips before responding.

"Okay, let's talk about the disconnect between perception and reality in art. And, by the way, this spaghetti is really good. Ever heard of Thomas

Percy?" she asks.

"Thanks, my mom is half Italian. I don't know Thomas Percy, but I do know Percy Sledge who, also, by the way, was not Motown."

"That was feeble. Not even close to funny. Actually, this guy predates him by a long way. Late eighteenth century, in fact, and he was an Irish bishop."

"Okay, what does he have to do with Aretha?"

"Nothing. But I did learn about him in an English literature course, and it is interesting how he got famous—or infamous. It makes my case. He published a book of early English folk songs that is often considered the foundation of English folk music. He claimed to have found the songs in a book that was lying on the floor of some British aristocrat whose maid was using the pages as fire starters. He sat on them for a while, until he realized he could make a lot of money by publishing them, which he did. It became a huge bestseller."

I am happy to let her take a turn at being arcane.

"Okay, what's the point, other than maybe something I'll try to remember the next time I play Trivial Pursuit?"

"It completely defeats your view that accuracy in cultural matters is so critical." She takes a bite and quickly swallows to finish making her point. "The Most Reverend Percy was eventually forced to share the originals, and it turned out he had added to most of the songs. He claimed he had to do so because they didn't make sense in their original form. But it created a huge scandal, because they were not the same songs he had claimed them to be."

"Okay, not the first or last person to do something like that. Imagine how many Homers embellished *Odyssey* and *Iliad* before they were published. Again, what's the point?"

"You make my case. Who really gives a shit whether Percy added to the songs if people enjoyed the music? Does it matter whether we know anything about Homer or whether he even existed? The point is, through whatever process, it resulted in great art—because at the end of the day, the only thing that matters is whether the product itself inspired people."

"Okay, I'll take your point, at least when it comes to eighteenth-century music. What are your contemporaries listening to these days?"

"Mostly crap, as has probably always been the case. Milli Vanilli–type garbage. And by the way, what's that playing right now? Very different."

"Guitar player named Django Reinhardt. He was a gypsy who originated the gypsy jazz genre. He lost two fingers in a fire in his wagon, but, as you can hear, that didn't stop him from being one of the greatest guitar players ever."

"Fascinating. Must be kind of old because the sound is so scratchy. But it's still pretty cool."

As dinner winds down, things again turn awkward as tell her I can clean things up. We both stand, and she moves toward me. Before we can touch, I gently block her advance.

"What?"

"Let's do this instead," I say, producing a pack of cards from my shirt pocket.

"What are those? Are we really going to play strip poker? That's a new one."

"No, we're just going to play cards. Any game you choose. Nothing more tonight or any other night. I just want to talk, and a card game gives me something to do with my hands while I look at you. That's good enough."

"Well, that's nice, J.D., but I really need the money I get from this."

"You'll get it."

She searches my eyes for the catch.

"Are you that rich you can pay these high prices just to talk?"

"Well, I don't really pay them. A relative does, and he's so rich he doesn't really care what the money is for. I'm not even sure he knows. He just likes to brag about his congressman cousin."

"Isn't it illegal for someone else to give a congressman that kind of money?"

"He's a family member whose business has no relationship whatsoever with any votes or positions I take. Is it legal? Well, this arrangement isn't. Or actually it is, if we just talk. But me getting the money from him—or, I should say, being the beneficiary—is fine. I assume it's still okay in this country for anyone to give financial assistance to a family member."

"Okay." She frowns, digesting the situation. I decide not to raise the obvious tax angle.

"There's still kind of an obvious question," she notes.

"What's that?"

"Well, why would you want to do this—even if it is your 'family member's' money—if you aren't getting what I am supposedly being paid for."

She walks over and sits on the sofa, making a show of pulling out her pager. She is making no attempt to hide her defensive posture.

"Don't worry, you're perfectly safe. Here, let's sit, and then tell me what your favorite game is."

After some consideration, she puts the pager away and returns to the table.

"Gin. What are the stakes?"

"Doesn't matter. How about five bucks a game, just to keep it interesting?" I shuffle and deal the cards.

"Rose, and I know that's not really your name, I know this is very strange, but my intentions are pure. Have you ever heard that LBJ once said if you want a friend in Washington, get a dog."

She looks up from her hand. "I'm a dog?"

"No, sorry, I didn't mean it that way. It's about me, not you. His point was, in DC, there are no friends. In fact, in politics there are no friends. Just connections that are both strategic and self-serving. Few, if any, go any deeper than that."

"Okay, but you'd still be paying for it. Is that real friendship?"

"I think it could be. I really enjoyed our last session, and the physical part didn't have to be part of it."

She peruses her hand, discards a two of clubs, and draws.

"You really want to just sit and talk? If we're such good friends, then, why should you pay me?"

I pick up the two and discard a four of hearts. I realize the cards are a distraction, so I stand and walk slowly to the window. There must be another car out there somewhere for her protection, but I only see her Impala.

"Because I care about you. And if it means helping you financially, that's a good thing."

"So, if I don't show up, I don't get paid?"

"Well, no, you wouldn't. Sorry, I still need someone who will listen to me without needing some sort of political favor or being able to brag about our relationship. Sorry, that wine went right through me, and I have to take a break. No cheating while I'm gone."

She is sitting with her chin on her hands and a frown on her face when I return. *Why wouldn't she be okay with this?* She's probably thinking "money for nothing," as the song goes.

I pick my hand back up when she discards and then break the silence.

"Look, part of this is going to be about you listening to me and letting me vent."

"Sure, that's pretty easy."

"But the other part is you opening up to me. I really want to know about you."

"That's going to be difficult. There are a lot of things I can't tell you."

"Yeah, I know, but I don't really need the details. I don't need to know where you're from, where you live, your day job, all that stuff. I just want to know what you're thinking."

She shrugs as she discards. "Okay, we can try. And, by the way, gin. You owe me five bucks."

"Okay, double or nothing." I reshuffle the cards before resuming the questioning.

"Let's start with the one most obvious question for me. Why the hell do you do this?"

She doesn't hesitate a bit. "For the money."

"That's not what I meant."

"Well, I certainly wouldn't do it without the money."

"I get that. Maybe my question is more along the lines of *how* can you do it? I'll be honest with you. One of the reasons I want this arrangement is so you can still get the money without . . ." I stop to see if she can finish the sentence for me.

"Degrading myself? Is that what you were going to say? You realize you're not my only customer? Whatever we arrange, I'm still going to have to do this with other people."

"I get that, but at least I can help. Or maybe we could even bump up the payments, and I could be your only customer." I propose.

She leans back in her chair and lets this sink in. She fixes her gaze on me and folds her arms, emphasizing the slight cleavage peeking out of her blouse. I really wish she would have fastened all of those buttons. Somehow, her body language in struggling with the concept is arousing me. After winning the second game, I reshuffle the cards. Several times.

"You didn't answer my question," I say as I finally deal a new hand.

She looks at her cards and immediately puts them down. She stands and paces before answering. I realize she could just as easily tell me it is none of my business, walk out the door, and rid herself of a very strange customer. Maybe she would do that if she didn't like me as well.

"It may not be as hard for me as you might think. I grew up in an area where there was a lot of sleeping around. It was sort of expected, and most of us girls got kind of used to it."

"But I assume you always did it with people you were attracted to and had some romantic relationship with, no matter how shallow."

Her eyebrows acknowledge the point. "That's what I always told myself, but I always ended up realizing that was all they were in it for. That's one of the reasons why I wanted to leave where I was."

"So, now you're doing this with people where the only connection is financial? That still doesn't explain it."

"I guess what I'm saying is I need the money, and it is something I can do. I'm not sure at this point there is anything else I can do that could make this much money. And I need the money. Besides, well, there's a bit of a family tradition. My father died when us kids were very young, and, um, let's just say my mother had to do things for money that most women would not do. You've heard the song 'Hickory Holler Tramp'?"

"Sure, O.C. Smith in 1968." Tough childhood, indeed. "Okay, I guess I get it. But it still seems like it would be difficult."

"Perhaps, but there is one other aspect that's going to sound a little crazy."

"Try me."

She has returned to her seat but is paying no attention to the cards.

"Okay. Growing up, I had two things going for me that set me apart from most of my friends. First, I was very smart and earned phenomenal grades, at least at that school. It was a shitty educational system, so I did a lot of self-teaching."

"Okay, good student. Maybe you still are, but I know you can't tell me that. You said there were two things."

She smiles toward the cabin's low ceiling before closing her eyes. She stands back up and takes long strides while talking, as if doing a subtle dance.

"I was a hell of a performer." Her voice is stronger now, and she almost seems to be talking to herself. "It's not just me bragging. I have always had people tell me when I'm on stage, whether singing or acting, I have a kind of unique magnetism. I'm grounded enough to know I can't hang my hat on that, so I have other career steps I'm taking. But I can always hope."

Her passion for what many would view as overly ambitious seems irrepressible to me. I need to do whatever I can to help this girl.

"Sure you can, and, yes, I can see why people would tell you that. I've always been told that too, and it's worked very well for me. But what does that have to do with this . . . work?"

She frowns as if it is a dumb question.

"Well, this is obviously an acting job. What could be more challenging than this? Or better training. If I can learn how to lose myself in doing this, I should be able to pull off just about any performance. I also try to portray different characters for each job."

This gives me pause.

"Oh, I thought I was dealing with the real you."

"Oh, you definitely are. I guess I had an immediate sense with you as well that this was different, so I've gone ahead and been myself. You should see my cheerleader portrayal. That works really well with some customers. So does the ditzy blonde, but the wig can be a challenge when we get to work."

"I'm sure it can be."

We resume the game and remain silent through two more games. I ponder why I am so taken with her. Typically, I am surrounded by people who have lived privileged lives, myself included. I have some constituents who are destitute, and I say all the right things to them. But I don't really know them.

No one in my circle of acquaintances has had to pull themselves up like this. She needs to succeed, and I want to do whatever I can to help her. That would be far more effective in helping someone than all those massive spending programs I always vote for. Sure, a cynic would ask whether I would do the same for a far less attractive woman in the same situation. I don't feel like I need to answer that question. For whatever reason, I have strong feelings for this woman, and she deserves my help. But I still want to try to stop the degradation, regardless of how she rationalizes it.

I declare gin, and her time is up, so I finally break the silence. “Do you really have to do this? I mean, if it was just me, would that be enough money?”

Her brow wrinkles while she ponders my question. “Well, not really. I mean, even if we do this regularly, my share isn’t enough for just one customer to suffice.”

“I’ll see if I can up the payments. Part of this is wanting to spend time with you. But part of it is also caring enough about you to help you get away from this. You are different from the other girls. I don’t know what their needs are, but you wouldn’t be doing this just to make more money. I want to try to save you from it.”

“Maybe if you got to know the other girls, you would feel the same way about them. And I *will* get away from it eventually. I just need the money for a while. And then it has to be over between you and me. Understood?”

I did anticipate that. All good things, and so on. I also know that my reason for constraining any further physical relationship with Rose is, ironically, based on my affection for her. With the other women, it was purely physical, and, given the limits of my marital situation, I have felt less guilt. That wouldn’t be true with someone I have feelings for. Yes, maybe even love. That would be cheating on Faith, which in my own awkward way, I have sworn myself against.

I dutifully give her fifteen dollars. She thanks me and gives me a gentle peck on the cheek. She leaves first, and I give her the requisite twenty minutes before leaving myself. She’s gone all of five minutes before I miss her.

I wish we had never met.

# FIFTEEN

# SAUNDRA

## Wally North

*September 1989*

When Saundra Gray first walked into the office, I immediately sensed trouble. Capitol Hill is full of beautiful women, but she is in another league entirely.

Her long black hair is what you first notice, with strands on both sides sweeping over her shoulders and then surfing to the tips of her breasts. They are perfectly formed, and the top of her blouse exposes enough cleavage that a guy has to force himself to look up. And when I do, she smiles, patiently awaiting my full attention. Meanwhile, the rest of her attire looks like it has been painted on.

"We really appreciate your dad's support, Saundra," I tell her after I've led her into my office after making a few introductions. I want to make it clear at the outset that the various fundraisers that her father, Dr. Aaron Gray, has either attended or hosted play no small part in her internship.

Even with the best spot in the office, my quarters are still cramped, so we have to sit very close, and it doesn't take but a few sentences before I feel like she and I are the only ones on an island.

"I'm so excited to be working for the congressman." Her eyes fix on mine.

"Well. I was impressed with your résumé." Indeed. High school valedictorian, president of the Latin club, homecoming queen runner-up (*Jesus, who the hell actually won?*), magna cum laude at Colgate, and second-year law student at Georgetown. Impressive, but no more so than hundreds of others that cross my desk on a regular basis.

I also know her knock-dead looks would be a strong selling point in other offices. With J.D.'s situation and a few other guys in the office, I am not comfortable with the potential distraction. But she is well connected and obviously very smart, a difficult combination for any AA to turn away.

As the interview continues, I keep having to ward off her questions about my personal life and get back to her professional attributes. We are stationed on the side of my desk, facing each other, and I keep noticing our knees are touching. I have to back up several times until I am braced against the wall like a target of a firing squad.

"I know you've been in DC awhile, so I assume you are well situated with the housing and transportation."

"Yes. I share a place with a student at American close to Rock Creek Park around the embassies. She works for a Connecticut senator, and we have similar hours, so it works well."

I shoot a glance over to Edna Pilkington, J.D.'s appointments secretary with whom I share the small office. Her desk is situated so she can see me over the hutch. I see her burying a smile, but I can't respond because Saundra's eyes are burrowed into mine.

I brief her on the various details about how we were set up, such as office hours and connections with the district office—all the standard stuff. She at least seems absorbed, but maybe more with me than the details.

"As you can imagine, we get a great deal of constituent mail, and we need some help with that. Are there any particular policy areas you are interested in or have strong views on?"

J.D. has always believed that it is a waste to have interns limited to menial work, especially if they are intelligent and could possibly be groomed as a future permanent staffer.

"Actually, I have very strong feelings about the environment. I think we have allowed the large companies to poison our environment. Back home, I am very concerned about the excessive use of pesticides the farmers are using. It's pretty clear the Reagan and Bush administrations haven't helped with this any more than any other environmental issue. I would love to take on that issue."

This is a very dicey issue for us, with the environmentalists, large companies, and the ag community all on different sides. A joint effort by industry and the eco freaks is excluding the farmers, who on a national level are far weaker politically. While J.D. has good environmental credentials, there is no way he is going to cross his farmers on something like this.

"Actually, we are pretty well staffed on those issues. How about foreign policy and defense?"

This is a much safer area. J.D. is well to the left of his fairly conservative constituency, but being a war hero has helped, and, since the end of the Vietnam War, the subject only arouses the passions of a limited few. And they are solid Republican votes, anyway.

"Um, well, I would love to learn more about them. Sure, as long as there's someone senior to guide me."

"Of course, we have great staff on that. We don't hear much concern about 'evil Commies' from the district. I think after Tiananmen Square everyone has pretty much become resigned to the fact that the Iron Curtain is built to last. But there are still those who think Bush may be squishy on nuclear disarmament and cutting back on military spending. Of course, we're all for those things but have to be a little careful on how we pitch it to the folks back home."

This clears things up, and I escape further distraction by commissioning Lucy, our office manager, and Rosa, the legislative director, to get her onboarded. The single guys in the office are going to have to be watched closely with her. I also assume J.D. will be okay given the arrangement we have with Starr, which I assume is going as planned.

SIXTEEN

# HOW OUR LAWS ARE MADE

**Wally North**

*October 1989*

Occasionally, amid all the fundraisers, constituent letters, town halls, internal personnel policies, staffing issues, budget issues, J.D. travel logistics, and all the other minutiae, I get to actually focus on public policy and legislative issues, which is what drew me to DC in the first place.

Today looks to be one of those days. The meeting in his office will not be a comfortable one. But his performance in situations like this reminds me of why I wanted to work for J.D. To the extent any politician can do so and get reelected, he is his own guy and rarely lets people push him around.

I have noticed this quality in a lot of moderates from both parties. If you are in a marginal district, which most moderates are, you can't just do the safe thing and always vote with the party leadership, no matter how much pressure they apply. You really don't have a "base" like those in a safe liberal or conservative district. So, you have to do your best to keep both ends of the spectrum at bay and occasionally stick with them on things they care about most. But J.D. is well suited for playing that game because he genuinely believes that compromise makes for better legislation—or at least ensures that it doesn't generate riots by those aggrieved.

Of course, this process makes it very challenging for the staff, since we have to actually read the various bills and ask all the questions beforehand so that we know what he will ask when we brief him. A lot of Hill staffers balk at this and just want to play the political version of "follow the leader." That type doesn't last long in our office.

Today's meeting is about the Family and Medical Leave Bill, which would guarantee employees twelve weeks of unpaid leave for childbirth and serious illnesses, among other things. We are nearing the end of the first session of the 101st Congress, and the proponents are lining up their ducks to make a big push for it to be an election-year issue in 1990. They want to get it through the House, keeping all the Democrats on board while adding some moderate Republicans. If by some miracle the Senate Republicans decide not to filibuster the bill, it will only take a majority there to pass it and send it to Bush. Otherwise, the bill will need sixty votes to invoke cloture and get past the filibuster. If the plan works, Bush can be expected to veto it, which will then position the Democrats as the "family first" party in the 1990 elections and, even better, in the 1992 presidential election.

But first things first, they need to get the bill passed by the House, and they need all Democrats on board. That's where J.D. comes into play as the leading voice among a large block of moderate Democrats. They have not yet taken a position on the bill, responding to their small business constituents, who fear the impact of high rates of absenteeism on their operations.

At the meeting in J.D.'s office with the bill's supporters, I've been called in urgently by Rosa, our legislative director. As soon as I walk in, I feel like going back and grabbing a fire extinguisher.

Susan Cady of Women United is holding court in full regalia. She has long been the face of the activist women's movement. I assume when I go home tonight and tell Gloria that I've been in a meeting with Susan, she will ask if I got her autograph.

Susan's long, straight, auburn hair and horn-rimmed glasses are iconic, popularized by political cartoonists. While many in the movement have shed the traditional trappings of beauty, she is ironically astute enough to know that she needs to appeal to men, however antediluvian that appeal may be, as well as to women. When she shows up on the *Today* show, *Meet the Press*, and others, she steals the show. She is drawn to cameras and microphones like a june bug to a floodlight but never seems to get burned.

The public continues to be transfixed by her. Like Dr. King, she has many detractors, but those who follow her are devoid of skepticism. Even those who fear her power respect her eloquence.

Most of Washington, on the other hand, generally despises her. Those of us who like getting things done know that Susan's and others' pyrotechnics always make that more difficult. But we still have to deal with her. In the case of the Family and Medical Leave Bill, J.D. really does want to get something done.

"Congressman, your failure to cosponsor this bill is disgraceful. You make it worse by holding us hostage to your proposal to gut it by eliminating a huge percentage of the population from its protections. You will pay for this among the women in your district." Susan's distaff version of Charlton Heston conjures visions of locusts immediately descending on our office.

However much folks dislike Susan and her ilk, I have long since learned that the most hated people in Washington are often the apostates—Democrats who only occasionally vote with business and Republicans who may side with labor or the other liberal groups. Everyone prefers to think the members in their aligned party are "in their pocket," and they usually are. If a business group has to sweat out the vote of a liberal Republican or vice versa on the other side, there is far more animosity toward them than anyone who consistently votes against them. It disrupts the natural order.

In the animal kingdom, they would be shunned by their herd. In Washington, though, they have one saving grace. In almost all of these cases, they have to be reelected in a marginal district and the leadership will go the extra distance—as long as it is a predictable length—to protect them. In the end, the leaders need their vote to retain or obtain the majority.

Meanwhile, the moderates ironically often do better than most in fund-raising since their votes are always in play, and therefore access to them is even more critical.

With regard to the Family and Medical Leave Bill, J.D. has a very simple and responsible demand for his vote. The bill would enable employees to take twelve weeks of unpaid leave for new parenthood, serious illnesses, and other things while having a legal right to reclaim their jobs when they return from leave. The proponents feel that they have already compromised by cutting the amount of leave back from the bill's original twenty-four weeks and, more importantly, making the leave unpaid. The latter would effectively make the full extent unavailable to a lot of employees. From the employer's perspective, making it unpaid reduces absenteeism by providing an incentive to return as soon as possible.

The bill has been cosponsored by the vast majority of Democrats, but the thirty-seven members of the Burnt Toast Coalition, led by J.D., have thus far withheld their support. The coalition was given its name by "Hap" Frawley, a Democrat from Oklahoma. When he resisted pressure to support a budget-busting bill, he famously said, "I know I'm going to get burned by saying no to this, but only slight burned, and slightly burned bread is still edible."

The coalition's demand would hardly gut the bill, but it would reduce its coverage by only applying it to employers with a minimum number of employees. If J.D. can get that number somewhere between fifty and one hundred, he thinks he can sell it to the small businesses in his district.

As Susan continues to fulminate, J.D. sits silently taking it in. I can see that Grady Collins from the Speaker's office is shaking his head silently while gazing at the carpet. He had worked with Rosa to put this meeting together when she told him she thought there was a way to break the stalemate.

J.D. lets Susan finish and then looks her straight in the eye. "What you are missing, Ms. Cady, is that right now, no American employees have this protection. Think about what it takes to make sure that most do, even if it requires that essential process of compromise. You've been around a while. Do you really not get that that's how things get done in this town?"

Nessie Moorhead of the American Federation of Labor and Congress of Industrial Organizations (AFL-CIO) speaks next. Both Rosa and Grady had agreed that she needed to be in the meeting, since she is among the most seasoned and reasonable lobbyists on the left and is a veteran of many compromises herself.

"Congressman, let me put this in more practical terms," says Nessie. The contrast between Nessie and Susan could not be sharper. Unlike Susan, Nessie is as usual "dressed for business," with her hair in a bun and a dark-blue vest buttoned almost to her collarbone and a light-blue skirt ending well below the knees. The winged rectangle of her glasses deprives her of any glamour whatsoever. She is actually a very attractive woman—at least as attractive as Susan—but she downplays it in her lobbying.

"True, people now don't have this protection," Nessie continues, "and I believe we all pray for the day that they do. But the issue will not get finally settled in the House. As you know, what you pass here will not be the final word. When it goes to the Senate, it will unfortunately need sixty votes."

J.D. rolls his eyes. "I know that, Nessie. But I'm here, not in the Senate. They'll do whatever they want."

She persists. "But the point is, to pass the Senate, it will require more compromises. So whatever minimum number you want is just going to get ratcheted up over there. We need to come out of the House with the strongest possible bill. Maybe you could support this with that understanding and even say so when it goes to the floor."

J.D. has a very high regard for Nessie, His face softens at her remarks. "I appreciate that, Nessie, and, as usual, your counsel is very wise. I totally get what you are saying, and I've had to deal with that on other bills."

Grady Collins looks up with this spark of hope, but it is immediately dashed by J.D.

"However, I am just one of thirty-seven in our coalition. I don't think I could sell that to all the others. Maybe a few, but not all of them, and you would still be short your votes. I have to stand with them on this."

The room falls silent. We are stuck. The various lobbyists look at each other with the blank stares they use to hide anger and frustration.

Grady starts to speak but is quickly interrupted by Susan.

"You know, Congressman, I'm just going to say what a lot of us are thinking. You are one of the few pro-life Democratic members. I actually prefer the term 'pro-life-of-misery-and-disgrace.' So, you start with two strikes against you on this, showing your true stripes on where you stand with women."

J.D. glares, and others in the room visibly freeze at this, knowing that chastising a member of Congress rarely works. J.D. starts to speak, but Susan holds her hand up, turning to Grady. "If it means bringing this to a vote and getting Congressman Clay and these other retrogrades on the record, I'd prefer a loss like that to watering the bill down even more."

She continues, looking directly at J.D. "We can try to fix things in the primaries."

Susan has moved beyond scolding to a threat, and the room erupts with one or two others jumping on her points but others urging restraint. Grady holds his hand up and literally shouts the room to silence.

"Let's be absolutely clear here. Speaker O'Connor has no desire to burn his members with this." He turns to Susan. "You clearly know where he stands on this and the other important women's issues, and—in fairness to Congressman Clay—he has been with us on all the other issues. The Speaker firmly believes we are here to pass legislation, not score political points. I think you owe the congressman an apology."

Her eyes almost jump out of her iconic horned rims. "The last thing I will ever do is apologize to him or anyone else who stands in the way of our rights. I also have my own distinct view on what pro-life means. Over my dead body will I apologize!"

Grady shakes his head and shifts into the traffic cop role that brought him here.

"Then I suggest you and anyone else in this room who shares your views leave. We are not going to have a productive discussion if it keeps going down this path."

J.D. says nothing. Susan is rarely put in her place, especially by a congressional staffer.

Susan stands abruptly and peers down her nose, which looks vaguely like a bird of prey's bill. "If you think this is your call, young man, you have a lot to learn about how Washington works."

She doesn't blink.

"It's not my call any more than it is yours or anyone else in this room except Congressman Clay and his colleagues."

She chuckles. "Well, we'll see about that, won't we? Come on, ladies, our next meeting is starting shortly."

Only Nessie remains after the others storm out.

In a city where most meetings with four or more people tend to be scripted, it is clear no one has a script beyond this point.

J.D. breaks the silence. "Grady, you and Rosa called this meeting. You can see where we are. Is that what you expected?"

Grady sits silent for a moment. "Honestly, Congressman, not really, but I did think it was a bit of a gamble. Susan likes to talk a big game, but I was hoping she would soften if she saw we really had a chance to move the ball here."

Nessie speaks. "Look, Congressman, we are trying everything we can to get this to the floor. Sometimes when things seem locked, you just have to get everyone in the same room and see if you can find a break."

J.D. stands from his seat on the couch and returns to his desk, making a point to start going through his pile of work. He is through with the discussion. But then he isn't.

"Well, folks, it was pretty goddam clear that they were opposed to any kind of movement. We didn't even talk about what the employer threshold could be. We can obviously negotiate that lower and then leave room for more movement in the Senate, but it's clearly a nonstarter with those folks. Why would we think they would even budge on the Senate side? This seems to be more about keeping the issue alive so they can identify their friends and enemies than actually getting something passed."

Grady thanks Nessie for her help, and she leaves the room. When it is just us and Grady, he looks straight at J.D. in a way that no congressional staffer who doesn't work for the leadership would do.

"Congressman, the speaker is very concerned about two things. First, we need to show progress on our agenda. Passing this will prove that the Democrats are clearly on the side of American women and families. It shows we not only say the right things but deliver on them as well. If we can somehow get this through the Senate and Bush vetoes it, that would not necessarily be a bad thing. Maybe it helps us wind up with a friendly administration where we can get even more things passed."

His voice softens. "Second, he is very concerned about you and the other Toasters. We get that you are in tough districts and walk a tightrope with your small businesses. But we are also concerned that you are making yourself very vulnerable with your own base, especially when you combine this with your pro-life position. We checked, and you got a lot of money from unions and the other groups in the coalition, but if you keep saying no to them, that will dry up, and we will lose your district."

I always know J.D. is really pissed when he smiles early into a long, silent pause while tugging his ear. I don't think Grady knows this and suspect he might interpret it as a measurement of the suggestion.

J.D. clears his throat forcibly. "Okay, Grady, you take this to the Speaker. First, I totally get your wanting to deliver on the agenda. I do, too, and I'd be pushing guys like me as well if I were in his shoes. But on your second point, don't you ever tell me how to win in my district. I am now in my fifth term, and I have mastered that tightrope. Keep in mind,

I'm the one showing flexibility here, not those 'one hundred percenters.' What I would suggest is that instead of putting the wood to his strong supporters like me, he should go back to the so-called base and tell them nothing gets done unless they bend."

Most seasoned congressional staffers know how to read the point where any more pushing of a member of Congress sparks a bridge fire, and Grady is astute enough to know he has reached that point.

"I will certainly take that message to him. Thank you, Congressman. I'll keep working with Rosa to get this worked out. Make no mistake, Speaker O'Connor values your support and that of all the Toasters in the highest possible terms."

J.D. lets a beat go by before he cracks a more genuine smile. "Shit, Grady, that kind of crap works in a floor speech, but you don't need to say it here. Look, I know he's fried with us, but we're just like everyone here. We all want to move the goddamn ball, but we also know we can't if we get benched by our voters. At the end of the day, I'm the one who has to make the read on where the voters in my district are. Now just make sure he's not so upset with me that he won't be coming to my fundraiser next week at Bullfeathers. Can you do that for me?"

"Sure, Congressman."

Grady leaves us alone. I speak first. "J.D., I am a little worried about his point on the base. We just can't win without getting that help from the libs."

Rosa nods. This insight is not foreign to her, since she is most often the one who has to deal with the lobbyists.

"Now don't worry, Wally, I got this all figured out. We only win if a bill passes with my business folks knowing I went to bat and got something for them. We just have to figure out a way to make sure it eventually passes."

Rosa and I exchange glances on our way out. Why would we need to say anything if we can finish each other's sentences?

SEVENTEEN

# IOWA STUBBORN

**Wally North**

*October 1989*

"Ever actually seen *The Music Man*?" J.D. asks as we are taking our seats at the Arena Stage.

As usual, it's a full house. Arena, down by the decrepit DC wharf area with its tired old seafood restaurants, is one of the most successful local theaters in the United States. Being more of a movie buff, I rarely attend, but, when I do, it is for some of the more serious productions, not the musicals. Nevertheless, I have to admit, Arena does a pretty good job with musicals, and it is their one tip of the hat to the masses. Less so their plays, which are more likely to be Ibsen or Chekhov than Neil Simon. But even those are more established plays. As with almost everything else in our local culture, Washington audiences are very well educated but not particularly adventurous.

"I watched the movie on TV a few years ago," I acknowledge. "Kind of hard to grow up in Iowa and not at some point see the most famous musical ever set there."

I know J.D.'s musical tastes are pretty eclectic, as one would expect of a former rock star of sorts, but I have never heard him talk about Broadway musicals. "Yeah, not really my thing, either," he says, "but I figured the local folks would want to know I attended. I watched it once with my dad, who said they only got Iowa half right. The good half, obviously."

With Faith back in Iowa—and limited by her disability even when in DC—J.D. often asks me to attend performances with him. It's more often that they're rock or country bands at the Birchmere in Alexandria or the Capital Center out in Largo. We have even done a couple of fundraisers in a sky suite at the latter. Springsteen and The Police are favorites of J.D.'s. Our "dates" are not uncommon among our colleagues. Mostly male members of Congress have mostly male AAs, with the wives only in town for the most demanding social or political events.

"I will give this musical credit for staying power," J.D. says. "It's almost thirty years old and still being revived. Wonder if any of the crap on Broadway these days will hold up as well."

The Iowa congressional caucus put together a block of seats, and there was a brief reception beforehand. The event has drawn several members of the bipartisan Iowa Federation, a formal organization of Iowans in DC—mostly current and former congressional staff—so J.D. and I are surrounded by a lot of familiar faces. The play is on the Fichandler Stage, which is in the round, so we are making visual contact with many of them. I can tell J.D. is ready for the play to begin so he can stop smiling and trying to nod to all those trying to get his attention from around the room.

"Well, J.D., I'm going to guess I've seen this one even more often than *My Fair Lady*," says Rep. W.H. "Chip" Wood, the dean of the Iowa delegation. He is sitting next to us with his wife, Vera. A staunch Republican, Chip was elected to his seat in southwest Iowa at the conclusion of World War II, when he returned to Iowa as a highly decorated war hero.

One of the most senior members of the House, he is little known outside of Iowa, except for a brief moment of infamy when he emerged as one of the leading opponents of the Civil Rights Act of 1964. His inflammatory speech on the House floor suggested the problem could have been avoided by "shipping those folks back to Africa to be with their original families." It would go down as one of the most outrageous congressional statements since the Civil War. Yet, throughout most of his career, Wood has been an otherwise mainstream Republican who bears no signs of overt racism, or at least not any going beyond the typical ignorance of many white people, especially those from mostly white communities.

Chip is "all Iowa," which helps explain his long tenure. Small-town bankers and drugstore owners approve that he never overdresses—tweed jackets and JCPenney ties are trademarks—and the farmers can't help but note his top-heavy build and a little red below his hairline in the back.

In reality, like J.D., he comes from an affluent family, with his father owning a highly successful John Deere franchise. His heft comes from a stellar high school wrestling career, not throwing bales of hay.

Vera's flowered dresses and traditional, black-rimmed eyeglasses don't hurt either. Chip never hesitates to offer that "she bakes a downright ornery cinnamon apple pie." Funny, I recently bumped into one of their adult children at an Iowa Federation event, and he said that she rarely cooked. In fact, her passion is professional boxing and one of her first jobs out of high school in Indiana was as an usher at a local sports arena, where she met Chip, an avid fan of martial arts.

As we are waiting for the play to begin, J.D. and Chip are talking about a potential bipartisan approach on pesticides. They both agree the issue is a difficult one for their districts. Issues affecting local businesses only occasionally break down along partisan lines, but both of them are trapped within their parties. J.D. by the environmentalists and Chip by the "no new regulations" folks who dominate his party. Yet, both are astute enough to know that it's always best to help shape something than to get rolled by it.

I forgot that the play has what must have been a very innovative opening for its time. Without any musical accompaniment, it is set in a single train car with several traveling salesmen chanting, in rhyme and rhythm, about a huckster—"Professor" Harold Hill—who is giving them all a bad name. Spoken words in rhythm, with no melody. I wonder if the rap music of Run DMC and others in that genre will ever make it to the Broadway stage.

As the play progresses, both J.D. and I reluctantly warm to it, particularly in the numerous references to Iowa, including an entire song called "Iowa Stubborn." When they sing the line, "You really ought to give Iowa a try," a third of the audience breaks into a cheer. How can J.D. not join? He gently nudges me to do so as well. Small price to pay to continue getting a paycheck as a congressional drone.

Meanwhile, Vera, who is sitting between J.D. and Chip, insists on singing along with many of the songs. She does this even when she doesn't seem to know the real words (except on "Gary, Indiana," which, it turns out, is where her father is from).

The evening has been entirely uneventful until J.D. momentarily gasps—just audible enough for me to hear—when one of the actresses enters the stage. I notice that J.D. has opened the program and is holding the cast list up to the light.

"Is everything okay?" I ask. He waves me off as he squints toward the page.

As the play continues, I see that whenever the young actress playing the mayor's daughter—Zaneeta Shinn—is on the stage, J.D. is fixed on her. It's a second- or third-tier part, but the part does have a speaking role and an annoying tendency to squeal "ee-gads," though this actress does it somewhat convincingly. At one point she briefly sees him in the audience and does ever the slightest double-take that no one else likely notices.

During the intermission, J.D. goes off to the men's room. I check the cast list, and "Zaneeta Shinn" is listed as Naomi Bridgewater, a George Washington University law student.

I wait in vain for J.D. to return to his seat, but right before the intermission ends, an usher comes down and tells me the congressman suddenly felt very ill and is heading home. I stay and enjoy the show more than I expected. I notice that whenever Naomi is on, she steals the scenes even with her small part.

EIGHTEEN

# CAREER PLANNING

**Naomi Bridgewater**

*October 1989*

I am not surprised when the first thing J.D. says to me when I enter the cabin is: "I saw you at the Arena."

"I know. I saw you out there. Did you enjoy the show?"

His eyes leave mine, a rare occurrence in these meetings.

"I enjoyed what I saw. I had to leave. You threw me into a total state of confusion, and I just couldn't sit there through the second act."

He continues staring at his feet. Has the revelation of my true identity broken the spell? Maybe this could be a good thing. The emergence of my own strong feelings for him has felt like a warning sign.

"I noticed you left." After I say this, he finally returns my gaze. "I guess that's it for my secret identity. I think under the rules, we should really make this the last visit."

"Not at all. They don't have to know," he says with a tinge of desperation.

"They don't. But part of the game here is that we are supposed to be two complete strangers with the whole thing built on a fantasy that has nothing to do with our real lives."

"But I feel that that fantasy is long gone. I don't have to know every detail of your life to know you, do I?"

"I guess not."

"Look, I have to tell you that you were astonishingly good out there.

You were an absolute eye magnet and not just for me. I don't know how serious you are about your legal career, but I really think you could make it as a performer if that's where you want to go."

He really seems convinced of this. He also probably has no idea of what a serious long shot a performance career is for anyone.

"Thank you for the compliment, but there are so many uncertainties around that, and I have to manage my expectations. My studies are going well, so, if all else fails, I should be able to get something there. I hear all the firms are trying to hire a lot of women to show they are progressive, so that should help."

"But law's not your first love?"

"Not at all. The intellectual challenge can be stimulating, but it is also draining. I would much prefer performing."

He thinks about that for a bit and then nods. For a moment, he feels more like a father than a lover, or maybe that's what it's been for me anyway.

"That's good," he says. "Continue on both tracks, and one of them should work. I just want to keep supporting you, and I like to think doing this does that, both financially and by being a friend."

We talk for a while about what he learned in his days as a "rock star" and how I have managed to juggle my studies and the show. I realize I have never felt this close to someone in my life, but is it the father who has long since left my life or the lover I've never had?

As I am leaving, he tries to give me his regular farewell peck on the cheek, but I cannot resist pulling him toward me. He relents only momentarily, then shakes his head, pushing me away gently.

"Okay, I get it, but not even a friendly peck? Friends do that all the time."

His eyes show a trace of pain. "I don't trust myself to keep it at that. You are just so beautiful, Naomi . . . I mean, Rose."

"Maybe right now I wish I wasn't."

I whisper my goodbye without looking in his eyes.

As I back my car out of the gravel drive, I wonder if it is time to end this one.

NINETEEN

# TEDDY ROOSEVELT ISLAND

**Saundra Gray**

*March 1, 1990*

I'm fried. Completely. My nerves are shot, and my head feels like it might explode. The congressional recess starts tomorrow, and I've tried reaching J.D. a dozen times, but he's making it painfully obvious he's done with me. *Fine. Let him go. I'll deal with him when I'm back.*

But right now, I just need to breathe—or run. A hard run through Rock Creek Park might burn some of this out of my system. It probably won't work, but what else can I do?

I lace up my trail shoes, glance at the Weather Channel one last time—still no rain—and grab my Walkman. My tape is a mix of The Police and Talking Heads. Perfect. Something familiar, something to drown out my thoughts.

The temperature's just low enough to be annoying, hovering in the low forties. I pull on my long-sleeve blue running shirt, layer it under a vest, and pair it with my black shorts. It's overkill at the start, but I'll heat up fast and tie anything extra to my fanny pack later. No way I'm getting caught out after dark, so I keep it light.

The anger hits hard the second my feet hit the pavement. My pace is fast—too fast. A 7:30 mile, maybe faster. I force myself to slow down once I hit the dirt path, my eyes scanning for stray branches and loose rocks. The plan is simple: three miles out, turn at the square near the Kennedy Center and head home.

*This is useless.* My brain keeps circling back to J.D. *What did I do wrong? What could I have done differently?* How could he choose *her*—a wife who can't even satisfy him—over me?

I can't stop. I won't. I decide to push farther. Maybe I'll loop through Teddy Roosevelt Island. I remember walking those trails with my parents once. Quiet. Secluded. It's perfect.

I glance at my watch. Yeah, I've got time. It'll tack on another two or three miles, but who cares? I need the extra burn. Avoiding the TR statue is a given—I'm in no mood for a politician's smug face, no matter how "honorable" history claims him to be. *Were any of them even honorable?*

The path into Georgetown requires concentration. I shut off Sting mid-verse—"This girl is half his age . . ." God, no—and focus on navigating the sidewalks.

I sense a jogger behind me before I see them. The faint rhythm of footsteps, the steady breath catching up behind me. My shoulders tense, my pace quickening before logic reminds me it's just someone out for a run. It always is. I lower my shoulders and shake out my hands. *Not everyone is out to get me.*

The bustle of Francis Scott Key Park distracts me for a moment. People bundled up against the cold, walking dogs or chatting on benches. Normally, their presence feels reassuring, but today I just want to be alone. My chest tightens as tears threaten to spill over, but I swallow them down. No one—not even strangers—gets to see me like that.

A dachshund lunges at me from a loose leash, nearly tripping me. I sidestep, biting back a sharp comment. No need to draw attention to myself. I just need to get across the bridge and find some peace.

The climb onto the Key Bridge feels like freedom. DC sprawls to my left, glowing faintly against the gray sky. For a moment, the sight lifts me. I have to remind myself to slow down. There's still three miles back, and I don't want to burn out.

Navigating down to the island entrance is easier than I expected. A few other runners pass by, their presence oddly comforting. By the time I cross the footbridge onto the island, I pause briefly to catch my breath. The Potomac stretches out below me, serene and endless. Even with the trees bare and brittle in late winter, the place feels untouched, almost sacred.

I veer right onto the Swamp Trail, away from the busier paths that lead to the statue. Solitude. That's all I want. I restart the Walkman, Sting diving straight into "Don't Stand So Close to Me," and let the music pull me into my rhythm.

The trail narrows quickly. Roots and rocks jut up like forgotten land mines, demanding I keep my focus sharp. My feet move instinctively—higher steps, quicker adjustments. The incline steepens near a massive beech tree, and I press forward, savoring the burn in my thighs.

Branches scrape against my arms, and I notice side trails branching off, tempting me with easier routes back to the main path. I stick to the loop. It's harder, quieter. Better.

The underbelly of the Roosevelt Bridge looms ahead, dark and hulking. A thick patch of fencing runs along its base, probably to keep people off the bridge. A gash in the wire catches my eye, just wide enough for someone to slip through. I shudder and look away, the thought too eerie to entertain.

My distraction costs me. My foot catches on a thick root, and the ground rushes up to meet me. Pain shoots through my hands and ribs as I slam down, my breath knocked out of me. I stay still, trying to gauge the damage. Nothing broken, I think. My palms throb, and my chest aches, but I can move.

I push up onto my knees and freeze. A figure in a dark jogging suit stands above me. My heart races—too fast.

Before I can scream, David Byrne's voice filters through the headphones. "Heaven is a place where nothing ever happens . . ."

And then, everything does.

# PART THREE

A few years ago, with little more public notice than a few obligatory obituaries, former Iowa Democratic Congressman J.D. Clay's life came to a violent end that remains shrouded in mystery. He had served in Congress from 1981 to 1991 and had many great legislative accomplishments, but that's not what the obituaries immediately gravitated toward.

Rather, it was his central role in the media-fed public frenzy surrounding the disappearance of a young intern in the nation's capital—a situation in which he was initially suspected of playing some role. Her body was eventually found, and the perpetrator was identified by circumstantial evidence following his suicide. But this was revealed too late for Clay, well after defeat in his primary. Though Clay was exonerated, those headlines were much smaller and nowhere near the front page. So, most people probably remember him as being guilty of the crime or having some direct

country—one who rises above partisan rhetoric in order to accomplish something, even if it means compromising. He did this on numerous occasions, whether the issue involved employment protections, environmental restrictions, regulation of large corporations, or any number of other areas where partisanship can paralyze needed action.

But now I have to ask myself: Did my genuine admiration for Clay prevent me from performing my role as a journalist with the right degree of probity and skepticism? Perhaps.

Recent events caused me to do a little quiet digging into what Clay's real role was and what I have learned is both disturbing and embarrassing.

First, let me make it clear that I have learned nothing that leads me to suspect Clay of either committing or conspiring in the murder of Saundra Gray. There is nothing connecting Clay with her murderer and my

TWENTY

# A SUNDAY MORNING CALL

**Wally North**

*March 1990*

The ringing phone wakes us both up. It is way too early on a Sunday morning for anyone to be calling with ordinary news. Usually, it is someone from the district office, so I assume whatever this is will take away the rest of my weekend. Gloria rolls her eyes and turns over. By this point in my career, she is very good at going back to sleep. I grab the phone before the second ring, hoping it won't wake the kids.

"Is this Wally North?" The voice on the other end sounds very distraught.

"Yes, it is."

"Oh, good, I was hoping this was the right number," a man says. I hear a woman in the background talking, though it is coming in and out. I can hear distress in her voice.

"It's Aaron Gray, Wally, Saundra's dad. You're Congressman Clay's top person, right?"

"Uh, yes, I'm his administrative assistant."

"Oh, his secretary?"

"Well, actually in Congress the chief of staff is usually called the administrative assistant, or AA. Is everything okay, Dr. Gray?" We briefly met at a fundraiser, well before we hired Saundra.

In our meeting, he impressed me as someone who relishes his status as a successful doctor. He also made it clear that his politics are well to the left of J.D.'s but that he is happy to have a Democrat representing him. His wife, Mrs. Lynne Gray, had seemed ill at ease, not looking me straight in the eye and acting like she resented having to give anyone money to be a public servant. I both agreed with and resented her.

Realizing this would not likely be a short conversation, I ask if I could call him back after transitioning to the kitchen phone. I could tell this tested his patience, but there is no reason for Gloria to get up this early on a Sunday. I call back and apologize quickly, then he resumes.

"We're calling about Saundra. She was supposed to arrive home yesterday. She wasn't on her flight to Des Moines, and we haven't heard from her."

I almost never have to deal with any of our staff's parents, except when they come to DC to visit. They are invariably grateful to have their son or daughter doing such important work, even if it is just working the constituent mail assembly line. I immediately assume it was probably just a miscommunication with Saundra. My mild annoyance dissipates when I realize I am probably one of their only connections in DC. I soften further at thinking about my reaction if my own kids missed a flight.

"I guess you tried calling her apartment?" I ask. "I think she has a roommate."

"We did and left several messages, but there was no response."

"Well, let's see, she doesn't come in on Thursdays or Fridays, and Wednesday would have been her last day in the office before the break. I do remember that she was in, and she told me she would see me when she got back. She seemed perfectly fine, Dr. Gray."

The noise in the background is still barely audible, but I can tell his wife is emphatically giving Gray directions about what to say. His hand is apparently working the transmitter hard, as her voice is coming in and out and I hear muffled pleas from him to calm down.

"Yes, we actually talked to her that evening, and she was fine. We were making sure we had the right flight to meet her. She was very eager to come home. Next weekend is her birthday, and we were planning something with her and her friends, so I know she was eager to return."

An invisible hand over my stomach is gradually squeezing. A fundamental skill for any congressional administrative assistant is to stay calm while trying to anticipate the worst, which this is beginning to resemble.

"Sure, well, I'm sure everything is fine. But, out of an abundance of caution, have you contacted the police?"

"Oh sure, they were a big help. We told them she was supposed to be on that flight. We had waited and waited at the gate and then baggage claim to see if she had checked anything. When we got home, we decided to call the police when there was no message on our answering machine. They gave us what I assume is their standard response: file a missing person report and then wait three days before contacting them again. They said most people do return within that time. We filed the claim, but there is absolutely nothing to indicate this is a normal situation."

I know there are any number of reasons a person can go missing, most of them innocent, and the police do this to conserve resources. As I am preparing coffee with the phone in the crook of my neck, I recognize there doesn't seem to be any reason Saundra would just decide to miss the flight and not tell her parents.

"Of course, I'm sure you're right," I say. "Do you know anything about her roommate? Maybe she's gone home, too, and we could try to contact her through her parents. We may have that information in our office, but, since we're not open today, that may slow things down, and I'm not even sure we have it."

"Well, Saundra told us her name was Emily something, but she never told us anything more, and it didn't seem important that we know."

Even forgiving hindsight realizations, I find that surprising. "Okay. So, what can I do to help?" It isn't clear to me there is anything, but I know I have to offer.

"Wally, we need to get the DC police to make this their top priority.

And since she works for a congressman, doesn't this make it a federal situation also? Shouldn't the FBI know?"

I don't have the heart to tell him how many times I have had to walk constituents back from trying to get the FBI involved in their problems. The muffled sounds of his wife's voice make me realize this is not going to be easy.

"I can try the DC police, but I have a feeling they do have pretty rigorous procedures they follow. I think the FBI would probably need a little more information before getting involved."

"I'm sorry, Mr. North, but you are sounding like them." The noise in the background is becoming more audible, and the shift from "Wally" to "Mr. North" is not a good sign. A cardinal rule in dealing with constituents is to never be an apologist for government action or inaction, even when the government may be acting reasonably. If they are, let them be the ones to explain why.

"At this point, Dr. Gray, that is probably all I can do. But I just woke up, so let me keep thinking. Excuse me a moment." I lay the phone down and step into the dining room to pour coffee and give myself a little more time. When I return, his voice has moved up a notch.

"Mr. North, the police would certainly listen to the congressman. Can't you get him involved?"

In the office, we refer to this in constituent cases as the "nuclear option." Of course, getting J.D. involved will always make a bigger difference, but we have to use it sparingly enough so that it remains effective. The other awkward thing is I have no idea what J.D.'s relationship with Saundra is. There have been rumors in the office, but I never gave them much credence. As far as I know, the arrangement I set up for him with Starr Fox is working fine. Why would J.D. do something foolish with an intern? But I still don't know for sure, so I have to be careful. But saying no would be difficult now that the request has been made.

"I can certainly let him know, and I am sure he will be concerned. As he would with any of our employees."

"So if Congress is in recess, is he back in the district? Maybe we could contact him directly."

This is awkward. He is, but he tries to keep Sunday mornings with Faith sacred. Sure, he will be talking to constituents there but holding off on any official business as much as possible. I can't lie, though, especially since it would be so easy to expose.

"Yes, he is. Let me check in with him. I'm certain right now he and Mrs. Clay are just getting up and planning to go to church."

"Do you know which one they attend? Maybe we could connect with him there?"

This is public information, so I give him the name of the church. I reassure him that I will reach out to J.D. immediately and make him aware, but I am careful not to promise anything more from J.D.

"Okay, thanks, we may try to find him there. Meanwhile, what about the DC police?"

My efforts to let Gloria sleep have failed. She comes in with a "what the hell" look on her face, which I wave off. She shrugs and grabs the mug of coffee out of my hand. Just another shitty day in the life of a congressional staffer's family.

"Let me see what I can do there, Dr. Gray. I'll get back to you as soon as I know anything."

We hang up on as good a note as I can expect. I know one of my next calls is going to be to Willow Milton's father, the DC cop who helped me get J.D. out of Northeast DC that dismal night a few years ago. But my next call has to be to J.D.

I hold my breath as the phone rings several times. I pray—well, to the extent that I do actually pray—that they are already up getting ready for church.

When he finally answers, his annoyance is as expected.

"Wally, it's Sunday morning."

"I know, sorry. Look, I just got a frantic call from Saundra Gray's parents. They think she has gone missing."

A long silence at the other end. He stammers a bit. "I thought she was going home for the break." This is generally a good assumption about our interns, but I wonder momentarily how he seems to know this for certain.

"She was supposed to be on the flight to Des Moines yesterday, but she didn't show up at the airport, and they've left several unanswered messages on her machine."

"Holy shit," he finally says after a long silence. The strength of his expression surprises me. It doesn't sound like he is hoping it was just a misunderstanding like I had hoped.

"They said the police told them they had to wait three days before doing anything, but now they want us to pressure them to act more quickly. They also want the FBI involved."

This time the silence is so protracted that I notice the ticking of our kitchen clock. I count sixteen ticks. By now, Gloria has picked up on what is going on, and I can tell the annoyance is replaced by parental solidarity.

"The FBI? That would only be for kidnapping," J.D. says.

"Well, they also think there could be some connection to her working for Congress."

"Well, maybe. What did you tell them?"

"I said I would follow up with the police. Actually, I think Willow's dad is still on the force, so I was going to try him."

"Good idea."

"But the main reason I called was because they are going to try to connect with you at church this morning."

"How the hell would they even know where we go?"

"J.D., you're a congressman. It's a matter of public record."

"Oh, of course. Look, I really don't want to see them right now. I'm going to tell Faith we're not going. I'll figure something out."

"Do you want me to call them and let them know?"

"No, they'll want to try to come here. Just keep working on the DC cops and tell them you couldn't get ahold of me."

"I can do that, but I'm pretty sure they are going to persist. They are going to want to talk to you today."

This time thirty-two ticks. He is thinking it through. I wonder why he isn't making himself so readily available. He finally speaks.

"Look, tell them I'm tied up with family all day today, and it would really be better if they just came by the district office. I'm going to be here all week, and I can work them in tomorrow. Set up a time and let them know. But wait until this afternoon so you can tell them you thought they'd be able to connect at the church."

This seems a lot more complicated than it needs to be, and I wonder why I wouldn't be able to get ahold of him if he didn't go to church. But, at this point, we just need a plan.

"Okay, I'll call Doris and set a time. The earlier tomorrow the better, I think."

"All right, but you keep pressing the DC cops, and let her parents know you are on it."

"Will do." The strangeness of the situation is sinking in. Normally, in a constituent matter, he's more proactive and I am trying to keep up with J.D. instead of having to lead him. I knew probing would be awkward, but I go ahead anyway.

"J.D., is there something going on here I should know about?"

He snaps back at me in a low whisper, obviously so Faith can't hear him.

"Now, what the hell would that be? Do I not tell you everything?"

J.D. usually at least tries to be cordial with me, so I am taken aback.

"Of course, you do. I'm just trying to think ahead here. If something really happened to Saundra, this is going to get some attention, and we need to be thinking about how we are going to handle appearances."

Gloria has been watching me closely and seems to be following. I see her mouth the question "appearances" with a frown. Often in politics, humanity takes a seat behind survival, but explain that to a parent who doesn't work for a politician.

J.D. chastises me. "Wally, we are, of course, very sorry for whatever has happened to her, and we'll do whatever we can to help. It's a matter for the police. There's only so much we can do."

"Sure. Do you think something happened to her?"

"Who knows? Maybe nothing has happened." He doesn't sound any more convinced than me. Disturbingly less so.

"Have they tried Emily?" he says after giving it more thought.

"Who's Emily?"

"Her roommate. I would assume they've reached out to her."

I then remember her name from my conversation with Gray. I wonder why J.D. would know who her roommate is when I don't. "They said they had no idea who it was and also wanted me to try to connect with her. They did recall her name was Emily something. Do you know her last name?"

"No. Why would I?" I decide not to ask why he would even know her first name.

"Okay, maybe the police can help with that, too. I'll keep you posted."

"Yes, please do." He hangs up abruptly. Before I can get back to my morning, I leave messages for Willow and Doris Knight, our district office manager.

I decide I'd better eat breakfast right away while I still have time.

## TWENTY-ONE

# A VISIT TO SAUNDRA'S APARTMENT

**Wally North**

*March 1990*

Walter Milton and I meet at Saundra's apartment. I am not at all surprised that he seems very on edge. I had learned from our previous encounter that he is very taciturn—not the stereotypical garrulous police type—so our conversation is minimal. He had warned me that while he was once again willing to help his daughter's coworker, anything we would do would have to be deniable and unofficial. He lets me do most of the work.

That morning, Walter was able to track down Emily, who was already at home in Connecticut. When he explained the situation, she was eager to help and called their neighbor to let us in. Emily told him she knew she had a legal right to a search warrant but didn't have anything to worry about for herself and was pretty sure about Saundra, too.

Emily told Walter that she had left earlier in the week for the break and knew Saundra was also planning to fly home. She told him Saundra often went running in nearby Rock Creek Park, so we might want to see if there were any signs she had gone running. The loose pile of clothes next to her dresser seems to confirm that. As does the empty bottle of Gatorade at the top of the garbage.

On her desk, I notice a few framed photographs. Saundra and her mother in thick wool coats and winter hats, beaming in Marienplatz with the Glockenspiel visible just over their shoulders. Saundra and her mother embracing on Colgate's football field at her graduation. The two of them lounging on beach chairs somewhere in the Mediterranean.

She also has a computer on her desk, and I ask Walter whether we can have someone at the station scrub it, but he says he would need a warrant. Before leaving, we ask a couple of questions of the neighbor who had let us in. She tells us she hasn't seen or heard from Saundra in several days, but that was not unusual, since she often goes home during the breaks. She expresses concern and volunteers to do whatever she can to help.

After trying unsuccessfully to reach J.D. at his home, I call the Grays and learn they had already been called by the district office to set up an appointment the following afternoon. They seem grateful that I had been able to use my DC police contact, but I am not surprised that our visit to her apartment fails to allay any of their fears.

"Isn't it clear something happened to her while she was out running?" Gray asks. "Shouldn't the police be searching the park you mentioned?"

"Mr. Gray, we really have nothing to go by other than an empty Gatorade bottle and what her roommate said. I don't know if you are familiar with it, but Rock Creek Park is a huge park that runs through a good part of the city. A lot of people drive and run through it every day, and as far as we know, nothing has been reported."

If anything, this increases his anxieties, and I can again hear Mrs. Gray in the background feeding more questions.

"Look, Wally, at this point I am holding out every hope that Saundra is somewhere safe. We have not received any calls from anyone asking for money. But we also have to assume that the worst could have happened, and we need to start looking for answers."

His politeness is starting to thin. And I know what the next request will be.

"Why can't the DC police search the park? Can't you and J.D. pressure them to do that? And, by the way," he seems to steel himself for a turn in the conversation, "why didn't you tell us he wouldn't be at church?"

"I honestly thought he would be. I wasn't able to reach him and assumed he had gone."

I have long since learned that in working for Congress, it just isn't possible to be honest with people 100 percent of the time. Eighty percent would be hall-of-fame level. In this case, I didn't have a very good feeling about my reasons for not being completely truthful. Other than keeping my job, of course.

"Is there any way we could go over to his house today to meet with him? Or at least give him a call at his home number, which you could give us?"

"Dr. Gray, I am very sorry, but only J.D. himself gives that out. I tried to reach him before calling you, and he wasn't there. I really think the best thing is for you to wait to meet with him tomorrow as scheduled. Meanwhile, I'll see what I can do with the DC police. A lot of people use the park, so if there was anything on or near the trail, it would have been reported. To get the police to do a thorough search of the park would take a lot of manpower, and I suspect that's not something they are going to do without more to go by. Meanwhile, let's hope you hear from Saundra."

"Mr. North." Once again, I am no longer Wally. "I think we would have heard from her by now. We'll certainly look forward to meeting with the congressman tomorrow, but I must say he isn't showing a lot of interest here in protecting one of his employees."

I shoot back immediately, maybe a little harder than I should but try to use a sympathetic tone. "Dr. Gray, I can't agree with that implication. J.D. cares very much about all of us and has always done everything he possibly can for us as employees. You have to realize there is only so much we can do here. I've used my best contact with the police, but we can't expect them to do anything outside normal procedures. They get missing person reports all the time, and most are resolved on their own within days. Meanwhile, if you hear from someone with a threat, we can get the FBI involved. But absent that, they're probably not going to take this on.

They get pressure from Congress on things like this all the time."

Here I am again violating the cardinal rule against being an apologist for the government, but I am starting to feel resentful that I am getting no credit for already going the extra mile. In my mind, it is still a matter for the police, though as a parent, I doubt I would be any less persistent than they are being.

I finally connect with J.D. an hour later, and he is upset that I had called them before filling him in. I apologize but do not regret my action, since Saundra is more their concern than his. I tell him everything I know, and we try to think about whether there is anything else we can do. I suggest that I should maybe try to call her roommate and see if she can add to anything we learned from the visit to their apartment, but he says he sees no value in that. I find that a little curious also. It's starting to feel like we aren't exactly leaving no stone unturned.

Gloria has returned from the movies with the kids, and the look on her face tells me it is time for stories, games, or any other bonding I could secure. I convince myself that this is just one crazy weekend, and I should be able to make up for it in the coming weeks.

TWENTY-TWO

# THE NEWS BREAKS

**Wally North**

*March 1990*

"Has J.D. called you yet?"

I am still rubbing sleep from my eyes when Doris in the district office calls with this question. No, "Good morning," "Sorry to wake you up," or any other pleasantries. Doris, as usual, goes right to the point.

"No. That would be highly unusual." I glance at the alarm, noting it isn't even 6:00 a.m. in Iowa.

"Well, brace yourself for something 'highly unusual.' The local morning paper has a story about Saundra's disappearance. Looks like her parents went to a reporter yesterday."

"I can't believe they would do that without knowing more."

"Well, here's the headline: 'Congressional Intern Missing Under Suspicious Circumstances.'"

"Good lord."

"Wait, here's the deck: 'Law Student Working for Rep. J.D. Clay Misses Flight Home with No Word to Parents; DC Police Disengaged.'"

"Well, I guess if they were going to do a story anyway, they had to mention us. Does it say anything about contacting us?"

"Nothing negative and maybe even a little positive. 'Miss Gray's parents indicated they had contacted Congressman Clay's office for assistance, and the office was able to enlist an off-duty policeman to check her apartment and verify her absence.' It doesn't give the officer's name, but it goes on to say: "Efforts by Miss Gray's parents to obtain additional police assistance were met with a standard response informing them of the large number of missing persons in the city.'"

"Crap, that's really going to help get the DC cops on our side. Was that it about us?"

"Well, they did say they would be looking for further help from Congressman Clay. 'Since she is one of his employees, they assume he will leave no stone unturned in efforts to find her.'"

"Yeah, they've definitely let me know that, but it's pretty obvious the whole point of the story is to put pressure on us to keep turning those stones."

Although I'm not the press secretary—and Darby does a great job at it—any competent AA knows how to handle the media. Ideally, you're proactive, but you also need to stay on the defense, which means anticipating the worst.

"We better be ready for them bringing that reporter with them to the meeting with J.D.," I tell Doris. "They may have also hired a lawyer already. These people are as desperate as you and I would be if it were one of our kids. But they have no idea how to handle the press beyond just getting its attention. We need to all get on the phone with J.D. and Darby to discuss how he is going to handle this. It is only a matter of time before the national press picks up on this, and we need to be doing everything we can to help the Grays."

I catch myself after saying that and add, "And, by the way, we are doing it because it is the right thing to do for both an employee and a constituent, not because we need to look good in this. Got that?"

"Oh, sure." It is typical of a statement we generally make, mostly for the record if not for our own comfort level. Cynics would, of course, never buy it, because the assumption is that everything a politician does is driven by optics. But in the best case, trying to "look good" is what motivates politicians and anyone else to "do good." How can you separate the two?

After I hang up with Doris, it occurs to me this could likely get Walter in trouble, so my next call is to him to give him a heads up. He is obviously annoyed but is not going to be too expressive with his daughter's boss. He thanks me and tells me he would report it to his superiors. Since we had been given permission by the neighbor, it could be worse, but he knows he will get reprimanded.

As I am showering and getting ready to go in for what could be yet another Monday from hell, something occurs to me. I recall that when I first spoke to the Grays, they indicated that they had left several messages on Saundra's answering machine. I am surprised that neither myself nor Walter thought to check the device, but then we were trying to get in and out quickly. Moreover, he is a beat cop, not a detective. But the device is still there, and someone eventually will be checking it.

I call Walter back, apologize, and ask him if he could give me the name and number of Saundra's roommate. I don't tell him what I am up to, just that I am following up to try to help the family. He obliges but pleads with me not to let anyone know how I had obtained it.

I reach Emily Norton at her parents' house later that morning. Fortunately, she doesn't ask how I got her number and doesn't seem surprised that I would be calling. She is very worried about Saundra and says she would do anything to help. I tell her I want to revisit the apartment to make sure there isn't anything pending that needs to be taken care of since Emily wouldn't be returning until after the break. She agrees to call the neighbor again.

I then decide to ask, "Emily, is there anything else about this that you think we should know?"

The long silence on the other end tells me there is.

"You work for Congressman Clay, right?"

"Yes, I'm his AA."

"Did he ever talk about Saundra?"

"Not any more than he would any other intern. Her duties are pretty menial, so there really isn't much need to."

Silence.

Then I add, "Why do you ask?"

"Let's just say she was a huge admirer of him."

This essentially confirms my suspicions about the rumors.

"Is there more?"

"Look, I am sworn to secrecy. If Saundra turns up, I can't say anything more."

"But if she doesn't?"

"I can't say anything more . . . right now."

I decide it would make more sense to go to Saundra's apartment before heading to the office, so I call our legislative director, Rosa, and tell her I'll be late and that she should lead the Monday morning stand-up if I am not in by nine thirty. I fill her in without mentioning where I'm headed. I want the news about Saundra to come to the staff from us before they hear it anywhere else.

TWENTY-THREE

# ANOTHER VISIT TO THE APARTMENT

**Wally North**

*March 1990*

Monday morning traffic is light with Congress in recess, so I make it to Saundra's apartment fairly quickly from our house on Capitol Hill. Seeing me again so soon generates visible concern on the neighbor's part, and she asks if there is anything she can do to help. I tell her we need something for the office and say little else, figuring it is only a matter of time before the press catches up with her.

With Walter out of the picture, I feel less rushed in looking for more clues before listening to the answering machine. Nothing out of the ordinary. On her bedstand is *The Russia House* by John le Carré, one of J.D.'s favorite authors, but that could be a coincidence.

I find the answering machine in the kitchen, which tells me she and Emily share the same phone. I start going backward and hear the various messages from Saundra's parents, starting with the most frantic. Finally, I get to Thursday. I hear J.D.'s voice.

"Saundra, if you are there, please call me before you do anything else. Maybe you have already left for Iowa, but, if not, do not go anywhere until we talk. Very urgent."

I note the time was Thursday afternoon at four thirty. Saundra was not supposed to have flown to Des Moines until Saturday morning. I listen to a few other messages before that, which have no relevance, several of them being for her roommate Emily.

I return to the four-thirty message. If something did happen to Saundra, the police will probably eventually listen to the machine. In my mind, it is completely out of the question that J.D. had anything to do with whatever happened to her. At the same time, she is an intern, and I am the AA, and I am completely unaware of any project she is working on directly for J.D., so this was likely to be personal.

I listen to the message three more times, writing it down word for word. Then I delete it. I'm not familiar with answering machine technology, so for all I know, someone could detect the deletion if they know how and look closely enough—if they think to check.

I realize that if a crime has occurred, I have just obstructed justice, whether J.D. was in fact responsible or not. I have crossed a line. It occurs to me that, until now, everything I have done for J.D. in connection with Saundra's disappearance has been completely legal and aboveboard, and, within the cynical world of DC, even ethical by its malleable standards. Now I can no longer say I am innocent of any criminal wrongdoing.

Okay, it is highly unlikely that there are many survivors in DC that can claim they have never transgressed any legal or ethical lines for their bosses. It is in many ways a throwback to the feudal society where the economic survival of the serfs was tied to that of their lord. It is a brutal place where one has to watch out for one's survival, and my star is completely pegged to J.D.'s. At least that's what I tell myself. And, again, I am only doing this because of my absolute conviction that if there has been any foul play regarding Saundra, J.D. has not been a part of it.

I look around for any other connections. At this point, if I were to find any, they would be destined for my trash bin at home. There is a very nice goldfinch brooch on her dresser, which happens to be the Iowa state bird. Could that have been a gift from J.D. or just a coincidence? Could Emily have seen her wearing it? Could it have been a gift from her parents? Its placement on top of her dresser suggests she has worn it recently and perhaps frequently. I decide it best to leave it, even though a recent gift could be tracked to where it was sold. And to whom it was sold.

There is a ticket to see *Fences* two weeks from now at the Kennedy Center. The playwright, August Wilson, is also a favorite of J.D.'s. Coincidence? No one would ask why this ticket is missing, so I slip it into my wallet, even though it seems highly unlikely that J.D. would take any chance of being seen publicly with her. If Saundra turns up, I'll figure out a way to get it back to her.

There is a knock at the door. It is her neighbor.

"Is everything okay?"

"Oh yes, I found what I was looking for." I grab a file that is conveniently on the table next to the door, having no idea what it is.

"It took me a while, but I finally found what I was looking for," I reassure her. "It's a writing project she is working on for the congressman that he needs today. I'll take it in and fax it to him. I was just on my way out."

I close the door, lock it, and give her back the key. If everything about J.D. remains above suspicion, no one will notice I have been there. But only if.

As I drive to the office, my self-doubts are squeezing my stomach like a vice. I could explain the visit to the apartment, but if the deletion is ever detected, I would be the immediate suspect, with the neighbor as a witness. More importantly, why hasn't J.D. come clean with me about Saundra? And, if as seems obvious, he is indeed having an affair with her, what happened with the Starr Fox solution?

TWENTY-FOUR

# SHARING THE NEWS

**Wally North**

*March 1990*

Once I get to the office, I call everyone together to bring them up to speed. Rosa has briefly shared news of Saundra's disappearance with them.

Although I know it is futile, I start by asking, "Does anyone here have any indication where Saundra may be or where she went last week?" I look around the room. I am not surprised that no one has seen or heard from her since her last day in the office last week. One of the legislative correspondents shares that she knows that Saundra is an avid runner, and I thank her.

There are a few gasps when I provide more details, and a couple of them visibly fight back tears. If Saundra has been missing since Thursday, all the worst-case scenarios seem far more likely than anything else.

"Look, this is a very touchy subject, and I want to make sure everyone is sensitized to things that could happen. Everyone should read the story in the local paper this morning and be aware that any story involving a member of Congress can quickly go national. When that happens, rumors start to replace facts in the public's mind, and we just need to be aware that J.D. can be portrayed as a hero or a villain. In this case, let's hope the story remains about Saundra with a happy ending."

This settles in with the staff, and the shaking heads and mumbled asides tell me the potential gravity is just starting to be appreciated.

Phil Lennon, our ag expert, jumps in. "I get the political concerns, but what can we do to help find Saundra?" This generates a lot of nods and "yeahs."

"Thanks, Phil. Saundra is, of course, the primary concern, and I apologize for having to cover the politics. First, we take our lead from the authorities. J.D. and I will be pressing the DC cops, and maybe even the FBI, to make this a high priority. As you can imagine, there are a lot of missing people in DC, so getting them to focus on this will not be easy. Any other leads anyone here has need to be shared with them, so let me know, and I'll pass them along."

Nods follow this as well.

"There is one thing I want to make absolutely clear to all of you. When the news gets out, both back home and here in DC, you are going to have a lot of friends and family who want to be 'in the know' since they have a connection with you. I can't emphasize this enough. Please just tell them the authorities are on it and the office is being as helpful as it can. It's fine to tell them how you feel about her as a coworker and any other anecdotes or thoughts that have no bearing on her disappearance. But any speculation you may offer quickly becomes a rumor and can completely undermine the efforts to find her."

I realize that if Saundra doesn't turn up soon, these instructions are probably hopeless, but, for now at least, they seem to get it. I close by reiterating there could very well be more press on this, and any of those queries need to go to our press secretary, Darby, or myself. I have been around long enough to know that any little thing involving a congressional office can blow up quickly, and this is more than just a *little thing.*

Everyone is in their casual clothes, as usual during recess, and there are several who have taken the day off, whom I will call later to fill in. Like most congressional offices, we usually stagger our staffing during recess, giving people relief from the chaos of when Congress is in session.

After briefing them, I head into J.D.'s office and close the door. This is the only place in a typically crowded congressional office where you can have any private conversation. I go in there frequently enough when he's not here, so I assume no one thinks it is unusual.

I ring the district office, and fortunately J.D. is already there. He answers with a curt greeting.

I bark back, "Close the door, J.D."

"It's closed. But why don't you tell me what the fuck is going on? I thought you told me you were handling this, then I wake up to a goddamn story about one of my employees missing, and we're now in the crosshairs."

I was advised early on by one of the more senior AAs in the Iowa delegation that, unlike most other congressional employees, the AA sometimes has to stand up to the congressman and tell him he is full of shit. Even with even-keeled members like J.D., the giant egos occasionally need to be deflated. The challenge is to know when to do this. I have no doubt this is one of those occasions. Going forward, J.D. may need me more than I need him. If he isn't astute enough to realize that now, he will soon enough.

"Look, J.D., after my Sunday got ruined, I spent my whole fucking day dealing with this. I can't control whatever stupid moves her parents want to make. But, more importantly, what are you not telling me about this?"

There is a long pause at the other end, and I can tell he is taken aback. I don't push back very often, and, by now, J.D. knows I only do it when it is in everyone's best interest.

He finally speaks. "What do you mean?"

I tell him about my second trip that morning and the message that had been left on the machine.

"Uh, yeah, I guess I did try to call her."

"Don't worry. I erased it. I don't have to tell you what that could mean for me if it's ever discovered that I destroyed what could be evidence."

"Evidence of what? I have *not* done anything criminal."

He gains control after that outburst and then continues. "Oh, Christ,

I'm sorry, Wally. I do appreciate that, and I'm sorry I barked at you. You would think after all this time in politics there wouldn't be anything that would rattle me. This sure is a different animal."

I am sitting at his desk while we are talking and can't avoid the adoring smile on Faith's face in their wedding picture. I wait for his explanation of the message, but there is only dead silence at his end.

I finally have to break it. "J.D., I want you to tell me what the message was about."

"Yes . . ." he trails off for a moment. "I guess I better tell you."

More silence, and I picture him tugging on his ear.

"Look, Wally, that woman is a shrew and has some serious mental issues. From the moment she started working for us, she was bound and determined to bed me down. She literally stalked me after work."

"Well, there were rumors among the staff that I tried to quell, but I have to say she—or maybe I should say *both of you*—did a pretty good job of hiding her tracks."

"I know she did. Well, I guess we both did. But, look, I was trying to end it. Two months ago, I told her in no uncertain terms it was over, but she kept pushing. I think she finally got it, but I'm not sure. Honestly, Wally, I think she actually had some delusions that I would leave Faith for her. I never gave her any indication that that was possible. It was purely physical."

"And I thought we had found a solution for that."

"Yes, I know, and I'm sorry. I'm a guy. I can only resist so much."

I don't ask how much resistance he really needs to put up while he is getting serviced by the most expensive call girls imaginable.

"J.D., she was an employee, young enough to be your daughter. Are you just another horny congressman here? No matter what happened to Saundra, this is bad. You and I know it is not uncommon in DC for members to have relations with their staff, but it's not going to play in Iowa."

"They will never know."

I can't believe he can be so sanguine. Unless Saundra shows up in the next day or so, this story is going to have legs, and their relationship is going to be a big part of it.

I stand at his desk. Sitting down wasn't helping firm up my resolve.

"Look, J.D., keeping this from getting out is going to be impossible. You're meeting with her parents later today. Here's what I suggest: You should tell them everything about your relationship with their daughter, that it has nothing to do with her disappearance, and you are ready to do whatever you can to help them find her."

"Absolutely not."

I probably should not be surprised, but I am taken aback. I have learned that J.D. can be moved off a position on a bill or campaign strategy, but I have never had to deal with him like this on a personal issue. And I can tell by the tone of his voice this is not going to be a persuadable issue.

"Of course, I'm going to help find her," he continues. "But I don't think they need to know about their daughter's sex life. It's going to be bad enough dealing with whatever happened to her."

"Okay, J.D., let me ask you one other question. Did her roommate know?"

"I honestly don't know."

"Well, I'm pretty sure she did based on a cryptic remark she made to me. Do you really think her parents are never going to talk to her roommate?"

"So, I guess Saundra talked to her, even though we both had a clear agreement on this."

"Well, agreements between lovers tend to evaporate after one gets brushed off."

"We weren't lovers."

"Apparently that wasn't how she saw it."

He asks me to hold long enough to brush off a knock on his door, probably reminding him of his next appointment.

"No, probably not. Look, I'm going to meet with them this afternoon. I'm not going to say anything about this. I'm going to promise to do whatever I can, including pressing the DC police and the FBI if it looks like it could be a kidnapping. I think I can handle this."

"Regardless of how today goes, at some point speculation on your relationship will come up in the press, especially if her roommate talks."

"I am not going to deny or confirm any relationship with Saundra to anyone. It is completely irrelevant to whatever happened to her, and it is nobody's business. I'm not going to do anything to hurt Faith or my family."

He quickly adds, "Or to hurt that poor woman's reputation."

I've lost this battle, so I leave it at that. But how will this affect my own situation? The primary and general elections are a few months away, and, with J.D.'s political fate potentially in the balance, everything I do from now on will determine how marketable I would be if J.D. loses. Going to jail for obstruction of justice would not be something I would want on my résumé.

How could I justify erasing that message?

In politics, one constantly has to reconcile ethics and ideals with necessity. And survival serves a larger purpose if you actually want to accomplish something. After a while, you realize that, in order to do that, you have to survive, or else some other schmuck will take your place and make a difference how they see fit.

The fact is, for all his shortcomings, I genuinely admire J.D. as a public servant. He tries to achieve good while being willing to compromise in order to get things done. The liberals view him as a sell-out. They have no idea how much he truly embraces their causes. They also don't appreciate that a pragmatist like him is the only kind of Democrat that can represent our district. The only people who hate him more than the far left are the far right, and they have enough cache in the district to knock J.D. off if he makes any false moves.

But it also isn't like he never clings to a principle tenaciously. Meanwhile, if he truly believes in something strongly, he is far less willing to play it politically safe, like with his advocacy for AIDS research. This is not a popular cause in rural Iowa, and even some Democrats are not on board with it. But when Faith's brother died, J.D. went from being moderately sympathetic to one of its true champions in Congress. He was one of the most prominent speakers at the presentation of the AIDS Memorial Quilt on the National Mall in 1987. Faith had sewn one of the panels commemorating her brother.

Can I abandon such a person, who in so many ways embodies my ideal of a heroic public servant, however humanly flawed he may be? Meanwhile, I am absolutely convinced that J.D. has done nothing to harm Saundra. That would not be him. If I thought he had, I would not do anything to protect him.

Of course, he never should have let himself get drawn into such an affair. But I also recognize it's harder for me to judge, since I am not by any means a "chick magnet" like J.D. Combine his Gary Cooper looks and the attraction of anyone—man or woman—to power, and of course, he is going to have people throwing themselves at him. It's easy for me to say I would deflect—easy to say in the absence of the temptation itself. I take his word that he finally gained control of himself and called a halt to things before it had gone too far. Even at that, it is difficult to reconcile J.D.'s affair with Saundra with the arrangement we have with Starr.

Look, if I can forgive Jefferson for his relationship with Sally Hemings, and Jackson for owning slaves and his treatment of the Indians, and Kennedy for his numerous transgressions, as well as FDR's and Eisenhower's long-standing affairs—all of which occurred long before the public eye was trained on every fault of its leaders—I can justify protecting J.D. Sure, he is no Jefferson, Jackson, or even Kennedy, but the nation needs people like him far more than some of those sanctimonious politicians who presumably do everything above board—or at least don't get caught—but coast through their service in government with no benefit to the public.

So, this is how I will manage any guilty feelings about erasing that message. But it doesn't alleviate the chill I feel about potentially getting caught, not to mention the pall regarding whatever the hell has happened to Saundra.

The only real certainty I have is that this is not going to get any better anytime soon.

## TWENTY-FIVE

# A CALL FROM A REPORTER

**Wally North**

*March 1990*

I have been reviewing draft responses to constituent mail—trying to keep my mind off Saundra's disappearance—when Doris finally calls from the district office to let me know how J.D.'s meeting with her parents went.

The call came just in time. I was having trouble focusing on one Iowan's view that the Social Security system could be fixed by requiring all recipients to work for minimum-wage jobs and decreasing their benefits accordingly. He claimed to have a bachelor's degree in economics and, in a PS, said he would be willing to be the Social Security Commissioner if the congressman wanted to forward his name to President Bush.

Doris sat in on the Gray meeting and says it had gone as well as could be expected. J.D. is a master of such situations and reassured them we would do everything we could, including pressing the police to get on it. He also indicated he would contact the FBI, but, absent signs of a kidnapping or some attempt to threaten a federal official, they probably could not get involved.

There were a lot of tears from Mrs. Gray, and J.D. hugged them both. Doris says she thinks all was fine until she saw them outside the office talking to the local reporter who had broken the story that morning about Saundra's disappearance.

The reporter then asked to see J.D., but Doris told him J.D. had no comment other than to confirm he had met with them and committed his office to doing everything to help.

I breathe a brief sigh of relief as everything seems to be under control. Then Clarissa asks if I want to take a call from Bebe Walker of the *Washington Post.* I have not heard her name in years. Bebe was a bit of a nemesis during J.D.'s presidential run. She had fancied herself as the next Sam Donaldson and had scored blows against several of the candidates after J.D. dropped.

She had even been one of the panelists during one of the debates. She bombed in that role, and her star has since declined. She is now a media has-been, mostly carrying minor stories in the local section. Normally, I would refer the call to Darby since it is a press inquiry, but I am curious as to why a reporter on the local DC beat would be calling an Iowa congressman. I have the call sent into J.D.'s office, where I can have some privacy.

Lesson one with any reporter: don't let caution override friendliness.

"Bebe, how are you? I don't think we've ever met, but I do remember you from J.D.'s presidential campaign in Iowa. I was just a lowly driver then."

I hear a click and realize the call has probably been recorded. Illegal, but not much I could do about that if it is never released. At least it may mean my words will be accurately transcribed.

As soon as she speaks, I remember how Bebe's forcibly endearing speaking voice is one step short of cloying. Several reviews of her performance in the debate had noted that.

"Well, congratulations," she begins. "Being an AA to a prominent member of Congress is always a great career move. That was a pretty exciting campaign, and, even though he didn't get the brass ring, he did get a lot of name recognition. Isn't that what most 'also rans' are going for in those campaigns?"

I take it as a jab. "Actually, J.D. really was serious about getting the nomination, and, honestly, I think he could have beat Reagan. But we'll never know, and, yes, it did increase his name recognition. Really, the only thing he cares about at this point is whether the voters in his district like him, and so far, it's pretty clear they do. What can I do for you?"

"I'm calling about a story that appeared in the Iowa papers over the weekend about a Saundra Gray who works for the congressman. Apparently, she's gone missing?"

I have to time my response carefully. Too long to respond will sound strategic; too short, defensive.

"Yes, we are very concerned about Saundra and are doing everything we can to find her. The congressman met with her parents today. At this point, we only know she is missing, and there really is nothing more to say."

"Okay, well, I just wanted to let you know that I have a source who indicates she has been having an affair with the congressman."

Now a pause is in order. This revelation—or trick—would be expected to be a shock, which it is. "Bebe, I'm completely unaware of any such situation." Okay, so another lie, but I view the question as irrelevant to her missing and don't think Bebe has any business asking.

"Can you confirm or deny it?"

"I can do neither. The congressman's personal life is outside my jurisdiction." Lie number two, of course.

Despite the recording, I hear her tapping away as we speak and try to envision each of my words on the front page of the *Post*, as all Hill employees are told to do early on.

"But as his AA, you would be concerned about him having any improper relationship with one of your employees, right?"

"Of course, I would. We have rules against that in our office, and they apply to the congressman as much as anyone else." That much, at least, is true.

"Then it really isn't 'outside your jurisdiction.'"

"What I meant was my relationship with J.D. is purely professional, so, of course, there are many things in his personal life that I am completely unaware of, as I should be. On something like this, absent evidence of something improper that impacts our office, I would have no reason to inquire."

"But now there is evidence, right?"

"Only hearsay from you. Can you tell me who told you this?"

"Wally, you know I'm going to protect my sources."

Rosa sticks her head in, and I wave her away. We are trying to get a press release out about J.D.'s position on a controversial pipeline in the eastern part of the district, and I assume that is what Rosa wants to talk about.

"Okay, well that doesn't give me much to go on," I say. "Can you at least tell me why this source would have some credibility with you?"

"Let me just say it is someone who is very familiar with the operations of your office and leave it at that."

"Sounds like a former employee." I feel confident that no one on our current staff would be the source. Loyalty to J.D. and each other—including Saundra, who is still a current staffer—is a trademark of our office.

"I didn't say that."

"No, I guess you didn't. But I am assuming, if it was, you would consider that there may be someone with an axe to grind."

She seems to think that gives her an opening. "Do you fire a lot of workers there?"

"Look, our turnover by Capitol Hill standards is among the best. But even the best office has to let people go, which rarely happens here. I'm sure that's the case even with a great employer like the *Washington Post*."

The conversation has gone long enough to avoid suspicion, so I try to bring it to a close.

"Bebe, I appreciate your checking on this. It's very busy here today with a lot going on. Please feel free to give me a call if you hear anything else."

"Wally, I can't tell you anything more than I have, but let the fact that

I am looking for a second source speak for itself. Let's say I do find one. Should I call you back for a comment?"

She is still digging, but I'm not going to cut her any slack.

"I don't really like talking about theoretical things. Notwithstanding anything someone may have told you, I have no reason to believe the congressman has done anything wrong. As I said, we are very concerned about Ms. Gray and are going to do whatever we can to help with that situation. Any other personal issues or allegations are totally irrelevant."

"So you are saying that if the congressman was having an affair with her, that could not possibly have any connection with her disappearance."

"Again, I am not going to address theoretical situations. The only thing I will say is that after working closely with J.D. for six years, I do know him well enough to know that he would never do anything to put another person in jeopardy. I will say that categorically, and it would apply to any allegation about any such action on his part."

I decide I'd better take notes on this. When I grab a notepad, I notice the sweat mark my hands leave.

"Well, let me just ask this, Wally. Let's say this story doesn't go away, for whatever reason. Maybe there was a relationship. Maybe the congressman isn't doing enough to find her. Don't you think that could hurt politically?"

"Bebe, I think our voters can handle a missing intern."

Rule two in any conversation with a reporter: don't let your anger respond. As soon as I say this, I hear her pecking away and immediately regret it.

"Look, Bebe, that didn't come out right and was not what I really meant. I was responding to your own attempt to politicize the very serious concerns about Ms. Gray's whereabouts. I'd like to retract it. First of all, your hypothetical is just that, so I don't see any relevance to politics here whatsoever. This is about one of our employees going missing, and until we know where she is and why it happened, we are going to leave no stone unturned. Politics do not play into this at all."

"Of course, they never do." Sometimes you can actually hear a smile.

A long pause allows my mind to wander, and seeing new buds sprouting on the tree outside my window reminds me I had promised to leave early enough to take the kids to the playground.

"Okay, we will leave it at that," she finally concedes. "Let's see where this goes. I may not be the last reporter you have to discuss this with."

She did not respond to my request for a retraction, and I decide if I press, it would just confirm for her that she had "gotten" me.

I decorously thank her, and we hang up. I immediately start thinking about all the people who have left the office in the past two months, regardless of the circumstances. There is a high rate of turnover in any congressional office because most of the employees are in the early stages of their careers. Very few want to work in a congressional office for more than a couple of years. It's a miserable, high-pressure job with little pay to justify the unforgiving hours and unceasing pressure. The fact that J.D. is a good boss—albeit one with high standards of performance—helps us keep the turnover rate down. But we still have our departures.

It occurs to me that the source could also be Emily, Saundra's roommate, but she doesn't sound like the type who would go first to the press, although she will pose a threat once any news starts to get out. It is more likely someone with a personal vendetta against J.D. who can claim some credibility from a history of working for him.

There are three former staffers whose tenure would have coincided with Saundra's. Fran Lebowski had gone to work for the Speaker with J.D.'s help, so she would clearly be loyal. Bob Parsons, our ag guy, left to work for the Nation's Farmers and is lobbying us hard on the next farm bill, so he wouldn't do anything to jeopardize that.

That leaves Judy Carricutt. Of the three, she is the only one who was actually fired, and for good reason. She had handled our health and labor issues, and, of anyone who has ever worked for J.D., she was the most frustrated with his centrist approach.

We had hired her from the Iowa Federation of Labor, thinking she would make a good bridge to labor, with which, like any moderate Democrat, we sometimes have a tenuous relationship. Unfortunately, she never really cut her ideological ties there and remained far more loyal to their cause than to J.D.

Things had gone particularly bad with her during a strike against one of the meatpackers in our district. J.D. had taken a neutral stand, and there were a lot of people in our district who resented the strikers. In reality, they were striking over much better pay and benefits than most of our constituents at a time when the Japanese were taking away a lot of jobs from middle America. During the strike, Judy pressed him hard to visit the picket line. Meanwhile, she was invariably giving J.D. drafts of floor statements that she knew did not represent his position. He started requiring that I review them first, and I had to do heavy edits, if not outright rejection, before they could go to him.

Bottom line, Judy was a cancer that no one in the office really liked, but we had to wait for a smoking gun to do anything about it. That finally came when one day we learned that J.D. had cosponsored a union-backed bill without his authorizing it. She insisted that he had, but I was sitting in his office when she briefed him and he had said, "They may have a point. Let's think about it."

Actually, the bill was not really that bad and he might have eventually cosponsored it, but anyone who works for Congress—anywhere on the political spectrum—would agree this was a fire-worthy offense. J.D. only learned about it when the sponsor thanked him on the House floor. When he got back to the office, he asked me to verify that his name was on the bill and, if so, terminate her immediately with three weeks' severance.

It was as ugly as I had thought it would be. She accused me of backstabbing her for her political views, insisted on meeting directly with J.D. (which I refused), and stormed out of the office. Most of the other staffers stayed silent, but a few quietly told me that day they were very relieved to finally see her go. I later heard even the Iowa Federation wasn't that upset with us. Apparently, they felt we had done them a favor by taking her off their hands earlier. Notably, they didn't rehire her after she left our office.

Despite all the bad blood, I was relieved to learn that she was able to get a job downtown with one of the far-left pro-labor groups. All Hill staffers know that getting fired is something that could happen to any of us at any moment for any number of reasons, so it was always good to hear when someone lands on their feet.

There was roughly a six-month overlap with her and Saundra, so they clearly knew each other, and it is possible they have stayed in touch after she left. As an intern, Saundra was not in any position to influence policy, and we all knew her views were decidedly to the left of J.D.'s. But she didn't make it an issue like Judy had.

Unless I am missing something, it seems pretty clear Judy is the likely leak. I call J.D. and explain the situation to him. I tell him the story about his affair with Saundra could surface at any time, and, at that point, all hell will break loose. We need to decide on a message. He tells me the only message he will ever provide is that his private life is his business, and the question is totally irrelevant.

I tell him I don't think that will work, but he insists. Meanwhile, we need to loop the staff in that this is out there even if we don't give them the whole story, which will be tricky. He initially resists but reluctantly agrees the worst thing would be for one of them to get blindsided.

I tell him I'll start with Rosa, our legislative director. Even if J.D. had vetoed my idea, I was going to tell Rosa anyway, because I know I will need at least one informed ally in the office. Moreover, she is my number two, and, if and when I ever leave, she will likely take my job. Plus, her loyalty to J.D. is not at all in question. But I do not plan to tell her about the deleted phone message. I figure she is going to have to do enough dissembling as it is, without crossing the line of criminality.

When Rosa comes in, the look on her face makes her question seem redundant, but she asks it anyway.

"Is she dead?"

"No. Well, not as far as we know. I sure hope not."

"Okay, I will keep my fingers crossed."

"Yeah, well, there's something else. Things could get really shitty here, and I need your help."

"The affair with J.D.?"

The question stuns me. Rosa has one of the most probing minds on the staff, and she would be one of the last to give credence to any rumors without enough evidence.

"Why do you say that?"

"Because I know the rumors are true."

"Is it that well known?"

"No, just a rumor for everyone else, but you can believe they're all thinking about that today."

"Then how do you know?"

"Because Saundra told me. I think she probably would have talked to you instead if you were a woman but assumed she would get more empathy from me. She asked to meet me for dinner one night, so as not to arouse any suspicions, and she unloaded on me."

I am a bit miffed at first that Rosa hadn't shared this with me, but I also understand the importance of discretion in her role. One of the reasons I value Rosa is her dispassionate approach to difficult issues. The emotions have to be there below the surface somewhere, but it never clouds her judgment.

"She was very upset—thought that J.D. had led her on and then dumped her. She was extremely bitter about the whole thing, but I talked her off the ledge. I also made it clear that if she didn't want to hurt her career, she needed to let it go and not talk to anyone else. I figured that if I appealed to her ambition, it would work, and I assume it did. As far as I know, she never told anyone else, at least on the staff."

"How long ago did you talk to her?"

"About a month ago. He had just cut her off, and it was pretty fresh. Why, do you know something?"

I tell her about my conversations with J.D. and Bebe, and she agrees we need to be more forthcoming.

She asks, "Who do you think the source was?"

"Our old pal Judy is my guess."

"Yep, that would make sense. And it's entirely possible she talked to her."

"Well, there was another one who would be an obvious source for the reporter. Her roommate."

"Has she talked?"

"I have talked to her, and she made a cryptic remark along the lines that she knew what was going on, but she didn't strike me as someone who would go running off to the press. If things heat up, though, she would be a wild card."

"So, what's next, Wally?"

I let it soak a bit and let her think about it as well. Rosa is one of the smartest people I have ever worked with and has a rare combination of smarts that applies both to policy and practicality.

"What do you think, Rosa?"

"Well, we obviously need to do all we can to help find Saundra, which we would do under any circumstances. Do her parents know about their relationship?"

"As far as we know, they don't have any suspicions, but eventually they will. I'm guessing an ambitious woman like Saundra would not be bragging to her parents about sleeping with a congressman, and they want to think the best of her. But, again, once the story starts getting out, who knows how they will respond?"

She agrees. "But that's not our only challenge," she adds. "We have an entire staff that suspected this in the first place, and they will be an obvious target for the press. We need to give them a heads up, but how much do we tell them?"

"How much do you advise?"

"To some extent, I agree that J.D.'s personal life is none of their business either. Since I told Saundra to keep it confidential, I think I should, too, as should you. I think we acknowledge to them that it has been a rumor in the office and the press is starting to pick up on the rumor. We tell them J.D. is saying his personal life is irrelevant and we all know he would never do anything to hurt Saundra or anyone else. How does that sound?"

It's good we are both of a similar mind, but I also know it is only a tourniquet.

"Okay, for now," I agree, "but it's only going to buy us some time. We can see how this evolves. Maybe she shows up—that's the best-case scenario. Maybe there is foul play, and, if so, hopefully it is clear that what happened has nothing to do with J.D., which you and I are convinced would be the case anyway. A lot of members have survived rumors of affairs, though with a young staffer it would be a career killer, especially in rural Iowa. Maybe people would cut him some slack because of Faith's situation, which is widely known. The reality is time works against us here. The sooner this is resolved the better. But the longer that it is out there with no one knowing what happened to her, the affair angle starts to have legs. It doesn't help we are in a slow news week with Congress out."

Rosa nods. "Agree. I think we should bring the staff in right now on this before anyone gets any calls from the reporters."

The staff meeting goes as well as could be expected. The "personal life" angle, if anything, confirms the rumors for them. They know J.D. prides himself on his honesty, and they have to assume if it wasn't true he would categorically deny it. But they seem comfortable with not pressing further. Rosa and I tell them in no uncertain terms that they should not talk to reporters—or anyone else for that matter.

Yeah, good luck with that absent quarantining them in the office. They are a loyal crew to a boss they admire, but in DC, career comes first, and, if things heat up, they will start looking. I am starting to feel I may need to as well at some point if this plays out for too long. But my first goal is to protect J.D. from any implication that he had anything to do with whatever happened to Saundra.

TWENTY-SIX

# TEMPERATURE RISING

**Wally North**

*March 1990*

I didn't sleep last night. My regrettable words to Bebe kept replaying in my flurried thoughts, and, until I can see the morning *Post*, I will have no peace. Even if she used the quote, at least it would dispel the agony of uncertainty.

As soon as I hear the slap of the paper on the doorstep below our bedroom window, I carefully withdraw from the covers so as not to awaken Gloria.

Knowing I will need something chemical to drink, I start coffee before settling in at the kitchen table with the paper. No surprise, there is nothing on the front page. Nor the rest of the A section. It is loaded with stories about the continuing dissolution of the Soviet domination over Eastern Europe, the battle over budget deficits, and whether Bush is going to renege on his "no new taxes" pledge.

It's not on the front page of the Metro section, either. A sigh of relief as I pour my coffee before going deeper. Finally, Bebe's story appears on page three of the Metro section, which is a defeat for her, no doubt.

A quick scan does not include my quote. I guess I either convinced her to ignore it or it just didn't fit with the story. I go back and read the whole story carefully. Quotes from the Grays expressing frustration with the DC police and a supportive quote from J.D.

The only troubling line notes the "office refused to comment on personal relationships with Saundra within the office." Maybe I am being overly paranoid, but this could imply a question of involvement with J.D. Otherwise, whew. Now we just need to have Saundra show up.

---

My day at the office starts uneventfully, until I get a call from Jake Talbott, the Grays' attorney from Des Moines. He is calling me from the airport in Omaha to let me know he and the Grays are on their way to DC. I recognize his name, as he has taken some notable cases in Iowa on behalf of citizens suing various localities.

I had not expected this so soon, but I tell him I am not at all surprised they are coming and say we will do whatever we can to help them.

"Well, the best way you could help us would be to join us in a press conference."

"On what? The *Post* ran a story this morning that I can fax to you. Not sure what your news angle will be."

"The Grays have asked for a meeting with the chief of police to urge him to become personally engaged in the search, and we are holding a press conference immediately afterward. It would be very helpful if you could join us for that. That would be right around the time of the local nightly news, so we are hoping we could get live coverage."

I have dealt many times with constituents with plans to "work" Washington with no clue whatsoever as to how the place really works.

"What specifically are you going to ask him to do?"

"We know Saundra was a runner and she lived close to Rock Creek Park, which is a popular jogging area. We want to ask the police to conduct a ground search of the park."

This is an ambitious request, but I don't want us to be viewed as the obstacle.

"Well, I'm not sure about being at the press conference. We are always very careful about engaging in local matters, especially outside our district. But it is federal property, so we can support the request they're making of the police. I'm not sure how the police operate there or if they defer to the Park Service. We can look into that before your meeting."

"It would be nice if you were there with the Grays," he repeats.

I am not quite sure why I wouldn't be able to do that, but I don't want to agree on the fly.

"I'll let you know on that. But I think you should try to help manage the Grays' expectations on this. The park is massive, runs maybe three to four miles in length. It is very narrow, and I assume if she was right off the path, something would have shown up by now. But spreading out beyond the path in an effective way is going to involve massive police resources."

He feigns incredulity. "Are you suggesting your employee's well-being is not worth those resources? Isn't it possible she's alive somewhere in the park waiting to be rescued?"

I assume he knows the total absurdity of this assumption, but I am not going to be the doomsayer. Since he had raised his voice, I assume he is also doing it for the benefit of the Grays, who are likely standing nearby. The contentious direction this is heading is not encouraging.

"Don't get me wrong, Mr. Talbott, we are completely supportive of this request." I'll let the cops be the ones to turn them down.

"I just want to make sure the Grays recognize what they are up against," I continue. "DC is a big city with numerous reports of missing persons filed every day with a lot of additional safety needs the police are addressing. Other than a pile of clothes and an empty Gatorade bottle, there isn't even any conclusive evidence that she had gone jogging, let alone where that would be or even if that is where she would have wound up."

"You're already being an apologist for the police failing to take action."

I am not afraid to bite back.

"Don't twist my words, Mr. Talbott. I said we would be supportive, and we will. Meanwhile, I have no police or detective experience, so I have no idea what the normal protocols are here. I am just hoping that as their lawyer, you are preparing the Grays for potential disappointment. Having worked in politics for almost a decade, one thing I do know about is managing expectations."

He tells me he will call when they arrive and repeats his hope that I will join them. With no words of farewell, he hangs up.

I immediately regret what I said. While trying to be helpful and explanatory, I had simply given him ammunition to make us part of the problem in the Grays' eyes. Any good lawyer, as I assume he is, would agree with everything I said. I should have just left it at "We're here to help." It was now even clearer that I need to be part of that meeting, and J.D. agrees after I explain to him what happened.

---

When I show up for the meeting with DC Chief of Police Oliver Sharp, the Grays are happy. He is not. He has served as police chief for five years, having been appointed by the notorious Marion Barry. For all his faults, Barry has made some laudable appointments, and Sharp has generally received praise given how tough his job is.

Physically, he is the stereotypical police chief of a crime-ridden city. Husky, with a broad mustachioed face—he reminds me of a lot of offensive linemen I played football with in high school. He is also tall enough to have played basketball at some point as well. Having seen him several times on local television, I know he has the brains to match his toughness. But he is also in his late fifties and probably looking to coast through his final months before retiring. The Gray situation won't help with that unless Saundra appears soon. Tough, comes with the job, pal.

His impatience with their request is not at all surprising, given the numbers of missing person cases filed regularly in the city and the limited resources. With a population that is almost half African American, with poor neighborhoods needing police protection—including many missing children related to domestic squabbles—he has obvious concerns about turning his department upside down for a wealthy white girl who isn't even from DC.

On the other hand, as a parent myself, I know I would probably be as aggressive and irrational as the Grays. As my inept conversation with Talbott that morning had made clear, my only role here is to be as supportive of our employee's parents/constituents as I can and let Sharp make his apologies. Meanwhile, I have a backup plan that Rosa suggested, which I am holding in reserve.

We are seated in Sharp's office facing his desk. Two other officers are sitting on a couch behind us. Talbott does most of the talking at the outset, but he is interrupted repeatedly by Mrs. Gray's tearful pleas and Dr. Gray's sharp condemnation of the police's inaction thus far. Talbott plays a more diplomatic role, but he clearly isn't giving Sharp any breathing room.

Sharp responds the way I expected him to—and the way the police are accustomed to in these situations. After patiently sitting through Talbott's theatrics, he explains that the police had to wait the standard number of days—which have now passed—before any kind of investigation. That investigation will now commence, but they have to balance it with other pending cases of missing persons, currently about two thousand of varying lengths of time since being reported, and mostly regarding young children.

Sharp says he is aware of my visit to Saundra's apartment with Walter Milton. He says it was highly improper on Milton's part. He has had to issue him a mild rebuke, but he understands how helpful it had been and had spoken informally with him to let him know it was all right under the circumstances.

Talbott jumps on this. "So, you know she probably was out jogging and most likely went to Rock Creek Park?"

"That's entirely possible, Mr. Talbott," Sharp responds. "But it's also speculation. Hundreds of joggers run through that park every day, and there have been no reports of anything unusual that could be connected to Ms. Gray."

Talbott stands and begins strolling around the office in full courtroom mode as his interrogation continues. Only the Grays seem to be swept up by it. I avoid Sharp's gaze.

"But, as I understand it," Talbott continues, "the park has many secluded areas with extensive vegetation that are well off the path. Is that correct?"

"Like most parks, yes."

"Shouldn't those be searched?"

"We have officers who regularly patrol the park, and just yesterday I asked one of them to follow the entire trail looking for any signs of Saundra. Nothing."

Talbott moves directly in front of Sharp's desk and spreads his hands.

"But surely they wouldn't have covered every single corner. No one officer could do that easily."

"That's correct, but to cover 'every single corner' would entail a ground search that would need multiple officers."

"How many?" I ask.

"To do the job right, probably thirty or so, starting at the top of the park and working all the way down to its end near the Kennedy Center. It would probably be an all-day affair."

This is the moment Rosa and I had anticipated.

"So, are you going to do it?" I press.

"Mr. North, we simply do not have the manpower to pull that many of our officers off their beat for that period of time. Every day, there are hundreds—sometimes thousands—of incidents throughout the city that need their attention."

"Does it have to be police?" I ask. "Could thirty private citizens do it?"

He pauses. He wasn't ready for this but decides to call my bluff.

"Maybe, if properly briefed."

"If I got thirty people together to help, could you at least provide someone to brief them?"

Sharp glares at me. The optics of having someone else do his job is grating. He erases his expression quickly, and I'm not sure anyone other than me and Talbott caught it.

"Mr. North, we very frequently use private citizens to help on things like this, but they have to be properly briefed and supervised. And this is actually National Park Service property, so the service would have to be involved as well. We can't just turn the park over to a large number of inexperienced people who have no idea what they are doing."

"Seems pretty simple. We've all seen it in the movies. Everyone spreads out, and you make sure every single square inch is covered, right?"

He swallows. The wheels were turning, but it is clear he sees no way out.

"Something like that."

"How much briefing does that require?" asks Talbott, who has now bought into my plan.

"Half hour maybe, but it should also be supervised. And then you have the heavy traffic that regularly uses the road running through the park. You would either have to shut it down or carefully manage the flow."

"So, it looks like we need a couple of people to brief the private citizens at the outset," I respond. "Maybe two cops on either side of the road to supervise and one or two more to help with traffic. Doesn't seem like you would need to shut it down. Just get people to slow down as they pass the searchers."

"Probably a little more complicated than you suggest, but, if you can get the people, I could probably free up a couple of folks to help. Now, I can't speak for the Park Service."

"Well, I work for a senior congressman who may have something to say about that. I'm guessing we could help align with the service."

"Okay, you think you have thirty people to do this?"

"Not a problem." I don't blink and hope he doesn't hear me swallow.

"Okay, well let's see if we can pull this together later this week. May take a little longer."

"Actually, I was thinking tomorrow."

Sharp has given me an opening, but I can feel the pressure in my stomach. Less than twenty-four hours to round up thirty people in DC . . . That's a lot of phone calls. I assume I will at least get credit for trying and maybe then the Grays will understand what they are up against. Again, always make it someone else's shortcomings when you can't deliver for a constituent.

"Tomorrow?" Sharp's annoyance is even more obvious now. His eyes are darting around the room. He looks beseechingly at his staff, but none are able to provide much help.

"Yes, I can get my thirty people lined up tonight, and they can all be there bright and early tomorrow morning."

I have been fully engaged with Sharp throughout this and haven't been paying any attention to the others, but I finally notice the Grays are looking at me with fresh eyes. I am now a hero figure to them. We'll see how long it lasts.

Before we leave Sharp's office to meet with the press, I ask if I can make a couple of phone calls. My call to Rosa is quick. She had already put the staff on alert, and, now that it is a go, she tells them to go ahead and call their other contacts on the Hill. With it being recess, we have a good chance of almost getting thirty.

I figure anything more than fifteen on such short notice would be forgivable. I also know Hill staffers love to get together. Also, with the park ending close to Georgetown, many will see some major party opportunities at the end of the search. After all, this could be as much fun as the softball games on the Mall, only with purpose.

My next call is to J.D., who was not yet aware of my plan. I wasn't sure how he would react, so I didn't want him to give me a counterorder. This is now in motion, and he can't stop it.

"You promised to do what?"

"J.D., this is something we need to do for a lot of obvious reasons. Rosa has checked with the staff, and everyone is on board. Now I need to ask one more thing."

"What's that?"

"You need to hop on the last plane to DC this evening and be there first thing in the morning for this."

"I can't. I have an important meeting with some constituents in Le Mars, and then I need to be back here to celebrate one of the kids' birthdays."

"Cancel those. You need to be here. J.D.—I'm really going out on a limb for you on this, and you need to do this. Your kids are old enough to understand why you would need to do this for someone else's kid."

"Goddammit, Wally, do I get to have a personal life?"

"In this case, J.D., no. But since when do any of us have one, least of all the guy whose name will be on the ballot?" I could have said more but decided it would be best to leave unspoken how this could have been avoided in the first place. He finally agrees and will be on the plane and at the park first thing. I have probably burned a chit, but he has already burned about fifty of them with me.

When we walk out of the police department, there are only five reporters waiting for us, including Bebe. I let Talbott do most of the talking, and he is as critical of Sharp as expected. I know by being involved I have sabotaged any potential alliance with Sharp, and that may come back to haunt me, but at this point our allegiance to the Grays is far more critical.

After Talbott has finished his tirade, he turns to me to make an announcement before having the Grays close the session. My announcement about the search the next day perks up the reporters, especially Bebe, who immediately recognizes that it could ramp up interest in the case.

The reporter from WRC4 is the only TV reporter on hand, but I figured once the word gets out about the next day, the other two local stations will be there.

I'm assuming if we find Saundra tomorrow, that will end it for us. A good resolution for us but tragedy for the Grays. Such is the cynical game of politics. If, on the other hand, we turn up nothing, the media circus around the case could become explosive. I tell myself not to wish for either. Just focus on what needs to be done.

TWENTY-SEVEN

# A DAY IN THE PARK AND A REVELATION ABOUT SAUNDRA

**Wally North**

*March 1990*

Today has been beyond anything I anticipated or have ever seen in DC until now. When I promised thirty people for the search, I did not factor in the local evening news and the front page of the Metro section. Not to mention the extensive Capitol Hill network that any Hill office has if you take its employees and multiply it by their contacts and theirs in turn.

Giving my fellow Hill staffers the benefit of the doubt, I believe the vast majority showed up to genuinely help. But there are always those who see any kind of crowd as a potential party in the making. And they have turned it into a circus, with disastrous results for the flora in Rock Creek Park.

The only ones likely to benefit are the bar owners in Georgetown, where, as expected, a good number of the "searchers" have wound up for a liquid lunch. It is, after all, recess. Oh, yes, and there is also Bebe, who I have to think is certain this is going to keep the story on the front page of some section, even if it is only the Metro.

If nothing else, we have accomplished our goal for the day. If Saundra's or any other missing person's remains were in the park, they sure as hell would have turned up. Which, of course, they didn't. The "briefing" by Chief Sharp was a ten-minute blast on a bullhorn, followed by a stream of young bodies canvassing the park high and low. Avoiding traffic wasn't an issue, because the staffers had brought so many cars that they had to close the road to turn it into a parking lot. Divvying up the volunteers into two groups—the North Park group and the South Park group—sped things up somewhat, and we have finished by early afternoon.

By now, everyone is exhausted, which, in the Grays' case, is a mixture of the relief and dread that always accompanies a missing person search that doesn't turn up a body. It only means the body isn't in the place that was searched. The mystery remains.

They are duly appreciative, and J.D. has said and done all the right things. Publicly, at least. Away from the cameras, he still seems annoyed with me. Probably for good reason. All we have accomplished is to draw more attention to a situation that contains dangerous hidden truths.

As the search is winding down, we are standing in Francis Park near the southern tip of Rock Creek, close to the edge of Georgetown. We are surrounded by a lot of staffers conspiring over their afternoon barhopping plans when a bookish young lady whose hair and designer "casual" clothes indicate a wealthy background walks toward us. When J.D. spots her about thirty feet away, he makes excuses and heads to one of the Don's Johns. It doesn't take long for me to figure out why.

"Mr. North?"

"Yes."

"Saundra's roommate, Emily Norton," she says, holding out her hand in a professional manner. She is wearing a Red Sox baseball cap with the ends of her pure blond hair furling below it. Like many other Hill professionals from wealthy families, she seems to be avoiding clothes emphasizing her physical beauty, but it is undeniable.

"Oh, Emily, very nice to meet you. I assumed you were still in Connecticut. We really appreciate your help the other day."

"Once I heard about this, I flew down to help. I know she ran here a lot, so I really thought this could bring some resolution, or at least some answers. Guess I should be glad it didn't turn anything up, but I'm still very worried about her."

The look on her face proves she isn't one of the ones who just came to party.

"Well, we will hope for the best," I say as reassuringly as I can. There is a long silence, and her eyes dart around to the others within earshot.

"Can we maybe talk somewhere after this?" she asks.

"Sure, we can get coffee later, if that works." I knew this conversation would need to happen eventually.

"That will. I've met the Grays, who obviously have a lot of questions, and I've already been contacted by the police for an interview. I'm an obvious source, I guess."

I nod in silent agreement; it is clear we both know what needs to be discussed.

"Yes, well, let's find a place later after this is all over," she says. "In addition to the Grays, I'm more than willing to be of help to you and the congressman." No hesitancy at all.

We agree to meet at a coffee shop in the Dupont Circle area later that afternoon.

---

Emily has changed out of her casual clothes into something more business-like. At first, I wonder if that means she is hoping for an interview, which would be very tacky, of course. But eventually I realize it's just who she is. She obviously comes from New England money and has probably had little trouble using connections to get her job with one of the Connecticut senators.

Not that she would need that kind of help long term. Clearly, if she wanted to flaunt it, she could look very seductive. As we speak, it occurs to me she is more interested in career advancement through her brains rather than her looks. But, of course, she does have both.

I figure it best to get right to the point.

"When we talked on the phone this weekend, you said there was something more. Is that what you wanted to talk about?" I ask.

"I know I hinted at this, but I wanted you to know that she and J.D. have been having an affair that he has broken off." It is the first time she doesn't look me directly in the eyes.

Her knowledge of the affair is no surprise. I decide if she isn't going to be coy, I won't either.

"I know about it," I acknowledge. "I guess the question is whether you think it is at all relevant to whatever happened to her."

"Absolutely not." No hesitation, which is reassuring. "Believe me, I'm as interested as anyone in finding out what happened, but I have absolutely no suspicion that Congressman Clay had anything to do with it. If I see anything else that indicates that, I'd be the first one to help nab him. But right now, I just don't see it."

"Okay, so what are you going to do with what you know?"

"For the moment, nothing. I did introduce myself to the Grays, and they had a lot of questions, obviously, but they didn't ask about that. I assume Saundra never said anything to them about the affair, so I didn't either. I figured if it turns out they are going to lose her, God forbid, why do they need to know something like that about her?"

"I agree and appreciate your discretion. Have you met with the police yet?" I assume she would agree that misleading the police would be an entirely different matter.

"They are supposed to come to the apartment tomorrow morning." I am glad the delay has given us a chance to talk, even if it does fuel the Grays' complaint about a slow official response. Talking to her, even by long-distance phone, should have been the first thing the police did.

"What are you going to say to them?"

She doesn't blink, but she is obviously troubled by what she is going to have to do.

"I'm not going to lie to the police. If they ask, I'll tell them, but I'm not going to volunteer it because I don't think it is relevant."

I couldn't see any other safe option for her.

"That's fine," I assure her. "I'm pretty sure any detective worth his salt is going to start looking for motives, so they are going to ask about people she knew and people she had relationships with."

"Yeah. Like I said, I'm not going to lie. I'll let them get there with their questions, and then I'll answer it. I'll also ask that they keep it confidential in the interests of the family."

"You shouldn't even have to ask. We can only hope they will honor that."

She continues sipping her coffee, and I can tell she wants to say more, but she is letting me take the lead.

"Let me ask you something, Emily. It seems like, in addition to the Grays, you are trying to protect the congressman. Obviously, that's much appreciated, but why would you do that if you knew what was going on between them?"

She takes another sip and a deep breath.

"Honestly, it's more about Saundra than him." She steadies herself with another breath.

"My relationship with Saundra took the same track as a lot of roommates thrown together. We were really good friends at first. How could we not be? She was so smart and funny and had that way of sucking you in and making you feel like you were her best friend. I could see why it would be easy for the congressman to fall for her."

"So, what happened? Did you stop being friends?"

"It wasn't so much that. I went from being infatuated with her to almost being afraid of her. Over time, I started to realize she was delusional and a threat to herself and others around her."

"For example?"

"Well, the congressman is the best example. As we got to know each other better, she started opening up more and told me the only way a woman was ever going to make it in Washington was to sleep with the right people and use that to land a spot where she could make a name for herself. I was kind of insulted by that, because I thought she knew me well enough to know that that clearly wasn't my agenda."

"Sadly, I'm not sure that's so delusional," I say. "Unfortunately, this city can be almost as bad as Hollywood in that respect."

"I'm not saying it's not true that there are women who do that and men who take advantage of it. But I don't think that's the only way it can be done. Hard work and taking full advantage of the right opportunity can work for a woman. Look at Sandra Day O'Connor and Jeane Kirkpatrick. It's clearly harder for a woman, but it's still possible."

There are some other names she could mention, but unfortunately few of them are as famous as the ones whose notorious scandals earned them a lucrative photo shoot in *Playboy*. I suspect Emily is being a bit naïve, but I admire her determination to separate herself from that path.

"True, but sadly Saundra's view was not all that uncommon," I say. "Hopefully, that's changing, but I think it is still common enough that I'm not sure I would say it's delusional on her part. And the attitudes of a lot of men in power don't help."

She shakes her head in obvious disapproval. The issue obviously touches a nerve that, until now, I had never fully appreciated with the other women I have worked with.

"I agree the strategy concept isn't uncommon, but how she approached it was," she continued. "She was playing the field for a while, but then she started hitting it off with Congressman Clay. She convinced herself that, with his wife's condition being what it is, she could draw him away from her. She really thought he would leave her. I tried very hard to talk her out of it, but she was totally determined. It became a very sore subject with us to the point where we weren't even speaking with each other. You could say it was none of my business, and I have no idea what she thought of me, but I started becoming very judgmental, which is not normal for me. The situation was just wrong, and I couldn't keep my mouth shut."

The coffee shop is becoming more crowded, so we have to lower our voices, even though I don't see any familiar faces. Who knows how many reporters live in the Dupont Circle area?

"Did you think about moving out?" I ask.

"We had a couple more months on the lease, and I just had no other options. But I did come close. A week or so before she disappeared, things got very scary. She was flying around the apartment throwing things. I came home one day, and from outside the front door I could hear her screaming into the phone at someone—maybe the congressman for all I know. When I opened the door, she banged the phone down and went into her room, slamming the door on her way. It became clear to me that he had broken things off, and instead of taking it gently, she was determined to take some action. I really started to fear for myself; she was so scary."

"So, you don't hold J.D. responsible at all?"

"Sure, to some extent. But I also know his situation with his wife, and I'm guessing that makes him pretty vulnerable in a town where women are constantly throwing themselves at him. I might have a different perspective too, because when I was a freshman in high school, my mom caught my dad having an affair with one of his assistants. Totally unforgivable situation, but he was very contrite."

"That must have been tough for you to deal with."

"I was really pissed at him for about six months, but finally my mom had a long talk with me and told me if she could forgive him, which she finally did, I could too. When he and I finally spoke, he tried to explain to me what compels men to do stupid and regrettable things when it comes to sex. He's kind of a nature buff, and he said that nature puts this incredible pressure on them to replicate themselves. It's just as true as it is of a male dog chasing after a female in heat or those ridiculous dances that some exotic male birds do to compete for the females. He thinks women just don't have the same degree of compulsion, because nature builds in them being overly protective against getting strapped down with offspring, which invariably lands on the mother, while the male has the freedom to move on. I don't know if I buy it, not being an anthropologist, but I forgave him anyway."

"Sounds like an excuse for bad behavior by men," I respond.

"I guess it is to some extent," she says. "But I also assume men have varying degrees of control over it. Up to a point, it's forgivable like any other transgression, but it's never clear when forgiveness is no longer justified."

"Well, then what about those of us who behave ourselves? I'm not going to say I've never said or done something stupid or, yes, probably even offensive. This may sound self-serving, and you can decide whether to believe me, but I've never cheated on my wife, and I would expect the same of my son if he ever gets married. But when men's bad behavior becomes understandable, does it become assumed that I'm also doing those things?"

"Of course not. Or at least I don't. I guess it's all a sliding scale. At some point, you go from understandable to unforgivable."

"And J.D. and your dad never crossed that line, even if they went farther than most of the rest of us?" I ask.

She ponders my question.

"Something like that. Like I said, it's all relative. Look, Dad was the number one man in my life growing up, and all those things I loved and admired him for were still true. How could I not forgive him?"

"I guess I can see that. Pretty sure my father never strayed, but I guess you never know. Living in a small town would have been a deterrent, I would think."

She lets that soak.

"I have another reason for not wanting to go after the congressman."

"What's that?"

"His affair with Saundra pales in comparison with what I see in my office. Let's just say my senator is no monk, and what I hear about a number of others is no better. Yet, they are all held up as fine examples of enlightened males because they are pro-choice and vote the right way on issues like family leave and discrimination. Of course, I strongly agree with those positions, but I don't think positions on issues define someone from a moral perspective. Their philandering and often downright abusive behavior do cross the line."

"Don't any of the women complain about it?"

"A few seem to like the attention and even goad him on at times, but most of us are afraid of losing our jobs."

"Maybe that will change someday. I doubt men's behavior will."

"One can hope."

It seems like we have covered everything, but there is still something bugging me.

"Emily, can I ask one other question? This behavior by Saundra is really hard to explain. She is such a smart and likable person that there is no reason to believe she would have to do this to get ahead. It almost sounds psychotic. How do you explain that?"

Emily looks down at her coffee and nervously glances around.

"What is it, Emily?"

She clears her throat haltingly. "There was something that happened that I've kept to myself. That family is in such pain now that I wasn't going to tell anyone, and it's just speculation on my part."

"We can keep it between us," I assure her. "You don't have to tell me, and I will hold it close either way."

"Well, it has been bugging me, and I do think I need to tell someone, so please keep this to yourself. It was late at night, and I think she assumed I was asleep, but I could hear strange noises in the kitchen. I cracked my door and realized it was her on the phone, and she was talking baby talk. I couldn't make out what she was saying, but it sounded something like 'Daddy's gonna get it' or something like that."

"Was it like a sex call?"

"I guess. I've obviously never done one of those calls, but if I had to imagine that would be it. I know that can be easy money if a girl wants to do it, but Saundra certainly didn't need any money."

"Well, maybe it was J.D. Who knows?"

"I don't think so. I think I know who it was."

After a few beats, I wonder if she is going to tell me.

"At the end, I thought I heard her say, 'Good night, Poppy.' Days later, I heard her on a call with her parents, and I heard her call her dad Poppy. But again, is this anything conclusive? Maybe not. I certainly don't plan to share it with the cops unless I hear more. But if there was a history there, that could explain her strange behavior."

"Maybe." I clear my throat. "Not sure I'm glad you told me this. It's going to be hard to deal with him knowing this. I guess I'd better assume we have no other proof and leave it be."

I thank her, and we go our separate ways. I trust that she will not go running to Bebe with her story, but it is now clear the police will find out about J.D. and Saundra after talking to Emily. I call J.D. that evening to report to him and get his take on the day's events. I don't mention Saundra's late-night phone call with her father.

He admits I probably made the right call on setting up the search as far as the Grays were concerned. But he also recognizes that we have just drawn more attention to the case. I tell him the police are going to know after talking to Emily, and it is just a matter of time before his affair gets out. I let him know I think he needs to be ready to say something more than "it's none of your business." Better to come clean early and have Faith's support. Being coy will only raise more suspicions. He totally disagrees and stands stubbornly by his plan.

I then ask him something I neglected to ask on the earlier call.

"J.D., one more thing I need to know. If you had already broken things off with Saundra, why was there a message on her machine asking her to call you right away?"

The length of time before his response convinces me I won't get the truth. "Oh, she had something I needed for work. I knew she was going to be heading back to Iowa shortly and wanted to make sure she got it to me."

As far as I know, Saundra was doing no direct work for J.D. on anything. Even if she was, given the awkwardness, he would have had me or someone else from the office reach out to her. I don't believe him. But I still am convinced that erased message has nothing to do with the disappearance. I realize I now know a whole lot more than I want or need to know.

TWENTY-EIGHT

# J.D. MEETS WITH THE POLICE

**Wally North**

*March 1990*

It's been several days since the search, which received massive coverage by the local media, as could be expected. All three local TV stations carried it, but Bebe's story in the *Post* the following day still remained stuck in the Metro section, albeit on the front page.

The quotes from the Grays and J.D. were fine, and Chief Sharp refrained from any comment on the event—whose circus-like atmosphere would have disturbed any cop, I assume—but instead he reiterated his commitment to finding Saundra. Most of Bebe's story highlighted the event as an exhibition of Hill staff solidarity, with various quotes from staffers. The staffers came across as purely altruistic, since Bebe ignored the massive postsearch party in Georgetown so she could make the deadline with her story.

The day after the search, they established a fund for a reward under the Iowa-based Missy Walker Foundation, named after a small Sioux City child who was abducted and murdered in the late sixties. The foundation supports families of crime victims not only with financial assistance but also by advising them on ways to keep their cases in the public eye.

J.D. and Faith donated $10,000, which got some good press, even including a good hit from Bebe. Given its strategy, the foundation could become a major thorn in our side. But even with their assistance, Saundra's case is not going to get any more attention than the thousands of other missing persons whose stories barely linger in memory until it is collectively assumed "we will just never know."

The Friday after the search, Emily gave me a call to see whether anything further had developed. The police had interviewed her, and she had responded truthfully about Saundra's relationship with J.D. Beyond that, it seemed to her there wasn't much urgency to the investigation.

But yesterday, J.D. called to tell me the police had asked for an interview. The House is back in session, so J.D. met with the police in his apartment this morning.

When he arrived at the office, there seemed to be a forced elan on his part. He went around the office to each staffer to get an update on what they are working on. He engaged one on one with staff members frequently, but I can't remember him ever doing that in one shot, clearly making rounds through the office almost performatively.

When we finally wind up in his office to discuss the day's agenda, I ask how it went with the police.

"It was very awkward. They kept looking around at everything in the room, as if maybe Saundra was hidden in a closet somewhere, and they sure weren't going to miss it."

"What did you tell them about your relationship?"

"They were obviously following up on what her roommate had said. What I told them was not a lie. I told them we had met a few times outside work socially. Had dinner together twice."

"Which, of course, led to an obvious question."

"Yes, and when they asked it, I said 'If you can tell me the relevancy of that question, I will answer it.' Of course, they couldn't, so we moved on."

"But it wasn't really a denial."

"I said I wouldn't lie. Why should I? They already knew anyway from talking to her roommate. I just didn't think they needed it directly from me. I have nothing to do with whatever happened to her, and I am sure once she is found—under whatever circumstances those may be—that will be proven."

After working so closely for so long with J.D., I have developed a sixth sense about when he is being direct with me. I am not reassured. The deleted phone message keeps weighing on me.

Meanwhile, with or without any connection to her disappearance, I still believe he needs to be honest about his relationship with Saundra, so I am not going to let it go.

"Well, at some point, you're going to get asked that question by the press. Or even the Grays."

"I'll cross that bridge when I come to it, but it will be the same response. I really do not want to hurt Saundra's reputation, so I'd prefer to keep it between us."

He starts leafing through his inbox, his usual signal to end an unpleasant conversation. He might be ready for this to end, but I'm not.

"By the way, I spoke with her roommate after the search," I interrupt his attempt at dismissal. "She thinks she is really unbalanced. Do you think Saundra would do anything to hurt herself over this?" I don't mention Emily's suspicion about her being abused.

"She is definitely unbalanced, but probably not suicidal. I'm not a shrink, though. But I would guess if she did that, she would do it in a way to make me and a lot of other people feel guilty. That probably wouldn't involve disappearing for a couple of weeks." He waves his hand.

"Look, this is a critical week, and we need to get over this distraction. Bring Rosa in and let's talk about the DOD bill on the floor tomorrow. I've got to start lining up support for my amendment."

As I start to leave, he interjects, "Wait, one more thing I keep forgetting to tell you. It sounds like our friend Bebe has been busy. Yesterday on the floor a couple members let me know they had been approached by her asking if they knew anything about the disappearance and my relationship with Saundra. They assured me they gave her nothing, so hopefully she'll realize that's a dry hole."

# TWENTY-NINE

# THE ENQUIRER

**Wally North**

*March 1990*

When I took the job as AA, I knew the worst calls would come to me first.

Instead of her usual practice of buzzing me, Clarissa walks into my cubicle with an uncommonly rattled look on her face.

"Wally, I have Dr. Gray on the phone, and he sounds pretty upset. He wants to talk to J.D. right away."

I tell her to send him through.

"Is this Wally? I don't want to talk to you. I want to talk to the congressman. Where is he?"

I have to remind myself that what Emily told me about Saundra's late-night call with Gray was only speculation. *Always be nice to constituents!*

"I'm sorry, Dr. Gray, right now he is voting, and there are supposed to be several votes, so we don't expect him back soon. I can have him call you when he returns, but maybe I can help you now."

This is not a lie. I really do have to wait for his return. When he is in and out of the office in DC, J.D. prefers not to use his pager. That can be annoying, but in this case, it is a blessing.

"I really want to ask him this directly, so he doesn't have a chance to make up a story."

"What do you mean by that?"

"I assume the word will get to him before he calls anyway, but I'll ask you, and I really hope you will be straight with me. Is he having an affair with my daughter?"

"What?"

"Is he having an affair with my daughter?"

Technically, no. He didn't ask if they had *had* an affair.

"Why would you ask that?"

"So, you aren't categorically saying no?"

"I didn't say that. That's a question only he could answer 'categorically.' As far as I know, he is not having an affair with Saundra." Again, technically, true. "But I asked why you would ask that."

"I got a call from a neighbor whose wife reads that filthy trash at the grocery stores, and she says there is a story in the *National Enquirer* this week claiming that the congressman and Saundra are having an affair and asking if there is any connection with her going missing."

"Dr. Gray, as we both know, there is no limit to what a periodical like that will publish, and their standards of proof are almost nil. The publicity around Saundra obviously gave them a chance to jump on it with their lurid speculation. Why would anyone believe them?"

"I don't think anyone will if the congressman categorically denies it. But people in this town are already talking. The story says its source is a former employee of his."

It was just a matter of time before they got hold of Judy Carricutt. And, unlike Bebe, the *Enquirer* wouldn't wait for a second source.

"Look, I will have J.D. call you right away when he gets back, but I can assure you any speculation based on comments from a former employee has nothing to do with Saundra's whereabouts. This town is full of disgruntled ex-employees who are always looking for ways to screw their ex-bosses." Poor choice of words, but I figure he is so rattled it will go past him.

"Well, maybe you can tell me whether you know anything about this."

"Dr. Gray, I am his AA. I deal with J.D. on a professional level. I'm not with him twenty-four hours a day. If you want me to make categorical statements about J.D.'s personal life when we aren't working, I can't do that."

"But, as his chief of staff, you would be concerned if he was having an affair with a current employee, right?"

"Of course, I would be concerned if I were aware of it. Look, J.D. will be back in about an hour, and I will have him call you right away."

"Fine. I will be here."

Coming from a relatively well-educated family, I have never paid much attention to the *National Enquirer*. Sure, one can't completely ignore the outrageous rumors it often tries to peddle on its cover about Jackie Onassis, Lady Di, or any other celebrity whose personal details the masses are presumably obsessed with. Stories like Caroline Kennedy being Elvis's baby were just a little too far-fetched for my imagination to embrace.

So these kinds of stories only get legs if there is some grain of truth that keeps them alive. Or if there is some reporter from a respectable news outlet who sees opportunity in it. Or some hypersensitive family member.

Members of Congress and their staffers—or the professional staffs at least—pay little attention to these stories. Only items in the *Post*, *New York Times*, *Wall Street Journal*, or the local papers back in the district get noticed. Respectable journalism, if we can agree to call it that.

But people outside our world of supposedly "responsible discourse" do read these, and certainly that is the case in northwest Iowa. It would have been nice if the story about the "Congressman Having a Passionate Affair with His Missing Intern (Does He Know Where She Is?)" had come to our attention before Dr. Gray called me about it.

But it didn't.

When J.D. returns after a couple of hours, he closets himself in his office to make the call to Gray, which he had tried unsuccessfully to convince me is unnecessary. He is in there awhile. Finally, he buzzes me to come in.

"How'd it go?"

"Not well. But I guess as good as it could."

"What does that mean?"

J.D. avoids eye contact and starts shuffling papers on his desk and checking his phone messages before he answers.

"It means I didn't answer their question."

"The crap about your personal life having nothing to do with her disappearance?"

"Something like that. And I'm sorry. It's not crap."

"And they didn't buy it?"

"Well, they hopefully bought that it has nothing to do with her disappearance."

I take a seat in the chair opposite him, and he still isn't looking directly at me. And J.D. is someone who probably makes eye contact with his dentist while getting his teeth drilled.

"I'm pretty sure that wasn't all they cared about," I say. "With or without her disappearance, they are wondering if their twenty-four-year-old daughter is having an affair with a man twice her age who is her boss. I'd be concerned, as I believe you would be too."

I don't bother to add that his refusal to categorically deny the affair likely only confirmed it with them. I assume he is astute enough to figure that out.

"I told them her connection to me and this office had nothing to do with it as far as I know."

"In other words, it was none of their business."

"I guess so."

"Would that work with you as a parent?"

"Probably not. But it also wouldn't work with me if someone told me my daughter was using sex in a predatory way to further their career, even if it meant trying to steal someone from their spouse. I feel like if I tell them anything, I have to tell them everything. If it has nothing to do with her disappearance, why do they need to know?"

Knowing what I know about Saundra's tactics, I can't argue with him on a principled level, but it still doesn't work on a strategic level.

We sit silent for a while. There are several voices coming from outside his door, and, from the occasional loud laughter, it sounds like it could be a group of constituents visiting DC and making the rounds to their delegation. J.D. would normally jump up and head right to the door so they aren't kept waiting.

Instead, he is buried in his thoughts, and I can tell he is no more satisfied with his response than I am. We are both hoping that she will be found. That old "hope as a strategy" dodge that every political consultant warns against.

I finally speak. "You know that looking like you are hiding something just plays into suspicion that it does have something to do with her going missing."

"Wally, as bad as this is, I still believe the truth will endure here. I'm now convinced someone has done something really bad to Saundra, and we need to find out who it was. It sure as hell wasn't me, and, eventually, when she is found, that will be clear."

"You honestly think that, even if you don't know what actually happened?"

"Of course, I do. There is no connection whatsoever between her disappearance and the affair. You have to believe me, Wally."

If any statement calls for eye contact, it is that one. But he is still looking away.

"Okay, well, if this story is in the *Enquirer* today, it's just a matter of time before it goes broader," I say. "You know why? Because it's true, at least in part, and you and I both know that. When an *Enquirer* story is based on a bold-faced lie, it usually goes nowhere. But Gary Hart will tell you when there is an element of truth, it starts taking on a life of its own."

"Unless she's found before it does."

I am starting to feel lost. I have tied my whole career to someone I have believed in, and his normal candor and integrity have been a big part of that. Voters rarely completely buy into any politician, so if even I am losing faith in him, what will happen with them?

"But what if she's not found?" I blurt, and my eyes speak as loudly as my voice. "You are acting like a complete idiot here, J.D.!"

I immediately realize the volume and tone have overstepped my bounds. J.D. gives me a hard look. It is clear he is trying to decide how much of the standard boss–employee relationship is going to survive this. I now have a great deal of leverage over him, but I am still his employee.

"Don't yell at me like that, Wally. You still work for me, and I'm not going to tolerate something like that."

I apologize, but we both know that the last thing he needs right now is a story about firing his top aide in a suspicious situation that could become an inferno with more kindling.

## THIRTY

# AND SO IT BEGINS

**Wally North**

*March 1990*

First thing yesterday morning, when J.D. got to the office from the House of Representatives gym, he called me in.

"I was followed by two black SUVs coming into work this morning."

"Law enforcement?"

"I don't think so. I shared this with one of my colleagues at the gym who's been through an investigation. He said when it's law enforcement, you don't notice them. The press, on the other hand, don't care whether you notice them or not."

"Why the hell would they be following you?"

"Looking for photo ops, I assume," he said. "I asked him if I had any rights in this area. He told me only people who have never had to deal with the press would believe that. He told me to brace myself because this would only be the beginning."

A quick beginning, indeed. The shit apparently has finally hit the fan. This morning, Bebe finally got her front-page headline in the *Post*. After trying unsuccessfully to call J.D., I am on my way out the door when the phone rings.

"J.D.?"

"Wally, I need you to come get me."

"What's up?"

"Well, I'm looking out my front window, and I count twenty reporters, three news vans with broadcasting dishes, and about fifteen cameramen. I've already been called by one of the neighbors asking me what the hell is going on. I can only assume there must be a story in the paper, but I can't get to it."

"There is, and it's not good. I already tried to call you, but you must have been in the shower. I guess I could have assumed something like this would happen. I'll be there as fast as I can."

I am a little ahead of the heaviest morning rush, so it only takes me twenty minutes to drive to J.D.'s townhouse. I try several news channels on the radio, including NPR, but there is nothing.

As I arrive, I am immediately swarmed. I guess most people like to be on TV and get their moment of fame, but this is not what I have in mind for myself.

It is easy dealing with the barrage of questions because I know there is nothing that would work, and I assume "no comment" wouldn't be an interesting sound bite. So I just don't say anything at all. I grab J.D.'s paper on the way in and slip past the last three reporters as J.D. edges the door open to let me in.

The stalking from the day before had probably removed any element of surprise, so his face registers no reaction as he reads the story. The headline reads, "Questions Raised in Missing Intern's Relationship to Congressman." This is how presumably respectable news publications deal with gossip. They never report the gossip as fact—the news is that the other, more salacious, publications do. The story repeats the "unsubstantiated" report from another former employee of an affair and runs a picture of J.D. and Saundra together that appeared in one of the tabloids. It fails to note that that picture was a standard official picture of J.D. and two new employees with the other employee cropped out.

Bebe had called me again asking for a reaction to the *Enquirer* story, and I had told her I never read the gossip rags. Her story includes a quote from me saying, "I have seen nothing inappropriate in the office."

Not exactly a firm denial. I just hadn't gotten comfortable with making bold-faced lies. I figure at some point, I may have to do that. Before reaching that point, would I resign? Did anyone on Kennedy's team ever wonder what they would say if the press started looking into his affair with Marilyn Monroe, who committed suicide while he was in office? Would they have lied to keep the New Frontier pristine?

But the worst part of Bebe's story is that she finally includes my previous quote saying, "I think our voters can handle a missing intern." I assume J.D.'s reading that line is what provokes his sharp look at me, but he says nothing. She clearly has been sitting on it for when it would punch the hardest, taking it completely out of context.

As we are about to leave, I caution J.D., "Just keep in mind that as difficult as this trek to my car is going to be, the footage is going to be carried on every channel, even if you don't say anything. No forced smile. We're still worried about where she is. Just walk through the phalanx. Anything you say will just lead to more questions."

It is about a thirty-foot walk, and it takes a while to wade our way through. Most of the questions are what you would expect. I get one asking if it is my normal job to drive the congressman to work and, if not, why today?

When we get in the car, I ask him how he is doing.

"How the fuck do you think?" Ever under control physically, I note from his hands he is now shaking but keeps his face passive as we are pulling away from the cameras.

We don't speak on the ride in. There is a forced quiet in the office as well, since everyone has either read the story or been told. Darby is already in J.D.'s office waiting for us.

"I've taken at least five calls, J.D., with messages from another fifteen asking for a comment," he says.

"Our comment is the only thing that matters is finding Saundra, okay?" J.D. snaps.

"Do we have an answer for the obvious question?" Darby presses.

J.D. doesn't even have to ask what the "obvious question" would be. "Yes, it's irrelevant to where Saundra is."

"So, we're not denying it."

"We don't have to affirm or deny. It's my personal life, and it's irrelevant." J.D. starts fishing through the paperwork, trying to signal he is done without having to lay down the law. It doesn't work for Darby and me.

"That's not going to stop the questions," Darby insists.

Having gone through the same exchange with J.D. several times, I watch to see if Darby can make any progress.

"Darby, I am fully aware that the only thing that is going to fucking stop the questions is Saundra showing up, which will make it absolutely clear that I had nothing to do with it."

"What if she never shows up? What if she's at the bottom of some river? What if she's starting a new life incognito somewhere in Europe?"

Darby's questions are disturbing. Actually, if she did turn up alive, it would not be the best result for us politically, given her temperament. I refuse to let my strategic mind go there. This is a tortured human being who, at this point, can likely only be in grave physical danger—or was. That is all that I will allow myself to feel. But I also have to protect J.D. He may have had the affair, but I refuse to believe any complicity in whatever her fate is—or was.

J.D. finally looks us both in the eyes. "If she never turns up again, then the story eventually goes away. We know how these news cycles work. Eventually something else shitty happens that overtakes this shitty thing, and the press starts obsessing over that shiny new shitty thing."

I realize "wait for something else shitty to happen" is probably a better strategy than "hope," because something shitty always happens to take away the focus of the media. You just never know when that would be and hope to hell it isn't the beginning of World War III. That is about the only thing I can think of that would be worse for us. At least we'd be in good company with the rest of the world.

I chime in. "J.D., I can assure you this story will never go away in the district. Fortunately, we have some time before the election, but between now and then, 'it's none of your business' is not going to work."

J.D. knows he doesn't have an answer for this.

"Yeah, well, you didn't exactly help by emphasizing the politics of the thing. What the hell were you thinking?"

"Totally out of context, J.D., and it was from a previous conversation that she was holding for an opportune time." Not that it makes any difference. I can tell from the look on Darby's face that he isn't any happier with it, but he isn't going to rebuff one of his only allies on it.

J.D. asks Darby to give him a draft statement within the next thirty minutes, and that will be it for the day. Darby and I exchange glances on the way out, and I tell him to give it his best shot.

Well, that is it for most of the rest of the day until, on our way to a vote this afternoon, a reporter asks whether J.D.'s wife's disability has created marital tensions. The footage of me restraining J.D. as he lunges for the reporter will undoubtedly make it on every news program tonight. Hopefully, most stations will at least be objective enough to include the reporter's question, but the image of a congressman under intense pressure will now be permanently seared in the public's consciousness.

## THIRTY-ONE

# UNRELENTING

**Wally North**

*April 1990*

The last few weeks have been pure hell for J.D. and the rest of us. My commute with J.D. has become a morning routine, with each day bringing a few more reporters, cameras, and new levels of tension with his neighbors, with whom I have stopped exchanging glances.

The creativity of the questions never ceases either.

"Is it true Saundra resembles your mother?"

"What is your position on sex crimes?"

"Is it true you and Saundra took a trip to Morocco?"

"Did Saundra ever meet your wife?"

"Is it true you have a tattoo of Saundra on your right buttock?"

Within a month, Saundra—just "Saundra" to everyone—has become the most famous Saundra ever. Pictures of her, most of which have likely been supplied by her parents, swarm the periodicals and news hours. And all of them are adorable. Saundra's ballet recital. Saundra playing dress-up with her siblings. Saundra with her prom date. Saundra with the family puppy. That was the picture one of the NASCAR drivers displayed on the hood of his race car. There are very few things the public would have thought it didn't know about Saundra. Other than her whereabouts, of course.

Now that the rumors about the affair have gone public, the Grays are giving us the cold shoulder. When they come to DC to meet with various officials, including both of their senators, they don't meet with J.D., which has been noted by the press. When asked about whether they are aware of an affair, they generally dodge the question (Who wants to talk about their daughter's sex life?), but they also refuse to deny any suspicions about whether he may have been involved in her disappearance. They simply urge the police and FBI to "leave no stone unturned." They clearly have no interest whatsoever in giving J.D. any excuses or cover. Which doesn't really surprise me.

Meanwhile, J.D.'s perfect voting record—something we tout in every reelection campaign—is toast. His frequent absenteeism is yet another source of criticism. There have been days where, after certain stories publish, he just doesn't want to go in.

Fortunately, we were able to escape for one long weekend to one of his Virginia colleagues' cabins in George Washington National Forest, about three hours southeast of the city. Just me and him and a phone on which we could call the office. The occasional rings (actually, more than occasional) cut into our ability to relax. We actually went fishing, hiking, and watched old movies on a nineteen-inch TV. Mostly it was vintage John Wayne movies and other Westerns. They aren't necessarily our type, but we did discover the beauty of some of the classics, like *Red River* and *The Searchers*.

All in all, it was a nice relief from the daily assault, and apparently the local press in nearby Lexington and Staunton had other things to worry about. Needless to say, this has been hell for Faith. So that she doesn't get blindsided, she asked the local postman, who is an old family friend, to give her advance copies of the tabloids. They have gone well beyond the Saundra allegations about J.D. to include his alleged relationships with other congresspersons—men and women—DC pole dancers, and even farm animals. The postman has warned her about staying away from the grocery stores on Thursdays, known as "Trash Thursdays," because that is the day the new editions come out.

J.D. tells me he has been completely honest with Faith about the brief affair. He said she was forgiving but told him he was "a complete moron" for allowing himself to be seduced by Saundra. He is assured she does not question his innocence in Saundra's disappearance.

Despite her disability and the slew of reporters camped on her doorstep every day, including those who regularly scour her trash bins every Wednesday before the pickups, Faith continues to go into the drugstore and manage the business. If nothing else, this has maintained a strong relationship with the townspeople with whom she and J.D. had grown up. In fact, the drugstore's business picked up slightly, perhaps due to the additional curiosity factor. One of the tabloids has actually printed a J.D. and Saundra Tour of the area, with the drugstore being one of the obvious stops. I have little doubt that, to the extent J.D. still has support in his part of the district, it is largely due to Faith's steadfastness.

But J.D.'s relationships in DC have become strained. With the neighbors, that's no surprise, given the disruptions to their daily lives. But even most of his congressional colleagues, who have their own self-preservation to worry about, keep their distance. Ever since the scandals involving Wilbur Mills, Wayne Hays, Gary Hart, and other notables, they have known it only takes one bad apple to make them all look bad in the public's eye. Any words or acts of solidarity with an accused colleague would make them publicly complicit.

The only ones who offer comfort are those who have been through similar situations—on both sides of the aisle—who tell him to keep his cool and assume his every action is being filmed or recorded in some way. They then assure him that they survived—but as far as either of us know, none of them had been through anything like this.

The most surprising support has come from Faith's fundamentalist parents. J.D. told me they have become more tolerant since her brother's death. J.D. mentioned a call from her father, who told him Faith had explained the situation to him. He still thinks J.D. is a sinner and needs to "find Christ," and that he will be there for him when he finds Him.

J.D. said it told him a lot about his father-in-law, whom he has always dismissed as a religious charlatan. He realized that the old haranguer really must have accepted Christ's teachings in his heart. Even with that, J.D. is unlikely to ever "find Christ" in the sense Faith's dad means, unlike some of Nixon's opportunistic Watergate scoundrels.

Every time we think interest in the case will subside, something else pops. It has become so unrelenting that I am getting up at 5:00 a.m. to drive to the nearest newsstand that has the *Post* so I won't have to wait for it to show up on my doorstep.

When an interview with Saundra's aunt is published one morning, I drive straight to J.D.'s townhouse. Fortunately, the paparazzi have not yet shown up. J.D. is wiping the sleep from his eyes when he answers my insistent doorbell.

"Now what?"

"Bebe published an interview with one of Saundra's aunts, who conveniently lives in Richmond. She claims that Saundra came down one weekend to visit and told her she was having a relationship with a 'very important official' in Washington but didn't name who it was. Saundra told her it was very serious, and the person was going to leave his wife for her."

"That's it?"

"Pretty much. Bebe then, of course, goes through all the background and the allegations of a relationship with you."

"Jesus. Total hearsay. Does the *Post* have any standards on this?"

I am surprised he is asking that at this point. But then, who does have standards? A congressman and his staffer who repeatedly mislead the press, the voters, and the general public?

## THIRTY-TWO

# GAMESMANSHIP

**Wally North**

*April 1990*

It's now unmistakable that, regardless of whether the suspicions are true, J.D. is politically vulnerable. In addition to the onslaught of the press, we are starting to see more and more demonstrations in the district.

Moreover, it is clearly being fed by both sides of the political spectrum, who have also managed to keep their fingerprints hidden. Those on the far left and their organized groups have always viewed J.D. as a turncoat who doesn't belong in the Democratic party. They would prefer a "true believer" as the Democratic nominee. Without a remote chance of one of their true believers winning in the general, they would at least have the pelt of an apostate. Of course, the party leadership has little patience for this approach, since it threatens its Democratic majority in the House, but they too have to stay on the good side of the activists.

Meanwhile, the Republicans are licking their chops. They had always viewed this as a truly Republican district gone wrong, and, in their eyes, J.D. is no better than any of the liberals. They know if he can be bumped off in the primary, especially by someone outflanking him on the left, the district can be recaptured. And they are absolutely correct.

The alignment of these strategies is so clear that we even wonder if they are coordinating. Of course, that would mean they have to speak to one another, so it seems unlikely. But these days our naïvete seems to know no bounds.

It's blatantly clear who organized each demonstration based on the signs people are holding, with both ends of the political spectrum represented. Signs like "RESIGN NOW, COWARD" and "MURDERER AND ADULTERER," are typical of either. But the left says things like "SHOULDN'T PRO-LIFE INCLUDE SAUNDRA?" and "HOW ABOUT STRIKING A BLOW <u>FOR</u> WOMEN NEXT TIME?" One of the demonstrations organized by the far right had a sign that said, "FIRST BABIES, NOW INTERNS," held by someone who apparently was unaware of J.D.'s pro-life position.

Eventually, when J.D. got back to DC one Monday, he told me to cancel his flights home for the indefinite future. Normally, when he stays in DC, Faith flies in to join him, but, with her condition, it makes her very visible, so they decide to stay apart those weekends. Even in his absence, though, the demonstrations back home blare on.

THIRTY-THREE

# ADVICE FROM A FRIEND

**Wally North**

*April 1990*

J.D. and I are going over a list of supporters he plans to reach out to when Darby comes in with a request from Isaiah Stone to do an interview.

I am mildly optimistic. J.D. and Stone got to know each other early in J.D.'s tenure in Congress, and Stone had written a very complimentary piece in a local paper that got some attention in DC. Stone's career has since progressed, and he is starting to make a name for himself in the Washington bureau of the *Des Moines Register*, the most prestigious of the regional newspapers. Given the Iowa connection, he and J.D. know each other well.

J.D.'s eyes narrow looking at Darby. "What does he want to talk about?"

Darby frowns but tries not to act like it is a dumb question from the boss. "He wants to talk about the Saundra situation."

"Why should I talk to him about that? What about the pesticide issue or anything else his readers in Iowa may actually care about? He's a good reporter. Why would he want to talk to me about this sordid gossip?"

As bullheaded as J.D. is being, one of the things I admire about him is that he truly does care more about the issues than what he considers gossip. But if anyone is going to give him a break, it would be Stone, who has never engaged in the pure character assassination many reporters have sunk to since Watergate.

"J.D., right now it's just about the only thing in Washington his readers in Iowa are paying attention to," Darby says. "Regardless of any support you may be getting in your district, most of the rest of Iowa doesn't like the attention it's bringing to their state."

"That's bullshit, Darby. Sure, the tabloid readers are titillated—let them be. But the serious voters who are the kind I appeal to would look beyond this and only care about my positions."

It is becoming clear how blind J.D. has become to political realities. Is it just a naïve belief that only issues matter, or is it a futile hope? Probably the latter. If any other member was in the same situation, I'm pretty sure J.D. would see things more clearly.

I have to jump in. "I wish that were so, J.D., but the world has changed since Kennedy's revolving door in the White House living quarters. Even voters who care about the issues see DC as a cesspool with their worst imaginations filling in the blanks on what you guys in Congress are up to. Stone is a good reporter, and he doesn't feed into that. If you are going to get a fair hearing from anyone, it will be him. I think you should give him the time."

J.D. rolls his eyes. He knows we are right.

"Okay, set it up. But tell him when he comes, I want to talk about the real issues of concern to Iowans."

---

J.D. and I leave his townhouse well before dawn. Our early departure avoids the usual trailing by the pack. The dazzling beauty of spring in DC is unsurpassed. Its briskness is edging warmer each day, and I always enjoy this part of the season between the chill and the swelter. Much of the vegetation is still bursting colorfully from its buds, and I wonder when we will ever have our own new beginning.

There is nowhere else we can meet without drawing attention, so the interview will take place at Darby's apartment near Foggy Bottom. J.D. asked both Darby and me to sit in on it. I had hoped we could spend the time before Stone's arrival talking message, but J.D. wants nothing to do with that. Instead, he buries himself in the morning paper and staff briefing memos.

I have never been to Darby's place. He lives by himself in his small apartment a few blocks from the Metro station. Most of the inhabitants are George Washington University students, so, externally at least, it's a pretty shoddy place. His apartment, though, is nicely furnished and relatively clean for a bachelor pad. *Well, he may have brought in a maid before this meeting, given the company,* I ponder.

Stone dresses better than most reporters and comes wearing a suit, which probably drew some attention from the students in the building. It's doubtful any would have recognized either him or J.D., though.

Darby grew up in the Quad City area of Iowa, which is on the border of Iowa and Illinois. Chicago is the closest major city, and I didn't realize Darby is such an avid Chicago sports fan and collector. His collection makes an immediate impression on Stone, who had grown up in the Windy City.

Stone steps closer to the display case, his eyes narrowing in admiration. "Is that an Ernie Banks autograph? Did you meet him?"

Darby nods, a trace of pride flickering across his face. "I did. He was doing a signing in Davenport. Got to shake his hand and everything."

Stone whistles, clearly impressed. "That's incredible. What about the Walter Payton poster? Same deal?"

Darby hesitates, rubbing the back of his neck. "Not quite. Bought that one at a sports card show. But hey, Payton was known for being a little salty about that Super Bowl, so he probably signed it with some reluctance."

Stone grins. "Still counts in my book. This is quite the collection."

Stone turns toward the group, clearly ready to get down to business. J.D. appears genuinely glad to see a friendly face from the press.

"Isaiah, it's great to see you." J.D.'s handshake is almost effusive.

"Good to see you as well, J.D. Hope you are holding up okay."

"Your colleagues are beating the shit out of me, Isaiah. There's literally a feeding frenzy going on on my front lawn, and it's really tough."

Stone allows that to sit and waits to see if J.D. will add anything. He finally breaks the awkward moment. "Is there anything you want to talk about off the record before we start?"

J.D. doesn't hesitate. "Isaiah, I have nothing to hide, so I have nothing to say off the record."

"Okay." Stone pulls pen and paper from his briefcase. Darby brings in coffee, and we take seats around his small dining room table.

"Let me start with a blunt question. Did or do you have anything to do with the disappearance of Saundra Gray?"

J.D. frowns. It is clear he is trying to appear surprised, but it doesn't look sincere. "Well, I was hoping we could talk about some substantive issues, but, to answer your question, absolutely not. And there is simply nothing to add."

"Is there anything that would lead someone to suspect you had anything to do with her disappearance?"

"Again, absolutely nothing, and I—*we*—are totally committed to doing whatever we can to help find out where she is and what may have happened to her. And we are doing that."

J.D. looks at both me and Darby, and we nod in agreement. You could say we did this obediently as well, but I also believe it is true.

Stone clearly expected this response. He now looks straight into J.D.'s eyes.

"Okay, that's consistent with everything you've said. Now let's talk about your relationship with her."

J.D. clears his throat and says what Darby and I have heard repeatedly for weeks.

"She works for me. She's an intern in my office. She's a good worker.

Extremely bright. I use the present tense because I have every hope she will be found safe and healthy any day now. We miss her in the office—both her and her work—and she is still on the payroll. We are considering this indefinite paid leave."

Stone lets this sit to make sure J.D. is finished. But he also gives J.D. a determined stare that makes it clear he isn't satisfied.

"Do you have a relationship with her that goes beyond work?"

J.D.'s eyes flare, but he catches himself and keeps his voice steady.

"Here we go again. What happens in my personal life has nothing to do with whatever may have happened to Saundra."

"J.D., I know this is an odd request from a reporter, but in this case, can I be the one to go off the record?" Stone asks.

None of us have ever heard this from a reporter.

"Sure," says J.D., angling his head slightly back with furrowed brow.

"Look, your refusal to answer that question is only adding fuel to the fire. You have a reputation as a very honest, straight-talking politician. That's brought you a long way. If there was nothing there, it seems you would deny a relationship in no uncertain terms. Yet you aren't denying it."

I am surprised at Stone's directness. Few reporters would so openly reveal their support for a politician. He is clearly trying to help.

"But I'm not confirming it either," J.D. retorts. "I'm simply saying the question has nothing to do with her disappearance or my job as a member of Congress."

Stone shakes his head slightly and taps his index finger on the table nervously.

"Okay, let me try again, J.D. Your refusal to address the issue head-on is leading everyone to the conclusion that there is a relationship and that you are hiding something. That's what makes people think there is a connection."

It is gratifying to Darby and me to hear the same advice coming from a neutral source. It also reminds me again of how J.D. continued to hide the reason behind his actions—and brings back the memory of his urgent call to Saundra on the day she disappeared.

"Let me ask you something, Isaiah," J.D. interrupts. "Is there anything, any shred of evidence whatsoever, that I have had anything to do with her disappearance?"

"No, but people look for motive. It's one of the first things a detective looks for. And these people watch a lot of *Murder Most Foul* episodes."

J.D. shakes his head. "Isaiah, I know I am innocent of any foul play. That's good enough for me."

"But look, J.D., this is off the record, so I'm going to cross the line here myself. You are a highly respected member of Congress with an immaculate record of solid service and not a hint of scandal until now. I think you could admit something like this, and you would survive politically. At some point, we will all find out whatever happened to Ms. Gray, and I believe you in saying that there will be no implications for you. Meanwhile, people would probably give you credit for being straight with them."

"Isaiah, I'm the politician here, who's been reelected four times. I don't think I need your political advice."

Stone has to notice things are on edge, but he then takes one step too far.

"J.D.—let's be honest here. Everyone knows your personal situation. I think they would be especially forgiving."

"Is that a reference to my wife?" J.D. is now pointing his finger directly at Stone. After seeing his violent reaction to another reporter's similar question, I move closer to him in case I have to restrain him.

Stone draws back. "Uh, look, let's go back on the record."

But J.D. isn't going to let go and stands so hard his chair clatters backward. "No, I want to know, Mr. Stone. Was that a reference to my wife?"

J.D. rarely calls anyone "mister."

"J.D., I'm trying to be helpful here. There's a larger picture that I don't think you are seeing."

"No, I see the picture, Isaiah. You're just like all of them. You want to be the one with the big scoop. 'I'm the one who finally got the confession because he thought I was a friend.' Pulitzer Prize, here we come."

Stone too stands abruptly, but with no furniture damage. He opens his briefcase and stuffs the pen and paper inside.

"That is not at all the case, J.D., and you know I'm not that kind of reporter. Goddamn it, I'm trying to help, but you're not letting me. Just go on with your strategy and see where it leads you. I can see this is getting nowhere. Thanks for the coffee, Darby."

## THIRTY-FOUR

# STONE WEIGHS IN

**Wally North**

*April 1990*

Two days after the meeting with Stone, Doris calls me first thing at home to let me know his column finally appeared in the *Register.*

"It's actually not bad," she declares.

"Really?"

"He says some positive things about J.D. I'll fax it to you, but let me read the salient parts. The headline is 'When Politicians Have to Prove Their Innocence.'"

"Would be great if he gave us a road map for that," I speculate.

"Well, he doesn't, but I think it is still helpful. Here you go:

"'In recent weeks, Iowa and, indeed, the entire United States have become obsessed with the disappearance of Saundra Gray and whether one of Iowa's most popular members of Congress is somehow implicated. Hopefully, she will turn up safe and healthy, but, as time goes by, it is hard to believe that foul play isn't involved.'

"'But, let's be clear. Most of the insinuations and crass demonstrations targeting Congressman Clay are likely being orchestrated by those who would like to drill him out of office because of his politics. Yet, there is not one shred of evidence of any involvement by him in the disappearance.'"

"That is obvious, but it's nice to see someone credible actually say it for once," I interrupt. "Keep going."

"'What is there instead? A suspicion that he has been having an affair with a young intern in his office. Granted, she is well of age—twenty-four years old—but it is never appropriate for an employer to take advantage of a relationship with one of his employees. And, yes, he is married.'"

"No mention of Faith's disability?" I interrupt again.

"Apparently not," Doris responds. "He must assume it's well enough known to let it go. Besides, he probably doesn't want to sound like he's making apologies. Adultery under any circumstances is still wrong in most people's books, even today."

"At least in Iowa, I assume."

"Yeah, let me go on. 'So far, Clay has neither denied nor admitted any inappropriate relationship with Ms. Gray. He has responded to salacious reports in the tabloids and unsubstantiated hearsay in the so-called respectable press by saying his personal life is no one's business and is irrelevant to her disappearance.'"

She reads to herself a little more.

"Here's where Stone starts to turn a bit, but it's hard to disagree with him: 'And that's where Congressman Clay is wrong. A member of Congress's personal life is always relevant to those who vote for him. Just ask those who lived in the districts of Wilbur Mills, Wayne Hays, Gerry Studds, and, well, the list goes on. And, if he was somehow involved in her disappearance as part of a cover-up, it is clearly relevant.'

"'But what if he's not? We can all jump to conclusions about an inappropriate affair and cast judgment on that. But, in the absence of evidence, it is quite another thing to assume guilt in a much more serious offense—and I'll let the reader speculate as to what that might be. Assuming he is innocent of such an offense (as we must so assume until Ms. Gray's fate is determined), how does Clay prove that innocence? Proving a negative can be almost impossible. Meanwhile, the daily hounding of him by hordes of reporters, photographers, and TV cameras is a disgrace to my profession.'

"'So where does that leave us? Congressman Clay's refusal to respond to questions about his relationship with Ms. Gray is only adding fuel to the fire. It is creating a suspicion that there is some connection. He should either assert there was no relationship beyond her employment, which the voters can choose whether or not to believe, or acknowledge that there was one and let his district balance that against all of the positives he has built up in almost ten years of service to them.'

She takes a breath.

"He then goes on for a couple of paragraphs with a very positive assessment of that record. And then he closes strong: 'Regardless of what Clay ever admits, in the absence of further developments, Iowa and my colleagues in the press need to move on from this issue. We all feel for the Grays, and any of us in their situation would want to make sure nothing is left unexamined in the search for her. But thousands of people disappear each day, most if not all under highly suspicious circumstances. Until we know what happened to her, it is far too early to cast aspersions on those connected to her—even if there are suspicions about those connections. There has to be a presumption of innocence, and not just from a legal perspective.'

"'Meanwhile, there are far greater issues at stake in the upcoming elections upon which we all need to focus, whether it is a faltering economy, a deteriorating ecology, or the turmoil in Europe from the dissolution of the Soviet bloc. An obsession with sordid innuendos and stretches of the truth will only distract us from finding those solutions.'

"That's it. Not bad for us, I think, under the circumstances," she asserts.

I agree. After what happened at Darby's, we could not have done any better than this. It will by no means put a wrap on the issue, but it is reassuring, nevertheless. Yet, I also assume that, despite Stone's exhortation, J.D. will continue to evade the issue. And Stone's far less conscientious colleagues will continue to keep it in the public eye. And I'm still wondering about that phone message from J.D. to Saundra.

# THIRTY-FIVE

# EVERETT "SHARK" FINN

**Wally North**

*April 1990*

"Mr. Finn will be with you shortly. He's just finishing up a call."

We are sitting in the law offices of Everett Finn, who has long since gained the obvious nickname of "Shark," even though he is more often on the defense side. His attractive assistant, who vaguely resembles Sissy Spacek, has that slight Southern accent—the kind common in DC among those who've long since left behind most traces of their regional roots.

After five weeks of daily news hits, wading through crowds of reporters and cameras at home and at work, awkward silences from just about everyone I know, and a total lack of effectiveness in J.D. doing his real job, he has finally agreed to meet with a lawyer.

It goes without saying that J.D. is no longer the person I signed up to work with and worked closely alongside for the past six years. Maybe the wear and tear is showing a side of him that was always hidden. Or maybe anyone who goes through what he is going through would be transformed. His refusal to acknowledge the affair with Saundra in the face of all kinds of public evidence, not to mention the truth, is contrary to the image he has constructed of always being straight with the voters.

Either way, I am thinking less and less about what is best for him and more and more about my own fate. Unfortunately, that fate is considerably dependent on his. So, I am trapped. I have to stay in the game to get this fixed for my sake as well as his. Even if he isn't coming clean with me on that strange phone message, the man is not a murderer.

Finn was recommended by the Speaker's office. After he represented a few of the second-tier targets in the wake of the Watergate break-in, he made a name for himself helping people in DC from both parties who were under a cloud of suspicion. Many had, indeed, been guilty of what they were accused of, but many were not. Meanwhile, he had had enough clients who had ultimately been vindicated that, unlike many other DC lawyers, hiring him wasn't viewed as an admission of guilt. As with many things in DC, the truth didn't really matter as long as there was a strategy and a spin. And that's what Finn was supposed to help us with.

Finn's is a one-man office with one employee, which tells me his work probably has a lot more to do with relationships and spins than copious legal research. The pictures in the anteroom advertise his prominence well. The only ones without a former president are with John Wayne and Paul Newman, irreproachable figures from both ends of the political spectrum.

When we finally enter his office, I see pictures of others with less stellar records, though all were ultimately exonerated—legally, at least, if not socially.

Finn is a tall man with the de rigueur sweep of a white mane barely touching his collar. His nickname is a bit of a misnomer when you first meet him. He effortlessly generates charismatic warmth with his own slight Southern accent that immediately draws you in. Before we talk business, he asks J.D. about his drugstores and whether small operations like his can withstand the charge of national chains like Walgreens and Rite Aid. He has obviously done some homework.

J.D. had agreed to let me call Finn in advance and fill him in on everything to that point, including his relationship with Saundra and his interrogation by the police, along with anything else relevant I could share with him.

After the brief small talk, Finn makes a sharp turn from the pleasantries into the business at hand. His first question is one any lawyer would ask, but I wasn't ready for his vehemence.

"So, you let the police talk to you without having a lawyer present. Why in the name of our Lord Christ and all he suffered would you do something so incredibly stupid? Are you also going to help them plant the cross on the hill?"

Members of Congress typically aren't subjected to such vitriol, especially from someone they may actually employ, so J.D. is taken aback. He speaks through clenched teeth.

"I am innocent. I have nothing to hide."

"Well, almost nothing. Except this little tryst with one of your young employees who then just happened to disappear under mysterious circumstances."

Finn says this with virtually no facial expression but a tone in his voice that could rattle a Queen's Guardsman at Buckingham Palace. I worry J.D. will stand up and walk out before getting anything done. The fact that he doesn't is a testament to his desperation and Finn's reputation. But it's still going to be a bit edgy.

"That affair had nothing to do with it," J.D. whispers.

Finn narrows his eyes but maintains the same tone in his voice. The last time I saw anyone confront J.D. like this was at a pro-life rally he had addressed where some participants didn't like his openness to exceptions in cases of rape and incest.

"So, if it didn't have anything to do with it, why don't you just own up to it publicly and stop looking like you're trying to hide something?"

"Because it is nobody's fucking business except mine and hers. And why does everyone assume she would want everyone to know about it?"

"Yet, you essentially admitted it to the police, even if, in your naïve view, you don't think you did, and that it wasn't relevant."

"That's the police. They are charged with investigating a crime, and I didn't have any problem talking to them."

"Even if you knew they were going to go there with their questioning.

If you had had your lawyer present, he could have been the one to tell them it was irrelevant, and you could have kept your damn mouth shut!"

At this, J.D. stands up. He turns and glares at me.

"Come on, Wally, this guy's just going to sit here and insult me. I'm getting enough of that these days, and I sure as hell don't have to put up with it from him."

Finn holds both hands up defensively in a deliberate show of softening.

"Sit down, Congressman. I was just testing you."

"Oh, like I haven't been fucking tested enough already over the past month."

J.D. continues glaring but finally sits back down.

"I know you have," Finn says, using his hands like a priest giving comfort to his flock. "I just need to know whether I can work with you. If you are going to be overly sensitive about anything I say to you, it's not going to work. If, on the other hand, we can have blunt conversations about what's going on and what you need to do, I may be able to help you. You know my record, I assume."

J.D. is gradually cooling off. "I do. But you can't blame me for taking offense at what you just said."

"Fair enough. Let's just assume there is going to be a lot of offense going on in our relationship, but keep telling yourself it's all about saving your skin."

J.D. looks at me, and I nod.

"Okay. What's your plan?"

"In my view, I have two jobs here. First, to keep you out of jail. Second, to try to rehabilitate your image. And that's not just about trying to get reelected, which may be a long shot at this point. It's also about you being able to either continue here in DC or go back to Iowa and have the kind of respect that a former congressman deserves, especially one with the admirable record of accomplishment you've established. I did a little research."

J.D. raises an eyebrow, looks over at me, and this time he's the one who nods. "Well, thank you. That seems to be playing second fiddle these days."

"These days it would. Does anyone really remember Nixon opening the door to China?"

I'm not quite sure J.D. has done anything quite that momentous, but it is a nice reference. Even if a lot of people actually do remember Nixon going to China.

Finn continues, "Now, on the first task, I believe you are completely innocent of any wrongdoing in the young lady's disappearance. Once she's found—and eventually she probably will be—that will be evident to everyone, and you won't have to worry about going to jail. But that may not be for a very long time. So, until she is, you and anyone else who might have a motive will be in play with the police."

J.D. considers this a moment, looking upward a bit in thought and returning his gaze to Finn.

"Sadly, I think you are correct."

"Okay. So task number one is actually the easy one. Comparatively speaking. It's the reputational part that is the challenge."

"Well, I'm all ears."

"Good. Let's start with the assumption that even if she is found, it could be a long time from now. It could be next week. It could be next month. It could be next year. Maybe the body has been completely disposed of—burned or shredded—and it is never found. One of those things where twenty years later, some witness comes forward on their deathbed. Shit, we haven't even had that happen yet with Hoffa. It's kind of rare, actually, but it does happen."

"Well, let's hope that's not the case here."

"Agree, but as is often said in this town, hope is not a strategy."

"I've said that myself a few times, right, Wally?"

I nod. A good sign. J.D. is starting to warm to Finn. That was not the kind of expression J.D. would make in a hostile situation.

"Let's talk about this fascination with the girl's disappearance. There are two focal points. The first is her disappearance. Where is she? What happened to her? Yet there are thousands of missing persons in the DC area alone, let alone the whole country, and their absences go on for any length of time. But there is no public obsession with these. Why not?"

J.D. is silent, listening.

"It wasn't a rhetorical question, J.D. Why is there no public obsession with those others?"

J.D. thinks awhile, avoiding the obvious, and then says, "She's a beautiful young lady. She's white and affluent. I would guess in DC, most of those missing are poor nonwhite people, not as interesting. Sadly, the public writes them off. People assume they lead shitty lives so shitty things happen to them. But when something happens to their own, they get alarmed. It's deplorable, but it is what it is."

"Agree. But, even with that, absent any developments giving clues to their whereabouts, the public attention goes away. Right?"

"Right."

"So, I ask again, what is different about this case?"

J.D. gives a sigh of annoyance and just stares at Finn, waiting for him to go on. But he doesn't. He just stares back at J.D.

Finally, J.D. caves. "Okay, I know where you're going. So what's your strategy?"

"First, you come clean on your relationship. Publicly. You haven't admitted it until now because it is irrelevant to her disappearance, and you were also protecting her reputation—some may buy that—but you now know it has created a distraction from the real issue—her disappearance. You up the reward, task one of your staffers with helping the police, put new pressure on the FBI and police, and throw it back in their court. Meanwhile, you are appalled at the rumors, but there is no limit to what you will do to help find her."

J.D. holds his gaze for a full minute.

"No to the first part. All that other stuff is fine, but there is nothing to 'come clean' on that has anything to do with her disappearance."

I don't care whether J.D. sees me sigh and shake my head.

Finn is unfazed.

"I expected that. You obviously feel strongly about this, and I understand why you would hold to your position. Do something for me, though. Think about it. Talk to Wally, talk to your wife, talk to anyone else you can trust. And then get back to me."

"I'll do that, but I can tell you right now, it's not going to change. So, you need to think about a different strategy."

"Well, I'm not sure there is one, but if you'll promise to consider my suggestion, I'll promise to consider yours." He stands, and we both shake his offered hand. I look at my watch. We've been here over an hour. Probably two thousand dollars already. Where is that going to come from, let alone any additional work?

We spend the rest of the day dealing with legislation and constituent issues, and I let him think about Finn's offer. He goes home early, wading through the paparazzi and presumably eating a quiet dinner at home.

THIRTY-SIX

# A POLYGRAPH

**Wally North**

*April 1990*

When I pick up J.D. for our usual morning commute, I give him time to settle into my car and take one sip of coffee before asking about Finn's suggestion.

"The answer is no," he says.

"Come on, J.D. What else are we going to do? Continue to plow through all these cameras and tape recorders every day? Do you have any other solution?"

"No, but for what we'll be paying him, he's supposed to. I'm going to tell him no. I am not going to say anything publicly about me and Saundra."

I had figured he would be obstinate and had been thinking about another possibility.

"What about a polygraph? Not about the affair, but about any complicity in any potential crime."

He takes another sip of coffee before quickly acknowledging that he had already thought of it.

"Well?"

"Well, what? In the past Congress, you'll recall that I voted for a widespread ban. A lack of reliability was a huge factor in that debate. So, now I'm going to embrace it for my own agenda?"

He is referring to the Polygraph Protection Act of 1988, which banned their use by employers. He's correct that reliability was one of the driving factors. I push back.

"Wasn't that because a lot of employers were using fly-by-night operations?"

"That and the privacy invasion," he agrees.

"But there were some exceptions, right? Like for national security? That means someone thought they were accurate in certain circumstances."

"I was subjected to one or two while in the service and generally found them pretty reliable."

"Well, what about it?"

He continues sipping his coffee, and I am encouraged by the silence.

"I did not cause her disappearance. I have no doubt I would pass that. But does it have to ask about our relationship?"

"I thought about that, J.D. It seems like we should be able to set it up so that we decide what direction the questions take—if not the actual questions themselves. We're not asking the police to do it. I'm sure Finn has done it before and knows who provides the most credible services."

"Even with that, what if it screws up and says I'm lying? Which I'm not."

By now, we should be at the office, but an accident on Independence Avenue has ground everything to a halt, enabling us to continue playing it out. J.D. is right about the danger of failing, but I think he is overstating things.

"Look, it's not like we're going to do this with Geraldo Rivera on *Geraldo at Large*. We do it with no one else knowing about it. If we get the results we want, we leak it ourselves or even do a press release announcing it. If you fail, we never say anything."

"And assume a bad result doesn't get leaked? That would be the worst possibility if everyone found out I took it and failed and then kept it quiet."

"Agree. That's just a chance we have to take."

"Let's see what Finn thinks. I don't have anything this morning that can't be canceled, so once we get freed up, let's go straight to his office."

Two hours later, we are sitting with Finn in Jed Leland's offices in a strip mall in Springfield. Leland is a former FBI agent Finn has used in the past and is considered one of the best in the business.

Neither the office nor Leland himself could be more nondescript, as befitting a retired FBI agent's operation. The strip mall looks like it primarily caters to the local Vietnamese population, including a small grocery shop, a tattoo parlor (specializing in dragons), and a hair salon.

Leland's office was at the very end of one of the rows. The décor—or lack thereof—reflects the fact that it's the kind of business where most action comes from referrals, so good first impressions don't matter. Or maybe Jed Leland is just a slob who focuses solely on wires and graphs. He doesn't seem to have an assistant—who would likely make sprucing up a priority—and comes out of his office into the foyer to greet us himself.

He is a short, gnomish man whose tortoise-shell glasses underscore his chelonian nature. But he is a mud turtle, not a snapper, and could have served as a very smart but docile pet in another life.

He ushers J.D., Finn, and me into the testing room so we can all observe the machinery and get more information on polygraphs than I will hopefully ever need in the future. The chair in the middle of the small room is right out of central casting with a bevy of wires and a couple of straps. Opposite is a desk that apparently holds the control panel, with a chair facing the subject's chair.

It doesn't seem necessary, but there is a certain degree of pride of authorship on Leland's part. I probably don't need to read carefully all the plaques and certificates on the wall for proof he is top in his field. Finn's word is sufficient for me. We spend a fair amount of time briefing him, though he acknowledges he has been following the situation in the press. We make it clear there are to be no questions about any relationship J.D. may have with Saundra. He reiterates a point Finn had made that we can't dictate the questions or let J.D. see them before the interview. But he promises to stay away from the relationship.

He then leads us back to the entry room and closes the door to his office while he composes the questions. It is a short wait before he calls J.D. back in.

I leaf through past issues of *Insighter* magazine, which is targeted to current and former federal law enforcement officials. The various issues' coverage of community relations, retirement opportunities, and how to conduct interviews "with confidence" can only hold my attention so long, given the wait.

Finn is not nearly as tense as I am. He brought all the various morning papers and is rushing through them like a disposable obstacle course. I wonder if he ever reads past the headlines. But maybe in his business, that would only cloud his perceptions. There is such a thing as too much understanding.

After an hour, J.D. emerges, looking far less than satisfied. I ask him what is wrong, and he mumbles all is fine. But it clearly isn't.

Eventually, Leland calls us all into his office to give us the results. He peers down at them one more time, leafing through them carefully before speaking.

"I'm going to go through every question and give you the results. I'm going to skip the standard questions like name, place of birth, etc., where there would be no reason to lie. On the following questions, the test indicates Mr. Clay gave a truthful response:

"'Did you take any actions facilitating the disappearance of Ms. Gray?' 'No.'

"'Did you physically harm or have someone physically harm Ms. Gray?' 'No.'

"'Do you know where Ms. Gray can be found?' 'No.'

"There was no indication of any deception whatsoever in any of these questions."

He finally lifts his eyes to us, showing no reaction of his own but gauging ours. I suspect if you conducted polygraph tests for a living, you would develop your own sixth sense as well, constantly watching body language for clues.

I feel relieved, thinking I had misread J.D.'s reaction. Finn maintains his usual poker face.

"That's terrific," I blurt. "Exactly what we wanted."

Leland holds his hand up. "That wasn't all the questions."

He shifts in his seat, and J.D. wipes his chin.

"There was one more that Mr. Clay answered in the negative, but the machine indicated his response was not truthful." I noted he avoided the use of the word "lie."

"I asked the following question: 'Do you have any indication of what may have led to the disappearance of Ms. Gray, with or without your involvement?' Mr. Clay said no. The machine registered a falsehood."

J.D. shoots back defensively. "But I clearly don't! I knew these machines are bullshit."

Finn isn't as convinced.

"Now wait, J.D. Leland is the best in the business, and my use of his services over the years has been flawless. Let's take a look at this. Is there anything at all that might have led you to give the wrong answer? Maybe you do know something that's relevant here that you don't want us to know. Or maybe something you know but only subconsciously."

Leland interjects, "Something like that would be unlikely to be a factor in most cases, but I wouldn't rule it out. Can't say I've ever seen it, though."

He starts to go on, but J.D. interrupts.

"No. Of course there is nothing I am not telling you guys."

"Think."

The message that I erased on the machine now seems to have a more-than-plausible connection. Especially since J.D. still hasn't adequately explained it to me. But I don't want to say anything in front of the others.

J.D. scratches his head, not entirely convincingly.

"I really don't know. Maybe in my mind I do somehow connect the affair with all this in some unarticulated way. Someone does the wrong thing—and we both clearly did—and it leads to bad results? I am so ashamed of the whole affair that maybe I just can't keep them separate myself."

Leland's face is characteristically unreadable, but Finn is clearly skeptical.

"Okay, if that's true, is that what you want to say publicly to explain that response?"

"Do we have to include that response if we release the test results?"

"Absolutely," Leland jumps in. "I have never given anything but full disclosure of all questions and responses. If I did, my credibility would be shot and, without that, I'd be out of business. We either provide the full transcript or nothing."

That is not what J.D. wants to hear, but there is no sign of flexibility on Leland's part.

"This is total bullshit," J.D. unloads somewhat more forcefully than he normally does when offended. "That was a total bullshit question that has no precision whatsoever. Couldn't my reaction have just been one of confusion that registered a physical response similar to a lie?"

Leland says, "It is unlikely, but if you were confused, why didn't you just ask me to clarify like you did on a couple of others? Instead, you answered 'no' right away."

Finn holds his hand up. "Okay, well, we're just going to have to accept that this didn't work. As Leland said, we can't release partial results. We're back to square one, guys. If anyone asks anything more about polygraphs, we tell them J.D. is concerned about their accuracy and doesn't believe it would prove anything. Jed is solid on this, and there will be no leak, right, Jed?"

"Absolutely not. We only disclose if the client asks us to. I'll put your bill in the mail this afternoon."

On the drive back to the office, I ask the question I avoided earlier.

"J.D., let me ask you again. What was the urgent voicemail about that you left for Saundra the afternoon she disappeared? Is there something you didn't tell me?"

"I told you. I needed to ask her a question about a bill she was supposed to be following."

I almost slam on the brakes.

"No, actually, J.D., that's not what you told me. You told me she had some papers you needed, and you were going to have her drop them off."

"Yeah, you're right—that was it. The papers were about that issue. Shit, Wally, that was over a month ago. How can I remember? If there was a connection, I sure as hell would remember, wouldn't I?"

I shoot back, "You sure as hell would, but you may not be willing to tell me."

He lets that go. We keep driving in silence. I once again wish I had never deleted that message from the machine.

## THIRTY-SEVEN

# THE GRAYS ACCUSE

**Wally North**

*May 1990*

The Grays are keeping the heat on, and I can't say I blame them. Whenever it looks like there might be a break in interest, they emerge with some new angle to keep the issue alive.

They set up a charity, simply named Find Saundra, which accepts anonymous donations. They don't have to disclose their donors, so it's entirely likely that J.D.'s antagonists on both the right and left are supporting it. Even though it was probably against his best interest, J.D. publicly made a significant donation. Either way, it seems there are no limits to the resources available to the Grays, both financial and strategic.

They have also been sporadically making the rounds on the various morning TV shows, in which they invariably blast the DC police for failing to give the case a priority. Then, this morning on the *Today* show, they finally broke their silence on the allegation of an affair between J.D. and Saundra.

Until now, they have simply deflected questions about the issue, saying they just want the truth and don't really care whether there was an affair as long as it had nothing to do with Saundra's disappearance. When asked whether they had spoken to J.D. about his relationship with Saundra, they simply say he has repeated claims to them that his private life is irrelevant.

This morning, they shifted gears.

They couldn't have found a better forum than the *Today* show. They appeared live in the studio with Susan Alexander, who has made a name for herself by using the morning show as a news breaker. Dr. Gray was looking as dapper and dour as ever in a dark suit, while Mrs. Gray was holding back tears in a black dress that would have fit right in at an Iowa funeral. I must say, though, it was only partly show. The imminent tears were not an act.

Alexander was, of course, a pro at empathy, nodding and shaking her head at all the right times. I was starting to wonder why the most-watched morning show would concern itself with a status report on the investigation, which was old news. Then things turned when Alexander asked the perennial question.

"Do you believe Congressman Clay was—or maybe is—having an affair with your daughter?"

The Grays exchanged glances, and Mrs. Gray nodded to her husband. They obviously were prepared.

"We believe the congressman needs to come clean on this," said Dr. Gray. "The longer he avoids this issue, the more likely it seems that he may have had something to do with it. We are all being kept totally in the dark here, and he's only making it worse."

Alexander jumped on this. "In the past, you have not pressed on this aspect of the case. Do you think if he is having an affair, there could be a connection to your daughter's disappearance?"

"Like I said. He needs to come completely clean on both issues. But, until he does, can we rule it out? Of course not."

"Would you believe him if he told you he was completely innocent regarding her disappearance?"

"At this point, we are not sure."

Alexander was doing a masterful job of containing her excitement. This was clearly going to refresh interest in the case.

"What would it take for you to believe him?"

"It seems like, in situations like this, people accused of wrongdoing often voluntarily agree to submit to a lie detector test. We think the congressman should be asked that question. Is he so sure of his innocence that he will agree to do that?"

The question had been asked before, and J.D. had ignored it. But now, coming from the Grays, we realize it will become part of the mantra.

We call Finn to get his take on the polygraph question. We knew it would come up at some point, but we didn't expect it so quickly after J.D. took the test. I have no reason to believe a leak from Finn or the polygrapher, but it is odd. Maybe we were followed without knowing it?

The decibels in Finn's voice crank up higher than usual.

"Look, J.D., you are going to get asked over and over again on the polygraph issue. What are you going to say? 'Well, I took it and mostly passed?' Even if you lie and say you took it and passed with flying colors, everyone is going to want to see the results, and Jed would only give the full results. We certainly don't want that."

"So, what are you suggesting?" I ask.

Finn clears his throat. I can hear what sounds like a pencil tapping on his desk.

"We're back to square one. J.D., you need to tell the truth on the affair. The Grays are leaving that card to you. Come clean, and that eliminates the mystery."

"Does it?" J.D. shoots back. "Don't they then continue with, 'What's the connection?' And they'll then want a polygraph even more."

The pencil stops tapping.

"I think you can handle that by attacking the credibility of polygraph tests. Didn't you say you voted for the law banning it?"

J.D. briefs him on his nuanced position when he voted, which didn't clearly rule out the veracity of polygraphs.

"Gee, that's pretty nuanced," Finn said. "Could you boil that down to one sentence?"

"I could try. But I'll go back to your original point. I am not going to say anything I haven't said about my relationship with Saundra. This intrusion into any public figure's private life just has to end, and I'm making a stand here."

I could make a case that this is an honorable position he is taking if it wasn't so self-serving. Not that I disagreed with his overall point about the vulnerability of public figures, but his refusal to come clean with me on the answering machine is starting to color my view of his responses.

Finn lets J.D.'s response sit, as if to give him a chance to rethink it. Which J.D. doesn't.

"J.D., I think I'm at my rope's end," Finn finally says. "I just can't think of any other approach here but telling the truth, since I think it would help your credibility. Now I know you've got a primary coming up and the knives are out. I don't really know the politics in your district, but as of now, I can't believe this is helping."

"It's not."

"Then I suggest you get the absolute best campaign advice you can get. If you can get past the primary and November, this will eventually go away, like it has with some—but not all—of your colleagues. At some point, she'll be found. But right now, it seems unlikely before the vote next month. I have to admit, I am done with this. I have never walked away from a client, but in this case, I feel like I'd be robbing you if I kept billing you for services that seem to be going nowhere."

J.D. frowns and shakes his head.

"Mr. Finn, you're supposed to be the best in DC at situations like this. I can't believe the only thing you can come up with is for me to do myself in by confessing something that is no one's business. Guess we're on our own here."

We exchange pleasantries and hang up. I wait for J.D. to say something or give me some direction, but he remains silent. It doesn't seem like he even knows I am still in the room, so I quietly get up and leave his office. There are some constituents in the foyer, and Maggie the receptionist gives me the usual inquiring look—"Can they stop in and say hi?" I subtly shake my head, and she gets the message.

## THIRTY-EIGHT

# ABANDONMENT

**Wally North**

*May 1990*

I can tell from the look on his face as soon as Rosa and I enter J.D.'s office, it isn't going to be good news. He has just taken a call from Speaker O'Connor, and he has that distant look on his face we only see when he feels defeated.

We sit. He exhales, then says, "He wants me to stay silent during the family leave debate."

I know what this means. J.D. often goes his own way, but he is also a team player when it comes to party solidarity and has never crossed swords with the leadership.

The Family Leave Bill is going to be voted out of committee and will then go to the House floor next week. The bill will be amended to establish that only employers of fifty or more will be required to provide job-protected unpaid leave to their employees. Though he is not on the committee, everyone involved in the bill knows that J.D.'s role in securing this compromise essentially guarantees passage of the bill by getting the thirty-seven moderate Democrat members of the Burnt Toast Coalition, of which J.D. is still the informal leader, to vote for the bill.

J.D. has hoped that giving some visibility to his role would help deflect some of the attention away from the Saundra controversy. It would demonstrate that his personal life is irrelevant to the necessary work of getting laws passed, especially those intended to help working mothers. Normally, in such a situation, the sponsors and various supporters of the bill would go out of their way to applaud his role, some of them through gritted teeth. These plaudits are often obligatory, praising some who had minimal involvement, but in J.D.'s case, they would be well deserved. With all but a handful of Republicans not expected to vote "aye," those thirty-seven votes will send the bill to the Senate.

The fifty-employee threshold insulates the small businesses in his district from the bill's impact on their operations. Meanwhile, most larger companies already provide the benefit, and J.D. has no sympathy for those who don't. His opponents on the left will still resent what they view as a watering down of the bill's impact, but most of his support on the center left—a solid majority of the Democrats in his district—would clearly appreciate his role in getting the bill passed. Well, they would if they knew about it.

J.D. is clearly disappointed but is suppressing any anger toward O'Connor.

"No one outside Congress knows anything about the role I've played, and he thinks giving me any visibility at all would deflect from the accomplishment and wrap it into the Saundra story, which the press seems to care more about. He didn't say it, but I'm sure he was getting a lot of pressure from Susan Cady and the women's groups to shut me up. They must be delighted that he's going along with them."

By now, in addition to covert support for the Saundra demonstrations, those groups have poured a lot of money into the campaign of J.D.'s primary opponent—State Senator Everett Bernstein—who gives them and every other liberal group unflinching support. The groups are surely astute enough to know that Bernstein wouldn't stand a chance against any credible Republican in our district, but they don't care as long as it means getting rid of J.D. One less Democratic vote, but it sends a message to other potential apostates.

Rosa and I wait to see if he is going to say anything more or dismiss us, but he does neither. Anything else we might want to discuss no longer matters, so it is as if we suddenly have all the time in the world. Is he already thinking of himself as a lame duck, even before the primary?

I break the silence. "If you were in O'Connor's situation, would you do it any differently?"

"Probably not." I marveled once again how, in a situation like this, J.D. can step outside his own circumstances and have an objective view, even if it is against his interest.

He sits silently. This is the most dejected I have seen him since Saundra first disappeared. It is only the latest affront. Most of his colleagues have been avoiding being seen with him, and only his truest friends—and only those who are politically safe on their own—have been ignoring those optics. But this seems to hurt even more.

"He can't prevent you from taking the floor and saying something," I offer.

"No, he can't, but right now that's a bridge I don't need to burn. I can put a statement in the Congressional Record, and we can trumpet it however much we want in the district."

We all know that can only go so far. Politicians touting their own victories are typically met with skepticism, and rightfully so. Genuine credit is only appreciated when it is heralded elsewhere, and now that isn't going to happen with this. In fact, Bernstein will probably try to turn it to his advantage by claiming that J.D. had been a drag on the bill and voted for it reluctantly only after it got watered down.

Inertia is calcifying with all three of us. The last reed we could hold onto before slipping down the current has broken.

When I try to break the silence, J.D. holds up his hand.

"We're already dead," he says.

Rosa and I exchange glances.

"Huh?"

"We're already dead."

His face softens, and I even see a slight smile. *Is it relief?* He takes a deep breath and sits back in his chair. It might be the most relaxed I have seen him since the scandal broke.

"It's something my first sergeant in Nam said a week after I'd been there," he continues. "We had just survived an attack from the Viet Cong, and I had watched a couple of my comrades go down, and I was badly shaken."

He is staring straight ahead.

"I was slipping into a panic attack when Sarge grabbed my wrists. He looked me straight in the eye and said, 'There is no such thing as fear when you are already dead. And you are. Deal with it.' After that moment, I was able to overcome the panic and handle the next several months."

He suddenly stops, realizing we are sitting there, and looks straight at us with a determined expression.

"That's how we are going to deal with this. We're already dead. We've lost this race."

"Gee, J.D., that's not much of a pep talk," I gently complain.

"Wally, we are beyond pep talks. At this point, we have nothing to lose. So, are we just going to fold? Hell, no. We're going to go back to basic blocking and tackling. We run our campaign like I did my first one. Forget all the noise from the media and the fringe attack dogs. I'm going to go out and meet my constituents face to face. No more hiding."

"So are you going to . . ."

He holds up his hand.

"No, I'm not going to admit anything. I'll tell them it's irrelevant to my service to them and they can draw whatever conclusions they want."

Rosa adds, "Well, we don't have much time."

He nods.

"Of course we don't. We're already dead. That's our new mantra. Well, maybe just among the three of us, okay? We just make do with the time we have. Wally, you're officially suspended from the congressional office and are now on the campaign payroll. Rosa, you're going to run the office. Wally and I are going to do some driving, just like when we first got to know each other."

Suddenly I feel a peculiar rush of adrenaline. I may already be dead, but gaining a new sense of purpose is like a breath of air following a near drowning. This is, of course, a long shot with no real expectation of winning, but polishing my résumé will have to wait. It feels like we are back in the game, and I now feel an absence of pressure that only a severe underdog can feel going into a boxing match.

THIRTY-NINE

# FORWARD TO THE PAST

**Wally North**

*June 1990*

The campaign has been going extremely well, and I was starting to think J.D. may actually pull it off.

The past few weeks will be long remembered as one of the most memorable periods in my relationship with J.D. We're still hounded by the press and demonstrators as we drive around northwest Iowa, but J.D.'s attitude makes all the difference. Since he said we were "already dead," I have given up on pressing him any further on coming clean on the affair. Ditto getting any explanation of the deleted phone message. We've spent our driving time talking about life in general while listening to Little Feat, the Allman Brothers, Willie Nelson, and Randy Newman. The logistical challenges of getting from place to place have been the only campaign-related issues that interrupt our reverie. Often, these travels have been in the dead of night from one town to the next with surprise visits the following morning in local diners, John Deere stores, and church gatherings.

Trouper that she is, Faith has continued to juggle managing the store while doing her own campaign events in the area surrounding Mitoka. Yet even though she has been doing these on her own, the vultures have been only a little gentler with her. She responds to the incessant questions with: "I love J.D. and believe my fellow constituents will agree that he is the best they can have in Washington." I heard that someone on the campaign staff suggested she quote Tammy Wynette about "standing by her man," but she thought that was a bit too mawkish.

Most of the voters are polite. The news onslaught has made J.D. the most famous person in northwestern Iowa, and people are naturally drawn toward celebrities, even antiheroes, but their unspoken doubts and disappointments are clear on their faces.

Those who go beyond polite are the many people J.D. has helped over the years, whether it was help with a small business loan, an Annapolis recommendation, or facilitating a White House tour. One of the reasons long-term incumbents have an advantage is the accumulation over the years of those whose lives they have touched. Those people in turn feel through their connection with the congressman some special access to the halls of power that they are privy to and that they can boast about to their friends. That is not something they want to give up lightly, however nebulous it may be.

But even after ten years, that's a finite number. Most of the time, people pay little attention to who represents them, and, in our case, an enormous number of Democratic primary voters know very little about J.D. except for the scandal.

He doesn't blink when asked about Saundra. Same response every time. Totally committed to helping in any way to find out what happened to her, reiterating everything we have done to that point. Personal questions are irrelevant, so let's talk about what's important to the people of the district. Oddly, I think people are taking this as an admission, but if he can move on from it, so can they.

Just yesterday, our polls started to show we were drawing even with State Senator Bernstein, who had taken a strong lead when the Grays started implying J.D.'s complicity in Saundra's disappearance. To our pleasant surprise, our new approach seemed to be working. Meanwhile, there has been nothing new on Saundra's disappearance, so voters are obviously tiring of the same questions being asked over and over. For his part, Bernstein just keeps repeating the same leftist diatribes. His core supporters like that, but the more centrist Democrats in our district will have to swallow hard before buying into it. For them it would have to be a "no" vote on J.D. instead of a "yes" for Bernstein.

But today, while we have been enjoying a luncheon with ten constituents at a supporter's home in Whistle Bend, the phone rang. Our host said it was Doris from the district office and she needed to speak to J.D. right away. When J.D. returned, he remained distracted through the rest of the lunch, and we departed quicker than usual.

He won't tell me right away what it was about, but he tells me we have to find a place for him to make a private call. I find a phone booth outside the post office, and he is on the phone for a very long time. He returns to the car ashen faced.

"Who was that?"

"Well, you might say it was an old girlfriend."

"You mean even before Faith?"

"Before we were married, while I was in college."

I let it sit for a bit while he is thinking. Then I ask if it was personal and whether I should mind my own business, which I doubt.

"I wish you could, but I need to loop you in. We need to go straight to Mitoka, so start driving. I told Doris to cancel everything else between now and the election Tuesday. You'll see why when I explain."

The drive to Mitoka was only going to be about fifty minutes, but it gives him enough time to fill me in on Astrid Gilbert.

"You really paid for an abortion? You, the pro-life congressman? And at a time when it was still illegal?"

"Wally, my views were no different than they are now. I thought then as I do now—that it was the taking of an innocent life."

"So, how could you facilitate it?"

"Because it was her choice. We both made a mistake, and it was just as much mine as hers. Left to me, we would have gotten married or put the child up for adoption, but she wouldn't do either. I couldn't just wash my hands of it. She was going to do it anyway, so the least I could do was agree to her request to pay for it. I certainly wasn't going to turn her in to the authorities."

"So, she's going to go public with it?"

"No, she herself is not, but she won't have to. That's why she told Doris to have me call her. She's a very prominent anthropologist at Cal Berkeley now. Has made quite a name for herself. Doesn't agree at all with my politics, but says she still appreciates how I handled it with her. It was very tense at the time, obviously, and we avoided each other through graduation, but she bears no animosity whatsoever."

"Okay, so what's the problem?"

"The problem is, she runs in very liberal circles. One night, over wine with a couple she thought were very good friends, she told them about us. The news about Saundra had made me somewhat famous—infamous—and she told them what she thought was a very interesting angle. That was a while back, and she forgot all about it until she got a call from a reporter yesterday. Apparently, her so-called friends were more politically connected than she realized and had told someone in one of the leftist groups, who had shared it with the reporter."

J.D. takes a long pause as he watches the road. His eyes track on a Bernstein for Congress sign.

I ask the obvious question.

"So, what's she going to do?"

"Say nothing. Like I said, she still appreciates what I did and doesn't want to hurt me."

"Even if it could help the liberal cause?"

"Honestly, if I can guess, I don't think that matters to her. She's very liberal socially. I mean, she's an anthropologist, right? But I'm also guessing she's not that engaged politically—probably thinks both parties are full of shit and politicians even more so. I would guess I'm the only one she ever knew well, so she probably thinks of me differently. Also, she's pissed that these 'friends' dragged her personal life into this for political gains. And, believe me, I know where she's coming from on that."

"So, problem solved then, right? If she's not going to verify this, it goes nowhere."

He looks at me.

"You think so? Guess you haven't been around this stuff long enough, Wally. I've seen this play out too many times. The story becomes the story."

"What do you mean?"

"Well, first of all, like my 'alleged' affair with Saundra, it gets published by one of the sketchy tabloids, without attribution to their source. It probably doesn't name Astrid—Professor Gilbert—but eventually someone finds out and it gets out. Meanwhile, the 'respectable' media, which has been starved for any new stories about me for a while, now has a new angle. They don't assess the allegation itself, but they run with the fact that it was made, whether true or not. It generates more questions from reporters for me and a whole lot of new signs and demonstrations. I've now entered the ranks of 'child killer' among my pro-life supporters and 'hypocrite' with the pro-choice crowd."

I see where this is going.

"So, you're just going to stick with the 'none of your business' line on this, too?"

"Not this time. I'm going to admit it."

"When?"

"Today. First, I need to talk to Faith and the kids. She knew nothing about this, but I think she'll forgive me since it was so long ago, and we had made no commitments to each other at the time. The kids will obviously be a bigger challenge, but I'm going to frame it as a lesson in life that they need to learn from so they don't make the same mistake. Then we're calling a press conference at the DO, and we're going to just say it's true. Obviously, I won't give them Astrid's name, respecting her privacy, or any hints about who it is. Once I've admitted it, there will no longer be a push to verify it with her."

This makes sense. But I immediately wonder how we are going to get through the remaining campaign events without it being a major distraction. Before I can ask, it is clear he has already figured that out.

"The statement will be my last public appearance. No more events after that. We just wait out the election results on Tuesday and let the voters speak. I think we both know now what that answer will be."

I sense the same kind of relief in his voice as when he gave the "we're already dead" speech to me and Rosa. But I am also wondering what the hell I am going to do. He anticipates my question.

"You're welcome to spend the weekend with us in Mitoka, or if you want to head home, that's fine, too. We still have several months in office to serve our constituents, and there will be no reason to let up. We'll also need to work on getting you and the rest of the staff relocated come December."

To some extent, I am starting to share his sense of relief. No "hide the ball" on this one. No dodging reporters' questions. No new polygraphs. Myriad anxieties suddenly dissipate. But I still have one obvious question.

"So, J.D., why are you now deciding to be completely honest? What is different about this than the Saundra situation?"

"Two things. First, it is relevant to me being a congressman. I can hold back on Saundra because it's not. From a legal perspective, I did nothing wrong with her, and whoever did is the culprit, not me. I also don't see how me admitting to the affair does anything for the poor girl's reputation, even if it is clouded under suspicion already.

"But that's not the case here. Not only is it true, but it is completely relevant to a high-profile issue that I have taken a firm stance on. I have to not only face that myself, but let the voters factor it into their decision whether to let me continue to serve."

"Okay, I get it, and far be it from me to second-guess you on it. Now what's the second?"

"The second is I owe it to both Astrid and Faith to put this thing to rest. With Astrid, who I still have a lot of affection and loyalty to even after such a long time, she doesn't need to get dragged into this. It's about me, not her, and hopefully admitting it will make it go away before anyone finds out who it is. If I decided to fight it, eventually the press would track her down. With Faith, it won't be as easy. I've already created a lot of pain in her life, and what I need to do now is try to mitigate any more from occurring. I can only do that by coming clean and putting an end to the story."

At the next stop, I call my parents and let them know I'll be in the area for the weekend. They're happy for the time with me, but I know they will also have a lot of questions about what the hell I am going to do with my own career after November.

FORTY

# PRIMARY ELECTION NIGHT

**Wally North**

*June 1990*

After spending the weekend with my parents, I return to Mitoka to spend election day here, as I have for the past six years.

J.D.'s admission and the shutdown of our campaigning had predictable results. The editorials from the papers Sunday came out unanimously in favor of Bernstein, noting J.D.'s "hypocrisy" on the abortion issue was just the final blow. Only the *Padua Patriot* stuck with him, with the editor Charlie Kane maintaining his loyalty to a congressional career he had helped burnish with a 1982 article by Isaiah Stone early in both Stone's and J.D.'s careers. Meanwhile, even Stone's *Des Moines Register* abandoned us, and we can at least hope it was against his wishes.

Of course, this was an easy call for the various Republican papers scattered around the district, and his collaboration in the abortion made that even easier. They knew a victory for Bernstein in the Democratic primary would mean almost certain victory for Republican State Senator Cody Riggins, as long as he is able to fend off a challenge from the far right by Council Bluffs City Councilman Donner Lennon in the primary.

J.D. decided to cancel his election night event, saving his supporters any further embarrassment. None of them protested the decision. It is just those few of us closest to him that are there at his house as we field the calls from the various precincts. It is clear by 9:00 p.m. that Bernstein is going to beat

J.D., though the 53–47 margin is a lot closer than I expected. I guess a lot of voters must have admired J.D. for facing the truth on at least one issue.

Shortly after J.D. called Bernstein to concede, the local news station cut to the victory celebration. Bernstein is dutifully gracious to J.D. but touts his victory as a clarion call for "true Democrats taking back the party." He lists family and medical leave as one of his top agenda items, going beyond the pending bill and making it paid leave. He also includes the usual litany of stronger union rights, a minimum wage increase, and restrictions on trade with Japan. Interestingly, J.D. is in agreement on all these, though at a more moderate pace, which, he would argue, makes them more achievable.

"Well, lefties all over the country are going to be celebrating this one," J.D. says after taking a sip of bourbon. Since the call with Bernstein, he has been pouring more generously, which is unusual for him. Even though we are at his home, he is dressed in a suit—as he would be at headquarters—but has already loosened his blue tie.

Meanwhile, the Republican race is even tighter, but it looks like Riggins is going to fend off Lennon. J.D. isn't in much of a mood for prognostication, but Faith is.

"All those Bernstein supporters look so happy, but they must realize this is going to make Riggins's election a cakewalk," she says, between sips of wine. She is also dressed for the occasion in a prim blue dress that flows graciously over her seated legs. Despite her disability, she has kept in good shape and is as attractive as the day I met her. Under any other circumstances, she could have run for J.D.'s vacant seat and maybe even exceeded his majority.

I agree with her assessment of the jubilant victors on the screen, noting, "I think they were hoping Lennon would pull it out and the folks in the middle would walk away from him and either hold their nose and vote for Bernstein or not vote at all. Clearly, the left underestimated Riggins in assuming all Republicans are the racist knuckle-draggers of their fantasies.

They don't realize that most Iowans, however conservative, want the rest of the country to know they are educated, reasonable people, and Riggins is a good representation of that."

"He is," J.D. finally joins in. "He is going to make a good congressman and hold this district for a very long time. And, however reasonable he may come across in his rhetoric, everyone knows he is unlikely to vote with the left on anything. My 80-percent record is as good as the libs could ever get from this district, but they want 100 percent or nothing."

We are watching two TVs—local coverage and one staying constant on CNN. The latter is now reporting Bernstein's victory over J.D., who "had been beleaguered throughout his campaign about suspicions regarding a possible role in the disappearance of his intern, Saundra Gray." At this point, they could simply say "Saundra," since she is likely the only Saundra anyone in the country other than literary aficionados knows.

Faith can see that J.D. is drinking too much, and she gives me the signal that it is time for us all to leave. I touch his shoulder as I rise, and he gives me a grateful look. An "I told you so" about being more open about Saundra would be out of line. He knows I was right. And I know if he had to do it over, he wouldn't play it any other way. And the revelation about the abortion would have been fatal anyway.

As I get up to leave, I wonder how the Grays would be able to keep the pressure on with the loss of J.D. as a target. There would be no more resources coming from the right or the left. Both have achieved their objective. Indeed, one could easily predict that, after a splash of news stories immediately following J.D.'s defeat, the public's Saundra obsession will recede into the chaotic fog of what seems to be turning into a twenty-four-hour news cycle in the media.

As I am the last of the group to leave, J.D. calls out to me when I reach the door and beckons me back. He stares at me for a long time without saying anything. I am wondering if he is about to slip into an alcoholic slumber when he finally speaks.

"I want you to know that I will make this right."

"Huh, J.D., what do you mean? You don't owe me anything."

He smiles in the pedagogic way he always does when he thinks I am clueless.

"I'm not talking about you."

As I start to ask for more, he waves me off and bids me good night.

# PART FOUR

A few years ago, with little more public notice than a few obligatory obituaries, former Iowa Democratic Congressman J.D. Clay's life came to a violent end that remains shrouded in mystery. He had served in Congress from 1981 to 1991 and had many great legislative accomplishments, but that's not what the obituaries immediately gravitated toward.

Rather, it was his central role in the media-fed public frenzy surrounding the disappearance of a young intern in the nation's capital—a situation in which he was initially suspected of playing some role. Her body was eventually found, and the perpetrator was identified by circumstantial evidence following his suicide. But this was revealed too late for Clay, well after defeat in his primary. Though Clay was exonerated, those headlines were much smaller and nowhere near the front page. So, most people probably remember him as being guilty of the crime or having some direct connection to it.

country—one who rises above partisan rhetoric in order to accomplish something, even if it means compromising. He did this on numerous occasions, whether the issue involved employment protections, environmental restrictions, regulation of large corporations, or any number of other areas where partisanship can paralyze needed action.

But now I have to ask myself: Did my genuine admiration for Clay prevent me from performing my role as a journalist with the right degree of probity and skepticism? Perhaps.

Recent events caused me to do a little quiet digging into what Clay's real role was and what I have learned is both disturbing and embarrassing.

First, let me make it clear that I have learned nothing that leads me to suspect Clay of either committing or conspiring in the murder of Saundra Gray. There is nothing connecting Clay with her murderer and my presumption of innocence still holds.

## FORTY-ONE

# A BELATED EXONERATION (OF SORTS)

**Wally North**

*January 1991*

They finally found Saundra's body on a cold Thursday in early January when a hiker's dog insisted on lunging through a gap in a fence at the base of the Roosevelt Bridge on Teddy Roosevelt Island. Her badly decomposed body was lying under the brush far enough off the path that it could have easily escaped detection for several more months or years, maybe forever.

Even if the body had not been found the very same day the United States launched Operation Desert Storm against Saddam Hussein, it's doubtful it would have received much notice from anyone other than the Grays, myself, J.D., and the northwest Iowa press. Even Bebe Walker has moved on. Another reporter covered the story for the *Post*, noting the J.D. connection for anyone who bothered to read the story, which at least made the first page of the Metro section.

Congressman Riggins had been sworn in two weeks earlier. I assume he had contacted the Gray family, as J.D. would have in similar circumstances. Though I vacated my role as AA when the new Congress arrived, I got the word out to the other former Clay staffers on the memorial service for Saundra. Though we all wanted to forget the sordid events of last year, she was still a colleague. Some attended the service, while most sent flowers or donations in lieu of attending. Though J.D. and Faith did not attend, I decided to. After a look of mild surprise on Dr. Gray's face from a distance,

I received a slight nod of acknowledgment. Mrs. Gray turned her glance away immediately. I avoided the receiving line, wondering why I had bothered to attend. Maybe expecting some sort of closure, but that seemed more obtainable for them than me.

The autopsy determined she had been strangled after receiving a gash on the forehead. They reported the decomposition was consistent with the date of her disappearance last March. After the spectacle of Rock Creek Park, a lot of us wondered why no one—the police especially—had speculated that a run in the park could easily be extended to the island. It just didn't occur to anyone.

The Grays were quoted in the press as expressing grief and hoping the quest for justice in Saundra's death would be revived, without mentioning J.D. As it turned out, the only thing the police had to go on was a bloody glove that had been discarded near the body. The glove was too large for Saundra, and there were fingerprints that reportedly didn't match anyone in the database. Trying to track down where the glove had been purchased was apparently too big a leap for the police. Chief Sharp said all the right things, but he knew, with everything else going on in the world, there would be little pressure for him to deliver. The body had been found, and the circumstances suggested a random assault.

J.D., in the process of starting a new career in the private sector, has refused to comment to the few reporters who have contacted him beyond expressing condolences to the family. He knew any sour grapes about now-disproven suspicions would not be helpful in restoring his reputation. Absent some additional evidence of a connection between J.D. and Saundra's assailant, few are likely to speculate publicly on any culpability on his part, especially since there is no longer any political gain for his adversaries. And I guess I'll never know what that deleted phone message was about.

One week after the memorial service, while the news world was obsessed with the daily maneuverings of the coalition troops in Iraq, a Ukrainian immigrant was found dead of an apparent suicide by a self-inflicted gunshot wound in a Northeast DC apartment. The gun was fingerprinted, and the prints matched those found on the glove.

Despite the war sucking the air out of most other news, the mysterious Ukrainian immigrant who had apparently murdered Saundra Gray received modest attention from the *Post* and other papers, along with a brief mention on CNN and the nightly news programs. But none of these matched the headlines from the previous spring. With very little fanfare, they did obligingly mention that this brings the sad story to its conclusion with a "likely" exoneration of former Congressman J.D. Clay.

Meanwhile, my search for a new job in DC continues. Gloria and I are so ready to turn the page.

FORTY-TWO

# RECOGNITION

**Isaiah Stone**

*February 1993*

## An Unsung Hero in the Family Leave Victory

by Isaiah Stone

The Reagan–Bush era has officially ended. There was much to celebrate this week when, in one of his first significant acts, President Clinton signed the Family and Medical Leave Act, giving job protection to millions of Americans who otherwise would have to choose between their job and their family. With this, the United States now joins most of the rest of the world in providing this protection, even though it still stands apart by not requiring that the leave be paid. Well, that's unfinished business for another day and another Congress.

As with any other success, there were many fathers engaging in self-heralding, from the president down to congressional leadership and the original sponsors. There were even a few Republicans claiming credit, despite their party's long-standing resistance to any new employment protections. Well, the Republicans can take some credit for not using the filibuster to pin the bill down in the Senate. Better late than never, one may suppose.

Yet, amid all the chest-beating and back-slapping, there was one forgotten figure who should get some measure of credit. Remember former Congressman J.D. Clay from Iowa? Oh yeah, that's the guy who lost his seat after a scandal involving a murdered intern with whom he was having an alleged affair. Didn't he also run for president at one point? That's pretty much anything anyone will remember, unless they also remember that he was a decorated Vietnam vet who was also a one-hit wonder on the pop charts after coming home.

A few may vaguely recall that he was eventually exonerated on the murder suspicion after the real culprit was found dead of an apparent suicide. We may never know whether Clay was actually having an affair with the intern, but the benefit of the doubt and presumption of innocence is rarely granted to high-profile politicians in such instances. Maybe deservedly, given all the perks that go with the job. And when was the last time a politician gave anyone else the benefit of the doubt if there was a chance to gain some headlines by beating up on some poor government bureaucrat for not being perfect?

Well, before you relegate Clay to the back bins of your cerebellum, there is one more piece to add to the Clay file. Without him, the Family and Medical Leave Act may never have become law. Don't try to go back to old *New York Times* and *Washington Post* articles to see how, because you won't find it there.

In 1990, when the liberal interest groups were pushing a huge boulder up a hill to get the bill considered on the House floor, there were a lot of moderate Democrats—let alone pretty much every Republican—who were very concerned about its impact on their small businesses. Given the stress of operating a small business with a small number of employees to begin with, it was not unreasonable to be concerned about how they would deal with the twelve-week absence of a key employee whom they would be barred from replacing.

The liberal groups were adamant. The clerk in a dry-cleaning shop needed the bill's protections every bit as much as a factory worker on a one-hundred-employee assembly line. They were not going to budge, and they threatened any Democrat who stood in their way with a primary challenge from a purer liberal.

Someone who understood that bills become law as much through compromise as harsh rhetoric and threats needed to stand up to them, but few were willing to engage. Maybe it took a war hero—and that's exactly what Clay did in an act of political heroism. The leader of a group of moderate Democrats known as the Burnt Toast Coalition, informed the bill's supporters that his backing was contingent on capping the number of employees at covered employers at fifty.

Those supporters howled and screamed, threatening to go after him in his next primary if he stood his ground. For several weeks, there was a pitched battle between the two sides, with all the bill's sponsors standing with the interest groups and moderate Democrats quietly urging Clay on while keeping their mouths shut.

As it turned out, Clay's closest ally in this was not those moderate Democrats but the very astute Speaker O'Connor, who resolved the matter by telling the House Education and Labor Committee that he would not schedule the bill for a floor vote unless they went along with Clay's demand.

The rest is celebrated history. The Democratic House and Senate passed the bill that year with the Clay limitation, but it would have to wait for a Democratic president for it to become law. In fact, many view George Bush's veto of the bill (twice) as one of many factors that doomed his futile quest for a second term.

As President Clinton launches his administration with a solid Democratic Congress, one would hope that there will be more legislators cut from the same cloth as Clay. He has now returned to his hometown of Mitoka and may be wishing he had never left. It's too bad. Washington could still use his uncanny abilities as a legislative strategist. If Clinton doesn't find a few of these up on Capitol Hill to help him with his agenda, the Family and Medical Leave Act, signed within weeks of his inauguration, may very well be one of his last major legislative accomplishments.

FORTY-THREE

# A FAVOR SOUGHT

**Ray Collins**

*June 2000*

"Mr. Collins, there's a Mr. Clay on the line."

I'm right in the middle of reviewing a brief. Does this have to be now?

"Mr. Clay? Did he say what it was regarding?"

"It's a Mr. J.D. Clay. He says he knows you."

I tell her to let him through.

"Wow, Congressman Clay. I haven't heard your name since, well . . ." I stammer.

He interrupts. "I know, Ray. It's okay. How about 'the debacle'? And call me J.D."

"Well, that's kind of hard after all those years of deference. On committee staff, we were sternly admonished by the staff director to call you guys 'congressman' or 'mister,' but I'll try. How in the world are you doing? Do you still have all those drugstores out there?"

J.D. Clay had always been one of my favorite members of the House Judiciary Committee—one of the few nonlawyers to serve there. We all took the scandal and his demise very hard, figuring he was innocent of Gray's disappearance, which turned out to be the case, though too late for his political survival.

"Oh, I let Faith handle that. The kids have just started their own careers and didn't even stay in Mitoka, so I guess she'll keep doing it for a while.

Mitoka isn't doing any better than any other small town in this part of the world in keeping its youth. I stay busy. I head up the local chamber and do some occasional political consulting. How about you?"

"Well, I guess you were able to track me down here at Justice. I came over from the Hill and am hoping after the election I'll be able to stay, assuming Gore wins. It's been a good gig. Not lucrative enough, according to my wife, but I won't be here forever. Assistant attorney general is not a bad thing to have on your résumé. By the way, do you stay in touch with Wally North? When I was AA for Congressman Coulouris before he moved me over to Judiciary, we got to be good friends."

"Oh yeah, Wally's doing fine downtown. I was so glad he was able to land on his feet. He was basically my guardian angel through a really rough period."

I expect him to continue, but there is a long silence. Guess I need to prompt him.

"What can I do for you, Mr. Clay—er—J.D.?"

I can hear him coughing and taking a couple of deep breaths. Finally, he starts quietly.

"Ray, this is not easy for me, and I may be taking a big risk. But hopefully by coming to you, I can get something done that should have been done a long time ago. As you might imagine, there was a lot more to Saundra's death than anyone knows, including the authorities. You may not be the right person to contact, but hopefully you can do something or at least point me in the right direction to someone who can."

When you work on Capitol Hill, it becomes ingrained in your DNA to try to be helpful to members of Congress of either party, even after their terms are over. I was once in an airport when I saw a senator standing next to a gift shop, looking a bit lost. I was a House staffer, and he was a conservative Republican whose politics I abhorred. Yet, I didn't think twice about asking him if I could help somehow. He was very appreciative and said he was fine, and I moved on. That's just what you do. So, of course,

I'll try to help Mr. Clay.

"Sure, J.D. It's been almost ten years since it happened, so may I ask, why now? You don't have to tell me. I'm just curious."

"No, that's fine. It's just that there could be some risk to me by coming forward. While the kids were still at home, I didn't want to take that risk for their sakes. Now they're gone, and Faith and I just have to take the risk. There was more than just the guy who presumably murdered Saundra. And, for her sake, I want to see justice done."

He tells me what he knows.

"Okay, thanks, J.D. Wow, that's pretty alarming, and I can see why you would want to do something about it. I think you came to the right person. Let me think about this for a bit and decide who could help. I can't make any promises, but I'll try to keep this as discreet as possible. You may have to take a deposition at some point and sign an affidavit, but I'll do whatever I can to protect you."

"Thank you," J.D. says simply. It sounds like he could be on the verge of tears, so I bring it to a close quickly before he breaks up.

After hanging up, I excuse myself from the office and head down to the third floor to a little-used pay phone. After dialing the number I had been given, a voice with a thick accent answers.

"I need Starr to call me right away at the following number." I give them the number on the phone.

## FORTY-FOUR

# J.D.'S FUNERAL

**Isaiah Stone**

*August 2000*

It has been eighteen years since I was last in Mitoka. It was when I wrote the profile of J.D. for the *Padua Patriot*. I guess I'm closing the loop by coming back for his funeral after the shocking news of his murder. Admittedly, I'm here out of curiosity as much as anything, but I keep telling myself I would have come out of respect, anyway. And maybe there's a story.

I now realize I have been ensconced in the Washington scene for so long, I have completely forgotten how small towns embrace the staid traditions that help maintain the stability and predictability that keep their denizens satisfied with rural life. Funerals are one of those. The dark suits and dresses I am surrounded by could just as easily have been worn to services thirty years earlier—and probably were. They had likely been bought for a single purpose, with only an expanding waistline requiring an occasional new purchase.

The brown stone façade of the Methodist church is comforting even to a nonresident like me. At times like this, I regret that the inherent skepticism that has made me such a successful journalist has also bred uncertainty as to any kind of afterlife.

It seems that J.D.'s funeral has brought out many of the town's citizens who have long since forgiven him of any indiscretions. But their devotion to Faith is obvious as well, as she tirelessly takes hugs and kisses from her wheelchair. Though we've never met, I paid my own respects to her, and she expressed appreciation for my laudatory articles about J.D. I am impressed with how Faith maintained her stoicism throughout what has to have been an excruciating ordeal. I wonder if her own brush with a violent death years before provided any preparation for this.

One of the residents told me Faith continued to run the pharmacy business, which had expanded to thirty locations throughout northwest Iowa and is a constant target of acquisition by the larger chains. She has resisted those efforts, knowing it would sever the communal and cultural connections that can only come with a locally owned business.

After the ceremony, I catch up with Wally North, J.D.'s loyal AA, who is still in DC working with an agricultural trade association. He fills in the blanks on all that has transpired since J.D. lost the primary in 1990. I knew that J.D. had returned to Mitoka and had been extensively involved in the community, including a stint as the president of the local Chamber of Commerce. As an astute former politician, J.D. also maintained a decent business as a political consultant for various candidates at the state and local levels. Bearing no grudges for getting dumped in 1990, he still had strong Democratic ties, but he was willing to help centrist Republicans as well.

I ask Wally if he knows anything about what happened to J.D.

"I'm not sure I know anything more than what has been in the papers. Someone told me he was a regular at the chamber conferences, and I'm not sure the stories picked up that he had actually been on a panel that afternoon in Chicago. Just headed back up to his room after dinner and was found the next morning strangled to death, but I assume you knew that."

"I did. Still no suspects or apparent motive, I assume? When he was in Congress, were you aware of any enemies that could have been motivated to do this?"

He pauses and looks me straight in the eyes when he answers, "Absolutely not." A bit too forcefully, it seems. And then he offers nothing else and makes an excuse about having to say hi to a former donor. I guess seeing me must have brought back some dark memories (as if the entire day wouldn't be doing that).

You could feel the shock of J.D.'s murder among the townspeople. Violent crime in small towns like Mitoka is typically limited to drunk-driving hit-and-runs and brawls. A townsperson being murdered in a distant city is probably unprecedented here. The whole event is scored by a soft undercurrent of sobs among family members and close friends. From my own interactions with J.D., I am not at all surprised that there are a lot of the latter.

Meanwhile, during the service I couldn't help noticing a raven-haired woman in her mid-thirties whose beauty was shrouded by a scarf, sunglasses, and modest attire. It is only after she is detained by several of the women for her autograph after the service that I realize it is the famous actress Naomi Bridges. She is one of those rare actors, like Sophia Loren and Laurence Olivier, whose art transcends their physical magnificence.

Born Naomi Bridgewater, she has also become a bit of a folk hero after the publication of a profile a couple of years ago, which included an account of her mother, a destitute widow in Appalachia who kept the family going as a local prostitute. Naomi then attended a small college nearby on a scholarship and completed two years of law school in Washington before leaving for Hollywood. In the interview, she shared an impassioned defense of sex workers, using her mother's desperation as a justification. Her honesty was risky, but it resulted in a strong following that pushed her box office success even higher.

Since then, there have been rumors about her taking up her mom's profession to get herself through law school, but she has never addressed them. Her many fans have dismissed those rumors as either completely baseless or irrelevant to an inspiring story of a courageous woman who rose above her origins. To me, the titillating rumors take a back seat to her acting talent, which has garnered her three Oscar nominations and a name that can sell a movie on its own.

But why the hell is she in Mitoka for J.D.'s funeral? I watch as she graciously extracts herself from the various well-wishers and ducks into a limousine that will probably never see the likes of Mitoka again.

Is there a story here? Even if there isn't, I would love to know the connection.

## FORTY-FIVE

# A CALL WITH NAOMI

**Isaiah Stone**

*August 2000*

I am pleasantly surprised when Naomi Bridges answers on the first ring. It's been a week since the memorial service, and I've had a hard time containing my curiosity. I was able to use my contacts to get ahold of her agent, who got back to me quickly with her number after checking with her first.

"Ms. Bridges, thank you so much for taking my call," I say, trying to control my enthusiasm. Even though we are surrounded by famous people in the political realm, I am like most Washingtonians in almost completely blowing my cool around movie stars and sports figures. Perhaps because we came to DC because of the allure of fame, then once we got here we discovered they are all just other humans. We still have that longing for the mythical, so we find it elsewhere.

"Call me Naomi. My agent knows I'm not usually this easy for reporters, but I generally don't turn down Pulitzer Prize winners. From my days in Washington, I'm still a bit of a political junkie and have read a couple of your books. *The Muddled Middle* was one of my favorites."

"That's surprising. I've never seen your name listed among the various Hollywood illuminati who have a high political profile."

When she chuckles at this on the other end of the line, my mind envisions the warm, engaging smile that has adorned so many movie screens.

"Well, that's probably because I am well to the right of them," she admits. "Actually, I'm an independent—pretty much in the middle, maybe even to the left, but to them I would be a fascist. I do have some strong opinions, but, unlike many of my colleagues, I don't really feel like my profession qualifies me to express them publicly."

Since her positioning with her peers is not all that dissimilar from mine, this acknowledgment is refreshing to hear.

"So, I do have to get to a shoot. What can I help you with, Mr. Stone?"

"Actually, you probably wouldn't recognize me by sight, but I did see you at the memorial service for J.D. Clay."

There is a brief moment of silence. Her voice drops to a near whisper.

"Yes, that was very sad. I was an admirer of his."

"As was I. Unfortunately, most people still remember him from the Gray situation if they remember him at all."

Another pause.

"Yes, that was sad also. I'm afraid he was one of the last of a dying breed who embraced realistic solutions from the middle, which made him vulnerable to attacks from the extremes. It didn't take long for the long knives to come out when that story broke."

There is a longer silence. She breaks it.

"So, what did you want to talk about?"

"Well, I guess there's an obvious question. Unless you coincidentally were filming somewhere in the middle of Iowa, why would you travel all the way to Mitoka for his memorial service?"

"Mr. Stone . . ."

"If I get to call you Naomi, you certainly should call me Isaiah."

"Isaiah, are you wanting to interview me for an article you're writing? I really don't have much to say."

"Actually, no. It's really more out of curiosity than anything. I assume whatever we would talk about could be completely off the record, unless you want it to be otherwise. I have a pretty good reputation for that if you want to check me out before we go any further."

"No need. I trust you."

Silence.

"Totally off the record, right?" she asks.

"Absolutely."

"Let's just say, he and I had a brief but very close relationship while I was a student at George Washington Law School."

"Okay."

"I assume you are aware of the rumors about how I worked my way through law school."

"Well, yes, but I've never really given them much credence, and, even if they were true, I really don't think it matters given all you have accomplished. If they are true, I think I admire you even more."

"Well, I don't know about that. The truth is I've never publicly acknowledged it, but informally with friends—and I hope we can be that—I've never denied it. The fact is, he was one of my customers."

Her admission is stunning. J.D. Clay was a charismatic, attractive figure combined with the allure of power that any congressman would have. Why would he need to hire a woman for sex? It also makes an affair with Saundra seem less likely.

"Okay. Wow. Well, I guess that explains the connection, but I assume you wouldn't normally go to a memorial service for one of your . . . customers."

"No, most of them were real creeps, actually. But not him. He was a dear, dear man, and we grew very close for a period of time. If you want to know how considerate he was, I can tell you one other thing."

"Okay."

"We stopped sleeping together but continued our encounters."

"For a long period of time?"

"Yes, we only slept together very early on and not many times. He didn't want to after that. It wasn't because he wasn't attracted to me.

Actually, I was probably just as attracted to him. He said he had entered into the arrangement with the service I worked for to satisfy his needs without having an affair. You know about his wife? He employed the service after her injury. When he started falling in love with me, which was against an agreement he'd had with his wife, he thought that he would then truly be cheating on her—and he loved her very much. So, he insisted on keeping it platonic, if that expression would still apply."

"So, by not sleeping with you, he was not having an affair, even though you both loved each other. Seems like kind of a tortured logic, doesn't it?"

"Yes, and I tried explaining that to him. Does an affair have to include sex to be an affair? Or can it be from a deep attachment that has everything else? I'm not sure I know the answer, but there was some attraction between us, and there were times where it was hard to remain physically separate. And, by the way, he kept paying me, though I'm not sure where that money came from."

My head is spinning. This sounds like one of her movies. But I had always thought of J.D. as a very principled person, and this does somehow fit. In a very bizarre way.

"So how did it end?"

"Well, it ended right around the time of Saundra's disappearance. I just never heard anything more from him after the news exploded. Obviously, he had to be careful at that point. I mean, he was obviously being followed by reporters. That was also about the same time I had decided to ditch law school and take my chances in Hollywood. I had recently been in some DC productions and was getting rave reviews and a lot of encouragement from the local theater folks. As it turned out, I made the right decision, obviously."

"Obviously. Did you ever reconnect with J.D.?"

"Never. I would have loved to do so, but I didn't want to complicate things with his family. I think if his wife had preceded him in death, I might have tried, but it wasn't meant to be. It's just as well. He loved her deeply. Which, as I say, was why he wanted to stay just friends. I know it is difficult to understand, but love can be complicated."

"Well, no matter how well disguised you were, I would assume his widow found out you were in attendance. Pretty small town."

"Oh, I figured that. I didn't connect with her there, but I sent a large donation in his name to the Vietnam veterans' charity they designated and sent her a note a couple of days later telling her he was one of the few politicians that I always admired. She may or may not believe that's why, but, based on my understanding of their relationship, she may also figure it out. That's fine. That's what she can tell others if they ask. I just felt I had to be there. Second only to my mother, I give him credit for helping me believe in myself at a very critical juncture in my life. I will always be grateful to him for that."

I let it soak in. Then the reporter in me speaks up.

"Can I ask one last question? Did you ever get any insight on Saundra from him?"

A slight sigh as she delays her response. Is it a hard question, or is she avoiding something?

"None whatsoever. I assumed like everyone else that he probably was having an affair with her. He certainly wasn't getting any physical fulfillment from me. But, like I say, after all that broke, I never saw or heard from him again. I read they found the body and the guy who did it, so I guess that's that. Really a tragedy that such a promising political career was cut short by that. He would have made a great president, even though he would never have been nominated."

"Agree. But maybe a cabinet position in the Clinton administration. He would have fit right in with the moderate image Clinton tries to convey."

"Maybe. And I'm guessing a lot of the Democrats would have finally forgiven him for what he did after they had to forgive Clinton."

Clearly, I'm not going to get anything more on J.D., but I'm reluctant to let this go.

"So, Naomi, what's next for you?"

"Well, right now I'm shooting a movie that we hope opens this fall in time for the Oscar nominations. I play the oldest daughter of a stern and righteous minister who is having to break the news to him and the rest of the family that she is gay. That's a new one for me. I love the part, and maybe I have another shot at some metal. We'll see."

"I look forward to it. This has been enjoyable and a real honor just to speak with you. And it's completely off the record."

"Oh, the honor is mine, Isaiah. Keep up the good work."

FORTY-SIX

# AN OBITUARY

**Washington Post**

*September 2013*

## Solomiya Kovalenko, restauranteur

Solomiya Kovalenko, seventy-six, owner of several successful Washington restaurants, died September 8 at her home in Great Falls, Virginia. The cause of death was a brain aneurysm, according to her son, Andriy Kovalenko.

Known to many of her friends as "Starr," Kovalenko opened several gourmet cuisine restaurants in the Washington area, including Cervantes (Dumfries), Bocaccio (Beltsville), and Petrarch (Lorton). Her upscale restaurants, named after famous writers, were noteworthy for their locations in modest areas, while drawing affluent patrons through reputation and quality.

A native of Ukraine born in Kiev, Kovalenko served in the Soviet Ministry of Arts before defecting in 1974 with her son Andriy. Her husband, a prominent member of the Soviet Party, disappeared soon thereafter, and she reportedly assumed he was either executed or sent to Siberia. She disclaimed any involvement or awareness by him in her defection until after the fall of the Soviet Union, when she acknowledged that he had assisted her. She never remarried.

Kovalenko established residency in the Washington area with the assistance of American contacts she had made through her work promoting Russian ballet troupes. She became a United States citizen in 1980. She was a benefactor of many other immigrants from Ukraine both during the Soviet era and after Ukraine gained its independence. She was also an active member of the Ukrainian American Society of Northern Virginia, serving as its president in the early 1990s.

Kovalenko is survived by her son, Andriy, her daughter-in-law, Maria Sloane, and three grandchildren.

## FORTY-SEVEN

# AN EXPOSÉ

**Wally North**

*February 2014*

The sunlight streaming through the thin curtains of my den feels harsh, almost accusatory, as I settle into my worn armchair with the morning paper. It's been years—decades, even—since I've felt this kind of tension coil through my chest. I unfold the *Washington Post* carefully, the smell of newsprint mingling with the faint aroma of coffee growing cold on the side table.

And there it is.

Five months after Solomiya Kovalenko's death, the story breaks. It's plastered across the page, complete with a grainy photo of Kovalenko from her younger days, captioned with her alias: Starr Fox. The exposé on the prostitution ring she led feels like a grenade tossed into my lap, and I fight the instinct to shove the paper away as if it might explode.

My hands tighten around the edges of the paper, creasing it. The words blur momentarily, but I blink hard and focus, willing myself to keep reading.

The story details everything: a network of enforcers, veiled threats, whispers of assassinations tied to the operation. *How has this stayed buried for so long?* Kovalenko's iron-fisted control, her reliance on young Ukrainian immigrants to police the ring, the disappearances—it all feels so painfully familiar.

I lean back, the chair groaning beneath me, as a sick twist of nausea curls in my stomach. My jaw clenches when I reach the line about members of Congress—clients of Kovalenko's operation. I trace the words with my eyes over and over, trying to convince myself they don't mean what I know they mean.

No names. Not yet.

But the omission of certain names is almost worse. There's no mention of Saundra or the Ukrainian man who "committed suicide" after her body was found. That silence feels deliberate, as if those details are waiting for someone to notice them. My chest tightens at the thought. *How long before the connection is made? How long before someone puts it all together?*

The air feels heavier, pressing down on my chest. There's nothing specific in the story that could tie back to me, but the unease is unmistakable. The article mentions the reporter's wife, one of Kovalenko's former workers, who had stepped forward to break the silence. Her bravery—or recklessness, depending on how you see it—lit the fuse for this revelation. And now, one by one, others are talking. It's only a matter of time before someone digs deeper. Before they find the threads. Before they find me.

I shift uncomfortably, a dull ache gnawing at my side. It's been months since the doctor's words settled like lead in my chest. "It's aggressive," he'd said. "We'll need to monitor it closely." He didn't have to explain. I'd seen the scans. The tumor, lurking deep in my abdomen, wasn't going to wait for me to sort out my life. It's growing fast, faster than I'd care to admit. Some days, I can almost pretend it's not there—until moments like this, when fear or stress twists the pain into something undeniable.

I press a hand to my side, but the ache in my gut feels like more than the tumor. It's the same gnawing fear I felt all those years ago, back when J.D. and I thought we could outrun this mess.

The noose is tightening again. I can feel it, even here in the supposed safety of my home.

I reach for my coffee, now stone cold, and take a sip anyway, my gaze drifting back to the article. The headline glares back at me, daring me to look away. But I don't. I can't. Not anymore.

## FORTY-EIGHT

# JUDY TALKS

**Isaiah Stone**

*March 2014*

During a long weekend at my beach house, I've been trying to disconnect from the outside world, letting Robert Penn Warren and Scott Turow provide my only company. Still, I've kept an eye on my personal email but just realized I've neglected to check the official account (istone@Register) listed at the end of my columns.

Being an editorial account, I don't monitor it closely or regularly. It is typically filled with the usual rants from readers on both ends of the spectrum. But it does include an occasional compliment from a centrist who welcomes my independence from the party line on either side. Those are my true fans, so I diligently respond to them. I once wrote that a centrist is someone who doesn't let someone else do their thinking for them. That column, in turn, generated both warmth and heat.

Not surprisingly, the official @Register inbox is full. I start deleting large chunks, but notice there are several emails from a Judy Carricutt, one each of the previous five days, the most recent being this morning. I go right to the last one, which notes with urgency that she wants to speak to me, giving me her cell number. I hate to give in to what is likely mere stalking. If it is, I can cut it off quickly and block further emails from that address.

My call goes into her voicemail, but she returns the call within fifteen minutes.

"Mr. Stone."

"Yes. Ms. Carricutt?"

"Yes. I appreciate you finally getting back to me. I work here in DC, and I thought an experience I had a few years ago would be of interest to you. In fact, I was thinking you might even want to pursue a story on it."

It isn't the first time I've received such a lead. Even on the rare occasion when they aren't wildly improbable, they almost invariably lead to a wild goose chase. Not always, though. So, I ask her to continue.

"It's been a while since I have read any of your articles, but I do recall back in the nineties you were following the J.D. Clay scandal involving his missing intern, Saundra Gray."

"That's correct. I think I've only written one thing on it since it faded from view. I was following his career fairly closely, since my first job was with a small Iowa paper near his hometown. Very tragic how things ended up for him. And it looks like another one of those crimes that may never get solved."

"Yes, very tragic. I do remember you writing some positive articles about him. I'm from Iowa myself, and I actually worked for him for a while."

Maybe not a wild goose chase after all.

"Oh, okay. I always heard he was good to work for. Were you still working for him when he lost in the primary?"

"Actually, no. I had left some time earlier. Yes, some people who worked for him were happy, but it just didn't work out for me."

"Sorry to hear that."

"Well, let's just say we didn't see eye to eye. I thought for a Democrat, he was way too willing to compromise our principles."

Her voice is quavering. *Nervousness or stifled anger? Could be either.*

"I know a lot of people felt that way," I acknowledge, "but I actually admired his pragmatism."

"Yes, I know. You were a big cheerleader for him."

This sounds more like an accusation than a statement of fact. I'm used to being badgered from either side.

"If you are challenging my objectivity, I'm going to have to protest. I actually think far too many of my colleagues in the press take sides and portray those whose positions they agree with as heroes and vice versa. I think that is a betrayal of journalistic principles. Regardless of whether I agreed with him or not, I saw him as someone who was just trying to do the job of legislating rather than posturing. And I think he was quite successful at that until the scandal broke."

"So, you just admitted you were a fan."

Touché. I'm not dealing with a dummy.

"Okay, I guess I did," I reluctantly admit. "Look, you are perfectly free to read or not read my columns. And I'm now in a position where I get to freely express my views via my opinion pieces, which are actually pretty widely read."

I regret being so thin-skinned but much prefer getting back to the Turow novel over getting into it with a critic.

"I really need to get started on my column. Is there something specific you wanted to discuss?"

"There is. And it's about Clay . . . There's more to the story than he ever let on."

Here comes the usual accusation. I'll head her off right away.

"Oh, I think most everyone assumed he was having the affair with Saundra. Some may argue he should have come clean on that. It may have given him more credibility on denying any connection with her disappearance. And, as it turned out, once her body was found and the culprit identified, most people assumed there was no connection. Case dismissed."

"But there was a connection. That's what I'm calling about."

My breath quickens at her statement, and I try to steady it. Silence at the other end while she lets me think this through. It is obviously coming from a biased source, but it seems unlikely she would take the trouble to track me down if there was nothing of substance to report. The old question comes back immediately to haunt me: *Was I naïve in sticking up for Clay?*

"I'm all ears. But, first, how would you know?"

"Saundra and I became very good friends while we worked together in his office. We stayed in touch after I left, and I actually tried to help her out with something."

"Before you go any farther, I have to ask, is this on the record?"

"I don't really care. You are going to see it as hearsay, but if you decide to write it, I'm fine with being identified. Enough time has passed."

Typically, someone deliberately giving a false lead would want to go off the record. However disagreeable this woman is, there may be some legitimacy to her story.

"So, before we go any further, why now?" I ask. "Shouldn't you have come forward back then?"

"Not if I valued my life."

"Are you suggesting Clay would have harmed you?"

"No. But he was involved in something that would."

This is not going to be a simple story. I take a deep breath and grab pen and paper. She likely heard me do this. Anyone who ever dealt with a reporter knows this is not done merely out of politeness.

"Let's start at the beginning."

"Well, actually, let's start more recently. I'm sure you saw the article last week in the *Post* about the Starr Fox prostitution ring."

"Of course. It's been the talk of the town."

"Did it occur to you that Clay may have been one of those customers?"

"Not really, but I wasn't ruling anyone out. I know that he had a disabled wife, so I guess that could make him seek other outlets. Though I'm not sure where he would have gotten the money. Those were some pretty expensive prices quoted. But if you are suggesting any of our readers would have any interest in a former congressman employing a prostitute twenty-five years ago while in office, I doubt you have ever read the *Register*."

"Oh, it's more than that, I can assure you. Did you not also recall when you saw that exposé that the guy they ultimately pegged with Saundra's murder was a Ukrainian immigrant?"

Indeed, I hadn't. Could be a coincidence, but it did seem strange.

"Are you suggesting Saundra was one of the girls they were using for the ring? She was a very attractive young aspiring professional, so she would fit the mold."

"No, she definitely wasn't. For one thing, those girls needed money, and Saundra clearly didn't. But that's where I can fill you in. And maybe you can do a little investigating based on what I tell you, unless you think Clay was such a saint that even being responsible for a person's murder is excusable."

I draw in a sharp breath, again too audible. "You're suggesting, then, that he had her murdered?"

"I didn't say that. I said he was responsible."

"Okay, you better explain to me the distinction."

She clears her throat. "First, she was not only having an affair with him, but, according to her, he told her he was going to leave his wife for her."

"Did you believe her?"

"Honestly, I wasn't sure, but what I thought didn't matter. I knew Saundra well enough to know she could talk herself into almost anything if she was fixated on it. She came to DC not only determined to rise as far as possible but also willing to leverage a romantic relationship if it helped her reach that goal. Look, I am a total feminist, but I can't ignore how some women will use their sex to accomplish their goals. I mean, why would they be any different from men in that regard? Women are human, too."

"Well, that's definitely something a lot of men think but leave unsaid."

"Yes, there are some things neither sex wants to acknowledge about itself. Anyway, regardless of whether he actually said it, she definitely believed he was going to leave his wife. And then he rather suddenly cut her off. I tried to tell her he was nothing more than a Don Juan and to learn her lesson and let it go. But she was the embodiment of the 'woman scorned' cliché. So, she did what a lot of jilted lovers do. She hired a detective."

"That could get expensive."

"Saundra came from a wealthy family, and her parents gave her a very generous allowance. Believe me, she could afford it."

"So, what did she learn?"

"I think he followed Clay to some hideaway where the Fox operation did their services and followed up from there. If the operation was as pervasive as it sounds, I suspect any savvy detective would have been aware of it, so he quickly put two and two together. Saundra told me he had had at least one other client where the same issue came up, so he really didn't have to do much digging. He told Saundra the whole story plus whatever else he knew about the operation."

I wonder if a naïve rich girl would be scared or intrigued by being confronted with DC's sordid side. Or both.

"Did this detective warn her to be careful?"

"I would certainly hope so, but if he did, she didn't heed it."

"So, Clay was seeing a prostitute, and he'd already told Saundra he was done with her. Why isn't that the end of it?"

"With anyone else it would have been, but not Saundra. She had something on J.D. So she decided to confront him with what she knew and threatened to expose him and thereby the entire operation."

I'm trying to imagine how J.D. would respond to such a threat. He had a reputation for not backing down easily on political matters. But he would have to recognize the danger of Saundra going public. And if she was as unbalanced as Judy was implying, he couldn't take it lightly.

"And how did he respond?"

"I don't know. I didn't hear back from her before she disappeared."

That was it? She knew nothing more than that? Clearly not enough for a jury or even an editor whose "reasonable doubt" would not be difficult to surpass.

"You think he had something to do with her murder just because of this?" I ask, trying to avoid any hint of disparagement in my voice. I need her to keep talking.

"Actually, much as I despise the man, I never thought him capable of that. But at the time, I was really scared of the whole situation and feared for my own safety if I said anything. I did ask around with some of my contacts in DC and learned something about the prostitution ring. There was a lot of speculation about it even back then. Some people thought there was some Ukrainian mob connection, too, and that anyone who knew anything about it was afraid to go public with it. When they finally identified the Ukrainian guy as her murderer, that confirmed it for me. I assumed it was the Ukrainian mob behind the whole thing. And the relationship with J.D. certainly was connected, even if he didn't order it."

Everything she says is clearly enough to arouse suspicion of such a connection, but how would the Ukrainians even know she was threatening J.D.? Or maybe they didn't. Or maybe J.D. tipped them off, but I just can't accept that. And it doesn't sound like she does, either. There had to be one more link, but it is clear she doesn't have it.

"Why are you willing to go public now?"

"Well, the whole story is finally out. Sounds like once the queen bee died, the whole thing's been shut down. If anyone's vulnerable to reprisals, it's the *Post* reporter. I'm small potatoes. At this point, I just want to get the truth out about Clay, and I figured I'd start with his strongest defender. I mean, you have won a Pulitzer Prize. Are you going to sit on the truth?"

I don't take the bait.

"At this point, I don't know what the truth is. As you said, a lot of what you've told me is hearsay and, for all we know, Saundra was never able to speak to J.D. Maybe the Ukrainians knew about the detective, and they got to her before she talked to J.D. This is all speculation, and I deal with facts."

"So, you're not going to pursue it?"

Of course, I have no option but to do so. But I'm not going to work with someone clearly out for revenge.

"I have a few places I can check. If I get some additional confirmation, I may. But I'm certainly not going to write a story based on conjecture. Based on what you say, I agree there is more to the story than what has been made public. But, as I said, a deceased member of Congress who was defeated over twenty years ago who also happened to be seeing a prostitute is of itself hardly something worth bringing to my readers."

"Even after all your paeans to him at the time, you don't feel you owe a little contrition to your readers?"

I drop my pencil impatiently and noisily, wishing she could see me do so. I am well aware that I may have been too lenient with J.D., but there is no need to acknowledge that to her.

"Look, my point to my readers, then and now, is that we need people in Congress who are willing to look at each issue on its merits and try to find solutions, not just posturing or scoring partisan points. For any faults he may have had, J.D. Clay is still one of the best examples of that kind of leadership I have ever seen. And I stand by my point that any flaws in his personal life take nothing away from that."

"Even if he was implicated in murder?"

"Of course not, but where's the proof?"

"I suspect if you dig deep enough, you may find that."

"Maybe or maybe not. Thanks for your insights, Ms. Carricutt."

## FORTY-NINE

# RECONNECTING WITH NAOMI

**Isaiah Stone**

*March 2014*

Naomi Bridges answers my call so quickly that I wonder if she had been anticipating it in the wake of the Starr Fox disclosures.

"Mr. Stone."

My name had obviously shown up on her phone, which meant she had saved my contact information.

"Yes, Ms. Bridges . . . er, Naomi, this is Isaiah."

"I figured you'd call at some point."

I've just returned from my beach house and am fully immersed in a story about the mixed congressional reactions to the Russian invasion of Crimea. I find the tepid reaction from the United States and the other NATO countries very frustrating and get the feeling no one is focusing on the long-term impact, as usual. At this point, I wonder if there is even a story I can write. Meanwhile, the conversation with Judy Carricutt has made it hard to concentrate on anything else.

"You heard about the *Washington Post* exposé on the Starr Fox operation?" I ask.

"I read it. And I assume you have guessed correctly that I was part of that. The reporter did a pretty good job as far as he went. Got nothing significant wrong. Obviously, I could have added a lot more, but there was also a lot there I didn't know. After I left DC, I put it completely out of my mind. Except I do have to acknowledge that that work was a pretty good way to hone my acting skills. At least that's what I tell myself." She gives a slight chuckle. "And, by the way, you may not know this, but in Victorian England, the ladies of the night were euphemistically referred to as 'actresses.'"

I tell her about the conversation with Carricutt.

"Yes, I can add to that, if that's what you're looking for. When you and I last spoke, I was probably even more afraid than she was of the Ukrainians. I almost told you the full story, but then I caught myself. I guess, like her, now that it's over, it's time to come clean. I also guess I need to tell you the full story to allay any suspicions you have about J.D.'s involvement in her death. There was an indirect involvement, but if anyone is to blame, it's me."

I hear her swallow and then put down a glass. It occurs to me I interrupted a meal, but she seems fine with it.

"What fault could you possibly have in this?"

"Well, you said the last your contact heard from Saundra was that she was going to confront Clay. She actually did contact him."

Another pause and another swallow. It's still early afternoon in Los Angeles, so I assume it is water or a soda. But maybe not.

"After Saundra approached him, he immediately contacted me through a covert communication system we had set up. He told me she was on to the whole setup and was threatening to blow the whistle on both him and the Fox operation unless he came back to her. I guess she somehow thought that would be an attractive proposition. She was obviously a very deluded individual. But that's when I screwed up."

"How?"

Another swallow. And a very long wait. Is she having second thoughts right as the solution to the mystery is in reach?

"Naomi?"

"Yes, I'm still here. I was just hoping I would never have to face this. After he told me about her threat, I immediately contacted the operation and gave them a heads up. I was thinking more about myself than her. I was trying to cover myself, since they would eventually connect things to me. I assumed they would probably just give her a credible threat and she would back off. Instead, the reaction I got from them sent chills down my spine. I knew they played hardball, but the threats they then gave me about staying silent alerted me that she was probably in grave danger. They were pretty graphic about what they would do to me."

"So, what did you do?"

"I had no way of contacting Saundra, nor did I think that would work. So, I immediately got back to J.D. and told him my fears. He thanked me and told me he was going to warn her. Wanted to get off the phone right away so he could do that. That was the last time we spoke."

"Do you remember what day that was?"

"Of course. How could I forget? It has haunted me ever since. It was the day she disappeared. I don't know whether he ever reached her."

"Whether he did or did not—and maybe it was too late—either way, once she disappeared, he had to know it was connected to him."

Now it is my turn to pause.

"And he clearly decided not to tell the police," I continue. "Had he done so, they might have prevented it, or at least they would have known what they were dealing with, instead of falling back on the protocols. He also would have known that any publicity about his connection would end his political career."

"Right, but consider also who he was dealing with. It was the same as it was for me. I suspect at that point he was probably more concerned about his personal safety and that of his family than he was his political career."

"Probably. But it certainly would have been the heroic thing to do."

I am used to dealing with political heroics, but they rarely have personal consequences beyond losing an election. This would have been a different kind of heroism.

"Yes, neither J.D. nor I was exactly a profile in courage. I struggled with it at the time. On the one hand, I was a great admirer and owed him so much. But then I watched him duck and weave throughout that whole ordeal, saying nothing that could help find out what happened to her. Clearly, that would mean putting himself in danger. I also kept asking myself what I would do in that situation. I still do. The truth is, I didn't come forward either, even though I pretty much knew what had happened to her. At the time, I also had my own career to worry about. So, I'm not a hero here either. Whenever I make a cloak-and-dagger movie, and I've made a few of those, it always brings that whole period back to me."

"Naomi, do you think there could be a connection with his murder?"

"Possibly, I suppose. It was in Chicago, but someone could easily travel there if they didn't already have operations there."

"I understand he was a panelist, so the agenda could have been available publicly. It'd be far easier getting to him discreetly there than in Mitoka. But why? Do you think he finally decided to blow the whistle after all that time and they found out?"

"No idea. Guess we'll never know."

Her long sigh, followed by another swallow, signals both relief and resignation. She asks me what my next move is.

"Well, I assume we still have an off-the-record relationship, and I think I have to honor that."

There is a long silence at the other end.

"You know what? Go ahead and tell it if you want. I'll just leave it with you. I assume the statute of limitations on any criminal culpability by me has long since expired, and I've accomplished everything I want to. If it turns off the studios, so be it. I've made enough to retire. It would be a scandal that would tarnish my name, but maybe that's a price I have to pay for being a coward."

I am somewhat astonished that she would let this go on the record. But I'm still not sure what I would do with it.

"I don't know what I'm going to do. There are a couple more calls I need to make. It is ancient history, and it's not like knowing who Deep Throat was, where there was still a lot of public interest. On the other hand, I really went to the mat for the guy and wonder if I owe a little penance myself."

"Like I said, I'll leave it with you," she says before hanging up. It sounded like she was stifling a sob, so I don't take the hasty dismissal personally.

## FIFTY

# CAM FIGG

**Isaiah Stone**

*March 2014*

Before taking things further, I decide to see if I can get ahold of the *Washington Post* reporter who broke the story about the Starr Fox operation. Other than for social purposes, I rarely call other reporters because of the awkwardness of protecting sources and general territorial suspicions. But when I do, there are ground rules, and I usually try to be completely up front about my interest. However, when it comes to J.D.'s case, I need to be more than a little indirect.

I have little trouble connecting with Cam "Porky" Figg, the reporter who did the exposé. I'd never met him until now, but I knew of him before the article and that he had acquired his nickname through some heft. I assume since Figg has let the nickname stick, he has a manageable ego with a sense of humor.

I start by congratulating him on the story.

"Well, thanks," he says graciously. "Coming from you, that means a lot. I've always been an admirer, and you are certainly one of the deans on the political beat."

"Well, longevity has its rewards, I guess."

Given Figg's receptivity, I decide not to jump right in but instead to ask him about his own background. He is more than happy to talk about himself but finally asks why I called.

"Your story intrigued me. The time frame obviously covers a lot of familiar ground for me, especially the implication of members of Congress, some of whom I remember well. So, what's next? Are you expecting some criminal investigations to follow?"

"Sounds like it. I've already been called by various authorities, but I have to protect my sources, of course. My guess is they will try to focus on those currently in office or still active in DC. I assume they'll start with women who participated in the operation and get some immunity deals going. That's where they wanted help from me. I couldn't really do anything for them, but I did suggest my wife since they were kind enough to ask me before contacting her directly. She's going to be cooperative, but it's been quite a while since she worked for them. Maybe some of those folks will come forward on their own, but it certainly wouldn't help their reputations."

"Are you going to do any follow-up stories?"

He chuckles, even though nothing funny had been said. This irrelevant response is common in DC as an endearment ploy that can be a failed device if used too often. This was the third chuckle from Figg, so it seems to have become a tic, even though it fits the jolly temperament he conveys.

"No, with my wife's connection, it's hard to appear objective, and I've already gotten some heat for that. I told the *Post* to give it to someone else, and I'll help in any way I can. Is there something I can help you with?"

"Well, I'm with the competition, so my expectations are low. Let me tell you the angle I'm looking into, and you can decide whether you want to share anything."

"Sure."

"As I mentioned, I've been following Congress for thirty years. Sounds like this operation goes at least that far back. I'm thinking about doing something that looks at how the congressional operation worked. How they connected with members of Congress. How they may have worked with congressional staff. That sort of thing. I know there will be some interplay there with the investigations, so I get it if it's best for you to hold it close. But what I'm mostly interested in is ancient history. See if maybe we can get something on the record that future historians could work with. Political scandals are always good historical topics. If the *Post* isn't going there, it wouldn't be competition."

There was a slight pause without a chuckle. Reporters are not just proprietary animals. They also are naturally curious. I'm hoping I have piqued Figg's interest.

"That's an interesting angle. You saw I covered that a bit in my story, but I suspect we'll mostly be focusing on the current situation and the recent past. Unfortunately, I don't know how I could help you since I can't reveal my sources."

"Of course."

I let it soak for a bit and am thinking it may be a dry hole after all. It is a long shot. But then Figg finally speaks up.

"Let me just tell you a little bit I got that wasn't in the story, and then you can feel free to pursue it on your own."

"Sure, anything would be great."

"It seems there was a pretty active network of chiefs of staff—they used to call them administrative assistants, or simply AAs. It may not have been a very large group. There wouldn't have been a huge demand. Most members who want to fool around generally don't have any trouble getting any action, with young staffers and lobbyists constantly throwing themselves at them. But there is always a group who wants to 'play it safe,' such as it is, by paying to play and not getting caught up in any dangerous relationships. Lord knows there have been plenty of those kinds of relationships over the years, going back to Wilbur Mills and Fanne Foxe."

I respond quickly before he adds J.D. as an example.

"Not sure much has changed since the first Congress in that regard."

"Absolutely not, and the pleasure houses were generally pretty easy to access early on. Then along came the late twentieth century, with all the moral scruples and reporting on the private affairs of members of Congress and other celebrities, so it got a lot riskier. Just ask Eliot Spitzer."

"For sure." Much better example, anyway.

Figg continues his discourse. "So for those who want to avoid relationships and do things the old-fashioned way, they need a product that is airtight in maintaining confidentiality and safety. That's what Fox offered, backed up by a very strict security system, as we've seen."

"I can see why that could be an attractive offer. But, like you said, it was very expensive, and congressional salaries have never been particularly lucrative."

"Right. Downtown, with those fees and salaries, not as much of an issue. But on the Hill, with those modest salaries, it was mostly the independently wealthy members of Congress, I assume. But there are always wealthy donors and lobbyists. Those who drew on that source are obviously the most vulnerable from a legal perspective."

"Makes sense."

"Like I said, I think it has always been a very closed network involving a very limited number of congressmen, though it sounds like it was bipartisan."

"Nice to know there's still some of that."

"Agree. Anyway, the Fox operation was apparently well underway downtown before it hit the Hill. I understand it started small up there. One office where an AA was desperate to help his boss. Then word quietly got around, and this guy became the facilitator. By the time he left the Hill, there was enough of a network that someone else was able to take it on. I don't know if our reporters are going to take it back that far since those involved are probably long gone, but I guess you never know."

"Well, maybe someone should look into it, for the historical record if nothing else."

Figg chuckles again, but this sounds more like amusement than anything.

"I also heard that these AAs weren't just helping their bosses but that there was also something in it for them. Some kind of payoff from the Fox operation, probably in cash. I mean they were playing the role of middlemen, and those folks don't make very much either. They are very prone to 'financial incentives,' shall we say. I never quite got a good handle on that, but I'm assuming that will be the other thing investigators will be looking at."

"How far back do you think they will go?"

"As far as they can, but you know how these things work. The public is a lot more interested in the current folks, especially those they've heard of. The statute of limitations is, of course, a problem, but even without it, nabbing a former congressman or someone who worked for them from the distant past doesn't garner many headlines. People tend to be less interested in those they've never heard of, to state the obvious."

"Sounds like maybe something I could start looking into. For the history books, of course."

"Sure. Go for it. I think I've told you about all I can. I can't really tell you any more because I either don't know it or I have to protect my sources. But maybe I could ask one favor in return."

"Sure, happy to help."

"Well, as you know, the one source I did identify was my wife. She told me she would be as helpful as she could, as long as I was the only reporter she had to talk to. She's going to help the authorities as much as she can, but she really wants to stay out of any more stories. I don't know if she could help you at all anyway, but if you could leave her alone, I would really appreciate it."

"Absolutely. That's an easy call. Really appreciate the help, Cam."

"Ah, call me Porky. I'm used to it. I did start running recently, so maybe the nickname won't fit anymore, but it'll be hard to shake it. Irony can be fun, too, I suppose."

## FIFTY-ONE

# RECONNECTING WITH WALLY

**Isaiah Stone**

*March 2014*

It didn't take long to find out where I could reach Wally North. After talking to Figg, I'm still not sure if I'm going to write anything or if I have enough to do so. But, if I'm going to capture the whole story—for my own edification at least—Wally is the final piece, given what Figg had said. Even if he wasn't the staff kingpin Figg was referring to, would he let me know of his involvement, if any?

Wally's contact information was easily available on the staff page of the American Agriculture Confederation, where he works as the vice president for congressional affairs.

"Wally, this is a voice from your past. Isaiah Stone. It's been a while."

"Sure has. J.D.'s funeral, right? It's been over ten years. How are you, Isaiah?"

"Doing fine, Wally. I think I have a few more years of doing this before I write my memoirs, if anyone is still interested at that point."

"Given your history, I suspect they may be. You have a lot of stories to tell, I'm sure."

"I guess I do. But how about you?"

Wally sighs. I notice there is a catch in the sigh, as if he is having trouble breathing or is in some pain.

"Still toiling away on K Street. Same place after I left the Hill, and I've done well here."

"Well, congratulations on landing so well after the debacle with J.D. Sounds like everything turned out for the best for you."

Another sigh, but this one sounds less physically strained.

"From a career perspective, yes. From a personal perspective, not so much. I was diagnosed with stage 4 kidney cancer a few months ago. Suspect I am on the final runway unless a miracle treatment emerges."

Yet another imminent death in the Clay saga. I feel bad for him, but also realize any chance of getting the full story is on its last legs.

"So sorry to hear that, Wally. If you're working, it sounds like it may be somewhat under control."

He excuses himself for a moment, and I hear a door shut in the background.

"Somewhat," he gets back to me. "But I'm on a reduced schedule, and they're winding me down. I understand I have some rights under the Americans with Disabilities Act, but I think they're doing the best they can, so I'm not talking to any lawyers. I've been given less than a year. So far, the treatments have been as tolerable as can be expected. Far more tolerable than the projected medical bills, I think. There's some pain that's manageable with medication, but I continue to have less and less energy. Hard to justify my salary, so, at some point, I'll have to take a leave. Fortunately, the kids are grown. I am worried that these bills could eat into the nest egg I'll be leaving my wife, but hopefully life insurance will help, too."

I wonder if he could be this fatalistic if he had not had to shepherd J.D. through the scandal.

"I admire the way you can talk about it, Wally. I've had a few friends go through it, and yours is the best attitude I've seen so far. I'm still very sorry you are having to deal with this."

"Thanks. So, what can I do for you?"

He seems clueless as to why I'm calling.

"Well, I'm calling about the *Washington Post* article on the Starr Fox operation. I'm planning to do a follow-up from a historical perspective on how it worked on Capitol Hill."

This is met with silence. I hear something tapping on his desk, which seems to increase in intensity.

"Why would you think I could be helpful?" Wally finally says in a much lower register. Maybe hostile, or it could just be caution.

"Look, Wally, I'm not going to hide anything. I know J.D. was a customer of Starr's at the time Saundra disappeared, and I've even talked to one of the girls he was involved with. I may even know more than you do, but I thought maybe I'd see if there was anything you could help me with."

More tapping. "I really don't have anything to contribute."

I'm not at all surprised he is not going to offer anything on his own.

"Well, let me share something with you that I have learned. Let's both start by acknowledging J.D. was involved with Saundra. What I have learned is that Saundra found out J.D. was one of their customers after he ended the relationship. She then threatened to blow the whistle on the whole operation if he didn't follow through on what she presumed was a promise to leave his wife for her. He then contacted the prostitute to give her a heads up, and she then told the Starr operation. When their reaction sounded a lot more brutal than she had anticipated, the prostitute got back to J.D. He said he was going to try to warn Saundra. That was the last time the prostitute spoke to J.D., and it was the very day Saundra disappeared."

Silence. I wonder if we've been cut off. He finally speaks.

"If that's true, that was between J.D. and her. I have nothing to add."

"Okay, but I also want to tell you why I'm pursuing this. As you know, I was a total apologist for J.D. Even tried to give him some advice. I have always maintained there was no connection between him and Saundra's disappearance, even if they were having an affair. Now it looks like there was."

"Maybe. But I really have nothing to add. Like I said, that was all between J.D. and the two women, if in fact what you say is even true."

"I think it is. I feel obligated to do a column on this. Maybe a bit of a *mea culpa*. I was thinking there may be a side I was missing, and you could help me."

"I don't think so."

Does a good reporter ask a question even if he knows he won't get a response? They do it all the time in press conferences. I am now dealing with a dying cancer victim who is in full stonewall mode. Moreover, it is probably just a matter of time before the investigators get to Wally about the staff operations. He was likely involved or may even have been the staffer running the whole thing. Would he take the Fifth at that point?

"Well, you were his chief of staff, so you may have known something was going on. Did you ever have any engagement with the Starr operation?"

"No."

The breathing on the other end now sounds even more forced. This is going nowhere, and I am now just torturing a suffering, dying man, even if he is at least as culpable as I am—perhaps far more so.

"Okay, well, take care of yourself, Wally. Very sorry to hear about your situation. Let me know if you change your mind or if there is anything I can do to help."

"Will do." And the phone goes silent. I guess he hung up.

---

Three days later, I am somewhat shocked when I read Wally's obituary. The story indicates his body was found in a car in a remote area of Loudoun County. A drug overdose. It also notes the cancer, and most readers would likely reach the obvious conclusion that he was just accelerating the inevitable to avoid more pain and expense. Or was he afraid of being exposed? I send an anonymous donation to the Cancer Research Institution as requested by the family.

EPILOGUE

# PUTTING IT TO REST

**Isaiah Stone**

*March 2014*

Since my conversation with Judy Carricutt, I have not had a moment's peace. The follow-up conversations with Naomi, Figg, and Wally only made things far worse. Have I been an enabler for those who had suppressed evidence in a critical investigation? On the other hand, would it have saved Saundra's life if they hadn't? Probably not, given the circumstances, but at least it would have given her family closure a lot sooner.

Finally, whether consciously or not, did I drive Wally to an early demise by zeroing in on his role? Probably. Wasn't he going to die a painful death anyway? Was he already contemplating suicide to avoid it?

Meanwhile, what do I owe my readers? What do I owe myself? Does anyone else even care about this anymore? And if I never say or do anything, will anyone else ever put the pieces together like I did? Likely not, so what am I worried about? What should come first, the truth or my reputation?

After finishing breakfast, I walk slowly into my office. My nicely furnished office in my nicely furnished home in Great Falls, Virginia. The Pulitzer hasn't hurt, boosting my salary, book sales, and speaking fees. As with all of J.D.'s good deeds in Congress, was all of this success undermined by my complicity in a single contemptuous situation?

When I awaken my computer, the screen shows the unfinished article about congressional reactions to Putin's invasion of Crimea. *Am I ever going to finish this article, or should I just move on?* Putin's actions seem like a big deal to me, but the rest of the world seems to be giving a collective yawn.

I open a new Word file on the screen and type the potential title of an op-ed:

**"What Is the Measure of a Person?"**

I stare at the screen for a while. A couple of birds are chirping outside, and my window displays the onset of another glorious Washington spring. This is the time of year I usually enjoy most.

I start typing:

> A few years ago, with little more public notice than a few obligatory obituaries, former Iowa Democratic Congressman J.D. Clay's life came to a violent end that remains shrouded in mystery. He had served in Congress from 1981 to 1991 and had many great legislative accomplishments, but that's not what the obituaries immediately gravitated toward.
>
> Rather, it was his central role in the media-fed public frenzy surrounding the disappearance of a young intern in the nation's capital—a situation in which he was initially suspected of playing some role. Her body was eventually found, and the perpetrator was identified by circumstantial evidence following his suicide. But this was revealed too late for Clay, well after defeat in his primary. Though Clay was exonerated, those headlines were much smaller and nowhere near the front page. So, most people probably remember him as being guilty of the crime or having some direct connection to it.
>
> Oh yes, in addition to his murder, the obituaries did mention how he had initially made a name for himself as a decorated Vietnam veteran fronting a one-hit-wonder band and then

> later ran for president in a large field of which he was one of the early casualties. But in a historically apathetic nation that probably doesn't even remember the name Walter Mondale, no one remembers or cares about things like that.

That was the easy part. Whatever guilt I may feel about my own role does not eclipse my disillusionment about the direction political discourse is taking. The *mea culpa* and the complications of the story are going to be far more difficult to write. Start with the former.

> During Clay's ordeal, some longtime readers may recall that I was one of the journalists who came to his defense. I not only felt a keen sense of the journalistically arcane notion of "innocent until proven guilty," but I also believed then, as I do now, that he was the kind of rare public servant who needed to be sustained in this country—one who rises above partisan rhetoric in order to accomplish something, even if it means compromising. He did this on numerous occasions, whether the issue involved employment protections, environmental restrictions, regulation of large corporations, or any number of other areas where partisanship can paralyze needed action.
>
> But now I have to ask myself: *Did my genuine admiration for Clay prevent me from performing my role as a journalist with the right degree of probity and skepticism?* Perhaps.

I read through that section twice, with minor corrections. I try to envision myself standing in front of my readers, delivering this as a speech. That last statement would definitely get their attention.

> Recent events caused me to do a little quiet digging into what Clay's real role was, and what I have learned is both

> disturbing and embarrassing.
>
> First, let me make it clear that I have learned nothing that leads me to suspect Clay of either committing or conspiring in the murder of Saundra Gray. There is nothing connecting Clay with her murderer and my presumption of innocence still holds.
>
> But apparently the situation was very likely far more complicated than I had suspected. First, at the time, it seemed Clay probably did have an affair with Gray. He never really denied it, nor did his defenders—present company included—really try to dispel any suspicions. Our point was that, absent any additional evidence, any affair he may have had, even if it provided a potential basis for a motive, simply did not prove him a murderer. And there still is no such evidence.
>
> But I now know that the affair did exist and that it did actually have a connection with the murder, and—without revealing my sources—let's just say I have corroborated this with some who knew Clay at the time.

I have always wondered how well I could perform as a mystery writer, and my attempt to unravel a complicated series of criminal events is not exactly bolstering any confidence that I could. I continue to write what I know about the facts, starting with a gentle reminder of Faith's situation, a mitigating factor if not an excuse. I then walk the reader through the various events, starting with J.D.'s employment of the Fox operation; Saundra's absurd pursuit of an assumed marriage promise, her reaction to its denial, and the threat to J.D. of exposure; his warning to Naomi (whom I only identify as one of Fox's workers); her warning to the Fox operation; her assumption regarding his unsuccessful attempt to warn Saundra; and finally the potential connection to his own unsolved murder.

So how do I want to close? Exoneration? Vilification? Self-flagellation?

None seem appropriate. Somewhere in between, as with most complicated moral dilemmas.

> If all of this is true, Clay clearly had no guilt in her eventual demise and tried his best to protect her. Belatedly, granted, but as timely as he could reasonably be expected to do so.
>
> Not a murderer or even an accomplice. But his repeated assertions that his alleged affair with Gray was irrelevant were clearly disingenuous. Okay, a "lie" would be a better term. Meanwhile, by never coming forward with what he knew, he was clearly obstructing justice and perhaps delaying the identification of the location of her body and prolonging the agony of her family and those who knew her.
>
> And one can hardly say his role was "irrelevant" if the murder never would have happened absent Clay's relationships with Gray and the prostitution ring. Both were illicit and had results, even if unforeseen by Clay.
>
> But how do we weigh his silence, particularly if there was a connection to his own murder? If he had spoken up, he may have survived politically, but what about his own safety and maybe even that of his family?

After a few rewrites, I feel I have threaded the needle on the moral conflicts. But what is my larger point, and how does it speak to my own role, as well as that of the other key players? That would have to be what I close with.

> As a longtime admirer of this public figure and all his accomplishments, can I forgive him his silence and his cowardice? I have to consider all the other public figures I have forgiven over the years in light of their service, starting with our slaveholding forefathers.

> We are all human with human foibles. We all make mistakes and commit sins and hope that our good deeds are good enough to counterbalance them. Without question, Clay performed many good deeds. The question is whether they counterbalance not only his sins of the flesh but also his silence in a matter of justice. The reality is, in addition to these known and suspected facts, there are so many other actions in a person's life—both good and bad—that go unreported and reported but forgotten. If we are unable to catalogue them, can we ever pass judgment on the whole person? And, if we can, are we simply limiting ourselves to what is actually remembered, even if it may not be what really happened? I wish I had the answers.

I reread what I've written one more time, make a few more grammatical corrections, and then print three copies. I address two envelopes, one to Faith Clay and one to Naomi Bridges, and put the third in an unaddressed envelope that I will send to Wally North's widow once I get her address. I then highlight the full text of the file and hit Delete.

# ACKNOWLEDGMENTS

Near the end of my junior year in college, my parents took me to dinner and asked me what I planned to do after graduation. (Notably, as with the main character in this book, my father's name was Joe and his nickname growing up in a small town in Kansas was J.D., to distinguish him from his own father named Joe.) The Vietnam War had ground down enough that, even though I was going to lose my student deferment, I didn't have to worry about the draft. Without pausing, I told them I planned to be a writer. After all, I had just received an A in a creative writing course at the University of Nebraska.

They nodded and told me that was fine, but they asked how was I going to support myself and any family that I wanted to raise. They had obviously scoped out the career possibilities for a writer much more than I had and told me that most writers, unless and until they achieve enormous success, have other occupations that pay the bills (even when they are marginally successful as a writer). I had no answer to that because, being a well-nurtured upper-middle-class kid, I assumed everything would proceed according to my wishes as it always had. So, they suggested law school, and that was what I did, giving me another three years to figure out what I really wanted to do (which, eventually, was not the traditional practice of law).

For that advice, and for all of their enormous caring and understanding (along with the foundational love and support of my brother Steve), I am forever grateful and indebted to them. As I have learned through the long and lonely ordeal of writing a novel (followed by the even more tortuous tribulations of getting it published), they could not have been more prophetic. As it turned out, my law degree was followed by a very nontraditional approach to law and policy (which also tested their belief in me at times) that produced an exciting and lucrative career that forms the basis for the insights (and a few of the stories) that make up this book. And, by the way, the time given to me by semiretirement didn't hurt!

This book was written by a fascinating and fulfilling life and career as much as anything, and there are so many people who have been a major part of that journey. Far more than I can list here, so I'll do my best to keep it succinct.

I will start with a heartfelt acknowledgment of two individuals who gave me the confidence to bring a very good draft over the hump to achieve the long-sought publication of *The Saundra Gray Affair.* First, Mikael Carlson, a highly successful author in his own right of several compelling political thrillers, was the first person to read the entire manuscript—and to tell me it was good enough to stick with it. Mikael also provided enormously valuable suggestions based on his own experience.

The second person was my long-lost law school friend Kim Houtchens, with whom I reconnected during COVID-19 and have since stayed in touch with on a regular basis. We share many passions (especially music), and he is exactly the audience I am trying to reach. His positive reaction to the manuscript and some vital suggestions and edits helped me put the finishing touches on the manuscript while further bolstering my confidence.

Those responses then paved the way for finally finding a home for the book at RealClear Publishing. Taking the book to the finish line has been an exhilarating experience for someone who waited a lifetime to accomplish this. Will Wolfslau and Brandon Coward have been an absolute joy to work with,  along with peerless editor Rebecca Andersen, whose rewrites of several passages in the book were a humbling comparison to my own writing. Rory Wagstaff and his team at Ease of Mind Productions have also been terrific in helping me make the audiobook version a family-and-friends affair—including best friend, Jeff McGuiness, granddaughter Milla, nephew Joey, and sister-in-law Claudia—that I will never forget.

The material and insights forming the basis of this book are grounded in a Washington, DC, career that lasted almost a half-century. There are many I have benefited from along the way, but none more than Jeff McGuiness. As the president and CEO of a highly respected trade association/think tank (HR Policy Association, née Labor Policy Association) which he founded, Jeff saw something in me that few others did. He hired me, pushed me, occasionally coddled me (actually, very occasionally), and honed in me the delicate art of influencing public policy. He then finished by preparing me to be his successor, which, in turn, capped off my own career prior to semiretirement. He is also a great writer and photographer and, with his book *Bear Me Into Freedom,* has become a renowned expert on Frederick Douglass. Significantly, he assisted me in finalizing this book. His input on content, the photo he took for the book jacket, and his participation in the audiobook are only the most recent gifts he has given me. Finally, his wife, Dorie, has been an irreplaceable companion for Linda and me in our journey through life and various parts of the world.

Tim Bartl, my own successor at the association, has literally been a brother in arms for thirty years and one whose solid character continues to inspire. The others I have worked with at the association over the past thirty-six years have given me a second family to love and cherish. There are too many to mention here, but, for their help with the book, a special thanks to Greg Hoff, who has kept me sane and relevant enough in semiretirement to stick with this project, Marie Murphy for her help in getting it ready for submission, and Shelly Carlin for her help with endorsements.

Through this connection, I have also benefited enormously from my association with some of the most accomplished human resource chiefs (and their teams) in American industry, including our association chairs Bill Conaty, the late Randy McDonald, Mirian Graddick-Weir, and Pam

Kimmet. HR performs a vital function in our culture and economy. It gets a lot of criticism and not nearly enough credit.

Prior to joining the association, I somehow survived eight challenging and exhausting years working for the US House of Representatives. Second only to Jeff, I owe my career to Marge Roukema, a moderate Republican congresswoman from New Jersey. Along with her first administrative assistant, Judy Gleason, she saw some promise in an out-of-work Hill staffer with very little expertise but acceptable writing skills. My work for her also connected me with some of the most conscientious, thoughtful legislators the United States could ask for, including (I'll let the reader add "The Honorable" before these names) Steve Gunderson, Steve Bartlett, Bill Goodling, John Erlenborn, Leon Panetta, Olympia Snowe, Carl Perkins, Gus Hawkins, Jim Jeffords, Bill Clay, Dale Kildee, and many others.

I also owe a great deal to Roger Honberger, who gave me my first job out of law school with the County of San Diego's Washington Office. He taught me the honorable and ethical side of the much-maligned lobbying profession, which, at its best, informs policymaking in a crucial way. While working for him, I also formed my two earliest friendships in my Washington career that are still sustained—Paul Hanafin and former Congressman John Faso, who also became a major force in the New York statehouse.

The other plethora of mentors to whom I owe so many thanks are from the employment law community—most notably Roger King, Andy Kramer, Wilma Liebman, Bill Kilberg, Johnna Torsone, Mark Wilson, John Irving, Sam Estreicher, Edie Baum, Fred Feinstein, Randy Johnson, Russ Mueller, Phyllis Borzi, Judy Conti, and so many other brilliant and generous people!

It may take a village to raise a child, but in my case at least, it took a family and close friendships to write a novel, and I have been blessed with so many. One of the most important groups grew out of a softball team in my starter-home neighborhood twenty-five miles south of DC. Most of this group had careers and lived lives far removed from the DC political scene, and, for me in one of the most turbulent periods of my life, they provided a refreshing retreat from the lonely pretensions of DC. We were friends because we liked (and loved) each other, and it had nothing to do with social- or career-climbing. Brad and Karen Strohecker, Doug and Maureen Smith, Alex and Sandy Scourby, and Dave and Rita Poppert were part of a core group that included so many other friends and teammates.

My other sanctuary of sanity outside the DC vortex was the glorified garage band—The Backyard Blues Band (Bruce, Jim, Dale, Raymon, George, Charles, and Steve)—that survived for thirty-five years (and maybe more if we can ever get back together). I should also note the immense pleasure I have had singing with the association's "staff band," Consensus, and my singing (and erstwhile business) partner, Ani Huang (the "Armenian Nightingale").

Ultimately, it's all about family. Linda and I have both been blessed with the most loving and supportive siblings—and their families—one could possibly ask for. My brother Steve has also been my closest friend for life. Linda's sisters Pam, Laurie, and Claudia—along with Steve's wife, Cathie—have been the sisters I never had, with husbands Jim and Mike along for the ride with me. (Love those guys!) And Linda's parents, Harvey and Glady Gorham, were a second set of supportive parents that, along with their daughters, give the lie to any negative connotations of the term "in-laws."

Our kids—Keegan/Eva and Elyse/Nate—have proven our success as parents. They have thankfully allowed us to remain a large part of their lives, and—in watching them with their kids, Milla, Cael, Liam, and Marley—whatever formula we passed along to them seems to be working. Always put the kids first, and whatever mistakes you make as a parent will surely be rectified. (And a special thanks to Elyse and Nate for including us in the Junior Hurricanes family, who have become lifelong friends for us and them!)

Others who deserve mention in getting through life's joys and traumas include Alice Manor (my guardian angel), Bob and Sue Williams, John Tysse, Monte Lake, Ed Potter, Doug McDowell, Jeff Norris, Christine Cooper, Ann Reesman, Marisa Milton, Mike Peterson, Peg and Jack Brendmoen, Paul Wilson (whose silence prompted some key edits), Henry the Younger, Tom Hayes, and Alan Wild. There are so many others that space simply does not allow. And thanks to my favorite presidential historian, Tevi Troy, who gave me great advice in finding a publisher (in addition to being a very engaging coworker).

Finally, I could have done no better with a companion for almost sixty years than Linda, whom I first dated in high school. She is a complex person who will do anything for those she loves and has shown me that there are so many aspects of love that rarely get noticed. She left me alone while I toiled away with this novel. I know it is not really the kind she normally reads, but the novel's themes of loyalty, compassion, forgiveness, and tolerance are as much a reflection of her as me.

# ABOUT THE AUTHOR

**Daniel Yager** is a fifty-year veteran of the Washington, DC, legislative arena and the former chief executive officer of HR Policy Association (HRPA). Before that, he served as minority counsel to the House Education and Labor Committee. He has authored several books on labor relations. He is a graduate of the University of Nebraska and received his JD, cum laude, from the University of Santa Clara School of Law in 1975.